A Hoosier Chronicle

by

Meredith Nicholson

Double9
BOOKS

A Hoosier Chronicle
by Meredith Nicholson

Copyright © 2024

All Rights reserved.

ISBN: 978-93-62760-50-0

Published by

DOUBLE 9 BOOKS

2/13-B, Ansari Road
Daryaganj, New Delhi – 110002
info@double9books.com
www.double9books.com
Tel. 011-40042856

ABOUT THE AUTHOR

Meredith Nicholson (December 9, 1866 - December 21, 1947) was an American politician, diplomat, and best-selling author from Indiana. Nicholson was born on December 9, 1866, in Crawfordsville, Indiana, to Edward Willis Nicholson and the former Emily Meredith. Nicholson, who was largely self-taught, began his newspaper career at the Indianapolis Sentinel in 1884. He moved to the Indianapolis News the next year, where he stayed until 1897. He wrote Short Flights in 1891 and continued to write poetry and prose until 1928. Nicholson joined the Democratic Party in 1928 and served on the Indianapolis City Council for two years. He progressed through the ranks of the Democratic Party, earning assignments as envoys to Paraguay, Venezuela, and Nicaragua. Nicholson married first Eugenie Clementine Kountze, Herman Kountze's daughter, and then Dorothy Wolfe Lannon, from whom he eventually divorced. Nicholson died in Indianapolis on December 21, 1947, at the age of 81, and was interred in Crown Hill Cemetery.

CONTENTS

TO EVANS WOOLLEN, ESQ

The wise know that foolish legislation is a rope of sand which perishes in the twisting; that the State must follow and not lead the character and progress of the citizen; the strongest usurper is quickly got rid of; and they only who build on Ideas, build for eternity; and that the form of government which prevails is the expression of what cultivation exists in the population which permits it. The law is only a memorandum. We are superstitious, and esteem the statute somewhat; so much life as it has in the character of living men is its force.

EMERSON: *Politics.*

CHAPTER I
MY LADY OF THE CONSTELLATIONS

Sylvia was reading in her grandfather's library when the bell tinkled. Professor Kelton had few callers, and as there was never any certainty that the maid-of-all-work would trouble herself to answer, Sylvia put down her book and went to the door. Very likely it was a student or a member of the faculty, and as her grandfather was not at home Sylvia was quite sure that the interruption would be the briefest.

The Kelton cottage stood just off the campus, and was separated from it by a narrow street that curved round the college and stole, after many twists and turns, into town. This thoroughfare was called "Buckeye Lane," or more commonly the "Lane." The college had been planted literally in the wilderness by its founders, at a time when Montgomery, for all its dignity as the seat of the county court, was the most colorless of Hoosier hamlets, save only as the prevailing mud colored everything. Buckeye Lane was originally a cow-path, in the good old times when every reputable villager kept a red cow and pastured it in the woodlot that subsequently became Madison Athletic Field. In those days the Madison faculty, and their wives and daughters, seeking social diversion among the hospitable townfolk, picked their way down the Lane by lantern light. An ignorant municipal council had later, when natural gas threatened to boom the town into cityhood, changed Buckeye Lane to University Avenue, but the community refused to countenance any such impious trifling with tradition. And besides, Madison prided herself then as now on being a college that taught the humanities in all soberness, according to ideals brought out of New England by its founders. The proposed change caused an historic clash between town and gown in which the gown triumphed. University forsooth!

Professor Kelton's house was guarded on all sides by trees and shrubbery, and a tall privet hedge shut it off from the Lane. He tended with his own hands a flower garden whose roses were the despair of all the women of the community. The clapboards of the simple story-and-a-half cottage had faded to a dull gray, but the little plot of ground in which the house stood was cultivated with scrupulous care. The lawn was always fresh and crisp, the borders of privet were neatly trimmed and the flower beds disposed effectively. A woman would have seen at once that this was a man's work; it was all a little too regular, suggesting engineering methods rather than polite gardening.

Once you had stepped inside the cottage the absence of the feminine touch was even more strikingly apparent. Book shelves crowded to the door, — open shelves, that had the effect of pressing at once upon the visitor the most formidable of dingy volumes, signifying that such things were of moment to the master of the house. There was no parlor, for the room that had originally been used as such was now shelf-hung and book-lined, and served as an approach to the study into which it opened. The furniture was old and frayed as to upholstery, and the bric-à-brac on an old-fashioned what-not was faintly murmurous of some long-vanished feminine hand. The scant lares and penates were sufficient to explain something of this shiplike trimness of the housekeeping. The broken half of a ship's wheel clung to the wall above the narrow grate, and the white marble mantel supported a sextant, a binocular, and other incidentals of a shipmaster's profession. An engraving of the battle of Trafalgar and a portrait of Farragut spoke further of the sea. If we take a liberty and run our eyes over the bookshelves we find many volumes relating to the development of sea power and textbooks of an old vintage on the sailing of ships and like matters. And if we were to pry into the drawers of an old walnut cabinet in the study we should find illuminative data touching the life of Andrew Kelton. It is well for us to know that he was born in Indiana, as far as possible from salt water; and that, after being graduated from Annapolis, he served his country until retired for disabilities due to a wound received at Mobile Bay. He thereafter became and continued for fifteen years the professor of mathematics and astronomy at Madison College, in his native state; and it is there that we find him, living peacefully with his granddaughter Sylvia in the shadow of the college.

Comfort had set its seal everywhere, but it was keyed to male ideals of ease and convenience; the thousand and one things in which women express themselves were absent. The eye was everywhere struck by the strict order of the immaculate small rooms and the snugness with which every article had been fitted to its place. The professor's broad desk was free of litter; his tobacco jar neighbored his inkstand on a clean, fresh blotter. It is a bit significant that Sylvia, in putting down her book to answer the bell, marked her place carefully with an envelope, for Sylvia, we may say at once, was a young person disciplined to careful habits.

"Is this Professor Kelton's? I should like very much to see him," said the young man to whom she opened.

"I'm sorry, but he isn't at home," replied Sylvia, with that directness which, we shall find, characterized her speech.

The visitor was neither a member of the faculty nor a student, and as her grandfather was particularly wary of agents she was on guard against the stranger.

"It is important for me to see him. If he will be back later I can come again."

The young man did not look like an agent; he carried no telltale insignia. He was tall and straight and decidedly blond, and he smiled pleasantly as he fanned himself with his straw hat. Where his brown hair parted there was a cowlick that flung an untamable bang upon his forehead, giving him a combative look that his smile belied. He was a trifle too old for a senior, Sylvia reflected, soberly studying his lean, smooth-shaven face, but not nearly old enough to be a professor; and except the pastor of the church which she attended, and the physician who had been called to see her in her childish ailments, all men in her world were either students or teachers. The town men were strange beings, whom Professor Kelton darkly called Philistines, and their ways and interests were beyond her comprehension.

"If you will wait I think I may be able to find him. He may have gone to the library or to the observatory, or for a walk. Won't you please come in?"

Her gravity amused the young man, who did not think it so serious a matter to gain an interview with a retired professor in a small college. They debated, with much formality on both sides, whether Sylvia should seek her grandfather or merely direct the visitor to places where he would be likely to find him; but as the stranger had never seen Professor Kelton, they concluded that it would be wiser for Sylvia to do the seeking.

She ushered the visitor into the library, where it was cooler than on the doorstep, and turned toward the campus. It is to be noted that Sylvia moves with the buoyant ease of youth. She crosses the Lane and is on her own ground now as she follows the familiar walks that link the college buildings together. The students who pass her grin cheerfully and tug at their caps; several, from a distance, wave a hand at her. One young gentleman, leaning from the upper window of the chemical laboratory, calls, "Hello, Sylvia," and jerks his head out of sight. Sylvia's chin lifts a trifle, disdainful of the impudence of sophomores. She has recognized the culprit's voice, and will deal with him later in her own fashion.

Sylvia is olive-skinned and dark of eye. And they are interesting eyes— those of Sylvia, luminous and eager—and not fully taken in at a glance. They call us back for further parley by reason of their grave and steady gaze. There is something appealing in her that takes hold of the heart, and we remember her after she has passed us by. We shall not pretend that her features are perfect, but their trifling irregularities contribute to an impression of individuality and character. Her mouth, for example, is a bit large, but it speaks for good humor. Even at fifteen, her lips suggest firmness and decision. Her forehead is high and broad, and her head is well set on straight shoulders. Her dark hair is combed back smoothly and braided and the braid is doubled and tied with a red ribbon. The same color flashes in a flowing bow at her throat. These notes will serve to identify Sylvia as she crosses the campus of this honorable seat of learning on a June afternoon.

This particular June afternoon fell somewhat later than the second consulship of Grover Cleveland and well within the ensuing period of radicalism. The Hoosiers with whom we shall have to do are not those set forth by Eggleston, but the breed visible to-day in urban marketplaces, who submit themselves meekly to tailors and schoolmasters. There is always corn in their Egypt, and no village is so small but it lifts a smokestack toward a sky that yields nothing to Italy's. The heavens are a soundingboard devised for the sole purpose of throwing back the mellifluous voices of native orators. At the cross-roads store, philosophers, perched upon barrel and soap-box (note the soap-box), clinch in endless argument. Every county has its Theocritus who sings the nearest creek, the bloom of the may-apple, the squirrel on the stake-and-rider fence, the rabbit in the corn, the paw-paw thicket where fruit for the gods lures farm boys on frosty mornings in golden autumn. In olden times the French *voyageur*, paddling his canoe from Montreal to New Orleans, sang cheerily through the Hoosier wilderness, little knowing that one day men should stand all night before bulletin boards in New York and Boston awaiting the judgment of citizens of the Wabash country upon the issues of national campaigns. The Hoosier, pondering all things himself, cares little what Ohio or Illinois may think or do. He ventures eastward to Broadway only to deepen his satisfaction in the lights of Washington or Main Street at home. He is satisfied to live upon a soil more truly blessed than any that lies beyond the borders of his own commonwealth. No wonder Ben Parker, of Henry County, born in a log cabin, attuned his lyre to the note of the first blue-bird and sang,—

'Tis morning and the days are long.

It is always morning and all the days are long in Indiana.

Sylvia was three years old when she came to her grandfather's. This she knew from the old servant; but where her earlier years had been spent or why or with whom she did not know; and when her grandfather was so kind, and her studies so absorbing, it did not seem worth while to trouble about any state of existence antedating her first clear recollections—which were of days punctuated and governed by the college bell, and of people who either taught or studied, with glimpses now and then of the women and children of the professors' households. There were times, when the winds whispered sharply round the cottage on winter nights, or when the snow lay white on the campus and in the woods beyond, when some memory taunted her, teasing and luring afar off; and once, as she walked with her grandfather on a day in March, and he pointed to a flock of wild geese moving *en échelon* toward the Kankakee and the far white Canadian frontier, she experienced a similar vague thrill of consciousness, as though remembering that elsewhere, against blue spring sky, she had watched similar migrant battalions sweeping into the north.

She had never known a playmate. The children of the college circle went to school in town, while she, from her sixth year, was taught systematically by her grandfather. The faithful oversight of Mary, the maid-of-all-work, constituted Sylvia's sole acquaintance with anything approximating maternal care. Mary, unknown to Sylvia and Professor Kelton, sometimes took counsel—the privilege of her long residence in the Lane—of some of the professors' wives, who would have been glad to help directly but for the increasing reserve that had latterly marked Professor Kelton's intercourse with his friends and neighbors.

Sylvia was vaguely aware of the existence of social distinctions, but in Buckeye Lane these were entirely negligible; they were, in fact, purely academic, to be studied with other interesting phenomena by spectacled professors in quiet laboratories. It may, however, be remarked that Sylvia had sometimes gazed, not without a twinge, upon the daughter of a village manufacturer whom she espied flashing through the Lane on a black pony, and this young person symbolized all worldly grandeur to Sylvia's adoring vision. Sylvia knew the world chiefly from her reading,—Miss Alcott's and Mrs. Whitney's stories at first, and "St. Nicholas" every month, on a certain day that found her meeting the postman far across the campus; and she had read all the "Frank" books,—the prized possessions of a neighbor's boy,— from the Maine woods through the gunboat and prairie exploits of that delectable hero. At fourteen she had fallen upon Scott and Bulwer and had devoured them voraciously during the long vacation, in shady corners of the deserted campus; and she was now fixing Dickens's characters ineffaceably in her mind by Cruikshank's drawings. She was well grounded in Latin and had a fair reading knowledge of French and German. It was true of Sylvia, then and later, that poetry did not greatly interest her, and this had been attributed to her undoubted genius for mathematics. She was old for her age, people said, and the Lane wondered what her grandfather meant to do with her.

The finding of Professor Kelton proves to be, as Sylvia had surmised, a simple matter. He is at work in a quiet alcove of the college library, a man just entering sixty, with white, close-trimmed hair and beard. The eyes he raises to his granddaughter are like hers, and there is a further resemblance in the dark skin. His face brightens and his eyes kindle as he clasps Sylvia's slender, supple hand.

"It must be a student—are you sure he isn't a student?"

Sylvia was confident of it.

"Very likely an agent, then. They're very clever about disguising themselves. I never see agents, you know, Sylvia."

Sylvia declared her belief that the stranger was not an agent, and the professor glanced at his book reluctantly.

"Very well; I will see him. I wish you would run down these references for me, Sylvia. Don't trouble about those I have checked off. It can't be possible I am following a false clue. I'm sure I printed that article in the 'Popular Science Monthly,' for I recall perfectly that John Fiske wrote me a letter about it. Come home when you have finished and we'll take our usual walk together."

Professor Kelton had relinquished his chair in the college when Sylvia came to live with him twelve years before the beginning of this history, and had shut himself away from the world; but no one knew why. Sylvia was the child of his only daughter, of whom no one ever spoke, though the older members of the faculty had known her, as they had known also the professor's wife, now dead many years. Professor Kelton had changed with the coming of Sylvia, so his old associates said; and their wives wondered that he should have undertaken the bringing-up of the child without other aid than that of the Irishwoman who had cooked his meals and taken care of the house ever since Mrs. Kelton's death. He was still a special lecturer at Madison, and he derived some income from the sale of his textbooks in mathematics, which he revised from time to time to bring them in touch with changing educational methods.

He had given as his reason for resigning a wish to secure leisure for writing, and he was known to suffer severely at times from the wounds that had driven him from active naval service. But those who knew him best imagined that he bore in his breast deeper wounds than those of war. These old friends of the college circle wondered sometimes at the strange passing of his daughter and only child, who had vanished from their sight as a girl, never to return. They were men of quality, these teachers who had been identified with the college so long; they and their households were like a large family; and when younger men joined the faculty and inquired, or when their wives asked perfectly natural questions about Professor Kelton and Sylvia, their inquiries were met by an evasion that definitely dismissed the matter. And out of this spirit, which marked all the social intercourse of the college folk, affection for Professor Kelton steadily increased, and its light fell upon Sylvia abundantly. There was a particular smile for her into which much might be read; there was a tenderness manifested toward her which communicated itself to the students, who were proud to win her favor and were forever seeking little excuses for bandying words with her when they met.

The tradition of Professor Kelton's scholarship had descended to Sylvia amusingly. She had never attended school, but he had taught her systematically at home, and his interests were hers. The students attributed to her the most abstruse knowledge, and stories of her precocity were repeated proudly by the Lane folk. Many evenings spent with her grandfather at the observatory had not been wasted. She knew the paths of the stars as she knew the walks of the campus. Dr. Wandless, the president emeritus, addressed her always as "My Lady of the Constellations," and told her solemnly that from much peering through the telescope she had coaxed the stars into her own eyes. Professor Kelton and his granddaughter were thus fully identified with the college and its business, which was to impart knowledge,—an old-fashioned but not yet wholly neglected function at Madison. She reckoned time by semesters; the campus had always been her playground; and the excitements of her life were those of a small and sober academic community. The darkest tragedies she had known had, indeed, been related to the life of the college,—the disciplining of the class of '01 for publishing itself in numerals on the face of the court-house clock; the recurring conflicts between town and gown that shook the community every Washington's birthday; the predatory habits of the Greek professor's cow, that botanized freely in alien gardens and occasionally immured herself in Professor Kelton's lettuce frames; these and like heroic matters had marked the high latitudes of Sylvia's life. In the long vacations, when most of the faculty sought the Northern lakes, the Keltons remained at home; and Sylvia knew all the trees of the campus, and could tell you just what books she had read under particular maples or elms.

Andrew Kelton was a mathematical scholar of high attainments. In the field of astronomy he had made important discoveries, and he carried on an extensive correspondence with observers of stellar phenomena in many far corners of the world. His name in the Madison catalogue was followed by a bewildering line of cabalistic letters testifying to the honor in which other institutions of learning held him. Wishing to devise for him a title that combined due recognition of both his naval exploits and his fine scholarship, the undergraduates called him "Capordoc"; and it was part of a freshman's initiation to learn that at all times and in all places he was to stand and uncover when Professor Kelton passed by.

Professor Kelton's occasional lectures in the college were a feature of the year, and were given in Mills Hall to accommodate the large audience of students and town folk that never failed to assemble every winter to hear him. For into discourses on astronomy he threw an immense amount of knowledge of all the sciences, and once every year, though no one ever knew when he would be moved to relate it, he told a thrilling story of how once, guided by the stars, he had run a Confederate blockade in a waterlogged ironclad under a withering fire from the enemy's batteries. And when he had finished and the applause ceased, he glanced about with an air of surprise and said: "Thank you, young gentlemen; it pleases me to find you so enthusiastic in your pursuit of knowledge. Learn the stars and you won't get lost in strange waters. As we were saying—" It was because of still other stories which he never told or referred to, but which are written in the nation's history, that the students loved him; and it was for this that they gave him at every opportunity their lustiest cheer.

The professor found the stranger Sylvia had announced waiting for him at the cottage. The young man did not mention his own name but drew from his pocket a sealed letter.

"Is this Professor Andrew Kelton? I am to give you this letter and wait for an answer."

Professor Kelton sat down at his desk and slit the envelope. The letter covered only one page and he read slowly to the end. He then re-read the whole carefully, and placed the sheet on his desk and laid a weight upon it before he faced the messenger. He passed his hand across his forehead, stroked his beard, and said, speaking slowly,—

"You were to bring this letter and bear back an answer to the writer, but you were instructed not to discuss it in any way or disclose the name or the residence of the person who sent you. So much I learn from the letter itself."

"Yes, sir. I know nothing of the contents of the letter. I was told to deliver it and to carry back the answer."

"Very good, sir. You have fulfilled your mission. Please note carefully what I say. The reply is *No*. There must be no mistake about that,—do you understand?"

"I am to report that you answered 'No'."

"That is correct, sir," replied Professor Kelton quietly. The young man rose, and the Professor followed him to the door.

"I thank you for your trouble; it has been a warm day, the warmest of the season. Good-afternoon, sir."

He watched the young fellow's prompt exit through the gate in the hedge to the Lane and then returned to the library, where he re-read the letter. Now that he was alone he relaxed somewhat; his manner expressed mingled trepidation and curiosity. The letter was type-written and was neither dated nor signed. He carried it to the window and held it against the sunlight, but there was not even a watermark by which it might be traced. Nor was there anything in the few straightforward sentences that proved suggestive. The letter ran:—

> Your granddaughter has reached an age at which her maintenance and education require serious consideration. A friend who cannot be known in the matter wishes to provide a sum of money to be held and expended by you for her benefit. No obligations of any sort will be incurred by you in accepting this offer. It is hardly conceivable that you will decline it, though it is quite optional with you to do so. It will not, however, be repeated.
>
> Kindly designate by a verbal "Yes" or "No" to the bearer whether you accept or decline. The messenger is a stranger to the person making the offer and the contents of this communication are unknown to him. If you wish to avail yourself of this gift, the amount will be paid in cash immediately, and it is suggested that you refrain from mentioning the matter to your granddaughter in any way.

Professor Kelton had given his answer to the messenger unhesitatingly, and the trouble reflected in his dark eyes was not due, we may assume, to any regret for his negative reply, but to the jangling of old, harsh chords of memory. He crossed and recrossed the room, lost in reverie; then paused at his desk and tore the letter once across with the evident intention of destroying it; but he hesitated, changed his mind, and carried it to his bedroom. There he took from a closet shelf a battered tin box marked "A. Kelton, U.S.N." which contained his commissions in the Navy. He sat down on the bed, folded the letter the long way of the sheet and indorsed it in pencil: "Declined." Then he slipped it under the faded tape that bound the official papers together, and locked and replaced the box.

Sylvia meanwhile had found the review article noted on her grandfather's memorandum, and leaving a receipt with the librarian started home with the book under her arm. Halfway across the campus she met her grandfather's caller, hurrying townward. He lifted his hat, and Sylvia paused a moment to ask if he had found her grandfather.

"Yes; thank you. My business didn't take much time, you see. I'm sorry I put you to so much bother."

"Oh, that was nothing."

"Is that new building the college library?"

"Yes," replied Sylvia. "Are you a Madison man?"

"No. I was never here before. I went to a very different college and" — he hesitated —"a little bigger one."

"I suppose there are bigger colleges," Sylvia remarked, with the slightest accent on the adjective.

The young man laughed.

"That's the right spirit! Madison needs no praise from me; it speaks for itself. Is this the nearest way to the station?"

It had been on Sylvia's tongue to ask him the name of his college, but he had perhaps read this inquiry in her eyes, and as though suddenly roused by the remembrance of the secrecy that had been imposed upon him, he moved on.

"Yes, I understand," he called over his shoulder. "Thank you, very much."

He whistled softly to himself as he continued on his way, still glancing about alertly.

The manner of the old professor in receiving the letter and the calmness with which he had given his reply minimized the importance of the transaction in the mind of the messenger. He was thinking of Sylvia and smiling still at her implication that while there were larger colleges than Madison there was none better. He turned to look again at the college buildings closely clasped by their strip of woodland. Madison was not a college to sneer at; he had scanned the bronze tablet on the library wall that published the roll of her Sons who had served in the Civil War. Many of the names were written high in the state's history and for a moment they filled the young man's mind.

As she neared home Sylvia met her friend Dr. Wandless, the former president, who always had his joke with her.

"Hail, Lady of the Constellations! You have been looting the library, I see. Hast thou named the stars without a gun?"

"That isn't right," protested Sylvia. "You're purposely misquoting. You've only spoiled Emerson's line about the birds."

"Bless me, I believe that's so!" laughed the old gentleman. "But tell me, Sylvia: 'Canst thou bind the sweet influences of Pleiades, or loose the bands of Orion? Canst thou bring forth Mazzaroth in his season? or guide Arcturus with his sons?'"

Sylvia, with brightening eyes and a smile on her lips, answered:—

"Knowest thou the ordinances of heaven? canst thou set the dominion thereof in the earth?"

"Ah, if only I could, Sylvia!" said the old minister, smiling gravely.

They came in high spirits to the parting of their ways and Sylvia kept on through the hedge to her grandfather's cottage. The minister turned once, a venerable figure with snowy beard and hair, and beat the path softly with his stick and glanced back, as Sylvia's red ribbon bobbed through the greenery.

"'Whose daughter art thou?'" he murmured gently.

Then, glancing furtively about, he increased his gait as though to escape from his own thoughts; but the question asked of Bethuel's daughter by Abraham's servant came again to his lips, and he shook his head as he repeated:—

"Whose daughter art thou?"

CHAPTER II
SYLVIA GOES VISITING

"How old did you say you were, Sylvia?"

"I'm sixteen in October, grandpa," answered Sylvia.

"Is it possible!" murmured the professor. "And to think that you've never been to school."

"Why, I've been going to school every day, almost, ever since I can remember. And haven't I had the finest teacher in the world, all to myself?"

His face brightened responsive to her laugh.

This was at the tea-table—for the Keltons dined at noon in conformity with local custom—nearly a week after the unsigned letter had been delivered to Andrew Kelton by the unknown messenger. Sylvia and her grandfather had just returned from a walk, prolonged into the cool dusk. They sat at the square walnut table, where they had so long faced each other three times a day. Sylvia had never doubted that their lives would go on forever in just this way,—that they would always be, as her grandfather liked to put it, "shipmates," walking together, studying together, sitting as they sat now, at their simple meals, with just the same quaintly flowered dishes, the same oddly turned teapot, with its attendant cream pitcher (slightly cracked as to lip) and the sugar-bowl, with a laboring ship depicted in blue on its curved side, which was not related, even by the most remote cousinship, to anything else in the pantry.

Professor Kelton was unwontedly preoccupied to-night. Sylvia saw that he had barely touched his strawberries—their first of the season, though they were fine ones and the cream was the thickest. She folded her hands on the edge of the table and watched him gravely in the light of the four candles whose flame flared in the breeze that swept softly through the dining-room windows. Feeling her eyes upon him the old gentleman suddenly roused himself.

"We've had good times, haven't we, Sylvia? And I wonder if I have really taught you anything. I suppose I ought to have been sending you to school with the other youngsters about here, but the fact is that I never saw a time when I wanted to part with you! You've been a fine little shipmate, but you're not so little any more. Sixteen your next birthday! If that's so it isn't best for us to go on this way. You must try your oar in deeper water. You've outgrown me—and I'm a dull old fellow at best. You must go where you will meet other girls, and deal with a variety of teachers,—not just one dingy old fellow like me. Have you ever thought what kind of a school you'd like to go to?"

"I don't believe I have; I don't know much about schools."

"Well, don't you think you'd like to get away from so much mathematics and learn things that will fit you to be entertaining and amusing? You know I've taught you a lot of things just to amuse myself and they can never be of the slightest use to you. I suppose you are the only girl of your age in America who can read the sextant and calculate latitude and longitude. But, bless me, what's the use?"

"Oh, if I could only—"

"Only what?" he encouraged her. He was greatly interested in getting her point of view, and it was perfectly clear that a great idea possessed her.

"Oh, if I could only go to college, that would be the finest thing in the world!"

"You think that would be more interesting than boarding-school? If you go to college they may require Greek and you don't even know what the letters look like!"

"Oh, yes, I know a little about it!"

"I think not, Sylvia. How could you?"

"Oh, the letters were so queer, I learned them just for fun out of an old textbook I found on the campus one day. Nobody ever came to claim it, so I read it all through and learned all the declensions and vocabularies, though I only guessed at the pronunciation."

Professor Kelton was greatly amused. "You tackled Greek just for fun, did you?" he laughed; then, after a moment's absorption: "I'm going to Indianapolis to-morrow and I'll take you with me, if you care to go along. In fact, I've written to Mrs. Owen that we're coming, and I've kept this as a little surprise for you."

So, after an early breakfast the next morning, they were off for the station in one of those disreputable, shaky village hacks that Dr. Wandless always called "dark Icarian birds," with their two bags piled on the seat before them. On the few railway journeys Sylvia remembered, she had been carried on half-fare tickets, an ignominy which she recalled with shame. To-day she was a full-grown passenger with a seat to herself, her grandfather being engaged through nearly the whole of their hour's swift journey in a political discussion with a lawyer who was one of the college trustees.

"I told Mrs. Owen not to meet us; it's a nuisance having to meet people," said the professor when they had reached the city. "But she always sends a carriage when she expects me."

As they stepped out upon the street a station wagon driven by an old negro appeared promptly at the curb.

"Mawnin', Cap'n; mawnin'! Yo' just on time. Mis' Sally tole me to kerry you all right up to the haouse. Yes, seh."

Sylvia did not know, what later historians may be interested to learn from these pages, that the station wagon, drawn by a single horse, was for years the commonest vehicle known to the people of the Hoosier capital. The panic of 1873 had hit the town so hard, the community's punishment for its sins of inflation had been so drastic, that it had accepted meekly the rebuke implied in its designation as a one-horse town. In 1884 came another shock to confidence, and in 1893, still another earthquake, as though the knees of the proud must at intervals be humbled. The one-horse station wagon continued to symbolize the quiet domesticity of the citizens of the Hoosier capital: women of unimpeachable social standing carried their own baskets through the aisles of the city market or drove home with onion tops waving triumphantly on the seat beside them. We had not yet hitched our wagon to a gasoline tank, but traffic regulations were enforced by cruel policemen, to the terror of women long given to leisurely manoeuvres on the wrong side of our busiest thoroughfares. The driving of cattle through Washington Street did not cease until 1888, when cobbles yielded to asphalt. It was in that same year that Benjamin Harrison was chosen to the seat of the Presidents. What hallowed niches now enshrine the General's fence, utterly disintegrated and appropriated, during that bannered and vociferous summer, by pious pilgrims!

Down the busy meridional avenue that opened before Sylvia as they drove uptown loomed the tall shaft of the soldiers' monument, and they were soon swinging round the encompassing plaza. Professor Kelton explained that the monument filled a space once called Circle Park, where the Governor's Mansion had stood in old times. In her hurried glimpses Sylvia was unable to account for the lack of sociability among the distinguished gentlemen posed in bronze around the circular thoroughfare; and she thought it odd that William Henry Harrison wore so much better clothes than George Rogers Clark, who was immortalized for her especial pleasure in the very act of delivering the Wabash from the British yoke.

"I wonder whether Mrs. Owen will like me?" said Sylvia a little plaintively, the least bit homesick as they turned into Delaware Street.

"Of course she will like you!" laughed Professor Kelton, "though I will say that she doesn't like everybody by any manner of means. You mustn't be afraid of her; she gets on best with people who are not afraid to talk to her. She isn't like anybody you ever saw, or, I think, anybody you are ever likely to see again!" And the professor chuckled softly to himself.

Mrs. Owen's big comfortable brick house stood in that broad part of Delaware Street where the maple arch rises highest, and it was surrounded by the smoothest of lawns, broken only by a stone basin in whose centre posed the jolliest of Cupids holding a green glass umbrella, over which a jet of water played in the most realistic rainstorm imaginable.

Another negro, not quite as venerable as the coachman, opened the door and took their bags. He explained that Mrs. Owen (he called her "Mis' Sally") had been obliged to attend a meeting of some board or other, but would return shortly. The guests' rooms were ready and he at once led the way upstairs, where a white maid met them.

Professor Kelton explained that he must go down into the city on some errands, but that he would be back shortly, and Sylvia was thus left to her own devices.

It was like a story book to arrive at a strange house and be carried off to a beautiful room, with a window-seat from which one could look down into the most charming of gardens. She opened her bag and disposed her few belongings and was exploring the bathroom wonderingly (for the bath at home was an affair of a tin tub to which water was carried by hand) when a maid appeared with a glass of lemonade and a plate of cakes.

It was while she munched her cakes and sipped the cool lemonade in the window-seat with an elm's branches so close that she could touch them, and wondered how near to this room her grandfather had been lodged, and what the mistress of the house was like, that Mrs. Owen appeared, after the lightest tap on the high walnut door. Throughout her life Sylvia will remember that moment when she first measured Mrs. Owen's fine height and was aware of her quick, eager entrance; but above all else the serious gray eyes that were so alive with kindness were the chief item of Sylvia's inventory.

"I thought you were older,—or younger! I didn't know you would be just like this! I didn't know just when you were coming or I should have tried to be at home—but there was a meeting,—there are so many things, child!"

Mrs. Owen did not sigh at the thought of her burdens, but smiled quite cheerfully as though the fact of the world's being a busy place was wholly agreeable. She sat down beside Sylvia in the window-seat and took one of the cakes and nibbled it while they talked. Sylvia had never been so wholly at ease in her life. It was as though she had been launched into the midst of an old friendship, and she felt that she had conferred the greatest possible favor in consenting to visit this house, for was not this dear old lady saying, —

"You see, I'm lonesome sometimes and I almost kidnap people to get them to visit me. I'm a terribly practical old woman. If you haven't heard it I must tell you the truth—I'm a farmer! And I don't let anybody run my business. Other widows have to take what the lawyers give them; but while I can tell oats from corn and horses from pigs I'm going to handle my own money. We women are a lot of geese, I tell you, child! I'm treasurer of a lot of things women run, and I can see a deficit through a brick wall as quick as any man on earth. Don't you ever let any man vote any proxy for you—you tell 'em you'll attend the stockholders' meetings yourself, and when you go, kick!"

Sylvia had not the faintest notion of what proxy meant, but she was sure it must be something both interesting and important or Mrs. Owen would not feel so strongly about it.

"When I was your age," Mrs. Owen continued, "girls weren't allowed to learn anything but embroidery and housekeeping. But my father had some sense. He was a Kentucky farmer and raised horses and mules. I never knew anything about music, for I wouldn't learn; but I own a stock farm near Lexington, and just between ourselves I don't lose any money on it. And most that I know about men I learned from mules; there's nothing in the world so interesting as a mule."

When Professor Kelton had declared to Sylvia on the way from the station that Mrs. Owen was unlike any other woman in the world, Sylvia had not thought very much about it. To be sure Sylvia's knowledge of the world was the meagrest, but certainly she could never have imagined any woman as remarkable as Mrs. Owen. The idea that a mule, instead of being a dull beast of burden, had really an educational value struck her as decidedly novel, and she did not know just what to make of it. Mrs. Owen readjusted the pillow at her back, and went on spiritedly: —

"Your grandpa has often spoken of you, and it's mighty nice to have you here. You see a good many of us Hoosiers are Kentucky people, and your grandpa's father was. I remember perfectly well when your grandpa went to the Naval Academy; and we were all mighty proud of him in the war."

Mrs. Owen's white hair was beautifully soft and wavy, and she wore it in the prevailing manner. Her eyes narrowed occasionally with an effect of sudden dreaminess, and these momentary reveries seemed to the adoring Sylvia wholly fascinating. She spoke incisively and her voice was deep and resonant. She was exceedingly thin and wiry, and her movements were quick and nervous. Hearing the whirr of a lawn-mower in the yard she drew a pair of spectacles from a case she produced from an incredibly deep pocket, put them on, and criticized the black man below sharply for his manner of running the machine. This done, the spectacles went back to the case and the case to the pocket. In our capital a woman in a kimono may still admonish her servants from a second-story window without loss of dignity, and gentlemen holding high place in dignified callings may sprinkle their own lawns in the cool of the evening if they find delight in that cheering diversion. Joy in the simple life dies in us slowly. The galloping Time-Spirit will run us down eventually, but on Sundays that are not too hot or too cold one may even to-day count a handsome total of bank balances represented in our churches, so strong is habit in a people bred to righteousness.

"You needn't be afraid of me; my bark is worse than my bite; you have to talk just that way to these black people. They've all worked for me for years and they don't any of 'em pay the slightest attention to what I say. But," she concluded, "they'd be a lot worse if I didn't say it."

We reckon time in our capital not from fires or floods or even *anno urbis conditæ*, but from seemingly minor incidents that have nevertheless marked new eras and changed the channels of history. Precedents sustain us in this. A startled goose rousing the sleeping sentinels on the ramparts; a dull peasant sending an army in the wrong direction; the mischievous phrase uttered by an inconspicuous minister of the gospel to a few auditors,— such unconsidered trifles play havoc with Fame's calculations. And so in our calendar the disbanding of the volunteer fire department in 1859 looms gloomily above the highest altitudes of the strenuous sixties; the fact that Billy Sanderson, after his father's failure in 1873, became a brakeman on the J.M. & I. Railroad and invested his first month's salary in a silver-mounted lantern, is more luminous in the retrospect than the panic itself; the coming of a lady with a lorgnette in 1889 (the scion of one of our ancient houses married her in Ohio) overshadows even the passing of Beecher's church; and the three-days' sojourn of Henry James in 1905 shattered all records and established a new orientation for our people. It was Sally Owen who said, when certain citizens declared that Mr. James was inaudible, that many heard him perfectly that night in the Propylæum who had always thought Balzac the name of a tooth-powder.

Mrs. Owen's family, the Singletons, had crossed the Ohio into Hoosier territory along in the fifties, in time for Sally to have been a student—not the demurest from all accounts—at Indiana Female College. Where stood the college the Board of Trade has lately planted itself, frowning down upon Christ Church, whose admirable Gothic spire chimed for Union victories in the sixties (there's a story about that, too!) and still pleads with the ungodly on those days of the week appointed by the Book of Common Prayer for offices to be said or sung. Mrs. Jackson Owen was at this time sixty years old, and she had been a widow for thirty years. The old citizens who remembered Jackson Owen always spoke of him with a smile. He held an undisputed record of having been defeated for more offices than any other Hoosier of his time. His chief assets when he died were a number of farms, plastered with mortgages, scattered over the commonwealth in inaccessible localities. His wife, left a widow with a daughter who died at fourteen, addressed herself zealously to the task of paying the indebtedness with which the lamented Jackson had encumbered his property. She had made a point of clinging to all the farms that had been so profitless under his direction, and so successfully had she managed them that they were all paying handsomely. A four-hundred-acre tract of the tallest corn I ever saw was once pointed out to me in Greene County and this plantation, it was explained, had been a worthless bog before Mrs. Owen "tiled" it; and later I saw stalks of this corn displayed in the rooms of the Agricultural Society to illustrate what intelligent farming can do.

At the State Fair every fall it was taken as a matter of course that "S. Owen" (such was her business designation) should win more red ribbons than any other exhibitor either of cereals or live stock. There was nothing that Sally Owen did not know about feeding cattle, and a paper she once read before the Short-Horn Breeders' Association is a classic on this important subject. Mrs. Owen still retained the active control of her affairs, though she had gradually given over to a superintendent much of the work long done by herself; but woe unto him who ever tried to deceive her! She maintained an office on the ground floor of her house where she transacted business and kept inventories of every stick of wood, every bushel of corn, every litter of pigs to which she had ever been entitled. For years she had spent much time at her farms, particularly through the open months of the year when farm tasks are most urgent; but as her indulgence in masculine pursuits had not abated her womanly fastidiousness, she carried with her in all her journeys a negro woman whose business it was to cook for her mistress and otherwise care for her comfort. She had acquired the farm in Kentucky to continue her ties with the state of her birth, but this sentimental consideration did not deter her from making the Lexington farm pay;

Sally Owen made everything pay! Her Southern ancestry was manifest in nothing more strikingly than in her treatment of the blacks she had always had about her. She called them niggers—as only a Southerner may, and they called her "Mis' Sally" and were her most devoted and obedient servants.

Much of this Sylvia was to learn later; but just now, as Mrs. Owen sat in the cool window-seat, it was enough for Sylvia to be there, in the company of the first woman—so it seemed to her—she had ever known, except Irish Mary at home. The wives of the professors in Buckeye Lane were not like this; no one was ever like this, she was sure!

"We shall be having luncheon at half-past twelve, and my grandniece Marian will be here. Marian is the daughter of my niece, Mrs. Morton Bassett, who lives at Fraserville. Marian comes to town pretty often and I've asked her down to-day particularly to meet you."

"I'm sure that is very kind," murmured Sylvia, though she would have been perfectly happy if just she and her grandfather had been left alone with Mrs. Owen.

"There's the bell; that must be Marian now," said Mrs. Owen a moment later, and vanished in her quick fashion. Then the door opened again instantly and she returned to the room smiling.

"What *is* your name, dear?" Mrs. Owen demanded. "How very stupid of me not to have asked before! Your grandpa in speaking of you always says my granddaughter, and that doesn't tell anything, does it?"

"My name is Sylvia—Sylvia Garrison."

"And that's a very nice name," said Mrs. Owen, looking at her fixedly with her fine gray eyes. "You're the first Sylvia I have ever known. I'm just plain Sally!" Then she seized Sylvia's hands and drew her close and kissed her.

As Sylvia had brought but one white gown, she decided that the blue serge skirt and linen shirt-waist in which she had traveled would do for luncheon. She put on a fresh collar and knotted a black scarf under it and went downstairs.

She ran down quickly, to have the meeting with the strange niece over as quickly as possible. Mrs. Owen was not in sight, and her grandfather had not returned from town; but as Sylvia paused a moment at the door of the spacious high-ceilinged drawing-room she saw a golden head bent over a music rack by the piano. Sylvia stood on the threshold an instant, shy and uncertain as to how she should make herself known. The sun flooding the windows glinted on the bright hair of the girl at the piano; she was very fair, and her features were clear-cut and regular. There was no sound in the room but the crisp rustle of the leaves of music as the girl tossed them about. Then as she flung aside the last sheet with an exclamation of disappointment, Sylvia made herself known.

"I'm Sylvia Garrison," she said, advancing.

They gravely inspected each other for a moment; then Marian put out her hand.

"I'm Marian Bassett. Aunt Sally told me you were coming."

Marian seated herself with the greatest composure and Sylvia noted her white lawn gown and white half-shoes, and the bow of white ribbon at the back of her head. Sylvia, in her blue serge, black ribbons, and high shoes, felt the superiority of this radiant being. Marian took charge of the conversation.

"I suppose you like to visit; I love it. I've visited a lot, and I'm always coming to Aunt Sally's. I'm in Miss Waring's School, here in this city, so I come to spend Sundays with Aunt Sally very often. Mama is always coming to town to see how I'm getting on. She's terribly ambitious for me, but I hate school, and I simply *cannot* learn French. Miss Waring is terribly severe; she says it's merely a lack of application in my case; that I *could* learn but won't. When mama comes she takes me to luncheon at the Whitcomb and sometimes to the matinée. We saw John Drew last winter: he's simply perfect—so refined and gentlemanly; and I've seen Julia Marlowe twice; she's my favorite actress. Mama says that if I just will read novels I ought to read good ones, and she gave me a set of Thackeray for my own; but you can skip a whole lot in him, I'm here to state! One of our best critics has said (mama's always saying that) that the best readers are those who know how to skip, and I'm a good skipper. I always want to know how it's going to come out. If they can't live happy forever afterward I want them to part beautifully, with soft music playing; and *he* must go away and leave *her* holding a rose as a pledge that *he* will never forget."

When Marian paused there was a silence as Sylvia tried to pick out of this long speech something to which she could respond. Marian was astonishingly wise; Sylvia felt herself immeasurably younger, and she was appalled by her own ignorance before this child who had touched so many sides of life and who recounted her experiences so calmly and lightly.

"This is the first time I ever visited," Sylvia confessed. "I live with my grandfather Kelton, right by Madison College, that's at Montgomery, you know. Grandfather was a professor in the college, and still lectures there sometimes. I've never been to school—"

"How on earth do you escape?" demanded Marian.

"It's not an escape," laughed Sylvia; "you see grandfather, being a professor, began teaching me almost before I began remembering."

"Oh! But even that would be better than a boarding-school, where they make you study. It would be easy to tell your grandfather that you didn't want to do things."

"I suppose it would," Sylvia acknowledged; "but it's so nice to have him for a teacher that I shouldn't know just how to do it."

This point of view did not interest Marian, and she recurred to her own affairs.

"I've been to Europe. Papa took us all last year. We went to Paris and London. It was fine."

"My grandfather was in the United States Navy, before he began teaching at Madison, so I know a good deal from him about Europe."

"Blackford—he's my brother—is going to Annapolis," said Marian, thus reminded of her brother's aspirations. "At least he says he is, though he used to talk about West Point. I hope he will go into the Army. I should like to visit West Point; it must be perfectly fascinating."

"I suppose it is. I think I should like college."

"Not for me!" exclaimed Marian. "I want to go to a convent in Paris. I know a girl right here in Indianapolis who did that, and it's perfectly fine and ever so romantic. To get into college you have to know algebra, don't you?"

"Yes; I think they require that," Sylvia replied, on guard against a display of too much knowledge.

"Do you know algebra?" demanded Marian.

"Sometimes I think I don't!"

"Well, there's no doubt about me! I'm sure I don't. It's perfectly horrid."

The entrance of Mrs. Owen and the return of Professor Kelton terminated these confidences. The four were soon at the luncheon table, where the array of crystal and silver seemed magnificent to Sylvia's unaccustomed eyes. She had supposed that luncheon meant some such simple meal as the suppers she had been used to at home; but it included fried chicken and cold ham, and there were several vegetables; and hot biscuits and hot corn bread; and it became necessary for Sylvia to decline an endless succession of preserves and jellies. For dessert there were the most fragrant red raspberries conceivable, with golden sponge cake. The colored man who served the table seemed to enjoy himself immensely. He condescended to make suggestions as he moved about. "A little mo' of the cold ham, Cap'n?" or, "I 'membah you like the sparrograss, Mis' Marian," he murmured. "The co'n bread's extra fine, Mis'"—to Sylvia. "The hossis is awdahed for three, Mis' Sally"—to Mrs. Owen.

"You still have Kentucky cooking, Sally," remarked Professor Kelton, who had praised the corn bread.

"I do, Andrew," replied the old lady; "everybody knows that the best things in Indiana came through Kentucky. That includes you and me!"

Prompted by Mrs. Owen's friendly questioning, Sylvia found herself talking. She felt that she was talking more than Marian; but she was much less troubled by this than by Marian's sophisticated manner of lifting her asparagus stalks with her fingers, while Sylvia resorted to the fork. But Sylvia comforted herself with the reflection that this was all in keeping with Marian Bassett's general superiority. Marian conducted herself with the most mature air, and she made it quite necessary for Professor Kelton to defend the Navy against her assertion that the Army was much more useful to the country. The unhurried meal passed, and after they had returned to the drawing-room Marian left to meet her mother at the dressmaker's and return with her to Fraserville.

"I hope to see you again," said Marian, shaking hands with Sylvia.

"I hope so, too," Sylvia replied.

CHAPTER III
A SMALL DINNER AT MRS. OWEN'S

Professor Kelton announced that he had not finished his errands in town, and begged to be excused from the drive which Mrs. Owen had planned.

"Very well, Andrew. Then I shall take your Sylvia for a longer drive than I should expect you to survive. We'll go out and see how the wheat looks."

In this new environment Sylvia was aware that despite his efforts to appear gay her grandfather was not himself. She was quite sure that he had not expected to spend the afternoon downtown, and she wondered what was troubling him. The novelty of the drive, however, quickly won her to the best of spirits. Mrs. Owen appeared ready for this adventure with her tall figure wrapped in a linen "duster." Her hat was a practical affair of straw, unadorned save by a black ribbon. As she drew on her gloves in the *porte-cochère* the old coachman held the heads of two horses that were hitched to a smart road wagon. When her gloves had been adjusted, Mrs. Owen surveyed the horses critically.

"Lift Pete's forefoot—the off one, Joe," she commanded, stepping down into the asphalt court. "Um,—that's just what I thought. That new blacksmith knows his business. That shoe's on straight. That other man never did know anything. All right, Sylvia."

Mrs. Owen explained as the trim sorrels stepped off smartly toward the north that they were Estabrook stock and that she had raised them herself on her Kentucky farm, which she declared Sylvia must visit some day. It was very pleasant to be driving in this way under a high blue sky, beside a woman whose ways and interests were so unusual. The spirited team held Mrs. Owen's attention, but she never allowed the conversation to flag. Several times as they crossed car lines it seemed to Sylvia that they missed being struck only by perilously narrow margins. When they reached the creek they paused on the bridge to allow the sorrels to rest, and Mrs. Owen indicated with her whip the line of the new boulevard and recounted the history of the region.

At the State Fair grounds Mrs. Owen drove in, explaining that she wanted to see what they were doing to the track. Sylvia noticed that the employees they passed grinned at Mrs. Owen as though she were a familiar acquaintance, and the superintendent came up and discussed horses and the track changes with Mrs. Owen in a strange vocabulary. He listened respectfully to what Mrs. Owen said and was impressed, Sylvia thought, by her opinions. She referred to other tracks at Lexington and Louisville as though they were, of course, something that everybody knew about. The sun was hot, but Mrs. Owen did not seem to mind the heat a particle. The superintendent looked the sorrels over carefully; they had taken no end of ribbons at fairs and horse shows. Here was a team, Mrs. Owen announced, that she was not afraid to show in Madison Square Garden against any competitors in its class; and the superintendent admitted that the Estabrooks were a fine stock. He nodded and kept repeating "You're right," or "you're mighty right," to everything the old lady said. It seemed to Sylvia that nobody would be likely to question or gainsay any opinions Mrs. Owen might advance on the subject of horses. She glanced over her shoulder as they were driving back toward the gate and saw the superintendent looking after them.

"He's watching the team, ain't he, Sylvia? I thought I'd touch up his envy a little. That man," continued Mrs. Owen, "really knows a horse from an elephant. He's been trying to buy this team; but he hasn't bid up high enough yet. It tickles me to think that some of those rich fellows down in New York will pay me a good price when I send 'em down there to the show. They need working; you can't do much with horses in town; the asphalt plays smash with their feet. There's a good stretch of pike out here and I'll show you what this team can do."

This promised demonstration was the least bit terrifying to Sylvia. Her knowledge of horses was the slightest, and in reading of horse races she had not imagined that there could be such a thrill in speeding along a stretch of good road behind a pair of registered roadsters, the flower of the Estabrook stock, driven by so intrepid and skillful a whip as Mrs. Sally Owen.

"I guess that mile would worry the boys some," observed Mrs. Owen with satisfaction as she brought the team to a walk.

This was wholly cryptic to Sylvia, but she was glad that Mrs. Owen was not disappointed. As they loitered in a long shady lane Mrs. Owen made it possible for Sylvia to talk of herself. Sally Owen was a wise woman, who was considered a little rough and peculiar by some of her townspeople, chiefly those later comers who did not understand the conditions of life that had made such a character possible; but none had ever questioned her kindness of heart. And in spite of her frank, direct way of speech she was not deficient in tact. Sally Owen had an active curiosity, but it was of the healthy sort that wastes no time on trifling matters. She was curious about Sylvia, for Sylvia was a little different from the young girls she knew. Quite naturally she was comparing the slim, dark-eyed girl at her side with Marian Bassett. Marian was altogether obvious; whereas Mrs. Owen felt the barriers of reserve in Sylvia. Sylvia embodied questions in the Kelton family history that she could not answer, though she had known Andrew Kelton all his life, and remembered dimly his only daughter, who had unaccountably vanished.

"Where do you go to school, Sylvia?" she asked.

"I don't go to school,—not to a real school,—but grandfather teaches me; he has always taught me."

"And you are now about—how old?"

"Sixteen in October. I've been talking to grandfather about going to college."

"They do send girls to college nowadays, don't they! We're beginning to have some of these college women in our town here. I know some of 'em. Let's see. What they say against colleges for women is that the girls who go there learn too much, so that men are afraid to marry 'em. I wonder how that is? But that's in favor of college, I think; don't you?"

Mrs. Owen answered her own question with a laugh; and having opened the subject she went on to disclose her opinions further.

"I guess I'm too old to be one of these new women we're hearing so much about. Even farming's got to be a science, and it keeps me hustling to learn what the new words mean in the agricultural papers. I belong to a generation of women who know how to sew rag carpets and make quilts and stir soft soap in an iron kettle and darn socks; and I can still cure a ham better than any Chicago factory does it," she added, raking a fly from the back of the "off" sorrel with a neat turn of the whip. "And I reckon I make 'em pay full price for my corn. Well, well; so you're headed for college."

"I hope so," said Sylvia; "then after that I'm going to teach."

"Poor pay and hard work. I know lots of teachers; they're always having nervous prostration. But you look healthy."

"Oh, I'm strong enough," replied Sylvia. "I think I should like teaching."

"Marian was at Miss Waring's school last winter and I couldn't see what she was interested in much but chasing to matinées. Are you crazy about theatres?"

"Why, I've never been to one," Sylvia confessed.

"You're just as well off. Actors ain't what they used to be. When you saw Edwin Booth in 'Hamlet' or Jefferson in 'Rip,' you saw acting. I haven't been in any theatre since I saw Jefferson in the 'Rivals' the last time he came round. There used to be a stock company at the Metropolitan about war-time that beat any of these new actor folks. I'd rather see a good circus any time than one of these singing pieces. Sassafras tea and a circus every spring; I always take both."

Sylvia found these views on the drama wholly edifying. Circuses and sassafras tea were within the range of her experience, and finding that she had struck a point of contact, Mrs. Owen expressed her pity for any child that did not enjoy a round of sassafras tea every spring. Sassafras in the spring, and a few doses of quinine in the fall, to eliminate the summer's possible accumulation of malaria, were all the medicine that any good Hoosier needed, Mrs. Owen averred.

"I'm for all this new science, you understand that," Mrs. Owen continued. "A good deal of it does seem to me mighty funny, but when they tell me to boil drinking-water to kill the bugs in it, and show me pictures of the bugs they take with the microscope, I don't snort just because my grandfather didn't know about those things and lived to be eighty-two and then died from being kicked by a colt. I go into the kitchen and I say to Eliza, 'Bile the water, Liza; bile it twice.' That's the kind of a new woman I am. But let's see; we were speaking of Marian."

"I liked her very much; she's very nice and ever so interesting," said Sylvia.

"Bless you, she's nice enough and pretty enough; but about this college business. I always say that if it ain't in a colt the trainer can't put it there. My niece—that's Mrs. Bassett, Marian's mother—wants Marian to be an intellectual woman,—the kind that reads papers on the poets before literary clubs. Mrs. Bassett runs a woman's club in Fraserville and she's one of the lights in the Federation. They got me up to Fraserville to speak to their club a few years ago. It's one of these solemn clubs women have; awful literary and never get nearer home than Doctor Johnson, who was nothing but a fat loafer anyhow. I told 'em they'd better let me off; but they would have it and so I went up and talked on ensilage. It was fall and I thought ensilage was seasonable and they ought to know about it if they didn't. And they didn't, all right."

Sylvia had been staring straight ahead across the backs of the team; she was conscious suddenly that Mrs. Owen was looking at her fixedly, with mirth kindling in her shrewd old eyes. Sylvia had no idea what ensilage was, but she knew it must be something amusing or Mrs. Owen would not have laughed so heartily.

"It was a good joke, wasn't it—talking to a literary club about silos. I told 'em I'd come back and read my little piece on 'Winter Feeding,' but they haven't called me yet."

They had driven across to Meridian Street, and Mrs. Owen sent the horses into town at a comfortable trot. They traversed the new residential area characterized by larger grounds and a higher average of architecture.

"That's Edward Thatcher's new house—the biggest one. They say it's easier to pay for a castle like that out here than it is to keep a cook so far away from Washington Street. I let go of ten acres right here in the eighties; we used to think the town would stop at the creek," Mrs. Owen explained, and then announced the dictum: "Keep land; mortgage if you got to, but never sell; that's my motto."

It was nearly six when they reached home, and dinner was appointed for seven. Mrs. Owen drove directly into the barn and gave minute instructions as to the rubbing-down and feeding of the horses. In addressing the negroes she imitated their own manner of speech. Sylvia had noticed that Mrs. Owen did not always pronounce words in the same way, but such variations are marked among our Southwestern people, particularly where, as in Mrs. Owen's case, they have lived on both sides of the Ohio River. Sometimes she said "hoss," unmistakably; and here, and again when she said "bile" for "boil," it was obviously with humorous intention. Except in long speeches she did not drawl; at times she spoke rapidly, snapping off sentences abruptly. Her fashion of referring to herself in the third person struck Sylvia as most amusing.

"Look here, you Joe, it's a nice way to treat yo' Mis' Sally, turning out that wagon with the dash all scratched. Don' you think I'm blind and can't tell when you boys dig a broom into a varnished buggy! Next time I catch yo' doing that I'll send you down to Greene County to plow co'n and yo'll not go to any more fancy hoss shows with me."

As she followed Mrs. Owen into the house Sylvia thought she heard suppressed guffawing in the stable. Mrs. Owen must have heard it too.

"A worthless lot," she muttered; "I'm going to clean 'em all out some day and try the Irish"; but Mrs. Sally Owen had often made this threat without having the slightest intention of carrying it into effect.

Professor Kelton had just reached the house, and he seemed so hot and tired that Sylvia was struck with pity for him. He insisted, however, that he was perfectly well, but admitted that his errands had proved to be more vexatious than he had expected.

"What kind of a time have you been having?" he asked as they went upstairs together.

"Oh, the finest in the world! I'm sure I've learned a lot to-day—a great many things I never dreamed about before."

"Horses?"

"I never knew before that there was anything to know about horses; but Mrs. Owen knows all about them. And that team we drove behind is wonderful; they move together perfectly and go like lightning when you want them to."

"Well, I'm glad you've enjoyed yourself. You'd better put on your white dress,—you brought one, didn't you? There will be company at dinner."

"Don't you scare that child about company, Andrew," said Mrs. Owen, coming up behind them with the linen duster flung over her arm. "If you haven't any white dress, Sylvia, that blue one's perfectly good and proper."

She followed Sylvia to her room, continuing to reassure her. She even shook out the gown, exclaiming, "Well, well" (Sylvia didn't know why), and went out abruptly, instructing Sylvia to ring for the maid if she needed help.

There were three other guests for dinner, and they were unlike any other people that Sylvia had known. She was introduced first to Admiral Martin, a retired officer of the Navy, who, having remained in the service of his country to the retiring age, had just come home to live in the capital of his native state. He was short and thick and talked in a deep, growling voice exactly as admirals should. The suns and winds of many seas had burned and scored his face, and a stubby mustache gave him a belligerent aspect. He mopped his brow with a tremendous handkerchief and when Mrs. Owen introduced Sylvia as Professor Kelton's granddaughter he glared fiercely.

"Well, I declare, Andy, your granddaughter; well, I declare." He held Sylvia's hand a moment and peered into her face. "I remember your mother very well. Andy, I recall distinctly that you and your wife were at Old Point in about the winter of '69 and your daughter was with you. So this is your granddaughter? Well, I declare; I wish she was mine."

"I'm glad to see you, Sylvia," said Mrs. Martin, a shy, white-haired little woman. "I remember that winter at Old Point. I was waiting for my husband there. You look like your mother. It's really a very striking resemblance. We were all so fond of Edna."

This was the first time that any one except her grandfather had ever spoken to Sylvia of her mother, and the words of these strangers thrilled her strangely and caused the tears to shine suddenly in her eyes. It was all over in a moment, for Mrs. Martin, seeing Sylvia's trembling lips, changed the subject quickly.

The last guest was just entering,—a tall trapper-like man who crossed the room to Mrs. Owen with a long, curious stride. He had shaken hands with Professor Kelton, and Mrs. Owen introduced him to the Martins, who by reason of their long absences had never met him before.

"Mr. Ware, this is Sylvia Garrison," said Mrs. Owen.

Sylvia was given then as later to quick appraisements, and she liked the Reverend John Ware on the instant. He did not look or act or talk in the least like a minister. He was very dark, and his mustache was only faintly sprinkled with gray. His hair still showed black at a distance, though he was sixty-five. He had been, sometime earlier, the pastor of the First Congregational Church, but after a sojourn in other fields had retired to live among his old parishioners in the city which had loved him best. It had been said of him in the days of his pastorate that he drew the largest congregations and the smallest collections of any preacher the community had ever known. But Ware was curiously unmindful of criticism. He had fished and hunted, he had preached charity and kindness, and when there was an unknown tramp to bury or some unfortunate girl had yielded to despair, he had officiated at the funeral, and, if need be, ridden to the cemetery on the hearse.

"I'm Mrs. Owen's neighbor, you know," he explained to Sylvia. "My family have gone for the summer; I'm hanging on here till my Indian sends me a postal that the fishing is right on the Nipigon. Nothing like getting off the train somewhere and being met by an Indian with a paddle on his shoulder. You can learn a lot from an Indian."

There were candles and flowers on the round table, and the dishes and silver were Mrs. Owen's "company best," which was very good indeed. The admiral and Professor Kelton sat at Mrs. Owen's right and left, and Sylvia found herself between the minister and the admiral. The talk was at once brisk and general. The admiral's voice boomed out tremendously and when he laughed the glasses jingled. Every one was in the best of spirits and Sylvia was relieved to find that her grandfather was enjoying himself immensely. The admiral's jokes harked back to old times, when he and Kelton were at the Naval Academy, or to their adventures in the war. It was odd to hear Mrs. Owen and the admiral calling her grandfather "Andrew" and "Andy"; no one else had ever done that; and both men addressed Mrs. Owen as "Sally." At a moment when Sylvia had begun to feel the least bit awkward at being the only silent member of the company, the minister spoke to her.

He had seemed at first glance a stoical person; but his deep-set, brown eyes were bright with good humor.

"These old sea dogs made a lot of history. I suppose you know a good deal about the sea from your grandfather."

"Yes; but I've never seen the sea."

"I've crossed it once or twice and tramped England and Scotland. I wanted to see Burns's country and the house at Chelsea where Carlyle smoked his pipe. But I like our home folks best."

"Mr. Ware," growled the admiral, "a man told me the other day that you'd served in the Army. I wish I'd had a chaplain like you in the Navy; I might have been a different man."

Mrs. Owen glanced at Ware with a twinkle in her eyes.

"Afraid I'm going to be discovered," he remarked to Sylvia as he buttered a bit of bread.

"Well, what part of the Army did you serve in?" demanded the admiral.

"Captain, Fifth New York Cavalry," replied the minister quietly, shrugging his shoulders.

"Captain! You were a fighting man?" the admiral boomed.

"Sort of one. We had a good deal of fun one way or another. Four years of it. Didn't begin fighting the Devil till afterward. How are things at the college, Doctor Kelton?"

Ware thus characteristically turned the conversation from himself. It was evident that he did not care to discuss his military experiences; in a moment they were talking politics, in which he seemed greatly interested.

"We've kept bosses out of this state pretty well," Professor Kelton was saying, "but I can see one or two gentlemen on both sides of the fence trying to play that game. I don't believe the people of Indiana will submit to it. The bosses need big cities to prey on and we aren't big enough for them to work in and hide in. We all live in the open and we're mostly seasoned American stock who won't be driven like a lot of foreign cattle. This city isn't a country town any longer, but it's still American. I don't know of any boss here."

"Well, Sally, how about Mort Bassett?" asked the admiral. "I hope you don't mind my speaking of him."

"Not in the slightest," Mrs. Owen replied. "The fact that Morton Bassett married my niece doesn't make it necessary for me to approve of all he does—and I don't. When I get a chance I give him the best licks I can. He's a Democrat, but I'm not; neither am I a Republican. They're all just as crooked as a dog's hind leg. I gave up when they beat Tilden out of the presidency. Why, if I'd been Samuel Tilden I'd have moved into the White House and dared 'em to throw me out. The Democratic Party never did have any gumption!" she concluded vigorously.

"A sound idea, Sally," grumbled the admiral, "but it's not new."

"Bassett isn't a bad fellow," remarked Ware. "You can hardly call him a boss in the usual sense of the term."

"Personally, he's certainly very agreeable," said Mrs. Martin. "You remember, Mrs. Owen, I visited your niece the last time I was home and I never saw a man more devoted to his family than Mr. Bassett."

"There's no complaint about that," Mrs. Owen assented. "And Morton's a very intelligent man, too; you might even call him a student. I've been sorry that he didn't keep to the law; but he's a moneymaker, and he's in politics as a part of his business."

"I've wondered," said Professor Kelton, "just what he's aiming at. Most of these men are ambitious to go high. He's a state senator, but there's not much in that. He must see bigger game in the future. I don't know him myself; but from what you hear of him he must be a man of force. Weak men don't dominate political parties."

"This political game looks mighty queer to me," the admiral remarked. "I've never voted in my life, but I guess I'll try it now they've put me on the shelf. Do you vote, Mr. Ware?"

"Oh, yes! I'm one of these sentimentalists who tries to vote for the best man. Naturally no man I ever vote for is elected."

"If I voted I should want to see the man first," Mrs. Owen averred. "I should ask him how much he expected to make out of the job."

"You'd be a tartar in politics, Sally," said the admiral. "The Governor told me the other day that when he hears that you're coming to the State House to talk about the Woman's Reformatory,—or whatever it is you're trustee of,—he crawls under the table. He says they were going to cut down the Reformatory's appropriation last winter, but that you went to the legislature and gave an example of lobbying that made the tough old railroad campaigners green with envy."

"I reckon I did! I told the members of that committee that if they cut that appropriation I'd go into their counties and spend every cent I've got fighting 'em if they ever ran for office again. Joshua, fill the glasses."

Sylvia was anxious to know the rest of the story.

"I hope they gave you the money, Mrs. Owen," she said.

Did they give it to me? Why, child, they raised it twenty thousand dollars! I had to hold 'em down. Then Morton Bassett pulled it through the senate for me. I told him if he didn't I'd cut his acquaintance."

"There's Ed Thatcher, too, if we're restricted to the Democratic camp," the minister was saying. "Thatcher has a fortune to use if he ever wants to try for something big in politics, which doesn't seem likely."

"He has a family that can spend his money," said Mrs. Martin. "What would he want with an office anyway? The governorship would bore him to death."

"It might tickle him to go to the senate, particularly if he had a score to clean up in connection with it," remarked Ware.

"Just what do you mean by that?" asked the admiral.

"Well," Ware replied, "he and Bassett are as thick as thieves just now in business operations. If some day it came about that they didn't get on so well,—if Bassett tried to drop him as they say he has sometimes dropped men when he didn't have any more use for them,—then Thatcher's sporting blood might assert itself. I should be sorry for Bassett if that time came."

"Edward Thatcher knows a horse," interposed Mrs. Owen. "I like Edward Thatcher."

"I've fished with Bassett," said the minister. "A good fisherman ought to make a good politician; there's a lot, I guess, in knowing just how to bait the hook, or where to drop the fly, and how to play your fish. And Bassett is a man of surprising tastes. He's a book collector,—rare editions and fine bindings and that sort of thing."

"Is it possible! The newspapers that abuse him never mention those things, of course," said Mrs. Martin.

A brief restraint fell upon the company, as they realized suddenly that they were discussing the husband of their hostess's niece, whom the opposition press declared to be the most vicious character that had ever appeared in the public life of the state. The minister had spoken well of him; the others did not know him, or spoke cautiously; and Mrs. Owen herself seemed, during Ware's last speech, to be a trifle restless. She addressed some irrelevant remark to the admiral as they rose and adjourned to the long side veranda where the men lighted cigars.

"I think I like this corner best," remarked Ware when the others had disposed themselves. "Miss Sylvia, won't you sit by me?" She watched his face as the match flamed to his cigar. It was deep-lined and rugged, with high cheek bones, that showed plainly when he shut his jaws. It occurred to Sylvia that but for his mustache his face would have been almost typically Indian. She had seen somewhere a photograph of a Sioux chief whose austere countenance was very like the minister's. Ware did not fit into any of her preconceived ideas of the clerical office. Dr. Wandless, the retired president of Madison College, was a minister, and any one would have known it, for the fact was proclaimed by his dress and manner; he might, in the most casual meeting on the campus, have raised his hands in benediction without doing anything at all extraordinary. Ware belonged to a strikingly different order, and Sylvia did not understand him. He had been a soldier; and Sylvia could not imagine Dr. Wandless in a cavalry charge. Ware flung the match-stick away and settled himself comfortably into his chair. The others were talking amongst themselves of old times, and Sylvia experienced a sense of ease and security in the minister's company.

"Those people across there are talking of the Hoosiers that used to be, and about the good folks who came into the wilderness and made Indiana a commonwealth. I'm a pilgrim and a stranger comparatively speaking. I'm not a Hoosier; are you?"

"No, Mr. Ware; I was born in New York City."

"Ho! I might have known there was some sort of tie between us. I was born in New York myself—'way up in the Adirondack country. You've heard of Old John Brown? My father's farm was only an hour's march from Brown's place. I used to see the old man, and it wasn't my fault I wasn't mixed up in some of his scrapes. Father caught me and took me home—didn't see any reason why I should go off and get killed with a crazy man. Didn't know Brown was going to be immortal."

"There must have been a good many people that didn't know it," Sylvia responded.

She hoped that Ware would talk of himself and of the war; but in a moment his thoughts took a new direction.

"Stars are fine to-night. It's a comfort to know they're up there all the time. Know Matthew Arnold's poems? He says 'With joy the stars perform their shining.' I like that. When I'm off camping the best fun of it is lying by running water at night and looking at the stars. Odd, though, I never knew the names of many of them; wouldn't know any if it weren't for the dippers,—not sure of them as it is. There's the North Star over there. Suppose your grandfather knows 'em all."

"I think he does," replied Sylvia. "He still lectures about them sometimes."

"Wonder what that is, just across the farthest tip of that maple? It's familiar, but I can't name it."

"That," said Sylvia, "is Cassiopeia."

"So? How many constellations do you know?"

Sylvia was silent a moment. She was not sure that it was polite to disclose her knowledge of the subject to a man who had just confessed his ignorance. She decided that anything beyond the most modest admission would be unbecoming.

"I know several, or I think I do. This is June. That's the North Star over the point of that tree, as you said, and above it is Ursa Minor, and winding in and out between it and the Big Dipper is Draco. Then to the east, higher up, are Cygnus, Lyra, and Aquila. And in the west—"

She paused, feeling that she had satisfied the amenities of conversation with this gentleman who had so frankly stated his lack of knowledge.

Ware struck his knee with his hand and chuckled.

"I should say you do know a few! You've mentioned some I've always wanted to get acquainted with. Now go back to Cygnus, the Swan. I like the name of that one; I must be sure to remember it."

Politeness certainly demanded that Sylvia should answer; and now that the minister plied her with questions, her own interest was aroused, and she led him back and forth across the starry lanes, describing in the most artless fashion her own method of remembering the names and positions of the constellations. As their range of vision on the veranda was circumscribed, Ware suggested that they step down upon the lawn to get a wider sweep, a move which attracted the attention of the others.

"Sylvia, be careful of the wet. Josephus just moved the sprinkler and that ground is soaked."

"Don't call attention to our feet; our heads are in the stars," answered Ware. "I must tell the Indian boys on the Nipigon about this," he said to Sylvia as they returned to the veranda. "I didn't know anybody knew as much as you do. You make me ashamed of myself."

"You needn't be," laughed Sylvia. "Very likely most that I've told you is wrong. I'm glad grandfather didn't hear me."

The admiral and Professor Kelton were launched upon a fresh exchange of reminiscences and the return of Ware and Sylvia did not disturb them. It seemed, however, that Ware was a famous story-teller, and when he had lighted a fresh cigar he recounted a number of adventures, speaking in his habitual, dry, matter-of-fact tone, and with curious unexpected turns of phrase. Conversation in Indiana seems to drift into story-telling inevitably. John Ware once read a paper before the Indianapolis Literary Club to prove that this Hoosier trait was derived from the South. He drew a species of ellipsoid of which the Ohio River was the axis, sketching his line to include the Missouri of Mark Twain, the Illinois of Lincoln, the Indiana of Eggleston and Riley, and the Kentucky that so generously endowed these younger commonwealths. North of the Ohio the anecdotal genius diminished, he declared, as one moved toward the Great Lakes into a region where there had been an infusion of population from New England and the Middle States. He suggested that the early pioneers, having few books and no newspapers, had cultivated the art of story-telling for their own entertainment and that the soldiers returning from the Civil War had developed it further. Having made this note of his thesis I hasten to run away from it. Let others, prone to interminable debate, tear it to pieces if they must. This kind of social intercourse, with its intimate talk, the references to famous public characters, as though they were only human beings after all, the anecdotal interchange, was wholly novel to Sylvia. She thought Ware's stories much droller than the admiral's, and quite as good as her grandfather's, which was a great concession.

The minister was beginning a new story. He knocked the ashes from his cigar and threw out his arms with one of his odd, jerky gestures.

"There's a good deal of fun in living in the woods. Up in the Adirondacks there was a lot for the boys to do when I was a youngster. I liked winter better than summer; school was in winter, but when you had the fun of fighting big drifts to get to it you didn't mind getting licked after you got there. The silence of night in the woods, when the snow is deep, the wind still, and the moon at full, is the solemnest thing in the world. Not really of this world, I guess. Sometimes you can hear a bough break under the weight of snow, with a report like a cannon. The only thing finer than winter is spring. I don't mean lilac time; but before that, the very earliest hint of the break-up. Used to seem that there was something wild in me that wanted to be on the march before there was a bud in sight. I'm a Northern animal some way; born in December; always feel better in winter. I used to watch for the northward flight of the game fowl—wanted to go with the birds. Too bad they're killing them all off. Wild geese are getting mighty scarce; geese always interested me. I once shot a gander in a Kankakee marsh that had an Eskimo arrow in its breast. A friend of mine, distinguished ethnologist, verified that; said he knew the tribe that made arrows of that pattern. But I was going to say that one night,—must have been when I was fourteen,—I had some fun with a bear . . ."

Sylvia did not hear the rest of the story. She had been sitting in the shadow of the porch, with her lips apart, listening, wondering, during this prelude. Ware's references to the North woods had touched lightly some dim memory of her own; somewhere she had seen moon-flooded, snowy woodlands where silence lay upon the world as soft as moonlight itself. The picture drawn by the minister had been vivid enough; for a moment her own memory of a similar winter landscape seemed equally clear; but she realized with impatience that it faded quickly and became dim and illusory, like a scene in an ill-lighted steropticon. To-night she felt that a barrier lay between her and those years of her life that antedated her coming to her grandfather's house by the college. It troubled her, as such mirages of memory trouble all of us; but Ware finished his story, and amid the laughter that followed Mrs. Martin rose.

"Late hours, Sylvia," said Professor Kelton when they were alone. "It's nearly eleven o'clock and time to turn in."

CHAPTER IV
WE LEARN MORE OF SYLVIA

Andrew Kelton put out his hand to say good-night a moment after Sylvia had vanished.

"Sit down, Andrew," said Mrs. Owen. "It's too early to go to bed. That draft's not good for the back of your head. Sit over here."

He had relaxed after the departure of the dinner guests and looked tired and discouraged. Mrs. Owen brought a bottle of whiskey and a pitcher of water and placed them near his elbow.

"Try it, Andrew. I usually take a thimbleful myself before going to bed."

The novelty of this sort of ministration was in itself sufficient to lift a weary and discouraged spirit. Mrs. Owen measured his whiskey, and poured it into a tall glass, explaining as she did so that a friend of hers in Louisville kept her supplied out of the stores of the Pendennis Club.

"It's off the wood. This bottled drug-store whiskey is poison. I'd just as lief take paregoric. I drew this from my own 'bar'l' this morning. Don't imagine I'm a heavy consumer. A 'bar'l' lasts me a long time. I divide it around among my friends. Remind me to give you some to take home. Try one of those cigars; John Ware keeps a box here. If they're cabbage leaf it isn't my fault."

"No, thanks, Sally. You're altogether too kind to me. It's mighty good to be here, I can tell you."

"Now that you are here, Andrew, I want you to remember that I'm getting on and you're just a trifle ahead of me on the dusty pike that has no turning."

"I wish I had your eternal youth, Sally. I feel about ninety-nine to-night."

"That's the reason I'm keeping you up. You came here to talk about something that's on your mind, and the sooner it's over the better. No use in your lying awake all night."

Professor Kelton played with his glass and moved uneasily in his chair.

"Come right out with it, Andrew. If it's money that worries you, don't waste any time explaining how it happened; just tell me how much. I had my bank book balanced yesterday and I've got exactly twelve thousand four hundred and eighteen dollars and eleven cents down at Tom Adams's bank. If you can use it you're welcome; if it ain't enough I'm about to sell a bunch o' colts I've got on my Lexington place and they're good for six thousand more. I can close the trade by a night telegram right now."

Kelton laughed. The sums she named so lightly represented wealth beyond the dreams of avarice. It afforded him infinite relief to be able to talk to her, and though he had come to the city for the purpose, his adventures of the day with banks and trust companies had given a new direction to his needs. But the habit of secrecy, of fighting out his battles alone, was so thoroughly established that he found it difficult to enter into confidences even when this kind-hearted friend made the way easy for him.

"Come, out with it, Andrew. You're the only person I know who's never come to me with troubles. I'd begun to think you were among the lucky ones who never have any or else you were afraid of me."

"It's not fair to trouble you about this, but I'm in a corner where I need help. When I asked you to let me bring Sylvia here I merely wanted you to look her over. She's got to an age where I can't trust my judgment about her. I had a plan for her that I thought I could put through without much trouble, but I found out to-day that it isn't so easy. I wanted to send her to college."

"You want to send her to college and you thought you would come over and let me give her a little motherly counsel while you borrowed the money of Tom Adams to pay her college bills. Is that what's happened?"

"Just about that, Sally. Adams is all right; he has to protect the bank."

"Adams is a doddering imbecile. How much did you ask him for?"

"Five thousand dollars. I offered to put up my life insurance policy for that amount and some stock I own. He said money was tight just now and they'd want a good name on the paper besides the collateral, and that I'd better try my home bank. I didn't do that, of course, because Montgomery is a small town and—well, I'd rather not advertise my affairs to a whole community. I'm not a business man and these things all seem terribly complicated and embarrassing to me."

"But you tried other places besides Adams? I saw it in your eye when you came home this evening that you had struck a snag. Well, well! So money is tight, is it? I must speak to Tom Adams about that. He told me yesterday they had more money than they could lend and that the banks were cutting down their dividends. He's no banker; he ought to be in the old-clothes business."

"I can't blame him. I suppose my not being in business, and not living here, makes a difference."

"Rubbish! But you ought to have come to me. You spoke of stock; what's that in?"

"Shares in the White River Canneries. I put all I had in that company. Everybody seemed to make money in the canning business and I thought it would be a good investment. It promised well in the prospectus."

"It always does, Andrew," replied the old lady dryly. "Let me see, Morton Bassett was in that."

"I believe so. He was one of the organizers."

"Um."

"Adams told me to-day there had been a reorganization and that my shares were valueless."

"Well, well. So you were one of the suckers that put money into that canning scheme. You can charge it off, Andrew. Let's drop the money question for a minute, I want to talk about the little girl."

"Yes I'm anxious to know what you think of her"

"Well, she's a Kelton; it's in the eyes; but there's a good deal of her Grandmother Evans in her, too. Let me see,—your wife was one of those Posey County Evanses? I remember perfectly. The old original Evans came to this country with Robert Owen and started in with the New Harmony community down there. There was a streak o' genius in that whole set. But about Sylvia. I don't think I ever saw Sylvia's mother after she was Sylvia's age."

"I don't think you did. She was away at school a good many years. Sylvia is the picture of her mother. It's a striking likeness; but their natures are wholly different."

He was very grave, and the despondency that he had begun to throw off settled upon him again.

"Andrew, who was Sylvia's father? I never asked you that question before, and maybe I oughtn't to ask it now; but I've often wondered. Let me see, what was your daughter's name?"

"Edna."

"Just what happened to Edna, Andrew?" she persisted.

Kelton rose and paced the floor. Thrice he crossed the room; then he flung himself down on the davenport beside Mrs. Owen.

"I don't know, Sally; I don't know! She was high-spirited as a girl, a little willful and impulsive, but with the best heart in the world. She lost her mother too soon; and in her girlhood we had no home—not even the half-homes possible to naval officers. She had a good natural voice and wanted to study music, so after we had been settled at Madison College a year I left her in New York with a woman I knew pretty well—the widow of a brother officer. It was a horrible, terrible, hideous mistake. The life of the city went to her head. She wanted to fit herself for the stage and they told me she could do it—had the gift and all that. I ought never to have left her down there, but what could I do? There was nothing in a town like Montgomery for her; she wouldn't listen to it."

"You did your best, Andrew; you don't have to prove that to me. Well—"

"Edna ran off—without giving me any hint of what was coming. It was a queer business. The woman I had counted on to look out for her and protect her seemed utterly astonished at her disappearance and was helpless about the whole matter when I went down there. It was my fault—all my fault!"

He rose and flung up his arms with a gesture of passionate despair.

"Sit down, Andrew, and let's go through with it," she said calmly. "I reckon these things are hard, but it's better for you to tell me. You can't tell everybody and somebody ought to know. For the sake of the little girl upstairs you'd better tell me."

"What I've said to you I've never said to a soul," he went on. "I've carried this thing all these years and have never mentioned it. My friends at the college are the noblest people on earth; they have never asked questions, but they must have wondered."

"Yes; and I've wondered, too, since the first time you came here and told me you had brought your daughter's child home. It's perfectly natural, Andrew, for folks to wonder. Go on and tell me the rest."

"The rest!" he cried. "Oh, that's the hardest part of it! I have told you all I know! She wrote me after a time that she was married and was happy, but she didn't explain her conduct in any way. She signed herself Garrison, but begged me not to try to find her. She said her husband wasn't quite prepared to disclose his marriage to his family, but that it would all be right soon. The woman with whom I had left her couldn't help me to identify him in any way; at least she didn't help me. There had been a number of young men boarding in the neighborhood—medical and law students; but there was no Garrison among them. It was in June that this happened, and when I went down to try to trace her they had all gone. I was never quite sure whether the woman dealt squarely with me or not. But it was my fault, Sally; I want you to know that I have no excuse to offer. I don't want you to try to say anything that would make my lot easier."

It was not Sally Owen's way to extenuate errors of commission or omission. Her mental processes were always singularly direct.

"Are you sure she was married; did you find any proof of it?" she asked bluntly.

He was silent for a moment before he met her eyes.

"I have no proof of it. All I have is Edna's assurance in a letter."

Their gaze held while they read each other's thoughts. She made no comment; there was nothing to say to this, nor did she show surprise or repugnance at the dark shadow his answer had flung across the meagre picture.

"And Garrison—who was he?"

"I don't know even that! From all I could learn I think it likely he was a student in one of the professional schools; but whether law or medicine, art or music—I couldn't determine. The whole colony of students had scattered to the four winds. Probably Garrison was not his real name; but that is wholly an assumption."

"It's clear enough that whoever the man was, and whether it was straight or not, Edna felt bound to shield him. That's just like us fool women. How did Sylvia come to your hands?"

"There was nothing in that to help. About four years had passed since I lost track of her and I had traveled all over the East and followed every clue in vain. I spent two summers in New York walking the streets in the blind hope that I might meet her. Then, one day,—this was twelve years ago,—I had a telegram from the superintendent of a public hospital at Utica that Edna was there very ill. She died before I got there. Just how she came to be in that particular place I have no idea. The hospital authorities knew nothing except that she had gone to them, apparently from the train, seriously ill. The little girl was with her. She asked them to send for me, but told them nothing of herself. She had only hand baggage and it told us nothing as to her home if she had one, or where she was going. Her clothing, the nurse pointed out, was of a style several years old, but it was clean and neat. Most surprising of all, she had with her several hundred dollars; but there was nothing whatever by which to reconstruct her life in those blank years."

"But she wrote to you—the letters would have given a clue of some kind?"

"The few letters she wrote me were the most fragmentary and all in the first year; they were like her, poor child; her letters were always the merest scraps. In all of them she said she would come home in due course; that some of her husband's affairs had to be straightened out first, and that she was perfectly happy. They were traveling about, she said, and she asked me not to try to write to her. The first letters came from Canada—Montreal and Quebec; then one from Albany; then even these messages ceased and I heard no more until the telegram called me to Utica. She had never mentioned the birth of the child. I don't know—I don't even know where Sylvia was born, or her exact age. The nurse at the hospital said Edna called the child Sylvia."

"I overheard Sylvia telling Ware to-night that she was born in New York. Could it be possible—"

"No; she knows nothing. You must remember that she was only three. When she began to ask me when her birthday came—well, Sally, I felt that I'd better give her one; and I told her, too, that she was born in New York City. You understand—?"

"Of course, Andrew. You did perfectly right. She's likely to ask a good many questions now that she's growing up."

"Oh," he cried despairingly, "she's already asked them! It's a heartbreaking business, I tell you. Many a time when she's piped up in our walks or at the table with some question about her father and mother I've ignored it or feigned not to hear; but within the past year or two I've had to fashion a background for her. I've surrounded her origin and antecedents with a whole tissue of lies. But, Sally, it must have been all right—I had Edna's own word for it!" he pleaded brokenly. "It must have been all right!"

"Well, what if it wasn't! Does it make any difference about the girl? All this mystery is a good thing; the denser the better maybe, as long as there's any doubt at all. Your good name protects her; it's a good name, Andrew. But go on; you may as well tell me the whole business."

"I've told you all I know; and as I've told it I've realized more than before how pitifully little it is."

"Well, there's nothing to do about that. I've never seen any sense in worrying over what's done. It's the future you've got to figure on for Sylvia. So you think college is a good thing for girls—for a girl like Sylvia?"

"Yes; but I want your opinion. You're the only person in the world I can talk to; it's helped me more than I can tell you to shift some of this burden to you. Maybe it isn't fair; you're a busy woman—"

"I guess I'm not so busy. I've been getting lazy, and needed a hard jolt. I've been wondering a good deal about these girls' colleges. Some of this new woman business looks awful queer to me, but so did the electric light and the telephone a few years ago and I can even remember when people were likely to drop dead when they got their first telegram. Sylvia isn't"— she hesitated for an instant—"from what you say, Sylvia isn't much like her mother?"

"No. Her qualities are wholly different. Edna had a different mind altogether. There was nothing of the student about her. The only thing that interested her was music, and that came natural to her. I've studied Sylvia carefully,—I'm ashamed to confess how carefully,—fearing that she would grow to be like her mother; but she's another sort, and I doubt if she will change. You can already see the woman in her. That child, Sally, has in her the making of a great woman. I've been careful not to crowd her, but she has a wonderful mind,—not the brilliant sort that half sees things in lightning flashes, but a vigorous mind, that can grapple with a problem and fight it out. I'm afraid to tell you how remarkable I think she is. No; poor Edna was not like that. She hated study."

"Sylvia's very quiet, but I reckon she takes everything in. It's in her eyes that she's different. And I guess that quietness means she's got power locked up in her. Children do show it. Now Marian, my grandniece, is a different sort. She's a forthputting youngster that's going to be hard to break to harness. She looks pretty, grazing in the pasture and kicking up her heels, but I don't see what class she's going to fit into. Now, Hallie,—my niece, Mrs. Bassett,—she's one of these club fussers,—always studying poetry and reading papers and coming up to town to state conventions or federations and speaking pieces in a new hat. Hallie's smart at it. She was president of the Daughters once, by way of showing that our folks in North Carolina fought in the Revolution, which I reckon they did; though I never saw where Hallie proved it; but the speech I heard her make at the Propylæum wouldn't have jarred things much if it hadn't been for Hallie's feathers. She likes her clothes—she always had 'em, you know. My brother Blackford left her a very nice fortune; and Morton Bassett makes money. Well, as I started to say, there's all kinds of women,—the old ones like me that never went to school much, and Hallie's kind, that sort o' walked through the orchard and picked the nearest peaches, and then starts in at thirty to take courses in Italian Art, and Marian, who gives her teachers nervous prostration, and Sylvia, who takes to books naturally."

"There are all kinds of girls, just as there are all kinds of boys. Good students, real scholars have always been rare in the world—men and women. I should like to see Sylvia go high and far; I should like her to have every chance."

"All right, Andrew; let's do it. How much does a college course cost for a girl?"

"I didn't come here to interest you in the money side of it, Sally; I expected—"

"Answer my question, Andrew."

"I had expected to give her a four-year course for five thousand dollars. The actual tuition isn't so much; it's railroad fare, clothing, and other expenses."

Mrs. Owen turned towards Kelton with a smile on her kind, shrewd face.

"Andrew, just to please me, I want you to let me be partners with you in this. What you've told me and what I've seen of that little girl have clinched me pretty strong. I wish she was mine! My little Elizabeth would be a grown woman if she'd lived; and because of her I like to help other people's little girls; you know I helped start Elizabeth House, a home for working girls—and I'm getting my money back on that a thousand times over. It's a pretty state of things if an old woman like me, without a chick of my own, and with no sense but horse sense, can't back a likely filly like your Sylvia. I want you to let me call her our Sylvia. We'll train her in all the paces, Andrew, and I hope one of us will live to see her strike the home stretch. Come into my office a minute," she said, rising and leading the way.

The appointments of her "office" were plain and substantial. A flat-topped desk stood in the middle of the room—a relic of the lamented Jackson Owen; in one corner was an old-fashioned iron safe in which she kept her account books. A print of Maud S. adorned one wall, and facing it across the room hung a lithograph of Thomas A. Hendricks. Twice a week a young woman came to assist Mrs. Owen with her correspondence and accounts,—a concession to age, for until she was well along in the fifties Sally Owen had managed these things alone.

"You've seen my picture-gallery before, Andrew? Small but select. I knew both the lady and the gentleman," she continued, with one of her humorous flashes. "I went to Cleveland in '85 to see Maud S. She ate up a mile in 2:08-3/4—the prettiest thing I ever saw. You know Bonner bought her as a four-year-old—the same Bonner that owned the 'New York Ledger.' I used to read the 'Ledger' clear through, when Henry Ward Beecher and

Fanny Fern wrote for it. None of these new magazines touch it. And you knew Tom Hendricks? That's a good picture. Tom looked like a statesman anyhow, and that's more than most of 'em do."

She continued her efforts to divert his thoughts from the real matter at hand, summoning from the shadows all the Hoosier statesmen of the post-bellum period to aid her, and she purposely declared her admiration of several of these to provoke Kelton's ire.

"That's right, Andrew; jump on 'em," she laughed, as she drew from the desk a check book and began to write. When she had blotted and torn out the check she examined it carefully and placed it near him on the edge of her desk. "Now, Andrew Kelton, there's a check for six thousand dollars; we'll call that our educational fund. You furnish the girl; I put in the money. I only wish I had the girl to put into the business instead of the cash."

"But I don't need the money yet; I shan't need it till fall," he protested.

"That's all right. Fall's pretty close and you'll feel better if you have it. Now, you may count on more when that's gone if you want it. In case anything goes wrong with you or me it'll be fixed. I'll attend to it. I look on it as a good investment. Your note? Look here, Andrew Kelton, if you mention that life insurance to me again, I'll cut your acquaintance. You go to bed; and don't you ever let on to that baby upstairs that I have any hand in her schooling." She dropped her check book into a drawer and swung round in her swivel chair until she faced him. "I don't want to open up that affair of Sylvia's mother again, but there's always the possibility that something may happen. You know Edna's dead, but there's always a chance that Sylvia's father may turn up. It's not likely; but there's no telling about such things; and it wouldn't be quite fair for you to leave her unprepared if it should happen."

"There's one more circumstance I haven't told you about. It happened only a few days ago. It was that, in fact, which crystallized my own ideas about Sylvia's education. A letter was sent to me by a stranger, offering money for Sylvia's schooling. The whole thing was surrounded with the utmost secrecy."

"So? Then some one is watching Sylvia; keeping track of her, and must be kindly disposed from that. You never heard anything before?"

"Never. I was asked to send a verbal answer by the messenger who brought me the letter, accepting or declining the offer. I declined it."

"That was right. But there's no hiding anything in this world; you must have some idea where the offer came from."

"I haven't the slightest, not the remotest idea. The messenger was a stranger to me; from what Sylvia said he was a stranger at Montgomery and had never seen the college before. Time had begun to soften the whole thing, and the knowledge that some one has been watching the child all these years troubles me. It roused all my old resentment; I have hardly slept since it occurred."

"It's queer; but you'd better try to forget it. Somebody's conscience is hurting, I reckon. I wouldn't know how to account for it in any other way. If it's a case of conscience, it may have satisfied itself by offering money; if it didn't, you or Sylvia may hear from it again."

"It's just that that hurts and worries me,—the possibility that this person may trouble Sylvia sometime when I am not here to help her. It's an awful thing for a woman to go out into the world followed by a shadow. It's so much worse for a woman; women are so helpless."

"Some of us, like me, are pretty tough, too. Sylvia will be able to take care of herself; you don't need to worry about her. If that's gnawing some man's conscience—and I reckon it is—you can forget all about it. A man's conscience—the kind of man that would abandon a woman he had married, or maybe hadn't married—ain't going to be a ghost that walks often. You'd better go to bed, Andrew."

Kelton lingered to smoke a cigar in the open. He had enjoyed to-night an experience that he had not known in years—that of unburdening himself to a kindly, sympathetic, and resourceful woman.

While they talked of her, Sylvia sat in her window-seat in the dark above looking at the stars. She lingered there until late, enjoying the cool air, and unwilling to terminate in sleep so eventful a day. She heard presently her grandfather's step below as he "stood watch," marking his brief course across the dim garden by the light of his cigar. Sylvia was very happy. She had for a few hours breathed the ampler ether of a new world; but she was unconscious in her dreaming that her girlhood, that had been as tranquil water safe from current and commotion, now felt the outward drawing of the tide.

CHAPTER V
INTRODUCING MR. DANIEL HARWOOD

On the day following the delivery to Andrew Kelton of the letter in which money for Sylvia's education was offered by an unknown person, the bearer of the message was to be seen at Indianapolis, in the law office of Wright and Fitch, attorneys and counselors at law, on the fourth floor of the White River Trust Company's building in Washington Street. In that office young Mr. Harwood was one of half a dozen students, who ran errands to the courts, kept the accounts, and otherwise made themselves useful.

Wright and Fitch was the principal law firm in the state in the period under scrutiny, as may readily be proved by an examination of the court dockets. The firm's practice was, however, limited. Persons anxious to mulct* wicked corporations in damages for physical injuries did not apply to Wright and Fitch, for the excellent reason that this capable firm was retained by most of the public service corporations and had no time to waste on the petty and vexatious claims of minor litigants. Mr. Wright was a Republican, Mr. Fitch a Democrat, and each of these gentlemen occasionally raised his voice loud enough in politics to emphasize his party fealty. In the seventies Mr. Wright had served a term as city attorney; on the other hand, Mr. Fitch had once declined the Italian ambassadorship. Both had been mentioned at different times for the governorship or for the United States Senate, and both had declined to enter the lists for these offices.

Daniel Harwood had been graduated from Yale University a year before we first observed him, and though the world lay before him where to choose, he returned to his native state and gave himself to the study of law by day and earned a livelihood by serving the "Courier" newspaper by night. As Mr. Harwood is to appear frequently in this chronicle, it may be well to summarize briefly the facts of his history. He was born on a farm in Harrison County, and his aversion to farm life had been colored from earliest childhood by the difficulties his father experienced in wringing enough money out of eighty acres of land to buy food and clothing and to pay taxes and interest on an insatiable mortgage held somewhere by a ruthless life insurance company that seemed most unreasonably insistent in its collections. Daniel had two older brothers who, having satisfied their passion for enlightenment at the nearest schoolhouse, meekly enlisted under their father in the task of fighting the mortgage. Daniel, with a weaker hand and a better head, and with vastly more enterprise, resolved to go to Yale. This seemed the most fatuous, the most profane of ambitions. If college at all, why not the State University, to support which the Harwood eighty acres were taxed; but a college away off in Connecticut! There were no precedents for this in Harrison County. No Harwood within the memory of man had ever adventured farther into the unknown world than to the State Fair at Indianapolis; and when it came to education, both the judge of the Harrison County Circuit Court and the presiding elder of the district had climbed to fame without other education than that afforded by the common schools. Daniel's choice of Yale had been determined by the fact that a professor in that institution had once addressed the county teachers, and young Harwood had been greatly impressed by him. The Yale professor was the first graduate of an Eastern university that Daniel had ever seen, and he became the young Hoosier's ideal of elegance and learning. Daniel had acquired at this time all that the county school offered, and he made bold to approach the visitor and ask his advice as to the best means of getting to college.

We need not trace the devious course by which, after much burning of oil during half a dozen winters, Dan Harwood attained to a freshman's dignity at New Haven, where, arriving with his effects in a canvas telescope, he had found a scholarship awaiting him; nor need we do more than record the fact that he had cared for furnaces, taken the night shift on a trolley car, and otherwise earned money until, in his junior year, his income from newspaper correspondence and tutoring made further manual labor unnecessary. It is with profound regret that we cannot point to Harwood as a football hero or the mainstay of the crew. Having ploughed the mortgaged acres, and tossed hay and broken colts, college athletics struck him as rather puerile diversion. He would have been the least conspicuous man in college if he had not shone in debate and gathered up such prizes and honors as were accessible in that field. His big booming voice, recognizable above the din in all *'varsity demonstrations, earned for him the sobriquet of "Foghorn" Harwood. For the rest he studied early and late, and experienced the doubtful glory, and accepted meekly the reproach, of being a grind.

History and the dismal science had interested him immensely. His assiduous attention to the classes of Professor Sumner had not gone unnoticed by that eminent instructor, who once called him by name in Chapel Street, much to Dan's edification. He thought well of belles-lettres and for a time toyed with an ambition to enrich English literature with contributions of his own. During this period he contributed to the "Lit" a sonnet called "The Clam-Digger" which began:—

At rosy dawn I see thine argosy;

and which closed with the invocation:—

Fair tides reward thy long, laborious days.

The sonnet was neatly parodied in the "Record," and that journal printed a gratuitous defense of the fisherman at whom, presumably, the poem had been directed. "The sonnet discloses nothing," said the "Record," "as to the race, color, or previous condition of servitude of the unfortunate clammer to justify a son of Eli in attacking a poor man laudably engaged in a perfectly honorable calling. The sonneteer, coming, we believe, from the unsalt waters of the Wabash, seems to be unaware that the fisherman at whom he has leveled his tuneful lyre is not seeking fair tides but clams. We therefore suggest that the closing line of the sextette be amended to read—

Fair clams reward thy long, laborious days."

Harwood was liked by his fellow students in the law office. Two Yalensians, already established there, made his lot easier, and they combined against a lone Harvardian, who bitterly resented Harwood's habit of smoking a cob pipe in the library at night. The bouquet of Dan's pipe was pretty well dispelled by morning save to the discerning nostril of the harvard man, who protested against it, and said the offense was indictable at common law. Harwood stood stoutly for his rights and privileges, and for Yale democracy, which he declared his pipe exemplified. There was much good-natured banter of this sort in the office.

Harwood was busy filing papers when Mr. Fitch summoned him to his private room on the day indicated. Fitch was short, thin, and bald, with a clipped reddish beard, brown eyes, and a turn-up nose. He was considered a better lawyer than Wright, who was the orator of the firm, and its reliance in dealing with juries. In the preparation of briefs and in oral arguments before the Supreme Court, Fitch was the superior. His personal peculiarities had greatly Interested Harwood; as, for example, Fitch's manner of locking himself in his room for days at a time while he was preparing to write a brief, denying himself to all visitors, and only occasionally calling for books from the library. Then, when he had formulated his ideas, he summoned the stenographer and dictated at one sitting a brief that generally proved to be the reviewing court's own judgment of the case in hand. Some of Fitch's fellow practitioners intimated at times that he was tricky. In conferences with opposing counsel, one heard, he required watching, as he was wary of committing himself and it was difficult to discover what line of reasoning he elected to oppose or defend. In such conferences it was his fashion to begin any statement that might seem even remotely to bind him with the remark, "I'm just thinking aloud on that proposition and don't want to be bound by what I say." The students in the office, to whom he was unfailingly courteous, apostrophized him as "the fox." He called them all "Mister," and occasionally flattered them by presenting a hypothetical case for their consideration.

Fitch was sitting before the immaculate desk he affected (no one ever dared leave anything on it in his absence) when Harwood entered. The lawyer's chair was an enormous piece of furniture in which his small figure seemed to shrink and hide. His hands were thrust into his pockets, as they usually were, and he piped out "Good-Morning" in a high tenor voice.

"Shut the door, please, Mr. Harwood. What have you to report about your errand to Montgomery?"

He indicated with a nod the one chair in the room and Harwood seated himself.

"I found Professor Kelton without difficulty and presented the letter."

"You delivered the letter and you have told no one of your visit to Montgomery."

"No one, sir; no one knows I have been away from town. I handed the letter to the gentleman in his own house, alone, and he gave me his answer."

"Well?"

"*No* is the answer."

Fitch polished his eyeglasses with his handkerchief. He scrutinized Harwood carefully for a moment, then asked:—

"Did the gentleman—whose name, by the way, you have forgotten—"

"Yes, sir; I have quite forgotten it," Harwood replied promptly.

"Did he show any feeling—indignation, pique, as he read the letter?"

"No; but he read it carefully. His face showed pain, I should say, sir, rather than indignation. He gave his negative reply coldly—a little sharply. He was very courteous—a gentleman, I should say, beyond any question."

"I dare say. What kind of an establishment did he keep?"

"A small cottage, with books everywhere, right by the campus. A young girl let me in; she spoke of the professor as her grandfather. She went off to find him for me in the college library."

"A young person. What did she look like?"

"A dark young miss, with black hair tied with a red ribbon."

Fitch smiled.

"You are sure of the color, are you? This man lives there with his granddaughter, and the place was simple—comfortable, no luxuries. You had no conversation with him."

"I think we exchanged a word about the weather, which was warm."

Fitch smiled again. His was a rare smile, but it was worth waiting for.

"What did the trip cost you?"

Harwood named the amount and the lawyer drew a check book from his impeccable desk and wrote.

"I have added one hundred dollars for your services. This is a personal matter between you and me, and does not go on the office books. By the way, Mr. Harwood, what are you doing out there?" he asked, moving his head slightly toward the outer office.

"I'm reading law."

"Is it possible! The other youngsters in the office seem to be talking politics or reading newspapers most of the time. How do you manage to live?"

"I do some work for the 'Courier' from time to time."

"Ah! You are careful not to let your legal studies get mixed with the newspaper work?"

"Yes, sir. They put me on meetings, and other night assignments. As to the confidences of this office, you need have no fear of my—"

"I haven't, Mr. Harwood. Let me see. It was of you Professor Sumner wrote me last year; he's an old friend of mine. He said he thought you had a sinewy mind—a strong phrase for Sumner."

"He never told me that," said Dan, laughing. "He several times implied quite the reverse."

"He's a great man—Sumner. I suppose you absorbed a good many of his ideas at New Haven."

"I hope I did, sir: I believe in most of them anyhow."

"So do I, Mr. Harwood."

Fitch pointed to a huge pile of manuscript on a table by the window. It was a stenographic transcript of testimony in a case which had been lost in the trial court and was now going up on appeal.

"Digest that evidence and give me the gist of it in not more than five hundred words. That's all."

Harwood's hand was on the door when Fitch arrested him with a word.

"To recur to this private transaction between us, you have not the remotest idea what was in that letter, and nothing was said in the interview that gave you any hint—is that entirely correct?"

"Absolutely."

"Very well. I know nothing of the matter myself; I am merely accommodating a friend. We need not refer to this again."

When the door had closed, the lawyer wrote a brief note which he placed in his pocket, and dropped later into a letter-box with his own hand. Mr. Fitch, of the law firm of Wright and Fitch, was not in the habit of acting as agent in matters he didn't comprehend, and his part in Harwood's errand was not to his liking. He had spoken the truth when he said that he knew no more of the nature of the letter that had been carried to Professor Kelton than the messenger, and Harwood's replies to his interrogatories had told him nothing.

Many matters, however, pressed upon his attention and offered abundant exercise for his curiosity. With Harwood, too, pleased to have for the first time in his life one hundred dollars in cash, the incident was closed.

CHAPTER VI
HOME LIFE OF HOOSIER STATESMEN

In no other place can a young man so quickly attain wisdom as in a newspaper office. There the names of the good and great are playthings, and the bubble reputation is blown lightly, and as readily extinguished, as part of the day's business. No other employment offers so many excitements; in nothing else does the laborer live so truly behind the scenes. The stage is wide, the action varied and constant. The youngest tyro, watching from the wings, observes great incidents and becomes their hasty historian. The reporter's status is unique. Youth on the threshold of no other profession commands the same respect, gains audience so readily to the same august personages. Doors slammed in his face only flatter his self-importance. He becomes cynical as he sees how easily the spot light is made to flash upon the unworthiest figures by the flimsiest mechanism. He drops his plummet into shoal and deep water and from his contemplation of the wreck-littered shore grows skeptical of the wisdom of all pilots.

Harwood's connection with the "Courier" brought him in touch with politics, which interested him greatly. The "Courier" was the organ of the Democratic Party in the state, and though his father and brothers in the country were Republicans, Dan found himself more in sympathy with the views represented by the Democratic Party, even after it abandoned its ancient conservatism and became aggressively radical. About the time of Harwood's return to his native state the newspaper had changed hands. At least the corporation which had owned it for a number of years had apparently disposed of it, though the transaction had been effected so quietly that the public received no outward hint beyond the deletion of "Published by the Courier Newspaper Company" from the head of the editorial page. The "policy" of the paper continued unchanged; the editorial staff had not been disturbed; and in the counting-room there had been no revolution, though an utterly unknown man had appeared bearing the title of General Manager, which carried with it authority in all departments.

This person was supposed to represent the unknown proprietor, about whom there had been the liveliest speculation. The "Courier's" rivals gave much space to rumors, real and imaginary, as to the new ownership, attributing the purchase to a number of prominent politicians in rapid succession, and to syndicates that had never existed. It was an odd effect of the change in the "Courier's" ownership that almost immediately mystery seemed to envelop the editorial rooms. The managing editor, whose humors and moods fixed the tone of the office, may have been responsible, but whatever the cause a stricter discipline was manifest, and editors, reporters and copy-readers moved and labored with a consciousness that an unknown being walked among the desks, and hung over the forms to the very last moment before they were hurled to the stereotypers. The editorial writers—those astute counselors of the public who are half-revered and half-despised by their associates on the news side of every American newspaper—wrote uneasily under a mysterious, hidden censorship. It was possible that even the young woman who gleaned society news might, by some unfortunate slip, offend the invisible proprietor. But as time passed nothing happened. The imaginable opaque pane that separated the owner from the desks of the "Courier's" reporters and philosophers had disclosed no faintest shadow. Occasionally the managing editor was summoned below by the general manager, but the subordinates in the news department were unable, even by much careful study of their subsequent instructions, to grasp the slightest thread that might lead them to the concealed hand which swayed the "Courier's" destiny. It must be confessed that under this ghostly administration the paper improved. Every man did his best, and the circulation statements as published monthly indicated a widening constituency. Even the Sunday edition, long a forbidding and depressing hodge-podge of ill-chosen and ill-digested rubbish, began to show order and intelligence.

In October following his visit to Professor Kelton, Harwood was sent to Fraserville, the seat of Fraser County, to write a sketch of the Honorable Morton Bassett, in a series then adorning the Sunday supplement under the title, "Home Life of Hoosier Statesmen." The object of the series was frankly to aid the circulation manager's efforts to build up subscription lists in the rural districts, and personal sketches of local celebrities had proved potent in this endeavor. Most of the subjects that had fallen to Harwood's lot had been of a familiar type—country lawyers who sat in the legislature, or county chairmen, or judges of county courts. As the "Sunday Courier" eschewed politics, the series was not restricted to Democrats but included men of all faiths. It was Harwood's habit to spend a day in the towns he visited, gathering local color and collecting anecdotal matter.

While this employment cut deeply into his hours at the law office, he reasoned that there was a compensating advantage in the knowledge he gained on these excursions of the men of both political faiths.

Before the train stopped at Fraserville he saw from the car window the name "Bassett" written large on a towering elevator,—a fact which he noted carefully as offering a suggestion for the introductory line of his sketch. As he left the station and struck off toward the heart of the town, he was aware that Bassett was a name that appealed to the eye frequently. The Bassett Block and Bassett's Bank spoke not merely for a material prosperity, rare among the local statesmen he had described in the "Courier," but, judging from the prominence of the name in Fraserville nomenclature, he assumed that it had long been established in the community. Harwood had not previously faced a second generation in his pursuit of Hoosier celebrities, and he breathed a sigh of relief at the prospect of a variation on the threadbare scenario of early hardship, the little red schoolhouse, patient industry, and the laborious attainment of meagre political honors—which had begun to bore him.

Harwood sought first the editor of the "Fraser County Democrat," who was also the "Courier's" Fraserville correspondent. Fraserville boasted two other newspapers, the "Republican," which offset the "Democrat" politically, and the "News," an independent afternoon daily whose function was to encourage strife between its weekly contemporaries and boom the commercial interests of the town. The editor of the "Democrat" was an extremely stout person, who sprawled at ease in a battered swivel chair, with his slippered feet thrown across a desk littered with newspapers, clippings, letters, and manuscript. A file hook was suspended on the wall over his shoulder, and on this it was his habit to impale, by a remarkable twist of body and arm, gems for his hebdomadal journal. He wrote on a pad held in his ample lap, the paste brush was within easy reach, and once planted on his throne the editor was established for the day. Bound volumes of the "Congressional Record" in their original wrappers were piled in a corner. A consular report, folded in half, was thrust under the editor's right thigh, easily accessible in ferocious moments when he indulged himself in the felicity of slaughtering the roaches with which the place swarmed. He gave Dan a limp fat hand, and cleared a chair of exchanges with one foot, which he thereupon laboriously restored to its accustomed place on the desk.

"So you're from the 'Courier'? Well, sir, you may tell your managing editor for me that if he doesn't print more of my stuff he can get somebody else on the job here."

Dan soothed Mr. Pettit's feelings as best he could; he confessed that his own best work was mercilessly cut; and that, after all, the editors of city newspapers were poor judges of the essential character of news. When Pettit's good humor had been restored, Dan broached the nature of his errand. As he mentioned Morton Bassett's name the huge editor's face grew blank for a moment; then he was shaken with mirth that passed from faint quivers until his whole frame was convulsed. His rickety chair trembled and rattled ominously. It was noiseless laughter so far as any vocal manifestations were concerned; but it shook the gigantic editor as though he were a mould of jelly. He closed his eyes, but otherwise his fat face was expressionless.

"Goin' to write Mort up, are you? Well, by gum! I've been readin' those pieces in the 'Courier.' Your work? Good writin'; mighty interestin' readin', as old Uncle Horace Greeley used to say. I guess you carry the whitewash brush along with you in your pilgrimages. You certainly did give Bill Ragsdale a clean bill o' health. That must have tickled the folks in Tecumseh County. Know Ragsdale? I've set with Bill in the lower house three sessions, and I come pretty near knowin' him. I don't say that Bill is crooked; but I suspect that if Bill's moral nature could be dug out and exposed to view it would be spiral like a bedspring; just about. It's an awful load on the Republican Party in this state, having to carry Bill Ragsdale. O Lord!"

He pursed his fat lips, and his eyes took on a far-away expression, as though some profound utterance had diverted his thoughts to remote realms of reverie. "So you're goin' to write Mort up; well, my God!"

The exact relevance of this was not apparent. Harwood had assumed on general principles that the Honorable Isaac Pettit, of the "Fraser County Democrat," was an humble and obedient servant of the Honorable Morton Bassett, and would cringe at the mention of his name. To be sure, Mr. Pettit had said nothing to disturb this belief; but neither had the editor manifested that meek submission for which the reporter had been prepared. The editor's Gargantuan girth trembled again. The spectacle he presented as he shook thus with inexplicable mirth was so funny that Harwood grinned; whereupon Pettit rubbed one of his great hands across his three-days' growth of beard, evoking a harsh rasping sound in which he seemed to find relief and satisfaction.

"You don't know Mort? Well, he's all right; he will he mighty nice to you. Mort's one of the best fellows on earth; you won't find anybody out here in Fraser County to say anything against Mort Bassett. No, sir; by God!"

Again the ponderous frame shook; again the mysterious look came into the man's curious small eyes, and Harwood witnessed another seismic disturbance in the bulk before him; then the Honorable Isaac Pettit grew serious.

"You want some facts for a starter. Well, I guess a few facts don't hurt in this business, providin' you don't push in too many of 'em."

A Hoosier Chronicle | 65

He pondered for a moment, then went on, as though summarizing from a biography: —

"Only child of the late Jeremiah Bassett, founder of Bassett's Bank. Old Jerry was pure boiler plate; he could squeeze ten per cent interest out of a frozen parsnip. He and Blackford Singleton sort o' divided things up in this section. Jerry Bassett corralled the coin; Blackford rolled up a couple of hundred thousand and capped it with a United States senatorship. Mort's not forty yet; married only child of Blackford F. Singleton—Jerry made the match, I guess; it was the only way he could get Blackford's money. Mort prepared for college, but didn't go. Took his degree in law at Columbia, but never practiced. Always interested in politics; been in the state senate twelve years; two children, boy and girl. I guess Mort Bassett can do most anything he wants to—you can't tell where he'll land."

"But the next steps are obvious," suggested Harwood, encouragingly—"the governorship, the United States Senate—ever onward and upward."

"Well, yes; but you never know anything from *him*. *We* don't know, and you might think we'd understand him pretty well up here. He declined to go to Congress from this district—could have had it without turning a hand; but he put in his man and stayed in the state senate. I reckon he cuts some ice there, but he's mighty quiet. Bassett doesn't beat the tom-tom to call attention to himself. I guess no man swings more influence in a state convention—but he's peculiar. You'll find him different from these yahoos you've been writin' up. I know 'em all."

"A man of influence and power—leading citizen in every sense—" Dan murmured as he scribbled a few notes.

"Yep. Mort's considered rich. You may have noticed his name printed on most everything but the undertaker's and the jail as you came up from the station. The elevator and the bank he inherited from his pap. Mort's got a finger in most everything 'round here."

"Owns everything," said Harwood, with an attempt at facetiousness, "except the brewery."

Mr. Pettit's eyes opened wide, and then closed; again he was mirth-shaken; it seemed that the idea of linking Morton Bassett's name with the manufacture of malt liquor was the most stupendous joke possible. The editor's face did not change expression; the internal disturbances were not more violent this time, but they continued longer; when the strange spasm had passed he dug a fat fist into a tearful right eye and was calm.

"Oh, my God," he blurted huskily. "Breweries? Let us say that he neither makes nor consumes malt, vinous nor spirituous liquor, within the meaning of the statutes in such cases made and provided. He and Ed Thatcher make a strong team. Ed started out as a brewer, but there's nothing wrong about that, I reckon. Over in England they make lords and dukes of brewers."

"A man of rectitude—enshrined in the hearts of his fellow-citizens, popular and all that?" suggested Harwood.

Yes. Mort rather *retains* his heat, I guess. Some say he's cold as ice. His ice is the kind that freezes to what he likes. Mort's a gentleman if we have one in Fraser County. If you think you're chasin' one of these blue jeans politicians you read about in comic papers you're hitting the wrong trail, son. Mort can eat with a fork without appearin' self-conscious. Good Lord, boy, if you can say these other fellows in Indiana politics have brains, you got to say that Mort Bassett has *intellect*. Which is different, son; a dern sight different."

"I shall be glad to use the word in my sketch of Mr. Bassett," remarked Dan dryly. "It will lend variety to the series."

Harwood thanked the editor for his courtesy and walked to the door. Strange creakings from the editorial chair caused him to turn. The Honorable Isaac Pettit was in the throes of another convulsion. The attack seemed more severe than its predecessors. Dan waited for him to invoke deity with the asthmatic wheeziness to which mirth reduced his vocal apparatus.

"It's nothin', son; it's nothin'. It's my temperament: I can't help it. Did you say you were from the 'Courier'? Well, you better give Mort a good send-off. He appreciates a good job; he's a sort o' literary cuss himself."

As another mirthful spasm seemed imminent Dan retired, wondering just what in himself or in his errand had so moved the fat editor's risibilities. He learned at the Bassett Bank that Mr. Bassett was spending the day in a neighboring town, but would be home at six o'clock, so he surveyed Fraserville and killed time until evening, eating luncheon and supper with sundry commercial travelers at the Grand Hotel.

Harwood's instructions were in every case to take the subjects of his sketches at their own valuation and to set them forth sympathetically. The ambitions of most of the gentlemen he had interviewed had been obvious— obvious and futile. Nearly every man who reached the legislature felt a higher call to Congress or the governor's chair. Harwood had already described in the "Courier" the attainments of several statesmen who were willing to sacrifice their private interests for the high seat at the state capitol. The pettiness and sordidness of most of the politicians he met struck him humorously, but the tone of his articles was uniformly laudatory.

When the iron gate clicked behind him at the Bassett residence, his notebook was still barren of such anecdotes of his subject as he had usually gathered in like cases in an afternoon spent at the court-house. Stories of generosity, of the kindly care of widows and orphans, gifts to indigent pastors, boys helped through college, and similar benefactions had proved altogether elusive. Either Harwood had sought in the wrong places or Morton Bassett was of tougher fibre than the other gentlemen on whom his pencil had conferred immortality. In response to his ring a boy opened the door and admitted him without parley. He had a card ready to offer, but the lad ran to announce him without waiting for his name and reappeared promptly.

"Papa says to come right in, sir," the boy reported.

Dan caught a glimpse of a girl at the piano in the parlor who turned to glance at him and continued her playing. The lad indicated an open door midway of the long hall and waited for Harwood to enter. A lady, carrying a small workbasket in her hand, bade the reporter good-evening as she passed out. On a table in the middle of the room a checkerboard's white and black belligerents stood at truce, and from the interrupted game rose a thick-set man of medium height, with dark hair and a close-trimmed mustache, who came toward him inquiringly.

"Good-evening. I am Mr. Bassett. Have a chair."

Harwood felt the guilt of his intrusion upon a scene so sheltered and domestic. The father had evidently been playing checkers with his son; the mother's chair still rocked by another table on which stood a reading lamp.

Harwood stated his errand, and Bassett merely nodded, offering none of those protestations of surprise and humility, those pleas of unworthiness that his predecessors on Dan's list had usually insisted upon. Dan made mental note at once of the figure before him. Bassett's jaw was square and firm—power was manifest there, unmistakably, and his bristling mustache suggested combativeness. His dark eyes met Harwood's gaze steadily— hardness might be there, though their gaze was friendly enough. His voice was deep and its tone was pleasant. He opened a drawer and produced a box of cigars.

"Won't you smoke? I don't smoke myself, but you mustn't mind that." And Harwood accepted a cigar, which he found excellent. A moment later a maid placed on the table beside the checkerboard a tray, with a decanter and glasses, and a pitcher of water.

"That's for us," remarked Bassett, nodding toward the glasses. "Help yourself."

"The cigar is all I need; thank you."

The reporter was prepared to ask questions, following a routine he had employed with other subjects, but Bassett began to talk on his own initiative—of the town, the county, the district. He expressed himself well, in terse words and phrases. Harwood did not attempt to direct or lead: Bassett had taken the interview into his own hands, and was imparting information that might have been derived from a local history at the town library. Dan ceased, after a time, to follow the narrative in his absorption in the man himself. Harwood took his politics seriously and the petty politicians with whom he had thus far become acquainted in his newspaper work had impressed him chiefly by their bigotry or venality. It was not for nothing that he had worshiped at Sumner's feet at Yale and he held views that were not readily reconcilable with parochial boss-ships and the meek swallowing of machine-made platforms. Bassett was not the vulgar, intimate good-fellow who slapped every man on the back—the teller of good stories over a glass of whiskey and a cigar. He was, as Pettit had said, a new type, not of the familiar *cliché*. The decanter was a "property" placed in the scene at the dictates of hospitality; the checkerboard canceled any suggestion of conviviality that might have been conveyed by the decanter of whiskey.

Bassett's right hand lay on the table and Dan found himself watching it. It was broad but not heavy; the fingers that opened and shut quietly on a small paperweight were supple. It was a hand that would deal few blows, but hard ones. Harwood was aware, at a moment when he began to be bored by the bald facts of local history, that Bassett had abruptly switched the subject.

"Parties are necessary to democratic government. I don't believe merely in my own party; I want the opposition to be strong enough to make a fight. The people are better satisfied if there's a contest for the offices. I'm not sorry when we lose occasionally; defeat disciplines and strengthens a party. I have made a point in our little local affairs of not fighting independents when they break with us for any reason. Believing as I do that parties are essential, and that schismatic movements are futile, I make a point of not attacking them. Their failures strengthen the party—and incidentally kill the men who have kicked out of the traces. You never have to bother with them a second time."

"But they help clear the air—they serve a purpose?" suggested Harwood. He had acquired a taste for the "Nation" and the New York "Evening Post" at college, and Bassett's frank statement of his political opinions struck Dan as mediæval. He was, however, instinctively a reporter, and he refrained from interposing himself further than was necessary to stimulate the talk of the man before him.

"You are quite right, Mr. Harwood. They serve an excellent purpose. They provide an outlet; they serve as a safety valve. Now and then they will win a fight, and that's a good thing too, for they will prove, on experiment, that they are just as human and weak in practical application of their ideas as the rest of us. I'd even go as far as to say that in certain circumstances I'd let them win. They help drive home my idea that the old parties, like old, established business houses, have got to maintain a standard or they will lose the business to which they are rightfully entitled. When you see your customers passing your front door to try a new shop farther up the street, you want to sit down and consider what's the matter, and devise means of regaining your lost ground. It doesn't pay merely to ridicule the new man or cry that his goods are inferior. Yours have got to be superior—or"—and the gray eyes twinkled for the first time—"they must be dressed up to look better in your show window."

Bassett rose and walked the length of the room, with his hands thrust into his trousers pockets, and before he sat down he poured himself a glass of water from the pitcher and drank it slowly, with an air of preoccupation. He moved easily, with a quicker step than might have been expected in one of his figure. The strength of his hand was also in the firm line of his vigorous, well-knit frame. And his rather large head, Dan observed, rested solidly on broad shoulders.

Harwood's thoughts were, however, given another turn at once. Morton Bassett had said all he cared to say about politics and he now asked Dan whether he was a college man, to which prompting the reporter recited succinctly the annals of his life.

"You're a Harrison County boy, are you? So you didn't like the farm, and found a way out? That's good. You may be interested in some of my books."

Dan was immediately on guard against being bored; the library of even an intelligent local statesman like Morton Bassett was hardly likely to prove interesting. One of his earlier subjects had asked him particularly to mention his library, which consisted mainly of government reports.

"I've been a collector of Americana," Bassett remarked, throwing open several cases. "I've gone in for colonial history, particularly, and some of these things are pretty rare."

The shelves rose to the ceiling and Bassett produced a ladder that he might hand down a few of the more interesting volumes for Dan's closer inspection.

"Here's Wainwright's 'Brief Description of the Ohio River, With some Account of the Savages Living Thereon'—published in London in 1732, and there are only three copies in existence. This is Atterbury's 'Chronicle of the Chesapeake Settlements'—the best thing I have. The author was an English sailor who joined the colonists in the Revolution and published a little memoir of his adventures in America. The only other copy of that known to exist is in the British Museum. I fished mine out of a pile of junk in Baltimore about ten years ago. When I get old and have time on my hands I'm going to reprint some of these—wide margins, and footnotes, and that sort of thing. But there's fun enough now in just having them and knowing the other fellow hasn't!"

He flung open a panel of the wainscoting at a point still free of shelves and disclosed a door of a small iron safe which he opened with a key. "This isn't the family silver, but a few little things that are more valuable. These are first editions of American authors. Here's Lowell's 'Fable for Critics,' first edition; and this is Emerson's 'Nature,' 1836—a first. These are bound by Orpcutt; had them done myself. They feel good to the hand, don't they!"

Harwood's pleasure in the beautiful specimens of the binder's art was unfeigned and to his questioning Bassett dilated upon the craftsmanship.

"The red morocco of the Emerson takes the gold tooling beautifully, and the oak-leaf border design couldn't be finer. I believe this olive-green shade is the best of all. This Whittier—a first edition of 'In War Time'—is by Durand, a French artist, and one of the best specimens of his work."

Those strong hands of his touched the beautiful books fondly. Harwood took advantage of a moment when Bassett carried to the lamp Lowell's "Under the Willows" in gold and brown, the better to display the deft workmanship, to look more closely at the owner of these lovely baubles. The iron hand could be very gentle! Bassett touched the volume caressingly as he called attention to its perfection. His face, in the lamp's full light, softened, but there was in it no hint of sensuousness to prepare one for this indulgence in luxurious bibliomania. There was a childlike simplicity in Bassett's delight. A man who enjoyed such playthings could not be hard, and Dan's heart warmed with liking.

"Are you a reader of poetry?" asked Dan, as Bassett carefully collected the books and returned them to the safe.

"No. That is something we leave behind us with our youth," he said; and looking down at the bent head and sturdy shoulders, and watching the strong fingers turning the key, Dan wondered what the man's youth had been and what elements were mixed in him that soft textures of leather and delicate tracings of gold on brown and scarlet and olive could so delight him.

His rather jaunty attitude toward the "Home Life of Hoosier Statesmen" experienced a change. Morton Bassett was not a man who could be hit off in a few hundred words, but a complex character he did not pretend to understand. Threads of various hues had passed before him, but how to intertwine them was a question that already puzzled the reporter. Bassett had rested his hand on Dan's shoulder for a moment as the younger man bent over one of the prized volumes, and Dan was not insensible to the friendliness of the act.

Mrs. Bassett and the two children appeared at the door a little later.

"Come in, Hallie," said the politician; "all of you come in."

He introduced the reporter to his wife and to Marian, the daughter, and Blackford, the son.

"The children were just going up," said Mrs. Bassett. "As it's Saturday they have an hour added to their evening. I think I heard Mr. Bassett talking of books a moment ago. It's not often he brings out his first editions for a visitor."

They talked of books for a moment, while the children listened. Then Bassett recurred to the fact, already elicited, that Harwood was a Yale man, whereupon colleges were discussed.

"Many of our small fresh-water colleges do excellent work," remarked Bassett. "Some educator has explained the difference between large and small colleges by saying that in the large one the boy goes through more college, but in the small one more college goes through the boy. Of course I'm not implying, Mr. Harwood, that that was true in your case."

"Oh, I'm not sensitive about that, Mr. Bassett. And I beg not to be taken as an example of what Yale does for her students. Some of the smaller colleges stand for the best things; there's Madison College, here in our own state—its standards are severely high, and the place itself has quality, atmosphere—you feel, even as a casual visitor, that it's the real thing."

"So I've always heard," remarked Mrs. Bassett. "My father always admired Madison. Strange to say, I have never been there. Are you acquainted in Montgomery?"

Bassett bent forward slightly at the question.

"I was there for an hour or so last spring; but I was in a hurry. I didn't even take time to run into my fraternity house, though I saw its banner on the outer wall."

"Your newspaper work must give you many interesting adventures," suggested the politician.

"Not always as pleasant as this, I assure you. But I'm a person of two occupations—I'm studying law, and my visit to Montgomery was on an errand for the office where I'm allowed to use the books in return for slight services of one kind and another. As a newspaper man I'm something of an impostor; I hope I'm only a passing pilgrim in the business."

Dan faced Mrs. Bassett as he made this explanation, and he was conscious, as he turned toward the master of the house, that Bassett was observing him intently. His gaze was so direct and searching that Harwood was disconcerted for a moment; then Bassett remarked carelessly,—

"I should think newspaper work a good training for the law. It drills faculties that a lawyer exercises constantly."

Mrs. Bassett now made it possible for Marian and young Blackford to contribute to the conversation.

"I'm going to Annapolis," announced the boy.

"You've had a change of heart," said his father, with a smile. "It was West Point last week."

"Well, it will be Annapolis next week," the lad declared; and then, as if to explain his abandonment of a military career, "In the Navy you get to see the world, and in the Army you're likely to be stuck away at some awful place on the Plains where you never see anything. The Indians are nearly all killed anyhow."

"We hear a good deal nowadays about the higher education of woman," Mrs. Bassett remarked, "and I suppose girls should be prepared to earn their own living. Mothers of daughters have that to think about."

Miss Marian, catching Dan's eye, smiled as though to express her full appreciation of the humor of her mother's remark.

"Mama learned that from my Aunt Sally," she ventured; and Dan saw that she was an independent spirit, given to daring sayings, and indulged in them by her parents.

"Well, Aunt Sally is the wisest woman in the world," replied Mrs. Bassett, with emphasis. "It would be to your credit if you followed her, my dear."

Marian ignored her mother's rebuke and addressed herself to the visitor.

"Aunt Sally lives in Indianapolis and I go there to Miss Waring's School. I'm just home for Sunday."

"Mrs. Owen is my aunt; you may have heard of her, Mr. Harwood; she was my father's only sister."

"Oh, *the* Mrs. Owen! Of course every one has heard of her; and I knew that she was Senator Singleton's sister. I am sorry to say I don't know her."

Unconsciously the sense of Morton Bassett's importance deepened. In marrying Mrs. Jackson Owen's niece Bassett had linked himself to the richest woman at the state capital. He had not encumbered himself with a crude wife from the countryside, but had married a woman with important connections. Blackford Singleton had been one of the leading men of the state, and Mrs. Owen, his sister, was not a negligible figure in the background against which the reporter saw he must sketch the Fraserville senator. Harwood had met the wives of other Hoosier statesmen—uninteresting creatures in the main, and palpably of little assistance to ambitious husbands.

It appeared that the Bassetts spent their summers at their cottage on Lake Waupegan and that Mrs. Owen had a farm near them. It was clear that Bassett enjoyed his family. He fell into a chaffing way with his children and laughed heartily at Marian's forwardness. He met his son on the lad's own note of self-importance and connived with him to provoke her amusing impertinences.

Bassett imposed no restrictions upon Harwood's pencil, and this, too, was a novel experience. His predecessors on the list of leaders in Hoosier politics had not been backward about making suggestions, but Bassett did not refer to Harwood's errand at all. When Dan asked for photographs of Mrs. Bassett and the children with which to embellish his article, Bassett declined to give them with a firmness that ended the matter; but he promised to provide photographs of the house and grounds and of the Waupegan cottage and send them to Harwood in a day or two.

Harwood gave to his sketch of Morton Bassett a care which he had not bestowed upon any of his previous contributions to the "Courier's" series of Hoosier statesmen. He remained away from the law office two days the better to concentrate himself upon his task, and the result was a careful, straightforward article, into which he threw shadings of analysis and flashes of color that reflected very faithfully the impression made upon his mind by the senator from Fraser. The managing editor complained of its sobriety and lack of anecdote.

"It's good, Harwood, but it's too damned solemn. Can't you shoot a little ginger into it?"

"I've tried to paint the real Bassett. He isn't one of these raw hayseeds who hands you chestnuts out of patent medicine almanacs. I've tried to make a document that would tell the truth and at the same time please him."

"Why?" snapped the editor, pulling the green shade away from his eyes and glaring at the reporter.

"Because he's the sort of man you feel you'd like to please! He's the only one of these fellows I've tackled who didn't tell me a lot of highfalutin rot they wanted put into the article. Bassett didn't seem to care about it one way or another. I rewrote most of that stuff half a dozen times to be sure to get the punk out of it, because I knew he hated punk."

"You did, did you! Well, McNaughton of Tippecanoe County is the next standard-bearer you're to tackle, and you needn't be afraid to pin ribbons on him. You college fellows are all alike. Try to remember, Harwood, that this paper ain't the 'North American Review'; it's a newspaper for the plain people."

Dan, at some personal risk, saw to it that the illustrations were so minimized that it became unnecessary to sacrifice his text to accommodate it to the page set apart for it. He read his screed in type with considerable satisfaction, feeling that it was an honest piece of work and that it limned a portrait of Bassett that was vivid and truthful. The editor-in-chief inquired who had written it, and took occasion to commend Harwood for his good workmanship. A little later a clerk in the counting-room told him that Bassett had ordered a hundred copies of the issue containing the sketch, and this was consoling. Several other subjects had written their thanks, and Dan had rather hoped that Bassett would send him a line of approval; but on reflection he concluded that it was not like Bassett to do so, and that this failure to make any sign corroborated all that he knew or imagined of the senator from Fraser.

CHAPTER VII
SYLVIA AT LAKE WAUPEGAN

The snow lay late the next year on the Madison campus. It had been a busy winter for Sylvia, though in all ways a happy one. When it became known that she was preparing for college all the Buckeye Lane folk were anxious to help. Professor Kelton would not trust his own powers too far and he availed himself of the offers of members of the faculty to tutor Sylvia in their several branches. Buckeye Lane was proud of Sylvia and glad that the old professor found college possible for her. Happiness reigned in the cottage, and days were not so cold or snows so deep but that Sylvia and her grandfather went forth for their afternoon tramp. There was nothing morbid or anæmic about Sylvia. Every morning she pulled weights and swung Indian clubs with her windows open. A mischievous freshman who had thrown a snowball at Sylvia's heels, in the hope of seeing her jump, regretted his bad manners: Sylvia caught him in the ear with an unexpected return shot. A senior who observed the incident dealt in the lordly way of his kind with the offender. They called her "our co-ed" and "the boss girl" after that. The professor of mathematics occasionally left on his blackboard Sylvia's demonstrations and pointed them out to his class as models worthy of their emulation.

Spring stole into the heart of the Wabash country and the sap sang again in maples and elms. Lilacs and snowballs bloomed, and Professor Kelton went serenely about among his roses. Sylvia passed her examinations, and was to be admitted to Wellesley without conditions,—all the Lane knew and rejoiced! The good news was communicated to Mrs. Owen, who wrote at once to Professor Kelton from the summer headquarters she had established on her farm in northern Indiana that just then required particular attention. It ran:—

> I want you to make me a visit. Sylvia must be pretty tired after her long, busy year and I have been tinkering the house here a little bit so you can both be perfectly comfortable. It's not so lonely as you might think, as my farm borders Lake Waupegan, and the young people have gay times. My niece, Mrs. Bassett, has a cottage on the lake only a minute's walk

from me. I should like Marian and Sylvia to get acquainted and this will be easy if only you will come up for a couple of weeks. There are enough old folks around here, Andrew, to keep you and me in countenance. I inclose a timetable with the best trains marked. You leave the train at Waupegan Station, and take the steamer across the lake. I will meet you at any time you say.

So it happened that on a June evening they left the train at Waupegan and crossed the platform to the wheezy little steamer which was waiting just as the timetable had predicted; and soon they were embarked and crossing the lake, which seemed to Sylvia a vast ocean. Twilight was enfolding the world, and all manner of fairy lights began to twinkle at the far edges of the water and on the dark heights above the lake. Overhead the stars were slipping into their wonted places.

"You can get an idea of how it is at sea," said her grandfather, smiling at her long upward gaze. "Only you can hardly feel the wonder of it all here, or the great loneliness of the ocean at night."

It was, however, wonder enough, for a girl who had previously looked upon no more impressive waters than those of Fall Creek, Sugar Creek, and White River. The steamer, with much sputtering and churning and not without excessive trepidation on the part of the captain and his lone deck hand, stopped at many frail docks below the cottages that hung on the bluff above. Every cottager maintained his own light or combination of lights to facilitate identification by approaching visitors. They passed a number of sailboats lazily idling in the light wind, and several small power boats shot past with engines beating furiously upon the still waters.

"The Bassetts' dock is the green light; the red, white, and blue is Mrs. Owen's," explained the captain. "We ain't stoppin' at Bassett's to-night."

These lights marked the farthest bounds of Lake Waupegan, and were the last points touched by the boat. Sylvia watched the green light with interest as they passed. She had thought of Marian often since their meeting at Mrs. Owen's. She would doubtless see more of her now: the green light and the red, white and blue were very close together.

Mrs. Owen called to them cheerily from the dock, and waved a lantern in welcome. She began talking to her guests before they disembarked.

"Glad to see you, Andrew. You must be mighty hungry, Sylvia. Don't smash my dock to pieces, Captain; it's only wood."

Mrs. Owen complained after a few days that she saw nothing of Sylvia, so numerous were that young person's engagements. Mrs. Bassett and Marian called promptly—the former a trifle dazed by Sylvia's sudden advent, and Marian genuinely cordial. Mrs. Bassett had heard of the approaching visit with liveliest interest. A year before, when Marian had reported the presence in Mrs. Owen's house at Indianapolis of a strange girl with Professor Kelton, her curiosity had been piqued, but she soon dismissed the matter. Marian had carried home little information, and while Mrs. Bassett saw her aunt often on her frequent excursions to the city, she knew by long experience that Mrs. Owen did not yield gracefully to prodding.

Mrs. Bassett had heard all her life of Professor Kelton and she had met him now and then in the Delaware Street house, but her knowledge of him and his family was only the most fragmentary. Nothing had occurred during the year to bring the Keltons again to her attention; but now, with a casualness in itself disconcerting, they had arrived at Mrs. Owen's farmhouse, where, Mrs. Bassett was sure, no guests had ever been entertained before. The house had just been remodeled and made altogether habitable, a fact which, Mrs. Bassett had been flattering herself, argued for Mrs. Owen's increasing interest in herself and her family. The immediate arrival of the Keltons was disquieting.

Through most of her life Hallie Bassett had assumed that she and her children, as Sally Owen's next of kin, quite filled the heart of that admirable though often inexplicable woman. Mrs. Bassett had herself inherited a small fortune from her father, Blackford F. Singleton, Mrs. Owen's brother, a judge of the Indiana Supreme Court and a senator in Congress, whose merits and services are set forth in a tablet at the portal of the Fraser County Court-House. The Bassetts and the Singletons had been early settlers of that region, and the marriage of Hallie Singleton to Morton Bassett was a satisfactory incident in the history of both families. Six years of Mrs. Bassett's girlhood had been passed in Washington; the thought of power and influence was dear to her; and nothing in her life had been more natural than the expectation that her children would enjoy the fortune Mrs. Owen had been accumulating so long and, from all accounts, by processes hardly less than magical. Mrs. Bassett's humor was not always equal to the strain to which her aunt subjected it. Hallie Bassett had, in fact, little humor of any sort. She viewed life with a certain austerity, and in literature she had fortified herself against the shocks of time. Conduct, she had read, is three fourths of life; and Wordsworth had convinced her that the world is too much with us. Mrs. Bassett discussed nothing so ably as a vague something she was fond of characterizing as "the full life," and this she wished to secure for her children. Her boy's future lay properly with his father; she had no wish to meddle with it; but Marian was the apple of her eye, and she was striving by all the means in her power to direct her daughter into pleasant paths and bright meadows where the "full life" is assured. Hers were no mean standards. She meant to be a sympathetic and helpful wife, the wisest and most conscientious of mothers.

Mrs. Bassett was immensely anxious to please her aunt in all ways; but that intrepid woman's pleasure was not a thing to be counted on with certainty. She not only sought to please her aunt by every means possible, but she wished her children to intrench themselves strongly in their great aunt's favor. The reports of such of Mrs. Owen's public benefactions as occasionally reached the newspapers were always alarming. No one ever knew just how much money Sally Owen gave away; but some of her gifts in recent years had been too large to pass unnoticed by the press. Only a few months before she had established a working-girls' home in memory of a daughter—her only child—who had died in early youth, and this crash from a clear sky had aroused in Mrs. Bassett the gravest apprehensions. It was just so much money said to be eighty thousand dollars—out of the pockets of Marian and Blackford; and, besides, Mrs. Bassett held views on this type of benevolence. Homes for working-girls might be well enough, but the danger of spoiling them by too much indulgence was not inconsiderable; Mrs. Bassett's altruism was directed to the moral and intellectual uplift of the mass (she never said masses) and was not concerned with the plain prose of housing, feeding, and clothing young women who earned their own living. Mrs. Owen, in turning over this home to a board of trustees, had stipulated that music for dancing should be provided every Saturday evening; whereupon two trustees, on whom the Christian religion weighed heavily, resigned; but Mrs. Owen did not care particularly. Trustees were only necessary to satisfy the law and to assure the legal continuity of Elizabeth House, which Mrs. Owen directed very well herself.

Mrs. Bassett encouraged Marian's attentions to Mrs. Owen's young visitor; but it must be said that Marian, on her own account, liked Sylvia and found delight in initiating her into the mysteries of Waupegan life. She taught her to ride, to paddle a canoe, and to swim. There were dances at the casino, and it was remarkable how easily Sylvia learned to dance. Marian taught her a few steps on the first rainy day at the Bassett house, and thereafter no one would have doubted that Sylvia had been to dancing-school with the boys and girls she met at the casino parties. Marian was the most popular girl in the summer colony and Sylvia admired her ungrudgingly. In all outdoor sports Marian excelled. She dived from a spring-board like a boy, she paddled a canoe tirelessly and with inimitable grace, and it was a joy to see her at the tennis court, where her nimbleness of foot and the certainty of her stroke made her easily first in all competitions. At the casino, after a hard round of tennis, and while waiting for cakes and lemonade to be served, she would hammer ragtime on the piano or sing the latest lyrical offerings of Broadway. Quiet, elderly gentlemen from Cincinnati, Louisville, and Indianapolis, who went to the casino to read the newspapers or to play bridge, grinned when Marian turned things upside down. If any one else had improvised a bowling-alley of ginger-ale bottles and croquet-balls on the veranda, they would have complained of it bitterly. She was impatient of restraint, and it was apparent that few restraints were imposed upon her. Her sophistication in certain directions was to Sylvia well-nigh incomprehensible. In matters of personal adornment, for example, the younger girl's accomplishments were astonishing. She taught Sylvia how to arrange her hair in the latest fashion promulgated by "Vogue"; she instructed her in the refined art of manicuring according to the method of the best shop in Indianapolis; and it was amazing how wonderfully Marian could improve a hat by the slightest readjustments of ribbon and feather. She tested the world's resources like a spoiled princess with an indulgent chancellor to pay her bills. She gave a party and ordered the refreshments from Chicago, though her mother protested that the domestic apparatus for making ice-cream was wholly adequate for the occasion. When she wanted new tennis shoes she telegraphed for them; and she kept in her room a small library of mail-order catalogues to facilitate her extravagances.

Marian talked a great deal about boys, and confided to Sylvia her sentimental attachment for one of the lads they saw from day to day, and with whom they played tennis at the casino court. For the first time Sylvia heard a girl talk of men as of romantic beings, and of love as a part of the joy and excitement of life. A young gentleman in a Gibson drawing which she had torn from an old copy of "Life" more nearly approximated Marian's ideal than even the actors of her remote adoration. She had a great number of gowns and was quite reckless in her use of them. She tried to confer upon Sylvia scarf pins, ties, and like articles, for which she declared she had not the slightest use. In the purchase of soda water and candy at the casino, where she scribbled her father's initials on the checks, or at the confectioner's in the village where she enjoyed a flexible credit, her generosity was prodigal. She was constantly picking up other youngsters and piloting them on excursions that her ready fancy devised; and if they returned late for meals or otherwise incurred parental displeasure, to Marian it was only part of the joke. She was always late and ingeniously plausible in excusing herself. "Mother won't bother; she wants me to have a good time. And when papa is here he just laughs at me. Papa's just the best ever."

Mrs. Bassett kept lamenting to Professor Kelton her husband's protracted delay in Colorado. He was interested in a mining property there and was waiting for the installation of new machinery, but she expected to hear that he had left for Indiana at any time, and he was coming direct to Waupegan for a long stay. Mrs. Owen was busy with the Waupegan farm and with the direction of her farms elsewhere. On the veranda of her house one might frequently hear her voice raised at the telephone as she gave orders to the men in charge of her properties in central and southern Indiana. Her hearing was perfect and she derived the greatest satisfaction from telephoning. She sold stock or produce on these distant estates with the market page of the "Courier" propped on the telephone desk before her, and explained her transactions zestfully to Professor Kelton and Sylvia. She communicated frequently with the superintendent of her horse farm at Lexington about the "string" she expected to send forth to triumph at county and state fairs. The "Annual Stud Register" lay beside the Bible on the living-room table; and the "Western Horseman" mingled amicably with the "Congregationalist" in the newspaper rack.

The presence of the old professor and his granddaughter at Waupegan continued to puzzle Mrs. Bassett. Mrs. Owen clearly admired Sylvia, and Sylvia was a charming girl—there was no gainsaying that. At the farmhouse a good deal had been said about Sylvia's plans for going to college. Mrs. Owen had proudly called attention to them, to her niece's annoyance. If Sylvia's advent marked the flowering in Mrs. Owen of some new ideals of woman's development, Mrs. Bassett felt it to be her duty to discover them and to train Marian along similar lines. She felt that her husband would be displeased if anything occurred to thwart the hand of destiny that had so clearly pointed to Marian and Blackford as the natural beneficiaries of the estate which Mrs. Owen by due process of nature must relinquish. In all her calculations for the future Mrs. Owen's fortune was an integer.

Mrs. Bassett received a letter from her husband on Saturday morning in the second week of Sylvia's stay. Its progress from the mining-camp in the mountains had been slow and the boat that delivered the letter brought also a telegram announcing Bassett's arrival in Chicago, so that he was even now on his way to Waupegan. As Mrs. Bassett pondered this intelligence Sylvia appeared at the veranda steps to inquire for Marian.

"She hasn't come down yet, Sylvia. You girls had a pretty lively day yesterday and I told Marian she had better sleep a while longer."

"We certainly have the finest times in the world," replied Sylvia. "It doesn't seem possible that I've been here nearly two weeks."

"I'm glad you're going to stay longer. Aunt Sally told me yesterday it was arranged."

"We really didn't expect to stay more than our two weeks; but Mrs. Owen made it seem very easy to do so."

"Oh, you needn't be afraid of outstaying your welcome. It's not Aunt Sally's way to bore herself. If she didn't like you very much she wouldn't have you here at all; Aunt Sally's always right straight out from the shoulder."

"Marian has done everything to give me a good time. I want you to know I appreciate it. I have never known girls; Marian is really the first girl I have ever known, and she has taught me ever so many things."

"Marian is a dear," murmured Mrs. Bassett.

She was a murmurous person, whose speech was marked by a curious rising inflection, that turned most of her statements into interrogatories. To Sylvia this habit seemed altogether wonderful and elegant.

"Suppose we take a walk along the lake path, Sylvia. We can pretend we're looking for wild flowers to have an excuse. I'll leave word for Marian to follow."

They set off along the path together. Mrs. Bassett had never seemed friendlier, and Sylvia was flattered by this mark of kindness. Mrs. Bassett trailed her parasol, using it occasionally to point out plants and flowers that called for comment. She knew the local flora well, and kept a daybook of the wildflowers found in the longitude and latitude of Waupegan; and she was an indefatigable ornithologist, going forth with notebook and opera glass in hand. She spoke much of Thoreau and Burroughs and they were the nucleus of her summer library; she said that they gained tang and vigor from their winter hibernation at the cottage. Her references to nature were a little self-conscious, as seems inevitable with such devotees, but we cannot belittle the accuracy of her knowledge or the cleverness of her detective skill in apprehending the native flora. She found red and yellow columbines tucked away in odd corners, and the blue-eyed-Mary with its four petals—two blue and two white—as readily as Sylvia's inexperienced eye discovered the more obvious ladies'-slipper and jack-in-the-pulpit. To-day Mrs. Bassett rejoiced in the discovery of the season's first puccoon, showing its orange-yellow cluster on a sandy slope. She plucked a spray of the spreading dogbane, but only that she might descant upon it to Sylvia; it was a crime, Mrs. Bassett said, to gather wild flowers, which were never the same when transplanted to the house. When they came presently to a rustic seat Mrs. Bassett suggested that they rest there and watch the lake, which had always its mild excitements.

"You haven't known Aunt Sally a great while, I judge, Sylvia? Of course you haven't known any one a great while!"

"No; I never saw her but once before this visit. That was when grandfather took me to see her in Indianapolis a year ago. She and grandfather are old friends."

"All the old citizens of Indiana have a kind of friendship among themselves. Somebody said once that the difference between Indiana and Kentucky is, that while the Kentuckians are all cousins we Hoosiers are all neighbors. But of course so many of us have had Kentucky grandfathers that we understand the Kentuckians almost as well as our own people. I used to meet your grandfather now and then at Aunt Sally's; but I can't say that I ever knew him. He's a delightful man and it's plain that his heart is centred in you."

"There was never any one like grandfather," said Sylvia with feeling.

"I suppose that as he and Aunt Sally are such old friends they must have talked a good deal together about you and your going to college. It would be quite natural."

Sylvia had not thought of this. She was the least guileful of beings, this Sylvia, and she saw nothing amiss in these inquiries.

"I suppose they may have done so; and Mrs. Owen talked to me about going to college when I visited her."

"Oh! If *she* undertook to persuade you, then it is no wonder you decided to go. She's a very powerful pleader, as she would put it herself."

"It wasn't just that way, Mrs. Bassett. I think grandfather had already persuaded me. Mrs. Owen didn't know of it till afterward; but she seemed to like the idea. Her ideas about girls and women are very interesting."

"Yes? She has a very decided way of expressing herself. I should imagine, though, that with her training and manner of life she might look a little warily at the idea of college training for women. Personally, you understand, I am heartily in favor of it. I have hoped that Marian might go to college. Aunt Sally takes the greatest interest in Marian, naturally, but she has never urged it upon us."

Sylvia gazed off across the lake and made no reply. She recalled distinctly Mrs. Owen's comments on Marian, expressed quite clearly on the day of their drive into the country, a year before. It was not for her to repeat those observations; she liked Marian and admired her, and she saw no reason why Marian should not go to college. Sylvia, guessing nothing of what was in Mrs. Bassett's mind, failed to understand that Mrs. Owen's approval of Marian's education was of importance. Nothing could have been more remote from her thoughts than the idea that her own plans concerned any one but herself and her grandfather. She was not so dull, however, but that she began to feel that Mrs. Bassett was speaking defensively of Marian.

"Marian's taste in reading is very unusual, I think. I have always insisted that she read only the best. She is very fond of Tennyson. I fancy that after all, home training is really the most valuable,—I mean that the atmosphere of the home can give a child what no school supplies. I don't mean, of course, that we have it in *our* home; but I'm speaking of the ideal condition where there *is* an atmosphere. I've made a point of keeping good books lying about the house, and the best magazines and reviews. I was never happier than the day I found Marian curled up on a lounge reading Keats. It may be that the real literary instinct, such as I feel Marian has, would only be spoiled by college; and I should like nothing better than to have Marian become a writer. A good many of our best American women writers have not been college women; I was looking that up only the other day."

Sylvia listened, deeply interested; then she laughed suddenly, and as Mrs. Bassett turned toward her she felt that it would do no harm to repeat a remark of Mrs. Owen's that had struck her as being funny.

"I just happened to remember something Mrs. Owen said about colleges. She said that if it isn't in the colt the trainer can't put it there; and I suppose the successful literary women have had genius whether they had higher education or not. George Eliot hadn't a college training, but of course she was a very great woman."

Mrs. Bassett compressed her lips. She had not liked this quotation from Mrs. Owen's utterances on this vexed question of higher education. Could it be possible that Aunt Sally looked upon Marian as one of those colts for whom the trainer could do nothing? It was not a reassuring thought; her apprehensions as to Sylvia's place in her kinswoman's affections were quickened by Sylvia's words; but Mrs. Bassett dropped the matter.

"I have never felt that young girls should read George Eliot. She doesn't seem to me *quite* an ideal to set before a young girl."

As Sylvia knew nothing of George Eliot, except what she had gleaned from the biographical data in a text-book on nineteenth-century writers, she was unable to follow Mrs. Bassett. She had read "Mill on the Floss," and "Romola" and saw no reason why every one shouldn't enjoy them.

Mrs. Bassett twirled her closed parasol absently and studied the profile of the girl beside her.

"The requirements for college are not really so difficult, I suppose?" she suggested.

Sylvia's dark eyes brightened as she faced her interlocutor. Those of us who know Sylvia find that quick flash of humor in her eyes adorable.

"Oh, they can't be, for I answered most of the questions!" she exclaimed, and then, seeing no response in her inquisitor, she added soberly: "It's all set out in the catalogue and I have one with me. I'd be glad to bring it over if you'd like to see it."

"Thank you, Sylvia. I should like to see it. I may want to ask you some questions about the work; but of course you won't say anything to Marian of our talk. I am not quite sure, and I'll have to discuss it with Mr. Bassett."

"Of course I shan't speak of it, Mrs. Bassett."

Marian's voice was now heard calling them, down the path, and the girl appeared, a moment later, munching a bit of toast stuccoed with jam, and eager to be off for the casino where a tennis match was scheduled for the morning.

"Don't be late for dinner this evening, Marian; your father will be here, and if you see Blackford, be sure to tell him to meet the 3.10."

"Yes, mama, I'll remember, and I'll try to meet the train too." And then to Sylvia, as she led the way to the boathouse to get the canoe, "I'm glad dad's coming. He's perfectly grand, and I'm going to see if he won't give me a naphtha launch. Dad's a good old scout and he's pretty sure to do it."

Marian's manner of speaking of her parents disclosed the filial relationship in a new aspect to Sylvia, who did not at once reconcile it with her own understanding of the fifth commandment. Marian referred to her father variously as "the grand old man," "the true scout," "Sir Morton the good knight," and to her mother as "the Princess Pauline," or "one's mama," giving to *mama* the French pronunciation. All this seemed to Sylvia to be in keeping with Marian's general precociousness.

Sylvia had formed the habit of stealing away in the long twilights, after the cheerful gathering at Mrs. Owen's supper-table, for a little self-communing. Usually Mrs. Owen and Professor Kelton fell to talking of old times and old friends at this hour and Sylvia's disappearances were unremarked. She felt the joy of living these days, and loved dearly the delaying hour between day and night that is so lovely, so touched with poetry in this region. There was always a robin's vesper song, that may be heard elsewhere than in Indiana, but can nowhere else be so tremulous with joy and pain. A little creek ran across Mrs. Owen's farm, cutting for itself a sharp defile to facilitate its egress into the lake; and Sylvia liked to throw herself down beside a favorite maple, with the evening breeze whispering over the young corn behind her, and the lake, with its heart open to the coming of the stars, quiet before her, and dream the dreams that fill a girl's heart in those blessed and wonderful days when the brook and river meet.

On this Saturday evening Sylvia was particularly happy. The day's activities, that had begun late, left her a little breathless. She was wondering whether any one had ever been so happy, and whether any other girl's life had ever been so pleasantly ordered. Her heartbeat quickened as she thought of college and the busy years that awaited her there; and after that would come the great world's wide-open doors. She was untouched by envy, hatred, or malice. There was no cloud anywhere that could mar; the stars that stole out into the great span of sky were not more tranquil than her own heart. The world existed only that people might show kindness one to another, and that all this beauty of wood, field, water, and starry sky might bring joy to the souls of men. She knew that there was evil in the world; but she knew it from books and not from life. Her path had fallen in pleasant places, and only benignant spirits attended her.

She was roused suddenly by the sound of steps in the path beneath. This twilight sanctuary had never been invaded before, and she rose hastily. The course of an irregular path that followed the lake was broken here by the creek's miniature chasm, but adventurous pedestrians might gain the top and continue over a rough rustic bridge along the edge of Mrs. Owen's cornfield. Sylvia peered down, expecting to see Marian or Blackford, but a stranger was approaching, catching at bushes to facilitate his ascent. Sylvia stepped back, assuming it to be a cottager who had lost his way. A narrow-brimmed straw hat rose above the elderberry bushes, and with a last effort the man stood on level ground, panting from the climb. He took off his hat and mopped his face as he glanced about. Sylvia had drawn back, but as the stranger could not go on without seeing her she stepped forward, and they faced each other, in a little plot of level ground beside the defile.

"Pardon me!" he exclaimed, still breathing hard; and then his eyes met hers in a long gaze. His gray eyes searched her dark ones for what seemed an interminable time. Sylvia's hand sought the maple but did not touch it; and the keen eyes of the stranger did not loosen their hold of hers. A breeze blowing across the cornfield swept over them, shaking the maple leaves, and rippled the surface of the lake. The dusk, deepening slowly, seemed to shut them in together.

"Pardon me, again! I hope I didn't frighten you! I am Mr. Bassett, Marian's father."

"And I am Sylvia Garrison. I am staying—"

"Oh," he laughed, "you needn't tell me! They told me at the supper-table all about you and that you and Marian are fast friends."

"I knew you were coming; they were speaking of it this morning."

They had drawn closer together during this friendly exchange. Again their eyes met for an instant, then he surveyed her sharply from head to foot, as he stood bareheaded leaning on his stick.

"I must be going," said Sylvia. "There's a path through the corn that Mrs. Owen lets me use. They'll begin to wonder what's become of me."

"Why not follow the path to the lane,—I think there is a lane at the edge of the field,—and I will walk to the house with you. The path through the corn must be a little rough, and it's growing dark."

"Yes, thank you, Mr. Bassett."

"I had no idea of meeting any one when I came out. I usually take a little walk after supper when I'm here, and I wanted to get all the car smoke out of my lungs. I was glad to get out of Chicago; it was fiercely hot there."

The path was not wide enough for two and she walked before him. After they had exhausted the heat as a topic, silence fell upon them. He still swung his hat in his hand. Once or twice he smote his stick smartly upon the ground. He timed his pace to hers, keeping close, his eyes upon her straight slender figure. When they reached the lane they walked together until they came to the highway, which they followed to the house. An oil lamp marked the walk that led through Mrs. Owen's flower garden.

"Aren't you coming in, Mr. Bassett?" asked Sylvia, as they paused.

Her hand clicked the latch and the little white-washed gate swung open. In the lamplight their eyes met again.

"I'm sorry, but I must go home. This is the first time I've been here this summer, and my stay is short. I must be off again to-morrow."

"Oh, that's too bad! Marian has been telling me that you would stay a month, she will be terribly disappointed"

"My Western trip took more time than I expected I have a good deal to do at Fraserville and must get back there"

She stepped inside, thinking he delayed out of courtesy to her, but to her surprise he fastened the latch deliberately and lingered.

"They tell me you and your grandfather live at Montgomery. It's a charming town, one of the most interesting in the state."

"Yes, Mr. Bassett. My grandfather taught in the college there."

"I have often heard of Professor Kelton, of course. He's a citizen our state is proud of. Mrs. Bassett says you're going to college this fall—to Wellesley, is it? Mrs. Bassett has an idea that Marian ought to have a college education. What do you think about it?"

He smiled kindly, and there was kindness in his deep voice.

"I think girls should go who want to go," answered Sylvia, her hands on the pickets of the gate.

"You speak like a politician," laughed Bassett. "That's exactly what I think; and I haven't seen that Marian is dying for a college career."

"She has plenty of time to think of it," Sylvia replied. "I'm ever so much older"; and this seemed to dispose of that matter.

"You are staying here some time?"

"Another week. It seems that we've hardly been here a day."

"You are fortunate in having Mrs. Owen for a friend. She is a very unusual woman."

"The most wonderful person I ever knew!" responded Sylvia warmly.

He still showed no haste to leave her, though he had just reached Waupegan, and was going away the next day.

"Your grandfather isn't teaching at Madison now, I believe?"

"No; but he lectures sometimes, and he has taught me; there was never a better teacher," she answered, smiling.

"You must have been well taught if you are ready for college so early; you are—you say you're older than Marian—do you mind my asking how old you are?"

"Nearly seventeen; seventeen in October."

"Oh! Then you are four years older than Marian. But I mustn't keep you here. Please remember me to Mrs. Owen and tell her I'll drop in before I go." He bent over the gate and put out his hand. "Good-night, Miss Garrison!"

Sylvia had never been called Miss Garrison before, and it was not without trepidation that she heard herself so addressed. Mr. Bassett had spoken the name gravely, and their eyes met again in lingering contact. When the door closed upon her he walked on rapidly; but once, before the trees had obscured Mrs. Owen's lights, he turned and glanced back.

CHAPTER VIII
SILK STOCKINGS AND BLUE OVERALLS

One night in this same June, Harwood was directed by the city editor of the "Courier" to find Mr. Edward G. Thatcher. Two reporters had failed at it, and it was desirable to verify reports as to certain transactions by which Thatcher, in conjunction with Morton Bassett, was believed to be effecting a merger of various glass-manufacturing interests. Thatcher had begun life as a brewer, but this would long since have been obscured by the broadening currents of fortune if it had not been for his persistent dabbling in politics. Whenever the Republican press was at a loss for something to attack, Thatcher's breweries—which he had concealed in a corporation that did not bear his name were an inviting and unfailing target. For years, though never seeking office, he had been a silent factor in politics, and he and Bassett, it was said, controlled their party. Mrs. Thatcher had built an expensive house, but fearing that the money her husband generously supplied was tainted by the remote beer vats, she and her two daughters spent most of their time in Europe, giving, however, as their reason the ill-health of Thatcher's son. Thatcher's income was large and he spent it in his own fashion. He made long journeys to witness prize fights; he had the reputation of being a poor poker player, but "a good loser"; he kept a racing-stable that lost money, and he was a patron of baseball and owned stock in the local club. He was "a good fellow" in a sense of the phrase that requires quotation marks. Mrs. Sally Owen, whose opinion in all matters pertaining to her fellow citizens is not to be slighted, fearlessly asked Thatcher to dinner at her house. She expressed her unfavorable opinion of his family for deserting him, and told him to his face that a man who knew as little about horses as he did should have a guardian.

"He's in town somewhere," said the city editor; "don't come back and tell me you can't find him. Try the Country Club, where he was never known to go, and the University Club, where he doesn't belong, and all the other unlikely places you can think of. The other boys have thrown up their hands."

Dan had several times been fortunate in like quests for men in hiding, and he had that confidence in his luck which is part of the good reporter's endowment. He called all the clubs and the Thatcher residence by telephone. The clubs denied all knowledge of Edward G. Thatcher, and his residence answered not at all; whereupon Harwood took the trolley for the Thatcher mansion in the new quarter of Meridian Street beyond the peaceful shores of Fall Creek. A humorist who described the passing show from the stern of a rubber-neck wagon for the instruction of tourists announced on every round that "This is Edward G. Thatcher's residence; it contains twelve bath-rooms, and cost seventy-five thousand dollars four years ago. The family have lived in it three months. Does it pay to be rich?"

As Harwood entered the grounds the house loomed darkly before him. Most of the houses in this quarter were closed for the summer, but Dan assumed that there must be some sort of caretaker on the premises and he began patiently punching the front-door bell. Failing of any response, he next tried a side door and finally the extreme rear. He had begun to feel discouraged when, as he approached the front entrance for a second assault, he saw a light flash beyond the dark blinds. The door opened cautiously, and a voice gruffly bade him begone.

"I have a message for Mr. Thatcher; it's very important—"

"Mr. Thatcher not at home; nobody home," growled a voice in broken English. "You get right off dis place, quick!"

Dan thrust his walking-stick into the small opening to guard against having the door slammed in his face and began a parley that continued for several minutes with rising heat on the part of the caretaker. The man's rage at being unable to close the door was not without its humor; but Dan now saw, beyond the German's broad shoulders, a figure lurking within, faintly discernible from the electric lamps in a bronze sconce on the wall.

The reporter and the caretaker were making no progress in their colloquy and Dan was trying to catch a glimpse of the other man, who leaned against the wall quite indifferent to the struggle for the door. Dan supposed him to be another servant, and he had abandoned hope of learning anything of Thatcher, when a drawling voice called out:—

"Open the door, Hans, and let the gentleman in: I'll attend to him."

Dan found himself face to face with a young man of about his own age, a slender young fellow, clad in blue overalls and flannel shirt. He lounged forward with an air of languor that puzzled the reporter. His dress was not wholly conclusive as to his position in the silent house; the overalls still showed their pristine folds, the shirt was of good quality and well-cut. The ends of a narrow red-silk four-in-hand swung free. He was clean-shaven save for an absurd little mustache so fair as to be almost indistinguishable.

His blond hair was brushed back unparted from his forehead. Another swift survey of the slight figure disclosed a pair of patent-leather pumps. His socks, revealed at the ankles, were scarlet. Dan was unfamiliar with the ménage of such establishments as this, and he wondered whether this might not be an upper servant of a new species peculiar to homes of wealth. He leaned on his stick, hat in hand, and the big blue eyes of the young man rested upon him with disconcerting gravity. A door slammed at the rear upon the retreating German, whom this superior functionary had dispatched about his business. At a moment when the silence became oppressive the young man straightened himself slightly and spoke in a low voice, and with amusement showing clearly in his eyes and about his lips,—

"You're a reporter."

"Yes; I'm from the 'Courier.' I'm looking for Mr. Thatcher."

"Suppose, suppose—if you're not in a great hurry, you come with me."

The pumps, with the scarlet socks showing below the overalls, turned at the end of the broad hall and began ascending the stairs. The young man's manner was perfectly assured. He had not taken his hands from his pockets, and he carried himself with an ease and composure that set Dan's conjectures at naught. In the absence of the family, a servant might thus conduct himself; and yet, if Thatcher was not at home, why should he be thus ushered into the inner sanctities of the mansion by this singular young person, whose silk hose and bright pumps were so utterly out of harmony with the rest of his garb. There might be a trick in it; perhaps he had intruded upon a burglarious invasion,—this invitation to the upper chambers might be for the purpose of shutting him in somewhere until the place had been looted. It was, in any case, a novel adventure, and his curiosity was aroused by the languid pace with which, without pausing at the second floor, the young man continued on to the third. Through an open door Dan saw a bedroom in order for occupancy; but the furniture in the upper and lower halls was draped, and a faint odor of camphor hung upon the air. It had occurred to Harwood that he might be stumbling upon material for a good "story," though just what it might prove to be was still a baffling question. His guide had not spoken or looked at him since beginning the ascent, and Harwood grasped his stick more firmly when they gained the third floor. If violence was in the programme he meant to meet it gallantly. His conductor passed through a spacious bedroom, and led the way to a pleasant lounging- and reading-room with walls lined with books. Without pausing he flung open a door that divulged a shop, with a bench and tools. The litter of carpentry on the bare floor testified to the room's recent use.

"Sit down, won't you, and have a cigar?"

Dan hesitated. He felt that he must be the victim of a practical joke, and it was time that his dignity asserted itself. He had accepted a cigar and was holding it in his fingers, still standing. His strange guide struck a match and held it, so that Dan perforce took advantage of the proffered flame; and he noticed now for the first time the young fellow's slender, nervous hands, which bore no marks of hard toil. He continued to watch them with interest as they found and filled a pipe. They were amazingly deft, expressive hands.

"Have a chair! It's a good one; I made it myself!"

With this the young gentleman jumped lightly upon the workbench where he nursed his knees and smoked his pipe. He was a graceful person, trimly and delicately fashioned, and in this strange setting altogether inexplicable. But Dan's time was important, and he had not yet learned anything as to Edward G. Thatcher's whereabouts. This languid young gentleman seemed wholly indifferent to the reporter's restlessness, and Dan's professional pride rebelled.

"Pardon me, but I must see Mr. Thatcher. Where is he, please?"

"He's gone, skipped! No manner of use in looking for him. On my honor, he's not in town."

"Then why didn't you say so and be done with it?" demanded Dan angrily.

"Please keep your seat," replied the young fellow from the workbench. "I really wish you would."

He drew on his pipe for a moment, and Dan, curiously held by his look and manner and arrested by the gentleness of his voice, awaited further developments. He had no weapons with which to deal with this composed young person in overalls and scarlet hose. He swallowed his anger; but his curiosity now clamored for satisfaction.

"May I ask just who you are and why on earth you brought me up here?"

"Those are fair questions—two of them. To the first, I am Allen Thatcher, and this is my father's house. To the second—" He hesitated a moment, then shrugged his shoulders and laughed. "Well, if you must know,—I was so devilish lonesome!"

He gazed at Harwood quizzically, with a half-humorous, half-dejected air.

"If you're lonesome, Mr. Thatcher, it must be because you prefer it that way. It can't be necessary for you to resort to kidnapping just to have somebody to talk to. I thought you were in Europe."

"Nothing as bad as that! What's your name, if you don't mind?"

When Dan gave it, Thatcher nodded and thanked him.

"College man?"

"Yale."

"That's altogether bully. I envy you, by George! You see," he went on easily, as though in the midst of a long and intimate conversation, "they took me abroad, and it never really counted. They always treated me as though I were an invalid; and kept me for a year or two squatting on an Alp on account of my lungs. It amused them, no doubt; and it filled in my time till I was too old to go to college. But now that I'm grown up, I'm going to stay at home. I've been here a month, having a grand old time; a little lonesome, and yet I'm a person of occupations and Hans cooks enough for me to eat. I haven't been down town much, but nobody knows me here anyhow. Dad's been living at the club or a hotel, but he moved up here to be with me. Dad's the best old chap on earth. I guess he liked my coming back. They rather bore him, I fancy. We've had a bully day or two, but dad has skipped. Gone to New York; be back in a week. Wanted me to go; but not me! I've had enough travel for a while. They gave me a dose of it."

These morsels of information fell from him carelessly. His "they," Dan assumed, referred to his mother and sisters somewhere on the other side of the Atlantic; and young Thatcher spoke of them in a curiously impersonal and detached fashion. The whimsical humor that twinkled in his eyes occasionally was interesting and pleasing; and Dan imagined that he was enjoying the situation. Silk socks and overalls were probably a part of some whim; they certainly added picturesqueness to the scene. But the city editor must be informed that Edward G Thatcher was beyond his jurisdiction and Dan rose and moved toward the door. Allen jumped down and crossed to him quickly.

"Oh, I say! I really wish you wouldn't go!"

There was no doubt of the pleading in his voice and manner. He laid a hand very gently on Dan's arm.

"But I've got to get back downtown, if your father has really gone and isn't hidden away here somewhere."

"I've cut you a slice right out of the eternal truth on that, old man. Father will be in New York for breakfast in the morning. Search the house all you please; but, do you know, I'd rather like you to believe me."

"Of course, I believe you; but it's odd the office didn't know you were here. They told me you and your mother and sisters were abroad, but that your father was in town. A personal item in the 'Courier' this morning said that you were all in the Hartz Mountains."

"I dare say it did! The newspapers keep them all pretty well before the public. But I've had enough junketing. I'm going to stay right here for a while."

"You prefer it here—is that the idea?"

"Yes, I fancy I should if I knew it; I want to know it. But I'm all kinds of crazy, you know. They really think I'm clear off, simply because their kind of thing doesn't amuse me. I lost too much as a kid being away from home. They said I had to be educated abroad, and there you see me—Dresden awhile, Berlin another while, a lot of Geneva, and Paris for grand sprees. And my lung was always the excuse if they wanted to do a winter on the Nile,—ugh! The very thought of Egypt makes me ill now."

"It all sounds pretty grand to me. I was never east of Boston in my life."

"By Jove! I congratulate you," exclaimed the young man fervidly. "And I'll wager that you went to school at a cross-roads school-house and rode to town in a farm wagon to see a circus that had lions and elephants; and you probably chopped wood and broke colts and went swimming in an old swimmin'-hole and did all the other things you read about in American biographies and story books. I can see it in your eye; and you talk like it, too."

"I dare say I do!" laughed Dan. "They've always told me that my voice sounds like a nutmeg grater."

"They filed mine off! Mother was quite strong for the Italian *a*, and I'm afraid I've caught it, just like a disease."

"I should call it a pretty good case. I was admiral of a canal boat in New Jersey one summer trying to earn enough money to carry my sophomore year in college, and cussing the mules ruined my hope of a reputable accent. It almost spoiled my Hoosier dialect!"

"By George, I wonder if the canal-boat people would take me! It would be less lonesome than working at the bench here. Dad says I can do anything I like. He's tickled to death because I've come home. He's really the right sort; he did all the horny-handed business himself—ploughed corn, wore red mittens to a red school-house, and got licked with a hickory stick. But he doesn't understand why I don't either take a job in his office or gallop the Paris boulevards with mother and the girls; but he's all right. We're great pals. But the rest of them made a row because I came home. For a while they had dad's breweries as an excuse for keeping away, and my lungs! Dad hid the breweries, so their hope of a villa at Sorrento is in my chest. Dad says my lungs have been their main asset. There's really nothing the matter with me; the best man in New York told me so as I came through."

His manner of speaking of his family was deliciously droll; he yielded his confidences as artlessly as a child.

"They almost got a steam yacht on me last year," he went on. "Hired a Vienna doctor to say I ought to be kept at sea between Gibraltar and the Bosphorus. And here, by George, is America the dear, bully old America of Washington, Franklin, Andrew Jackson, and Abraham Lincoln! And they want to keep me chasing around among ruins and tombs! I say to you, Mr. Harwood, in all solemnity, that I've goo-gooed my last goo-goo at the tombs of dead kings!"

They stood near the shop door during this interchange. Dan forgot, in his increasing interest and mystification, that the "Courier's" city editor was waiting for news of Thatcher, the capitalist. Young Thatcher's narrative partook of the nature of a protest. He was seriously in rebellion against his own expatriation. He stood erect now, with the color bright in his cheeks, one hand thrust into his pocket, the other clenching his pipe.

"I tell you," he declared, "I've missed too much! Life over here is a big thing!—it's wonderful, marvelous, grand, glorious! And who am I to spend winters on the dead old Nile when history is being made right here on White River! I tell you I want to watch the Great Experiment, and if I were not a poor, worthless, ignorant ass I'd be a part of it."

Dan did not question the young fellow's sincerity. His glowing eyes and the half-choked voice in which he concluded gave an authentic stamp to his lament and pronouncement. A look of dejection crossed his face. He had, by his own confession, asked Dan into the house merely to have some one to talk to; he was dissatisfied, unhappy, lonely; and his slender figure and flushed cheeks supported his own testimony that his health had been a matter of concern. The Nile and the Alps against which he had revolted might not be so unnecessary as he believed.

The situation was so novel that Harwood's mind did not respond with the promptness of his heart. He had known the sons of rich men at college, and some of them had been his friends. It was quite the natural and accepted order of things that some children should be born to sheltered, pampered lives, while others were obliged to hew their own way to success. He had observed in college that the sons of the rich had a pretty good time of it; but he had gone his own way unenviously. It was not easy to classify young Thatcher. He was clearly an exotic, a curious pale flower with healthy roots and a yearning for clean, free air. Dan was suddenly conscious that the young fellow's eyes were bent upon him with a wistfulness, a kind of pleading sweetness, that the reporter had no inclination to resist. He delayed speaking, anxious to say the right word, to meet the plea in the right spirit.

"I think I understand; I believe I should feel just as you do if I were in your shoes. It's mighty interesting, this whole big scheme we're a part of. Over there on the other side it's all different, the life, the aims, and the point of view. And here we've got just what you call it—the most wonderful experiment the world ever saw. Great Scott!" he exclaimed, kindling from the spark struck by Thatcher's closing words, "it's prodigious, overwhelming! There mustn't be any question of losing!"

"That's right!" broke in Thatcher eagerly; "that's what I've been wanting somebody to say! It's so beautiful, so wonderful; the hope and promise are so immense! You believe it; I can see you do!" he concluded happily.

His hand stole shyly from the pocket that seemed to be its inevitable hiding-place, and paused uncertainly; then he thrust it out, smiling.

"Will you shake hands with me?"

"Let us be old friends," replied Dan heartily. "And now I've got to get out of here or I'll lose my job."

"Then I should have to get you another. I never meant to keep you so long. You've been mighty nice about it. I suppose I couldn't help you—I mean about dad? All you wanted was to see father or find you couldn't."

"I had questions to ask him, of course. They were about a glass-factory deal with Bassett."

"Oh, I dare say they bought them! He asked me if I didn't want to go into the glass business. He talks to me a lot about things. Dad's thinking about going to the Senate. Dad's a Democrat, like Jefferson and Jackson. If he goes to the Senate I'll have a chance to see the wheels go round at Washington. Perfectly bully for me!"

Harwood grinned at the youth's naïve references to Edward Thatcher's political ambitions. Thatcher was known as a wealthy "sport," and Dan had resented his meddling in politics. But this was startling news—that Thatcher was measuring himself for a senatorial toga.

"You'd better be careful! There's a good story in that!"

"But you wouldn't! You see, I'm not supposed to know!"

"Bassett and your father will probably pull it off, if they try hard enough. They've pulled off worse things. If you're interested in American types you should know Bassett. Ever see him?"

Allen laughed. His way of laughing was pleasant; there was a real bubbling mirth in him.

"No; but I read about him in the 'Courier,' which they always have follow them about—I don't know why. It must be that it helps them to rejoice that they are so far away from home; but I always used to read it over there, I suppose to see how much fun I missed! And at a queer little place in Switzerland where we were staying—I remember, because our landlord had the drollest wart on his chin—a copy of the 'Courier' turned up on a rainy day and I read it through. A sketch of Bassett tickled me because he seemed so real. I felt that I'd like to be Morton Bassett myself,—the man who does things,—the masterful American,—a real type, by George! And that safe filled with beautiful bindings; it's fine to know there are such fellows."

"Your words affect me strangely; I wrote the piece!"

"Now that is funny!" Allen glanced at Dan with frank admiration. "You write well—praise from Sir Hubert—I scribble verses myself! So our acquaintance really began a long time ago. It must have been last October that we were at that place."

"Yes; it was in the fall sometime. It's pleasant to know that anything printed in a newspaper is ever remembered so long. Bassett is an interesting man all right enough."

"It must be bully to meet men like that—the men who have a hand in the big things. I must get dad to introduce me. I suppose you know everybody!" he ended admiringly.

They retraced their steps through the silent house and down to the front door, continuing their talk. As Dan turned for their last words on the veranda steps he acted on an impulse and said:—

"Have supper with me to-morrow night—we won't call it dinner—at the Whitcomb House. I'll meet you in the lobby at six o'clock. The honorable state committee is in town and I'll point out some of the moulders of our political destiny. They're a joy to the eye, I can tell you!"

Allen's eager acquiescence, his stumbling, murmured thanks, emphasized Dan's sense of the forlorn life young Thatcher had described.

"So the old boy's skipped, has he?" demanded the city editor. "Well, that's one on us! Who put you on?"

"I kept at the bell until the door opened and then I saw Thatcher's son. He told me."

"Oh, the family idiot let you in, did he? Then there's no telling whether it's true or not. He's nutty, that fellow. Didn't know he was here."

"I believe he told me the truth. His father's on his way to New York."

"Well, that sounds definite; but it doesn't make any difference now. We've just had a tip to let the deal alone. For God's sake, keep at the law, Harwood; this business is hell." The city editor bit a fat cigar savagely. "You no sooner strike a good thing and work on it for two days than you butt into a dead wall. What? No; there's nothing more for you to-night."

CHAPTER IX
DANIEL HARWOOD RECEIVES AN OFFER

A brief note from Morton Bassett, dated at Fraserville, reached Harwood in July. In five lines Bassett asked Dan to meet him at the Whitcomb House on a day and hour succinctly specified.

Harwood had long since exhausted the list of Hoosier statesmen selected for niches in the "Courier's" pantheon. After his visit to Fraserville, he had met Bassett occasionally in the street or at the Whitcomb House; and several times he had caught a glimpse of him passing through the reception room of the law office into Mr. Fitch's private room. On these occasions Dan was aware that Bassett's presence caused a ripple of interest to run through the office. The students in the library generally turned from their books to speak of Bassett in low tones; and Mr. Wright, coming in from a journey on one of these occasions and anxious to see his partner forthwith, lifted his brow and said "Oh!" meaningfully when told that it was Morton Bassett who engaged the time of the junior member. Bassett's name did not appear in the office records to Dan's knowledge nor was he engaged in litigation. His conferences were always with Fitch alone, and they were sometimes of length.

Harwood was not without his perplexities these days. His work for the "Courier" had gradually increased until he found that his time for study had diminished almost to the vanishing point. The home acres continued unprofitable, and he had, since leaving college, devoted a considerable part of his earnings to the relief of his father. His father's lack of success was an old story and the home-keeping sons were deficient in initiative and energy. Dan, with his ampler outlook, grudged them nothing, but the home needs were to be reckoned with in the disposition of his own time. He had now a regular assignment to the county courts and received a salary from the "Courier." He was usually so tired at the end of his day's work that he found it difficult to settle down to study at night in the deserted law office. The constant variety and excitement of newspaper work militated against the sober pondering of legal principles and Dan had begun to realize that, with the necessity for earning money hanging over him, his way to the bar, or to a practice if he should qualify himself, lay long and bleak before him.

Dan had heard much of Morton Bassett since his visit to Fraserville. His conviction, dating from the Fraserville visit, that Bassett was a man of unusual character, destined to go far in any direction in which he chose to exert his energies, was proved by Bassett's growing prominence. A session of the legislature had intervened, and the opposition press had hammered Bassett hard. The Democratic minority under Bassett's leadership had wielded power hardly second to that of the majority. Bassett had introduced into state politics the bi-partisan alliance, a device by virtue of which members of the assembly representing favored interests cooperated, to the end that no legislation viciously directed against railways, manufacturers, brewers and distillers should succeed through the deplorable violence of reformers and radicals. Apparently without realizing it, and clearly without caring greatly, Bassett was thus doing much to destroy the party alignments that had in earlier times nowhere else been so definitely marked as in Indiana. Partisan editors of both camps were glad when the sessions closed, for it had been no easy matter to defend or applaud the acts of either majority or minority, so easily did Republicans and Democrats plot together at neutral campfires. It had not been so in those early post-bellum years, when Oliver Morton of the iron mace still hobbled on crutches. Harrison and Hendricks had fought no straw men when they went forth to battle. Harwood began to be conscious of these changes, which were wholly irreconcilable with the political ideals he had imbibed from Sumner at Yale. He had witnessed several political conventions of both parties from the press table, and it was gradually dawning upon him that politics is not readily expressed in academic terminology.

The silver lining of the Democratic cloud had not greatly disturbed Morton Bassett. He had been a delegate to the national convention of 1896, but not conspicuous in its deliberations; and in the subsequent turbulent campaign he had conducted himself with an admirable discretion. He was a member of the state committee and the chairman was said to be of his choosing. Bassett stood for party regularity and deplored the action of those Democrats who held the schismatic national convention at Indianapolis and nominated the Palmer and Buckner ticket on a gold-standard platform. He had continued to reelect himself to the senate without trouble, and waited for the political alchemists of his party to change the silver back to gold. The tariff was, after all, the main issue, Bassett held; but it was said that in his business transactions during these vexed years he had stipulated gold payment in his contracts. This was never proved; and if, as charged, he voted in 1896 for Republican presidential electors it did not greatly matter when a considerable number of other Hoosier Democrats who, to outward view were virtuously loyal, managed to run with both hounds and hare. Bassett believed that his party would regain its lost prestige and come into power again; meanwhile he prospered in business, and wielded the Democratic minority at the state house effectively.

Dan presented himself punctually at the Whitcomb House where Bassett, with his bag packed, sat reading a magazine. He wore a becoming gray suit without a waistcoat, and a blue négligé shirt, with a turnover collar and a blue tie. He pulled up his creased trousers when he sat down, and the socks thus disclosed above his tan Oxfords proved to be blue also. His manner was cordial without effusiveness; when they shook hands his eyes met Dan's with a moment's keen, searching gaze, as though he sought to affirm at once his earlier judgment of the young man before him.

"I'm glad to see you again, Mr. Harwood. I was to be in town for the day and named this hour knowing I should be free."

"I supposed you were taking it easy at Lake Waupegan. I remember you told me you had a place there."

Bassett's eyes met Dan's quickly; then he answered:—

"Oh, I ought to be there, but I've only had a day of it all summer. I had to spend a lot of time in Colorado on some business; and when I struck Waupegan I found that matters had been accumulating at home and I only spent one night at the lake. But I feel better when I'm at work. I'm holding Waupegan in reserve for my old age."

"You don't look as though you needed a vacation," remarked Dan. "In fact you look as though you'd had one."

"The Colorado sun did that. How are things going with you?"

"Well, I've kept busy since I saw you in Fraserville. But I seem doomed to be a newspaper man in spite of myself. I like it well enough, but I think I told you I started out with some hope of landing in the law."

"Yes, I remember. I'm afraid the trouble with you is that you're too good a reporter. That sketch you wrote of me proved that. If I had not been the subject of it I should be tempted to say that it showed what I believe they call the literary touch. Mrs. Bassett liked it; maybe because there was so little of her in it. We both appreciated your nice feeling and consideration in the whole article. Well, just how are you coming on in the law?"

"Some of my work at college was preliminary to a law course, and I have done all the reading possible in Wright and Fitch's office. But I have to eat and the 'Courier' takes care of that pretty well; I've had to give less time to study. I don't know enough to be able to command a position as law clerk,—there aren't many pay jobs of that sort in a town like this."

"I suppose that's true," assented Bassett. "I suppose I shall always regret I didn't hang on at the law, but I had other interests that conflicted. But I'm a member of the bar, as I probably told you at Fraserville, and I have a considerable library stored away."

"That," laughed Dan, "is susceptible of two interpretations."

"Oh, I don't mean it's in my head; it's in a warehouse in Fraserville."

The grimness of Bassett's face in repose was an effect of his close-trimmed mustache. He was by no means humorless and his smile was pleasant. Dan felt drawn to him again as at Fraserville. Here was a man who stood four square to the winds, undisturbed by the cyclonic outbursts of unfriendly newspapers. In spite of the clashing winter at the state house and all he had heard and read of the senate leader since the Fraserville visit, Dan's opinion of Bassett stood. His sturdy figure, those firm, masterful hands, and his deep, serious voice all spoke for strength.

"It has occurred to me, Mr. Harwood, that we might be of service to each other. I have a good many interests. You may have gathered that I am a very practical person. That is wholly true. In business I aim at success; I didn't start out in life to be a failure."

Bassett paused a moment and Dan nodded. It was at the tip of his tongue to say that such should be every man's hope and aim, but Bassett continued.

"I'm talking to you frankly. I'm not often mistaken in my judgments of men and I've taken a liking to you. I want to open an office here chiefly to have a quiet place from which to keep track of things that interest me. Fraserville is no longer quite central enough and I'm down here a good deal. I need somebody to keep an office open for me. I've been looking about and there are some rooms in the Boordman Building that I think would be about right. You might call the position I'm suggesting a private secretaryship, as I should want you to take charge of correspondence, make appointments, scan the papers, and keep me advised of the trend of things. I'm going to move my law library down here to give the rooms a substantial look, and if you feel like joining me you'll have a good deal of leisure for study. Then when you're ready for practice I may be in a position to help you. You will have a salary of, say, twelve hundred to begin with, but you can make yourself worth more to me."

Dan murmured a reply which Bassett did not heed.

"Your visit to my home and the article in the 'Courier' first suggested this to me. It struck me that you understood me pretty well. I read all the other sketches in that series and the different tone in which you wrote of me gave me the idea that you had tried to please me, and that you knew how to do it. How does the proposition strike you?"

"It couldn't be otherwise than gratifying, Mr. Bassett. It's taken my breath away. It widens all my horizons. I have been questioning my destiny lately; the law as a goal had been drawing further away. And this mark of confidence—"

"Oh, that point, the confidence will have to be mutual. I am a close-mouthed person and have no confidants, but of necessity you will learn my affairs pretty thoroughly if you accept my offer. You have heard a good deal of talk about me—most of it unflattering. You have heard that I drive hard bargains. At every session of the legislature I am charged with the grossest corruption. There are men in my own party who are bent on breaking me down and getting rid of me. I'm going to give them the best fight I can put up. I can't see through the back of my head: I want you to do that for me."

"I don't know much about the practical side of politics; it's full of traps I've never seen sprung, but I know they're planted."

"To be perfectly frank, it's because you're inexperienced that I want you. I wouldn't trust anybody who had political ambitions of his own, or who had mixed up in any of these local squabbles. And, besides, you're a gentleman and an educated man, and that counts for something."

"You are very kind and generous. I appreciate this more than I can tell you. And I'd like—"

"Don't decide about it now. I'd rather you didn't. Take a week to it, then drop me a line to Fraserville, or come up if you want to talk further."

"Thank you; I shan't want so much time. In any event I appreciate your kindness. It's the most cheering thing that ever happened to me."

Bassett glanced at his watch. He had said all he had to say in the matter and closed the subject characteristically.

"Here's a little thing I picked up to-day,—a copy of Darlington's 'Narrative,'—he was with St. Clair, you know; and practically all the copies of the book were burned in a Philadelphia printing-office before they were bound; you will notice that some of the pages are slightly singed. As you saw at my house, I'm interested in getting hold of books relating to the achievements of the Western pioneers. Some of these bald, unvarnished tales give a capital idea of the men who conquered the wilderness. They had the real stuff in them, those fellows!"

He took the battered volume—a pamphlet clumsily encased in boards, and drew his hand across its rough sides caressingly.

"Another of my jokes on the State Library. The librarian told me I'd never find a copy, and this was on top of a pile of trash in a second-hand shop right here in this town. It cost me just fifty cents."

He snapped his bag shut on the new-found treasure and bade Dan good-bye without referring again to the proposed employment.

Dan knew, as he left the hotel, that if an answer had been imperatively demanded on the spot, he should have accepted Bassett's proposition; but as he walked slowly away questions rose in his mind. Bassett undoubtedly expected to reap some benefit from his services, and such services would not, of course, be in the line of the law. They were much more likely to partake of the function of journalism, in obtaining publicity for such matters as Bassett wished to promulgate. The proposed new office at the capital marked an advance of Bassett's pickets. He was abandoning old fortifications for newer and stronger ones, and Dan's imagination kindled at the thought of serving this masterful general as aide-de-camp.

He took a long walk, thinking of Bassett's offer and trying to view it from a philosophical angle. The great leaders in American politics had come oftener than not from the country, he reflected. Fraserville, in Dan's cogitations, might, as Bassett's star rose, prove to be another Springfield or Fremont or Canton, shrouding a planet destined to a brilliant course toward the zenith. He did not doubt that Bassett's plans were well-laid; the state senator was farseeing and shrewd, and by attaching himself to this man, whose prospects were so bright, he would shine in the reflected glory of his successes. And the flattery of the offer was not in itself without its magic.

However, as the days passed Dan was glad that he had taken time for reflection. He began to minimize the advantages of the proposed relationship, and to ponder the ways in which it would compel a certain self-effacement. He had sufficient imagination to color the various scenes in which he saw himself Bassett's "man." In moods of self-analysis he knew his nature to be sensitive, with an emotional side whose expressions now and then surprised him. He rallied sharply at times from the skeptical attitude which he felt journalism was establishing in him, and assured himself that his old ideals were safe in the citadel his boyhood imagination had built for them. Dan's father was a veteran of the Civil War and he had been taught to believe that the Democratic Party had sought to destroy the Union and that the Republican Party alone had saved it. Throughout his boyhood on the Harrison County farm, he had been conscious of the recrudescence of the wartime feeling in every political campaign. His admiration for the heroes of the war was in no wise shaken at New Haven, but he first realized there that new issues demanded attention. He grew impatient of all attempts to obscure these by harking back to questions that the war had finally determined, if it had served any purpose whatever. He broke a lance frequently with the young men who turned over the books in Wright and Fitch's office, most of whom were Republicans and devout believers that the furnace fires of America's industries were brought down from Heaven by Protection, a modern Prometheus of a new order of utilitarian gods. In the view of these earnest debaters, Protection was the first and last commandment, the law and the prophets. The "Indianapolis Advertiser" and protection newspapers generally had long attacked periodically those gentlemen who, enjoying the sheltered life of college and university, were corrupting the youth of the land by questioning the wisdom of the fire-kindling god. There was a wide margin between theory and practice, between academic dilletantism and a prosperous industrial life fostered and shielded by acts of Congress. It required courage for young men bred in the popular faith to turn their backs upon the high altar, so firmly planted, so blazing with lamps of perpetual adoration.

While Dan was considering the politician's offer, a letter from home brought a fresh plea for help, and strengthened a growing feeling that his wiser course was to throw in his fortunes with Bassett. In various small ways Mr. Fitch had shown an interest in Harwood, and Dan resolved to take counsel of the lawyer before giving his answer.

The little man sat in his private room in his shirt sleeves, with his chair tipped back and his feet on his desk. He was, in his own phrase, "thinking out a brief." He fanned himself in a desultory fashion with a palm leaf. Dan had carried in an arm load of books which Fitch indicated should be arranged, back-up, on the floor beside him.

Dan lingered a moment and Fitch's "Well" gave him leave to proceed. He stated Bassett's offer succinctly, telling of his visit to Fraserville and of the interview at the Whitcomb. When he had concluded Fitch asked:—

"Why haven't you gone ahead and closed the matter? On the face of it it's a good offer. It gives you a chance to read law and to be associated with a man who is in a position to be of great service to you."

"Well, to tell the truth, sir, I have had doubts. Bassett stands for some things I don't approve of—his kind of politics, I mean."

"Oh! He doesn't quite square with your ideals, is that it?"

"I suppose that is it, Mr. Fitch."

The humor kindled in the little man's brown eyes, and his fingers played with his whitening red beard.

"Just how strong are those ideals of yours, Mr. Harwood?"

"They're pretty strong, I hope, sir."

Fitch dropped his feet from the desk, opened a drawer, and drew out a long envelope.

"It may amuse you to know that this is the sketch of Bassett you printed in the 'Courier' last fall. I didn't know before that you wrote it. No wonder it tickled him. And—er—some of it is true. I wouldn't talk to any other man in Indiana about Bassett. He's a friend and a client of mine. He doesn't trust many people; he doesn't"—the little man's eyes twinkled—"he doesn't trust Wright!—and he trusts me because we are alike in that we keep our mouths shut. You must have impressed him very favorably. He seems willing to take you at face value. It would have been quite natural for him to have asked me about you, but he didn't. Do you know Thatcher—Edward G.? He has business interests with Bassett, and Thatcher dabbles in politics just enough to give him power when he wants it. Thatcher is a wealthy man, who isn't fooling with small politics. If some day he sees a red apple at the top of the tree he may go for it. There'd be some fun if Bassett tried to shake down the same apple."

"I know Thatcher's son."

"Allen? I met him the other day. Odd boy; I guess that's one place where Ed Thatcher's heart is all right."

After a moment's reflection with his face turned to the open window Fitch added:—

"Mr. Harwood, if you should go to Bassett and in course of time, everything running smoothly, he asked you to do something that jarred with those ideals of yours, what should you do?"

"I should refuse, sir," answered Dan, earnestly.

Fitch nodded gravely.

"Very well; then I'd say go ahead. You understand that I'm not predicting that such a moment is inevitable, but it's quite possible. I'll say to you what I've never said before to any man: I don't understand Morton Bassett. I've known him for ten years, and I know him just as well now as I did the day I first met him. That may be my own dullness; but ignoring all that his enemies say of him,—and he has some very industrious ones, as you know,—he's still, at his best, a very unusual and a somewhat peculiar and difficult person."

"He's different, at least; but I can't think him half as bad as they say he is."

"He isn't, probably," replied Fitch, whose eyes were contemplating the cornice of the building across the street. Then, as though just recalling Dan's presence: "May I ask you whether, aside from that 'Courier' article, you ever consciously served Bassett in any way—ever did anything that might have caused him to feel that he was under obligations?"

"Why, no, sir; nothing whatever."

"—Or—" a considerable interval in which Fitch's gaze reverted to the cornice—"that you might have some information that made it wise for him to keep his hand on you?"

"Absolutely nothing," answered Dan, the least bit uncomfortable under this questioning.

"You're not aware," the lawyer persisted deliberately, "that you ever had any dealings of any kind even remotely with Mr. Bassett."

"No; never, beyond what I've told you."

"Then, if I were in your place, and the man I think you are, I'd accept the offer, but don't bind yourself for a long period; keep your mouth shut and hang on to your ideals,—it's rather odd that you and I should be using that word; it doesn't get into a law office often. If you feel tempted to do things that you know are crooked, think of Billy Sumner, and act accordingly. It's getting to be truer all the time that few of us are free men. What's Shakespeare's phrase?—'bound upon a wheel of fire';—that, Mr. Harwood, is all of us. We have valuable clients in this office that we'd lose if I got out and shouted my real political convictions. We're all cowards; but don't you be one. As soon as I'm sure I've provided for my family against the day of wrath I'm going to quit the law and blow the dust off of some of my own ideals; it's thick, I can tell you!"

This was seeing Fitch in a new aspect. Dan was immensely pleased by the lawyer's friendliness, and he felt that his counsel was sound.

Fitch broke in on the young man's thoughts to say:—

"By the way, you know where I live? Come up and dine with me to-morrow at seven if you're free. My folks are away and I'd like to swap views with you on politics, religion, baseball, and great subjects like that."

Dan wrote his acceptance of Bassett's offer that night.

CHAPTER X
IN THE BOORDMAN BUILDING

Harwood opened the office in the Boordman Building, and settled in it the law books Bassett sent from Fraserville. The lease was taken in Dan's name, and he paid for the furniture with his own check, Bassett having given him five hundred dollars for expenses. The Boordman was one of the older buildings in Washington Street, and as it antedated the era of elevators, only the first of its three stories was occupied by offices. Its higher altitudes had fallen to miscellaneous tenants including a few telegraph operators, printers, and other night workers who lodged there for convenience. Dan's immediate neighbors proved to be a shabby lawyer who concealed by a professional exterior his real vocation, which was chattel mortgages; a fire insurance agency conducted by several active young fellows of Dan's acquaintance; and the office of a Pittsburg firm of construction contractors, presided over by a girl who answered the telephone if haply it rang at moments when the heroes of the novels she devoured were not in too imminent peril of death.

This office being nearest, Dan went in to borrow a match for his pipe while in the midst of his moving and found the girl rearranging her hair before a mirror.

"That's as near heart disease as I care to come," she said, turning at his "Beg pardon." "There hasn't been a man in this place for two weeks, much less a woman. Yes, I can stake you for a match. I keep them for those insurance fellows—nice boys they are, too. You see," she continued, not averse to prolonging the conversation, "our business is mostly outside. Hear about the sky-scraper we're building in Elwood? Three stories! One of the best little towns in Indiana, all right. Say, the janitor service in this old ark is something I couldn't describe to a gentleman. If there's anything in these microbe fairy stories we'll all die early. You might as well know the worst:—they do light housekeeping on the third floor and the smell of onions is what I call annoying. Oh, that's all right; what's a match between friends! The last man who had your office—you've taken sixty-six?—well, he always got his matches here, and touched me occasionally for a pink photo of George Washington—stamp, ha! ha! see! He was real nice and when his wife dropped in to see him one day and I was sitting in there joshing him and carrying on, he was that painfully embarrassed! I guess she made him move; but, Lord, they have to bribe tenants to get 'em in here. To crawl up one flight of that stairway you have to be a mountain climber. I only stay because the work's so congenial and it's a quiet place for reading, and all the processions pass here. The view of that hairdressing shop across the way is something I recommend. If I hadn't studied stenography I should have taken up hairdressing or manicuring. A little friend of mine works in that shop and the society ladies are most confidential. I'm Miss Rose Farrell, if you tease me to tell. You needn't say by any other name it's just as sweet— the ruffle's a little frayed on that."

Bassett had stipulated that his name should not appear and he suggested that Dan place his own on the door. Later, when he had been admitted to the bar it would be easy to add "attorney at law," Bassett said. Each of the three rooms of what the agent of the building liked to call a suite opened directly into the hall. In the first Harwood set up a desk for himself; in the second he placed the library, and the third and largest was to be Bassett's at such times as he cared to use it. Throughout the summer Harwood hardly saw Bassett, and he began to regret his reluctant assent to a relationship which conferred so many benefits with so little work. He dug hungrily at the law, and felt that he was making progress. Fitch, who was braving the heat in town, had outlined a course of reading for him, and continued his manifestations of friendliness by several times asking him to dinner, with a motor ride later to cool them off before going to bed.

Bassett kept pretty close to Fraserville, running into the city occasionally for a few hours. He complained now and then because he saw so little of his family, who continued at the lake. Dan had certain prescribed duties, but these were not onerous. A great many of the country newspapers began to come to the office, and it was Harwood's business to read them and cut out any items bearing upon local political conditions. Bassett winnowed these carefully, brushing the chaff into his wastebasket and retaining a few kernels for later use. He seemed thoroughly familiar with the state press and spoke of the rural newspapers with a respect that surprised Harwood, who had little patience with what he called the "grapevine dailies," with their scrappy local news, patent insides, and servile partisan opinions. Still, he began to find in a considerable number of these papers, even those emanating from remote county seats, a certain raciness and independence. This newspaper reading, which Dan had begun perfunctorily, soon interested him. It was thus, he saw, that Bassett kept in touch with state affairs. Sporadic temperance movements, squabbles over local improvements, rows in school boards, and like matters were not beneath Bassett's notice. He discussed these incidents and conditions with Harwood, who was astonished to find how thoroughly Bassett knew the state.

Through all this Dan was not blind to the sins charged against Bassett. There were certain corporations which it was said Bassett protected from violence at the state house. But as against this did not the vast horde of greedy corporations maintain a lobby at every session and was not a certain amount of lobbying legitimate? Again, Bassett had shielded the liquor interests from many attacks; but had not these interests their rights, and was it not a sound doctrine that favored government with the least restraint? Rather uglier had been Bassett's identification with the organization of the White River Canneries Company, a combination of industries on which a scandalous overissue of stock had been sold in generous chunks to a confiding public, followed in a couple of years by a collapse of the business and a reorganization that had frozen out all but a favored few. Still, Bassett had not been the sole culprit in that affair, and was not this sort of financiering typical of the time? Bassett and Thatcher had both played the gentle game of freeze-out in half a dozen other instances, and if they were culpable, why had they not been brought to book? In his inner soul Dan knew why not: in the bi-partisan political game only the stupid are annoyed by grand juries, which take their cue tamely from ambitious prosecuting attorneys eager for higher office.

Bassett's desk stood against the wall and over it hung a map of Indiana. It was no unusual thing for Dan to find Bassett with his chair tipped back, his eyes fixed upon the map. The oblong checkerboard formed by the ninety-two counties of the Hoosier commonwealth seemed to have a fascination for the man from Fraserville. When Dan found him thus in rapt contemplation Bassett usually turned toward him a little reluctantly and absently. It was thus that Morton Bassett studied the field, like a careful general outlining his campaigns, with ample data and charts before him.

This was an "off" year politically, or, more accurately, the statutes called for no state election in Indiana. For every one knows that there is no hour of the day in any year when politics wholly cease from agitating the waters of the Wabash: somewhere some one is always dropping in a pebble to see how far the ripple will widen. In the torrid first days of September the malfeasance of the treasurer of an Ohio River county afforded the Republican press an opportunity to gloat, the official in question being, of course, a Democrat, and a prominent member of the state committee.

For several days before the exposure Bassett had appeared fitfully at the Whitcomb and in the Boordman Building. On the day that the Republican

"Advertiser" screamed delightedly over the Democratic scandal in Ranger County, Bassett called Dan into his office. Bassett's name had been linked to that of Miles, the erring treasurer, in the "Advertiser's" headlines; and its leading editorial had pointed to the defalcation as the sort of thing that inevitably follows the domination of a party by a spoilsman and corruptionist like the senator from Fraser.

Bassett indicated by a nod a copy of the "Advertiser" on his desk.

"The joke was on us this time. They're pinning Miles on me, and I guess I'll have to wear him like a bouquet. I've been in Louisville fixing this thing up and they won't have as much fun as they thought. It's a simple case: Miles hadn't found out yet that corn margins are not legitimate investments for a county's money. He's a good fellow and will know better next time. We couldn't afford to have a member of the state committee in jail, so I met the bondsmen and the prosecuting attorney—he's a Republican—in Louisville and we straightened it all out. The money's in bank down there. It proves to be after all a matter of bookkeeping,—technical differences, which were reconciled readily enough. Miles got scared; those fellows always do. He'll be good now."

Dan had been standing. Bassett pointed to a chair.

"I want you to write an interview with me on this case, laying emphasis on the fact that the trouble was all due to an antiquated system of keeping the accounts, which Miles inherited from his predecessors in office. The president of the bank and the prosecutor have prepared statements,—I have them in my pocket,—and I want you to get all the publicity you know how for these things. Let me see. In my interview you'd better lay great stress on the imperative need for a uniform accounting law for county officials. Say that we expect to stand for this in our next platform; make it strong. Have me say that this incident in Ranger County, while regrettable, will serve a good purpose if it arouses the minds of the people to the importance of changing the old unsatisfactory method of bookkeeping that so frequently leads perfectly trustworthy and well-meaning officials into error. Do you get the idea?"

"Yes; perfectly," Dan replied. "As I understand it, Miles isn't guilty, but you would take advantage of the agitation to show the necessity for reform."

"Exactly. And while you're about it, write a vigorous editorial for the 'Courier,' on the same line, and a few ironical squibs based on the eagerness of the Republican papers to see all Democrats through black goggles." The humor showed in Bassett's eyes for an instant, and he added: "Praise the Republican prosecutor of Ranger County for refusing to yield to partisan pressure and take advantage of a Democrat's mistakes of judgment. He's a nice fellow and we've got to be good to him."

This was the first task of importance that Bassett had assigned to him and Dan addressed himself to it zealously. If Miles was not really a defaulter there was every reason why the heinous aspersions of the opposition press should be dealt with vigorously. Dan was impressed by Bassett's method of dealing with a difficult situation. Miles had erred, but Bassett had taken the matter in hand promptly, secretly, and effectively. His attitude toward the treasurer's sin was tolerant and amiable. Miles had squandered money in bucket-shop gambling, but the sin was not uncommon, and the amount of his loss was sufficient to assure his penitence; he was an ally of Bassett's and it was Bassett's way to take care of his friends. Bassett had not denied that the culprit had been guilty of indiscretions; but he had minimized the importance of his error and adorned the tale with a moral on which Dan set about laying the greatest emphasis. He enjoyed writing, and in the interview he attributed ideas to Bassett that would have been creditable to the most idealistic of statesmen. He based the editorial Bassett had suggested upon the interview; and he wrote half a dozen editorial paragraphs in a vein of caustic humor that the "Courier" affected. In the afternoon he copied his articles on a typewriter and submitted them to Bassett.

"Good, very good. Too bad to take you out of the newspaper business; you have the right point of view and you know how to get hold of the right end of a sentence. Let me see. I wish you would do another interview changing the phraseology and making it short, and we'll give the 'Advertiser' a chance to print it. I'll attend to these other things. You'd better not be running into the 'Courier' office too much now that you're with me. They haven't got on to that yet, but they'll give us a twist when they do."

Dan had been admitted to the ante-chamber of Bassett's confidence, but he was to be permitted to advance a step further. At four o'clock he was surprised by the appearance of Atwill, the "Courier's" manager. Dan had no acquaintance with Atwill, whose advent had been coincident with the "Courier's" change of ownership shortly after Dan's tentative connection with the paper began. Atwill had rarely visited the editorial department, but it was no secret that he exercised general supervision of the paper. It had been whispered among the reporters that every issue was read carefully in proof by Atwill, but Dan had never been particularly interested in this fact. As Atwill appeared in the outer office, Bassett came from his own room to meet him. The door closed quickly upon the two and they were together for half an hour or more. Then Bassett summoned Dan.

"Mr. Atwill, this is Mr. Harwood. He was formerly employed on the 'Courier.' It was he that wrote up the Hoosier statesmen, you may remember."

Atwill nodded.

"I remember very well. Those articles helped business,—we could follow your pencil up and down the state on our circulation reports. I jumped the city editor for letting you go."

Atwill was a lean, clean-shaven man who chewed gum hungrily. His eyes were noticeably alert and keen. There was a tradition that he had been a "star" reporter in New York, a managing editor in Pittsburg, and a business manager in Minneapolis before coming to supervise the "Courier" for its new owner.

"Atwill, you and Harwood had better keep in touch with each other. Harwood is studying law here, but he will know pretty well what I'm doing. He will probably write an editorial for you occasionally, and when it comes in it won't be necessary for the regular employees of the 'Courier' to know where it comes from. Harwood won't mind if they take all the glory for his work."

When Atwill left, Bassett talked further to Harwood, throwing his legs across a chair and showing himself more at ease than Dan had yet seen him.

"Harwood," he said,—he had dropped the mister to-day for the first time in their intercourse,—"I've opened the door wider to you than I ever did before to any man. I trust you."

"I appreciate that, Mr. Bassett."

"I've been carrying too much, and it's a relief to find that I've got a man I can unload on. You understand, I trust you absolutely. And in coming to me as you did, and accepting these confidences, I assume that you don't think me as wicked as my enemies make me out."

"I liked you," said Dan, with real feeling, "from that moment you shook hands with me in your house at Fraserville. When I don't believe in you any longer, I'll quit; and if that time comes you may be sure that I shan't traffic in what I learn of your affairs. I feel that I want to say that to you."

"That's all right, Harwood. I hope our relations will be increasingly friendly; but if you want to quit at any time you're not tied. Be sure of that. If you should quit me to-morrow I should be disappointed but I wouldn't kick. And don't build up any quixotic ideas of gratitude toward me. When you don't like your job, move on. I guess we understand each other."

If Dan entertained any doubts as to the ethics involved in Bassett's handling of the situation in Ranger County they were swept away by the perfect candor with which Bassett informed their new intimacy. The most interesting and powerful character in Indiana politics had made a confidant of him. Without attempting to exact vows of secrecy, or threatening vengeance for infractions of faith, but in a spirit of good-fellowship that appealed strongly to Harwood, Bassett had given him a pass-key to many locked doors.

"As you probably gathered," Bassett was saying, "Atwill represents me at the 'Courier' office."

"I had never suspected it," Dan replied.

"Has anybody suspected it?" asked Bassett quickly.

"Well; of course it has been said repeatedly that you own or control the 'Courier.'"

"Let them keep on saying it; they might have hard work to prove it. And—" Bassett's eyes turned toward the window. His brows contracted and he shut his lips tightly so that his stiff mustache gave to his mouth a sinister look that Dan had never seen before. The disagreeable expression vanished and he was his usual calm, unruffled self. "And," he concluded, smiling, "I might have some trouble in proving it myself."

Dan was not only accumulating valuable information, but Bassett interested him more and more as a character. He was an unusual man, a new type, this senator from Fraser, with his alternating candor and disingenuousness, his prompt solutions of perplexing problems. It was unimaginable that a man so strong and so sure of himself, and so shrewd in extricating others from their entanglements, could ever be cornered, trapped, or beaten.

Bassett's hands had impressed Dan that first night at Fraserville, and he watched them again as Bassett idly twisted a rubber band in his fingers. How gentle those hands were and how cruel they might be!

The next morning Dan found that his interview with Bassett was the feature of the first page of the "Courier," and the statement he had sent to the "Advertiser" was hardly less prominently displayed. His editorial was the "Courier's" leader, and it appeared *verbatim et literatim*. He viewed his work with pride and satisfaction; even his ironical editorial "briefs" had, he fancied, something of the piquancy he admired in the paragraphing of the "New York Sun." But his gratification at being able to write "must" matter for both sides of a prominent journal was obscured by the greater joy of being the chief adjutant of the "Courier's" sagacious concealed owner.

The "Advertiser" replied to Bassett's statement in a tone of hilarity. Bassett's plea for a better accounting system was funny, that was all. Miles, the treasurer of Ranger County, had been playing the bucket shops with public moneys, and the Honorable Morton Bassett, of Fraserville, with characteristic zeal in a bad cause, had not only adjusted the shortage, but was craftily trying to turn the incident to the advantage of his party. The text for the "Advertiser's" leader was the jingle: —

"When the devil was sick, the devil a monk would be;
When the devil got well, the devil a monk was he!"

Bassett had left town, but the regular staff of the "Courier" kept up the fight along the lines of the articles Dan had contributed. The "Advertiser," finding that the Republican prosecuting attorney of Ranger County joined with the local bank in certifying to Miles's probity, dropped the matter after a few scattering volleys.

However, within a week after the Miles incident, the "Advertiser" gave Harwood the shock of an unlooked-for plunge into ice-water by printing a sensational story under a double-column headline, reading, "The Boss in the Boordman Building." The Honorable Morton Bassett, so the article averred, no longer satisfied to rule his party amid the pastoral calm of Fraser County, had stolen into the capital and secretly established headquarters, which meant, beyond question, the manifestation of even a wider exercise of his malign influence in Indiana politics. Harwood's name enjoyed a fame that day that many years of laborious achievement could not have won for it. The "Advertiser's" photographers had stolen in at night and taken a flashlight picture of the office door, bearing the legend

Harwood's personal history was set forth in florid phrases. It appeared that he had been carefully chosen and trained by Bassett to aid in his evil work. His connection with the "Courier," which had seemed to Dan at the time so humble, assumed a dignity and importance that highly amused him. It was quite like the Fraserville boss to choose a young man of good antecedents, the graduate of a great university, with no previous experience in politics, the better to bend him to his will. Dan's talents and his brilliant career at college all helped to magnify the importance of Bassett's latest move. Morton Bassett was dangerous, the "Advertiser" conceded editorially, because he had brains; and he was even more to be feared because he could command the brains of other men.

Dan called Bassett at Fraserville on the long distance telephone and told him of the disclosure. Bassett replied in a few sentences.

"That won't hurt anything. I'd been expecting something of the kind. Put you in, did they? I'll get my paper to-night and read it carefully. Better cut the stuff out and send it in an envelope, to make sure. Call Atwill over and tell him we ignore the whole business. I'm taking a little rest, but I'll be in town in about a week."

Dan was surprised to find how bitterly he resented the attack on Bassett. The "Advertiser" spoke of the leader as though he were a monster of immorality and Dan honestly believed Bassett to be no such thing. His loyalty was deeply intensified by the hot volleys poured into the Boordman Building; but he was not disturbed by the references to himself. He winced a little bit at being called a "stool pigeon"; but he thought he knew the reporter who had written the article, and his experience in the newspaper office had not been so brief but that it had killed his layman's awe of the printed word. When he walked into the Whitcomb that evening the clerk made a point of calling his name and shaking hands with him. He was conscious that a number of idlers in the hotel lobby regarded him with a new interest. Some one spoke his name audibly, and he enjoyed in some degree the sensation of being a person of mark.

He crossed University Square and walked out Meridian Street to Fitch's house. The lawyer came downstairs in his shirt sleeves with a legal envelope in his hand.

"Glad to see you, Harwood. I'm packing up; going to light out in the morning and get in on the end of my family's vacation. They've moved out of Maine into the Berkshires and the boys are going back to college without coming home. I see the 'Advertiser' has been after you. How do you like your job?"

"I'm not scared," Dan replied. "It's all very amusing and my moral character hasn't suffered so far."

Fitch eyed him critically.

"Well, I haven't time to talk to you, but here's something I wish you'd do for me. I have a quit-claim deed for Mrs. Owen to sign. I forgot to tell one of the boys in the office to get her acknowledgment, but you're a notary, aren't you? I've just been telephoning her about it. You know who she is? Come to think of it, she's Bassett's aunt-in-law. You're not a good Hoosier till you know Aunt Sally. I advise you to make yourself solid with her. I don't know what she's doing in town just now, but her ways are always inscrutable."

Dan was soon ringing the bell at Mrs. Owen's. Mrs. Owen was out, the maid said, but would be back shortly. Dan explained that he had come from Mr. Fitch, and she asked him to walk into the parlor and wait.

Sylvia Garrison and her grandfather had been at Montgomery since their visit to Waupegan and were now in Indianapolis for a day on their way to Boston. The Delaware Street house had been closed all summer. The floors were bare and the furniture was still jacketed in linen. Sylvia rose as Harwood appeared at the parlor door.

"Pardon me," said Dan, as the maid vanished. "I have an errand with Mrs. Owen and I'll wait, if you don't mind?"

"Certainly. Mrs. Owen has gone out to make a call, but she will be back soon. She went only a little way down the street. Please have a chair."

She hesitated a moment, not knowing whether to remain or to leave the young man to himself. Dan determined the matter for her by opening a conversation on the state of the weather.

"September is the most trying month of the year. Just when we're all tired of summer, it takes its last fling at us."

"It has been very warm. I came over from Montgomery this afternoon and it was very dusty and disagreeable on the train."

"From Montgomery?" repeated Dan, surprised and perplexed. Then, as it dawned upon him that this was the girl who had opened the door for him at Professor Kelton's house in Montgomery when he had gone there with a letter from Fitch, "You see," he said, "we've met before, in your own house. You very kindly went off to find some one for me—and didn't come back; but I passed you on the campus as I was leaving."

He had for the moment forgotten the name of the old gentleman to whom he had borne a letter from Mr. Fitch. He would have forgotten the incident completely long ago if it had not been for the curious manner in which the lawyer had received his report and the secrecy so carefully enjoined. It was odd that he should have chanced upon these people again. Dan did not know many women, young or old, and he found this encounter with Sylvia wholly agreeable, Sylvia being, as we know, seventeen, and not an offense to the eye.

"It was my grandfather, Professor Kelton, you came to see. He's here with me now, but he's gone out to call on an old friend with Mrs. Owen."

Every detail of Dan's visit to the cottage was clear in Sylvia's mind; callers had been too rare for there to be any dimness of memory as to the visit of the stranger, particularly when she had associated her grandfather's subsequent depression with his coming.

Dan felt that he should scrupulously avoid touching upon the visit to Montgomery otherwise than casually. He was still bound in all honor to forget that excursion as far as possible. This young person seemed very serious, and he was not sure that she was comfortable in his presence.

"It was a warm day, I remember, but cool and pleasant in your library. I'm going to make a confession. When you went off so kindly to find Professor Kelton I picked up the book you had been reading, and it quite laid me low. I had imagined it would be something cheerful and frivolous, to lift the spirit of the jaded traveler."

"It must have been a good story," replied Sylvia, guardedly.

"It was! It was the 'Æneid,' and I began at your bookmark and tried to stagger through a page, but it floored me. You see how frank I am; I ought really to have kept this terrible disclosure from you."

"Didn't you like Madison? I remember that I thought you were comparing us unfavorably with other places. You implied"—and Sylvia smiled—"that you didn't think Madison a very important college."

"Then be sure of my contrition now! Your Virgil sank deep into my consciousness, and I am glad of this chance to render unto Madison the things that are Madison's."

His chaffing way reminded her of Dr. Wandless, who often struck a similar note in their encounters.

Sylvia was quite at ease now. Her caller's smile encouraged friendliness. He had dropped his fedora hat on a chair, but clung to his bamboo stick. His gray sack suit with the trousers neatly creased and his smartly knotted tie proclaimed him a man of fashion: the newest and youngest member of the Madison faculty, who had introduced spats to the campus, was not more impressively tailored.

"You said you had gone to a large college; and I said—"

"Oh, you hit me back straight enough!" laughed Harwood.

"I didn't mean to be rude," Sylvia protested, coloring.

They evidently both remembered what had been said at that interview.

"It wasn't rude; it was quite the retort courteous! My conceit at being a Yale man was shattered by your shot."

"Well, I suppose Yale is a good place, too," said Sylvia, with a generous intention that caused them both to laugh.

"By token of your Virgilian diversions shall I assume that you are a collegian, really or almost?"

"Just almost. I'm on my way to Wellesley now."

"Ah!" and his exclamation was heavy with meaning. A girl bound for college became immediately an integer with which a young man who had not yet mislaid his diploma could reckon. "I have usually been a supporter of Vassar. It's the only woman's college I ever attended. I went up there once to see a girl I had met at a Prom—such is the weakness of man! I had arrayed myself as the lilies of the field, and on my way through Pokip I gathered up a beautiful two-seated trap with a driver, thinking in my ignorance that I should make a big hit by driving the fair one over the hills and far away. The horses were wonderful; I found out later that they were the finest hearse horses in Poughkeepsie. She was an awfully funny girl, that girl. She always used both 'shall' and 'will,' being afraid to take chances with either verb, an idea I'm often tempted to adopt myself."

"It's ingenious, at any rate. But how did the drive go?"

"Oh, it didn't! She said she couldn't go with me alone unless I *was* or *were* her cousin. It was against the rules. So we agreed to be cousins and she went off to find the dean or some awful autocrat like that, to spring the delightful surprise, that her long-lost cousin from Kalamazoo had suddenly appeared, and might she go driving with him. That was her idea, I assure you,—my own depravity could suggest nothing more euphonious than Canajoharie. And would you believe it, the consent being forthcoming, she came back and said she wouldn't go—absolutely declined! She rested on the fine point in ethics that, while it was not improper to tell the fib, it would be highly sinful to take advantage of it! So we strolled over the campus and she showed me the sights, while those funeral beasts champed their bits at so much per hour. She was a Connecticut girl, and I made a note of the incident as illustrating a curious phase of the New England conscience."

While they were gayly ringing the changes on these adventures, steps sounded on the veranda.

"That's Mrs. Owen and my grandfather," said Sylvia.

"I wonder—" began Dan, grave at once.

"You're wondering," said Sylvia, "whether my grandfather will remember you."

She recalled very well her grandfather's unusual seriousness after Harwood's visit; it seemed wiser not to bring the matter again to his attention.

"I think it would be better if he didn't," replied Dan, relieved that she had anticipated his thought.

"I was only a messenger boy anyhow and I didn't know what my errand was about that day."

"He doesn't remember faces well," said Sylvia, "and wouldn't be likely to know you."

As Mrs. Owen asked Dan to her office at once, it was unnecessary for Sylvia to introduce him to her grandfather.

Alone with Mrs. Owen, Dan's business was quickly transacted. She produced an abstract of title and bade him read aloud the description of the property conveyed while she held the deed. At one point she took a pen and crossed a *t*; otherwise the work of Wright and Fitch was approved. When she had signed her name, and while Dan was filling in the certificate, she scrutinized him closely.

"You're in Mr. Fitch's office, are you?" she inquired.

"Not now; but I was there for a time. I happened to call on Mr. Fitch this evening and he asked me to bring the deed over."

"Let me see, I don't believe I know any Harwoods here."

"I haven't been here long enough to be known," answered Dan, looking up and smiling.

Mrs. Owen removed her hat and tossed it on a little stand, as though hats were a nuisance in this world and not worthy of serious consideration. She continued her observation of Dan, who was applying a blotter to his signature.

"I'll have to take this to my office to affix the seal. I'm to give it to Mr. Wright in the morning for recording."

"Where is your office, Mr. Harwood?" she asked flatly.

"Boordman Building," answered Dan, surprised to find himself uncomfortable under her direct, penetrating gaze.

"Humph! So you're Morton Bassett's young man who was written up in the 'Advertiser.'"

"Mr. Bassett has given me a chance to read law in his office. He's a prominent man and the 'Advertiser' chose to put its own interpretation on his kindness to me. That's all," answered Dan with dignity.

"Sit still a minute. I forget sometimes that all the folks around here don't know me. I didn't mean to be inquisitive, or disagreeable; I was just looking for information. I took notice of that 'Advertiser's' piece because Mr. Bassett married my niece, so I'm naturally interested in what he does."

"Yes, Mrs. Owen, I understand."

Dan had heard a good deal about Mrs. Sally Owen, in one way or another, and persuaded now, by her change of tone, that she had no intention of pillorying him for Bassett's misdeeds, he began to enjoy his unexpected colloquy with her. She bent forward and clasped her veined, bony hands on the table.

"I'm glad of a chance to talk to you. It's providential, your turning up this way. I just came to town yesterday and Edward Thatcher dropped in last night and got to talking to me about his boy."

"Allen?"

Dan was greatly surprised at this turn of the conversation. Mrs. Owen's tone was wholly kind, and she seemed deeply in earnest.

"Yes, I mean Allen Thatcher. His father says he's taken a great shine to you. I hardly know the boy, but he's a little queer and he's always been a little sickly. Edward doesn't know how to handle him, and the boy's ma—well, she's one of those Terre Haute Bartlows, and those people never would stay put. Edward's made too much money for his wife's good, and the United States ain't big enough for her and the girls. But that boy got tired o' gallivanting around over there, and he's back here on Edward's hands. The boy's gaits are too much for Edward. He says you and Allen get on well together. I met him in the bank to-day and he asked me about you."

"I like Allen;—I'm even very fond of him, and I wish I could help him find himself. He's amusing"—and Dan laughed, remembering their first meeting—"but with a fine, serious, manly side that you can't help liking."

"That's nice; it's mighty nice. You be good to that boy, and you won't lose anything by it. How do you and Morton get on?"

"First-rate, I hope. He's treated me generously."

Then she fastened her eyes upon him with quizzical severity.

"Young man, the 'Advertiser' seems to think Morton Bassett is crooked. What do you think about it?"

Dan gasped and stammered at this disconcerting question.

She rested her arms on the table and bent toward him, the humor showing in her eyes.

"If he *is* crooked, young man, you needn't think you have to be as big a sinner as he is! You remember that Sally Owen told you that. Be your own boss. Morton's a terrible persuader. Funny for me to be talking to you this way; I don't usually get confidential so quick. I guess"—and her eyes twinkled—"we'll have to consider ourselves old friends to make it right."

"You are very kind, indeed, Mrs. Owen. I see that I have a responsibility about Allen. I'll keep an eye on him.

"Drop in now and then. I eat a good many Sunday dinners alone when I'm at home, and you may come whenever you feel like facing a tiresome old woman across the table."

She followed him into the hall, where they ran into Sylvia, who had been upstairs saying good-night to her grandfather. Mrs. Owen arrested Sylvia's flight through the hall.

"Sylvia, I guess you and Mr. Harwood are already acquainted."

"Except," said Dan, "that we haven't been introduced!"

"Then, Miss Garrison, this is Mr. Harwood. He's a Yale College man, so I read in the paper."

"Oh, I already knew that!" replied Sylvia, laughing.

"At Wellesley please remember, Miss Garrison, about the Kalamazoo cousins," said Dan, his hand on the front door.

"I guess you young folks didn't need that introduction," observed Mrs. Owen. "Don't forget to come and see me, Mr. Harwood."

CHAPTER XI
THE MAP ABOVE BASSETT'S DESK

Sometimes, in the rapid progress of their acquaintance, Allen Thatcher exasperated Harwood, but more often he puzzled and interested him. It was clear that the millionaire's son saw or thought he saw in Dan a Type. To be thought a Type may be flattering or not; it depends upon the point of view. Dan himself had no illusions in the matter. Allen wanted to see and if possible meet the local characters of whom he read in the newspapers; and he began joining Harwood in visits to the hotels at night, hoping that these wonderful representatives of American democracy might appear. Harwood's acquaintance was widening; he knew, by sight at least, all the prominent men of the city and state, and after leaving the newspaper he still spent one or two evenings a week lounging in the hotel corridors. Tradition survived of taller giants before the days of the contemporaneous Agamemnons. Allen asked questions about these and mourned their passing. Harrison, the twenty-third President; Gresham, of the brown eyes, judge and cabinet minister; Hendricks, the courtly gentleman, sometime Vice-President; "Uncle Joe" McDonald and "Dan" Voorhees, Senators in Congress, and loved in their day by wide constituencies. These had vanished, but Dan and Allen made a pious pilgrimage one night to sit at the feet of David Turpie, who had been a Senator in two widely separated eras, and who, white and venerable, like Aigyptos knew innumerable things.

The cloaked poets once visible in Market Street had vanished before our chronicle opens, with the weekly literary journals in which they had shone, but Dan was able to introduce Allen to James Whitcomb Riley in a bookshop frequented by the poet; and that was a great day in Allen's life. He formed the habit of lying in wait for the poet and walking with him, discussing Keats and Burns, Stevenson and Kipling, and others of their common admirations. One day of days the poet took Allen home with him and read him a new, unpublished poem, and showed him a rare photograph of Stevenson and the outside of a letter just received from Kipling, from the uttermost parts of the world. It was a fine thing to know a poet and to speak with him face to face,—particularly a poet who sang of his own soil as Allen wished to know it. Still, Allen did not quite understand how it happened that a poet who wrote of farmers and country-town folk wore eyeglasses and patent-leather shoes and carried a folded silk umbrella in all weathers.

The active politicians who crossed his horizon interested Allen greatly; the rougher and more uncouth they were the more he admired them. They were figures in the Great Experiment, no matter how sordid or contemptible Harwood pronounced them. He was always looking for "types" and "Big" Jordan, the Republican chief, afforded him the greatest satisfaction. He viewed the local political scene from an angle that Harwood found amusing, and Dan suggested that it must be because the feudal taint and the servile tradition are still in our blood that we submit so tamely to the rule of petty lordlings. In his exalted moments Allen's ideas shot far into the air, and Dan found it necessary to pull him back to earth.

"I hardly see a Greek frieze carved of these brethren," Dan remarked one night as they lounged at the Whitcomb when a meeting of the state committee was in progress. "These fellows would make you weep if you knew as much about them as I do. There's one of the bright lights now—the Honorable Ike Pettit, of Fraser. The Honorable Ike isn't smart enough to be crooked; he's the bellowing Falstaff of the Hoosier Democracy. I wonder who the laugh's on just now; he's shaking like a jelly fish over something."

"Oh, I know him! He and father are great chums; he was at the house for dinner last night."

"What!"

Harwood was unfeignedly surprised at this. The editor of the "Fraser County Democrat" had probably never dined at the Bassetts' in his own town, or at least Dan assumed as much; and since he had gained an insight into Bassett's affairs he was aware that the physical property of the "Fraser County Democrat" was mortgaged to Morton Bassett for quite all it was worth. It was hardly possible that Thatcher was cultivating Pettit's acquaintance for sheer joy of his society. As the ponderous editor lumbered across the lobby to where they sat, Dan and Allen rose to receive his noisily cordial salutations. On his visits to the capital, arrayed in a tremendous frock coat and with a flapping slouch hat crowning his big iron-gray head, he was a prodigious figure.

"Boys," he said, dropping an arm round each of the young men, "the Democratic Party is the hope of mankind. Free her of the wicked bosses, boil the corruption out of her, and the grand old Hoosier Democracy will appear once more upon the mountain tops as the bringer of glad tidings. What's the answer, my lads, to Uncle Ike's philosophy?"

"Between campaigns we're all reformers," said Harwood guardedly. "I feel it working in my own system."

"Between campaigns," replied the Honorable Isaac Pettit impressively, "we're all a contemptible lot of cowards, that's what's the matter with us. Was Thomas Jefferson engaged in manipulating legislatures? Did he obstruct the will of the people? Not by a long shot he did *not*! And that grand old patriot, Andrew Jackson, wasn't he satisfied to take his licker or let it alone without being like a heathen in his blindness, bowing down to wood and stone carved into saloons and distilleries?"

"It's said by virtuous Republicans that our party is only a tail to the liquor interests. If you're going back to the Sage of Monticello, how do you think he would answer that?"

"Bless you, my dear boy; it's not the saloons we try to protect; it's the plain people, who are entitled to the widest and broadest liberty. If you screw the lid down on people too tight you'll smother 'em. I'm not a drinkin' man; I go to church and in my newspaper I preach the felicities of sobriety and domestic peace. But it's not for me to dictate to my brother what he shall eat or wear. No, sir! And look here, don't you try to read me out of the Democratic Party, young man. At heart our party's as sweet and strong as corn; yea, as the young corn that leapeth to the rains of June. It's the bosses that's keepin' us down."

"Your reference to corn throws us back on the distilleries," suggested Harwood, laughing.

But he was regarding the Honorable Isaac Pettit attentively. Pettit had changed his manner and stood rocking himself slowly on his heels. He had been a good deal at the capital of late, and this, together with his visit to Thatcher's house, aroused Harwood's curiosity. He wondered whether it were possible that Pettit and Thatcher were conspiring against Bassett: the fact that he was so heavily in debt to the senator from Fraser seemed to dispose of his fears. Since his first visit to Fraserville Dan had heard many interesting and amusing things about the editor. Pettit had begun life as a lawyer, but had relapsed into rural journalism after a futile effort to find clients. He had some reputation as an orator, and Dan had heard him make a speech distinguished by humor and homely good sense at a meeting of the Democratic State Editorial Association. Pettit, having once sat beside Henry Watterson at a public dinner in Louisville, had thereafter encouraged as modestly as possible a superstition that he and Mr. Watterson were the last survivors of the "old school" of American editors. One of his favorite jokes was the use of the editorial "we" in familiar conversation; he said "our wife" and "our sanctum," and he amused himself by introducing into the

"Democrat" trifling incidents of his domestic life, beginning these items with such phrases as, "While we were weeding our asparagus bed in the cool of Tuesday morning, our wife—noble woman that she is—" etc., etc. His squibs of this character, quoted sometimes in metropolitan newspapers, afforded him the greatest glee. He appeared occasionally as a lecturer, his favorite subject being American humor; and he was able to prove by his scrap-book that he had penetrated as far east as Xenia, Ohio, and as far west as Decatur, Illinois. Once, so ran Fraserville tradition, he had been engaged for the lyceum course at Springfield, Missouri, but his contract had been canceled when it was found that his discourse was unillumined by the stereopticon, that vivifying accessory being just then in high favor in that community.

Out of his own reading and reflections Allen had reached the conclusion that Franklin, Emerson, and Lincoln were the greatest Americans. He talked a great deal of Lincoln and of the Civil War, and the soldiers' monument, in its circular plaza in the heart of the city, symbolized for him all heroic things. He would sit on the steps in the gray shadow at night, waiting for Dan to finish some task at his office, and Harwood would find him absorbed, dreaming by the singing, foaming fountains.

Allen spoke with a kind of passionate eloquence of This Stupendous Experiment, or This Beautiful Experiment, as he liked to call America. Dan put Walt Whitman into his hands and afterwards regretted it, for Allen developed an attack of acute Whitmania that tried Dan's patience severely. Dan had passed through Whitman at college and emerged safely on the other side. He begged Allen not to call him "camerado" or lift so often the perpendicular hand. He suggested to him that while it might be fine and patriotic to declaim

"When lilacs last in the dooryard bloom'd,"

from the steps of the monument at midnight, the police might take another view of the performance. He began to see, however, that beneath much that was whimsical and sentimental the young fellow was sincerely interested in the trend of things in what, during this Whitman period, he called "these states." Sometimes Allen's remarks on current events struck Harwood by their wisdom: the boy was wholesomely provocative and stimulating. He began to feel that he understood him, and in his own homelessness Allen became a resource.

Allen was a creature of moods, and vanished often for days or weeks. He labored fitfully in his carpenter shop at home or with equal irregularity at a bench in the shop of Lüders, a cabinetmaker. Dan sometimes sought him at the shop, which was a headquarters for radicals of all sorts. The workmen showed a great fondness for Allen, who had been much in Germany and spoke their language well. He carried to the shop quantities of German books and periodicals for their enlightenment. The shop's visitors included several young Americans, among them a newspaper artist, a violinist in a theatre orchestra, and a linotype expert. They all wore large black scarfs and called each other "comrade." Allen earnestly protested that he still believed in the American Idea, the Great Experiment; but if democracy should fail he was ready to take up socialism. He talked of his heroes; he said they all owed it to the men who had made and preserved the Union to give the existing government a chance. These discussions were entirely good-humored and Harwood enjoyed them. Sometimes they met in the evening at a saloon in the neighborhood of the shop where Allen, the son of Edward Thatcher, whom everybody knew, was an object of special interest. He would sit on a table and lecture the saloon loungers in German, and at the end of a long debate made a point of paying the score. He was most temperate himself, sipping a glass of wine or beer in the deliberate German fashion.

Allen was a friendly soul and every one liked him. It was impossible not to like a lad whose ways were so gentle, whose smile was so appealing. He liked dancing and went to most of the parties—our capital has not outgrown its homely provincial habit of calling all social entertainments "parties." He was unfailingly courteous, with a manner toward women slightly elaborate and reminiscent of other times. There was no question of his social acceptance; mothers of daughters, who declined to speak to his father, welcomed him to their houses.

Allen introduced Dan to the households he particularly fancied and they made calls together on Dan's free evenings or on Sunday afternoons. Snobbishness was a late arrival among us; any young man that any one vouched for might know the "nicest" girls. Harwood's social circle was widening; Fitch and his wife said a good word for him in influential quarters, and the local Yale men had not neglected him. Allen liked the theatre, and exercised considerable ingenuity in devising excuses for paying for the tickets when they took young women of their acquaintance. He pretended to Dan that he had free tickets or got them at a discount. His father made him a generous allowance and he bought a motor car in which he declared Dan had a half interest; they needed it, he said, for their social adventures.

At the Thatcher house, Harwood caught fitful glimpses of Allen's father, a bird of passage inured to sleeping-cars. Occasionally Harwood dined with the father and son and they would all adjourn to Allen's shop on the third floor to smoke and talk. When Allen gave rein to his fancy and began descanting upon the grandeur of the Republic and the Beautiful Experiment making in "these states," Dan would see a blank puzzled look steal into

Thatcher's face. Thatcher adored Allen: he had for him the deep love of a lioness for her cubs; but all this idealistic patter the boy had got hold of—God knew where!—sounded as strange to the rich man as a discourse in Sanskrit.

Thatcher had not been among Bassett's callers in the new office in the Boordman, but late one afternoon, when Dan was deep in the principles of evidence, Thatcher came in.

"I'm not expecting Mr. Bassett to-day, if you wish to see him," said Dan.

"Nope," Thatcher replied indifferently, "I'm not looking for Mort. He's in Fraserville, I happen to know. Just talking to him on the telephone, so I rather guessed you were alone, that's why I came up. I want to talk to you a little bit, Harwood. It must be nearly closing time, so suppose you lock the door. You see," he continued, idling about the room, "Mort's in the newspapers a good deal, and not being any such terrible sinner as he is I don't care to have his labels tacked on me too much. Not that Mort isn't one of my best friends, you know; but a family man like me has got to be careful of his reputation."

Harwood opened his drawer and took out a box of cigars. Thatcher accepted one and lighted it deliberately, commenting on the office as he did so. He even strolled through the library to the open door of Bassett's private room beyond. The map of Indiana suspended above Bassett's desk interested him and he stood leaning on his stick and surveying it. There was something the least bit insinuating in his manner. The room, the map, the fact that Morton Bassett of Fraserville had, so to speak, planted a vedette in the heart of the capital, seemed to afford him mild, cynical amusement. He drew his hand across his face, twisted his mustache, and took the cigar from his mouth and examined the end of it with fictitious interest.

"Well," he ejaculated, "damn it all, why not?"

Harwood did not know why not; but a man as rich as Edward Thatcher was entitled to his vagaries. Thatcher sank into Bassett's swivel chair and swung round once or twice as though testing it, meanwhile eyeing the map. Then he tipped himself back comfortably and dropped his hat into his lap. His grayish brown hair was combed carefully from one side across the top in an unsuccessful attempt to conceal his baldness.

"I guess Mort wouldn't object to my sitting in his chair provided I didn't look at that map too much. Who was the chap that the sword hung over by a hair—Damocles? Well, maybe that's what that map is—it would smash pretty hard if the whole state fell down on Mort. But Mort knows just how many voters there are in every township and just how they line up election morning. There's a lot of brains in Bassett's head; you've noticed it?"

"It's admitted, I believe, that he's a man of ability," said Dan a little coldly.

Thatcher grinned.

"You're all right, Harwood. I know you're all right or Mort wouldn't have put you in here. I'm rather kicking myself that I didn't see you first."

"Mr. Bassett has given me a chance I'd begun to fear I shouldn't get; you see I'm studying law here. Mr. Bassett has made that possible. He's the best friend I ever had."

"That's good. Bassett usually picks winners. From what I hear of you and what I've seen I think you're all right myself. My boy has taken quite a great fancy to you."

Thatcher looked at the end of his cigar and waited for Dan to reply.

"I've grown very fond of Allen. He's very unusual; he's full of surprises."

"That boy," said Thatcher, pointing his cigar at Dan, "is the greatest boy in the world; but, damn it all, I don't make him out."

"Well, he's different; he's an idealist. I'm not sure that he isn't a philosopher!"

Thatcher nodded, as though this were a corroboration of his own surmises.

"He has a lot of ideas that are what they call advanced, but it's not for me to say that he isn't right about them. He talks nonsense some of the time, but occasionally he knocks me down with a big idea—or his way of putting a big idea. He doesn't understand a good deal that he sees; and yet he sometimes says something perfectly staggering."

"He does; by George, he does! Damn it, I took him to see a glassworks the other day; thought it would appeal to his sense of what you call the picturesque; but, Lord bless me, he asked how much the blowers were paid and wanted me to raise their pay on the spot. That was one on me, all right; I'd thought of giving him the works to play with, but I didn't have the nerve to offer it to him after that. 'Fraid he'd either turn it down or take it and bust me."

Thatcher had referred to this incident with unmistakable pride; he was evidently amused rather than chagrined by his son's scorn of the gift of a profitable industry. "I offered him money to start a carpenter shop or furniture factory or anything he wanted to tackle, but he wouldn't have it. Said he wanted to work in somebody else's shop to get the discipline. Discipline? That boy never had any discipline in his life! I've kept my nose to the grindstone ever since I was knee-high to a toad just so that boy wouldn't have to worry about his daily bread, and now, damn it all, he runs a carpenter shop on the top floor of a house that stands me, lot, furniture, and all, nearly a hundred thousand dollars! I can't talk to everybody about this; my wife and daughters don't want any discipline; don't like the United States or anything in it except exchange on London; and here I am with a boy who wears overalls and tries to callous his hands to look like a laboring man. If you can figure that out, it's a damn sight more than I can do! It's one on Ed Thatcher, that's all!"

"If I try to answer you, please don't think I pretend to any unusual knowledge of human nature; but what I see in the boy is a kind of poetic attitude toward America—our politics, the whole scheme; and it's a poetic strain in him that accounts for this feeling about labor. And he has a feeling for justice and mercy; he's strong for the underdog." "I suppose," said Thatcher dryly, "that if he'd been an underdog the way I was he'd be more tickled at a chance to sit on top. When I wore overalls it wasn't funny. Well, what am I going to do with him?"

"If you really want me to tell you I'd say to let him alone. He's a perfectly clean, straight, high-minded boy. If he were physically strong enough I should recommend him to go to college, late as it is for him, or better, to a school where he would really satisfy what seems to be his sincere ambition to learn to do something with his hands. But he's all right as he is. You ought to be glad that his aims are so wholesome. There are sons of prosperous men right around here who see everything red."

"That boy," declared Thatcher, pride and love surging in him, "is as clean as wheat!"

"Quite so; no one could know him without loving him. And I don't mind saying that I find myself in accord with many of his ideas."

"Sort of damned idealist yourself?"

"I should blush to say it," laughed Dan; "but I feel my heart warming when Allen gets to soaring sometimes; he expresses himself with great vividness. He goes after me hard on my *laissez-faire* notions."

"I take the count and throw up the sponge!"

"Oh, that's a chestnut that means merely that the underdog had better stay under if he can't fight his way out."

"It seems tough when you boil it down to that; I guess maybe Allen's right—we all ought to divide up. I'm willing, only"—and he grinned quizzically—"I'm paired with Mort Bassett."

The light in his cigar had gone out; he swung round and faced the map of Indiana above Morton Bassett's desk, fumbling in his waistcoat for a match. When he turned toward Harwood again he blew smoke rings meditatively before speaking.

"If you're one of these rotten idealists, Harwood, what are you doing here with Bassett? If that ain't a fair question, don't answer it."

Harwood was taken aback by the directness of the question. Bassett had always spoken of Thatcher with respect, and he resented the new direction given to this conversation in Bassett's own office. Dan straightened himself with dignity, but before he could speak Thatcher laughed, and fanned the smoke of his cigar away with his hands.

"Don't get hot. That was not a fair question; I know it. I guess Bassett has his ideals just like the rest of us. I suppose I've got some, too, though I'd be embarrassed if you asked me to name 'em. I suppose" — and he narrowed his eyes — "I suppose Mort not only has his ideals but his ambitions. They go together, I reckon."

"I hope he has both, Mr. Thatcher, but you are assuming that I'm deeper in his confidence than the facts justify. You and he have been acquainted so long that you ought to know him thoroughly."

Thatcher did not heed this mild rebuke; nor did he resort to propitiatory speech. His cool way of ignoring Dan's reproach added to the young man's annoyance; Dan felt that it was in poor taste and ungenerous for a man of Thatcher's years and position to come into Bassett's private office to discuss him with a subordinate. He had already learned enough of the relations of the two men to realize that perfect amity was essential between them; he was shocked by the indifference with which Thatcher spoke of Bassett, of whom people did not usually speak carelessly in this free fashion. Harwood's own sense of loyalty was in arms; yet Thatcher seemed unmindful that anything disagreeable had occurred. He threw away his cigar and drew out a fresh one which he wobbled about in his mouth unlighted. He kept swinging round in his chair to gaze at the map above Bassett's desk. The tinted outlines of the map — green, pink, and orange — could not have had for him any novelty; similar maps hung in many offices and Thatcher was moreover a native of the state and long familiar with its configuration. Perhaps, Dan reflected, its juxtaposition to Bassett's desk was what irritated his visitor, though it had never occurred to him that this had any significance. He recalled now, however, that when he had arranged the rooms the map had been hung in the outer office, but that Bassett himself had removed it to his private room — the only change he had made in Dan's arrangements. It was conceivable that Thatcher saw in the position of the map an adumbration of Bassett's higher political ambition, and that this had affected the capitalist unpleasantly.

Thatcher's manner was that of a man so secure in his own position that he could afford to trample others under foot if he liked. It was—not to put too fine a point upon it—the manner of a bully. His reputation for independence was well established; he was rich enough to say what he pleased without regard to the consequences, and he undoubtedly enjoyed his sense of power.

"I suppose I'm the only man in Indiana that ain't afraid of Mort Bassett," he announced casually. "It's because Mort knows I ain't afraid of him that we get on so well together. You've been with him long enough by this time to know that we have some interests together."

Dan, with his fingers interlocked behind his head, nodded carelessly. He had grown increasingly resentful of Thatcher's tone and manner, and was anxious to be rid of him.

"Mort's a good deal closer-mouthed than I am. Mort likes to hide his tracks—better than that, by George, Mort doesn't *make* any tracks! Well, every man is bound to break a twig now and then as he goes along. By George, I tear down the trees like an elephant so they can't miss me!"

As Dan made no reply to this Thatcher recurred in a moment to Allen and Harwood's annoyance passed. It was obvious that the capitalist had sought this interview to talk of the boy, to make sure that Harwood was sincerely interested in him. Thatcher's manner of speaking of his son was kind and affectionate. The introduction of Bassett into the discussion had been purely incidental, but it was not less interesting because of its unpremeditated interjection. There was possibly some jealousy here that would manifest itself later; but that was not Dan's affair. Bassett was beyond doubt able to take care of himself in emergencies; Dan's admiration for his patron was strongly intrenched in this belief. The bulkier Thatcher, with the marks of self-indulgence upon him, and with his bright waistcoat and flashy necktie transcending the bounds of good taste, struck him as a weaker character. If Thatcher meditated a break with Bassett, the sturdier qualities, the even, hard strokes that Bassett had a reputation for delivering, would count heavily against him.

"I'm glad you get on so well with the boy," Thatcher was saying. "I don't mind telling you that his upbringing has been a little unfortunate—too much damned Europe. He's terribly sore because he didn't go to college instead of being tutored all over Europe. It's funny he's got all these romantic ideas about America; he's sore at me because he wasn't born poor and didn't have to chop rails to earn his way through college and all that. The rest of my family like the money all right; they're only sore because I didn't make it raising tulips. But that boy's all right. And see here—" Thatcher seemed for a moment embarrassed by what was in his mind. He fidgeted in his chair and eyed Harwood sharply. "See here, Harwood, if you find after awhile that you don't get on with Bassett, or you want to change, why, I want you to give me a chance at you. I'd like to put my boy with you, somehow. I'll die some day and I want to be sure somebody'll look after him. By God, he's all I got!"

He swung round, but his eyes were upon the floor; he drew out a handkerchief and blew his nose noisily.

"By George," he exclaimed, "I promised Allen to take you up to Sally Owen's. You know Mrs. Owen? That's right; Allen said she's been asking about you. She likes young folks; she'll never be old herself. Allen and I are going there for supper, and he's asked her if he might bring you along. Aunt Sally's a great woman. And"—he grinned ruefully—"a good trader. She has beat me on many a horse trade, that woman; and I always go back to try it again. You kind o' like having her do you. And I guess I'm the original easy mark when it comes to horse. Get your hat and come along. Allen's fixed this all up with her. I guess you and she are the best friends the boy's got."

CHAPTER XII
BLURRED WINDOWS

With Sylvia's life in college we have little to do, but a few notes we must make now that she has reached her sophomore year. She had never known girls until she went to college and she had been the shyest of freshmen, the least obtrusive of sophomores.

She had carried her work from the start with remarkable ease and as the dragons of failure were no longer a menace she began to give more heed to the world about her. She was early recognized as an earnest, conscientious student whose work in certain directions was brilliant; and as a sophomore her fellows began to know her and take pride in her. She was relieved to find herself swept naturally into the social currents of the college. She had been afraid of appearing stiff or priggish, but her self-consciousness quickly vanished in the broad, wholesome democracy of college life. The best scholar in her class, she was never called a grind and she was far from being a frump. The wisest woman in the faculty said of Sylvia: "That girl with her head among the stars has her feet planted on solid ground. Her life will count." And the girlhood that Sylvia had partly lost, was recovered and prolonged. It was a fine thing to be an American college girl, Sylvia realized, and the varied intercourse, the day's hundred and one contacts and small excitements, meant more to her than her fellow students knew. When there was fun in the air Sylvia could be relied upon to take a hand in it. Her allowance was not meagre and she joined zestfully in such excursions as were possible, to concerts, lectures, and the theatre. She had that reverence for New England traditions that is found in all young Westerners. It was one of her jokes that she took two Boston girls on their first pilgrimage to Concord, a joke that greatly tickled John Ware, brooding in his library in Delaware Street.

A few passages from her letters home are illuminative of these college years. Here are some snap-shots of her fellow students:—

"I never knew before that there were so many kinds of
people in the world—girls, I mean. All parts of the country
are represented, and I suppose I shall always judge different

cities and states by the girls they send here. There is a California freshman who is quite tall, like the redwood trees, I suppose. And there is a little girl in my class—she seems little—from Omaha who lives on a hilltop out there where she can see the Missouri River—and when her father first settled there, Indians were still about. She is the nicest and gentlest girl I know, and yet she brings before me all those pioneer times and makes me think how fast the country has grown. And there is a Virginia girl in my corridor who has the most wonderful way of talking, and there's history in that, too,—the history of all the great war and the things you fought for; but I was almost sorry to have to let her know that you fought on the other side, but I *did* tell her. I never realized, just from books and maps, that the United States is so big. The girls bring their local backgrounds with them— the different aims and traits. . . . I have drawn a map of the country and named all the different states and cities for the girls who come from them, but this is just for my own fun, of course. . . . I never imagined one would have preferences and like and dislike people by a kind of instinct, without really knowing them, but I'm afraid I do it, and that all the rest of us do the same. . . . Nothing in the world is as interesting as people—just dear, good folksy people!"

The correspondence her dormitory neighbors carried on with parents and brothers and sisters and friends impressed her by its abundance; and she is to be pardoned if she weighed the letters, whose home news was quoted constantly in her hearing, against her own slight receipts at the college post-office. She knew that every Tuesday morning there would be a letter from her grandfather. Her old friend Dr. Wandless sent occasionally, in his kindly humorous fashion, the news of Buckeye Lane and the college; and Mrs. Owen wrote a hurried line now and then, usually to quote one of John Ware's sayings. The minister asked about Sylvia, it seemed. These things helped, but they did not supply the sympathy, of which she was conscious in countless ways, between her fellow students and their near of kin. With the approach of holiday times, the talk among her companions of the homes that awaited them, or, in the case of many, of other homes where they were to visit, deepened her newly awakened sense of isolation. Fathers and mothers appeared constantly to visit their daughters, and questions that had never troubled her heart before arose to vex her. Why was it, when these other girls, flung together from all parts of the country, were so blest with kindred, that she had literally but one kinsman, the grandfather on whom all her love centred?

It should not be thought, however, that she yielded herself morbidly to these reflections, but such little things as the receipt of gifts, the daily references to home affairs, the photographs set out in the girls' rooms, were not without their stab. She wrote to Professor Kelton:—

"I wish you would send me your picture of mother. I often wondered why you didn't give it to me; won't you lend it to me now? I think it is put away in your desk in the library. Almost all the girls have pictures of their families—some of them of their houses and even the horse and dog—in their rooms. And you must have a new picture taken of yourself—I'd like it in your doctor's gown, that they gave you at Williams. It's put away in the cedar chest in the attic—Mary will know where. And if you have a picture of father anywhere I should like to have that too."

She did not know that when this reached him—one of the series of letters on which the old gentleman lived these days, with its Wellesley postmark, and addressed in Sylvia's clear, running hand, he bowed his white head and wept; for he knew what was in the girl's heart—knew and dreaded this roused yearning, and suffered as he realized the arid wastes of his own ignorance. But he sent her the picture of her mother for which she asked, and had the cottage photographed with Mills Hall showing faintly beyond the hedge; and he meekly smuggled his doctor's gown to the city and sat for his photograph. These things Sylvia proudly spread upon the walls of her room. He wrote to her—a letter that cost him a day's labor:—

"We don't seem to have any photograph of your father; but things have a way of getting lost, particularly in the hands of an old fellow like me. However, I have had myself taken as you wished, and you can see now what a solemn person your grandfather is in his *toga academica*. I had forgotten I had that silk overcoat and I am not sure now that I didn't put the hood on wrong-side-out! I'm a sailor, you know, and these fancy things stump me. The photographer didn't seem to understand that sort of millinery. Please keep it dark; your teachers might resent the sudden appearance in the halls of Wellesley of a grim old professor *emeritus* not known to your faculty."

The following has its significance in Sylvia's history and we must give it place—this also to her grandfather:—

"The most interesting lecture I ever heard (except yours!) was given at the college yesterday by Miss Jane Addams, of Hull

House, the settlement worker and writer on social reforms. She's such a simple, modest little woman that everybody loved her at once. She made many things clear to me that I had only groped for before. She used an expression that was new to me, 'reciprocal obligations,' which we all have in this world, though I never quite thought of it before. She's a college woman herself, and feels that all of us who have better advantages than other people should help those who aren't taught to climb. It seems the most practical idea in the world, that we should gather up the loose, rough fringes of society and weave the broken threads into a common warp and woof. The social fabric is no stronger than its weakest thread. . . . To help and to save for the sheer love of helping and saving is the noblest thing any of us can do—I feel that. This must be an old story to you; I'm ashamed that I never saw it all for myself. It's as though I had been looking at the world through a blurred window, from a comfortable warm room, when some one came along and brushed the pane clear, so that I could see the suffering and hardship outside, and feel my own duty to go out and help."

Professor Kelton, spending a day in the city, showed this to Mrs. Owen when she asked for news of Sylvia. Mrs. Owen kept the letter that John Ware might see it. Ware said: "Deep nature; I knew that night she told me about the stars that she would understand everything. You will hear of her. Wish she would come here to live. We need women like that."

Professor Kelton met Sylvia in New York on her way home for the holidays in her freshman year and they spent their Christmas together in the cottage. She was bidden to several social gatherings in Buckeye Lane; and to a dance in town. She was now Miss Garrison, a student at Wellesley, and the good men and women at Madison paid tribute to her new dignity. Something Sylvia was knowing of that sweet daffodil time in the heart of a girl before the hovering swallows dare to fly.

In the midyear recess of her sophomore year she visited one of her new friends in Boston in a charming home of cultivated people. The following Easter vacation her grandfather joined her for a flight to New York and Washington, and this was one of the happiest of experiences. During the remainder of her college life she was often asked to the houses of her girl friends in and about Boston; her diffidence passed; she found that she had ideas and the means of expressing them. The long summers were spent at the cottage in the Lane; she saw Mrs. Owen now and then with deepening attachment, and her friend never forgot to send her a Christmas gift—once a silver purse and a twenty-dollar gold piece; again, a watch—always something carefully chosen and practical.

Sylvia arranged to return to college with two St. Louis girls after her senior Christmas, to save her grandfather the long journey, for he had stipulated that she should never travel alone. By a happy chance Dan Harwood, on his way to Boston to deliver an issue of telephone bonds in one of Bassett's companies, was a passenger on the same train, and he promptly recalled himself to Sylvia, who proudly presented him as a Yale man to her companions. A special car filled with young collegians from Cincinnati and the South was later attached to the train, and Dan, finding several Yalensians in the company, including the year's football hero, made them all acquainted with Sylvia and her friends. It was not till the next day that Dan found an opportunity for personal talk with Sylvia, but he had already been making comparisons. Sylvia was as well "put up" as any of the girls, and he began to note her quick changes of expression, the tones of her voice, the grace of her slim, strong hands. He wanted to impress himself upon her; he wanted her to like him.

"News? I don't know that I can give you any news. You probably know that Mrs. Owen went to Fraserville for Christmas with the Bassetts? Let me see, you do know the Bassetts, don't you?"

"Yes. I was at Waupegan three summers ago at Mrs. Owen's, and Mrs. Bassett and all of them were very good to me."

"You probably don't know that I'm employed by Mr. Bassett. He has an office in Indianapolis where I'm trying to be a lawyer and I do small jobs for him. I'm doing an errand for him now. It will be the first time I've been east of the mountains since I left college, and I'm going to stop at New Haven on my way home to see how they're getting on without me. By the way, you probably know that Marian is going to college?"

"No; I didn't know it," exclaimed Sylvia. "But I knew her mother was interested and I gave her a Wellesley catalogue. That was a long time ago!"

"That was when you were visiting Mrs. Owen at Waupegan? I see, said the blind man!"

"What do you see?" asked Sylvia.

"I see Mrs. Bassett and Marian, niece and grandniece respectively, of Aunt Sally Owen; and as I gaze, a stranger bound for college suddenly appears on Mrs. Owen's veranda, in cap and gown. Tableau!"

"I don't see the picture," Sylvia replied, though she laughed in spite of herself.

"I not only see," Dan continued, "but I hear the jingle of red, red gold, off stage."

This was going a trifle too far. Sylvia shook her head and frowned.

"That isn't fair, Mr. Harwood, if I guess what you mean. There's no reason why Marian shouldn't go to college. My going has nothing to do with it. You have misunderstood the whole matter."

"Pardon me," said Dan quickly. "I mean no unkindness to any of them. They are all very good to me. It's too bad, though, that Marian's preparation for college hadn't been in mind until so recently. It would save her a lot of hard digging now. I see a good deal of the family; and I'm even aware of Marian's doings at Miss Waring's school. Master Blackford beguiles me into taking him to football games, and I often go with all of them to the theatre when they're in town. Mr. Bassett is very busy, and he doesn't often indulge himself in pleasures. He's the kind of man whose great joy is in work—and he has many things to look after."

"You are a kind of private secretary to the whole family, then; but you work at the law at the same time?"

Harwood's face clouded for a moment; she noticed it and was sorry she had spoken; but he said immediately:—

"Well, I haven't had much time for the law this winter. I have more things to do outside than I had expected. But I fear I need prodding; I'm too prone to wander into other fields. And I'm getting a good deal interested in politics. You know Mr. Bassett is one of the leading men in our state."

"Yes, I had learned that; I suppose he may be Senator or Governor some day. That makes it all the more important that Marian should be fitted for high station."

"I don't know that just that idea has struck her!" he laughed, quite cheerful again. "It's too bad it can't be suggested to her. It might help her with her Latin. She tells me in our confidences that she thinks Latin a beast. It's my rôle to pacify her. But a girl must live up to her mother's ambitions, and Mrs. Bassett is ambitious for her children. And then there's always the unencumbered aunt to please into the bargain. Mrs. Owen is shrewd, wise, kind. Since that night I saw you there we've become pals. She's the most stimulating person I ever knew. She has talked to me about you several times"—Dan laughed and looked Sylvia in the eyes as though wondering how far to go—"and if you're not the greatest living girl you have shamefully fooled Mrs. Owen. Mr. Ware, the minister, came in one evening when I was there and I never heard such praise as they gave you. But I approved of it."

"Oh, how nice of you!" said Sylvia, in a tone so unlike her that Dan laughed outright.

"You are the embodiment of loyalty; but believe me, I am a loyal person myself. Please don't think me a gossip. Marian's mother still hopes to land her in college next year, but she's the least studious of beings; I can't see her doing it. Mrs. Bassett's never quite well, and that's been bad for Marian. College would be a good thing for her. I've seen many soaring young autocrats reduced to a proper humility at New Haven, and I dare say you girls have your own way of humbling a proud spirit."

"I don't believe Marian needs humbling; one can't help liking her; and she's ever so good to look at."

"She's certainly handsome," Dan admitted.

"She's altogether charming," said Sylvia warmly; "and she's young—much younger than I am, for example."

"How old is young, or how young is old? I had an idea that you and she were about the same age."

"You flatter me! I'm nearly four years older! but I suppose she seems much more grown-up, and she knows a great many things I don't."

"I dare say she does!" Dan laughed. And with this they turned to other matters.

Dan sat facing her, hat in hand, and as the train rushed through the Berkshires Sylvia formed new impressions of him. She saw him now as a young man of affairs, with errands abroad—this in itself of significance; and he had to do with politics, a subject that had begun to interest Sylvia. The cowlick where his hair parted kept a stubborn wisp of brown hair in rebellion, and it shook amusingly when he spoke earnestly or laughed. His gray eyes were far apart and his nose was indubitably a big one. He laughed a good deal, by which token one saw that his teeth were white and sound. Something of the Southwestern drawl had survived his years at New Haven, but when he became earnest his eyes snapped and he spoke with quick, nervous energy, in a deep voice that was a little harsh. Sylvia had heard a great deal about the brothers and young men friends of her companions at college and was now more attentive to the outward form of man than she had thought of being before.

When they reached Boston, Harwood took Sylvia and her companions to luncheon at the Touraine and put them on their train for Wellesley. His thoughtfulness and efficiency could not fail to impress the young women. He was an admirable cavalier, and Sylvia's companions were delighted with him. He threatened them with an early visit to college, suggesting the most daring possibilities as to his appearance. He repeated, at Sylvia's instigation, the incident of the hearse horses at Poughkeepsie, with new flourishes, and cheerfully proposed a cousinship to all of them.

"Or, perhaps," he said, when he had found seats for them and had been admonished to leave, "perhaps it would be more in keeping with my great age to become your uncle. Then you would be cousins to each other and we should all be related."

Speculations as to whether he would ever come kept the young women laughing as they discussed him. They declared that the meeting on the train had been by ulterior design and they quite exhausted the fun of it upon Sylvia, who gained greatly in importance through the encounter with Harwood. She was not the demure young person they had thought her; it was not every girl who could produce a personable young man on a railway journey.

Sylvia wondered much about Marian and dramatized to herself the girl's arrival at college. It did not seem credible that Mrs. Bassett was preparing Marian for college because she, Sylvia Garrison, was enrolled there. Sylvia was kindly disposed toward all the world, and she resented Harwood's insinuations. As for Mrs. Owen and Dan's intimations that Marian must be educated to satisfy the great aunt's ideals as represented in Sylvia—well, Sylvia had no patience whatever with any such idea.

CHAPTER XIII
THE WAYS OF MARIAN

The historian may not always wait for the last grain of sand to mark the passing of an hour; he must hasten the flight of time frequently by abrupt reversals of the glass. Much competent evidence (to borrow from the lawyers) we must reject as irrelevant or immaterial to our main issue. Harwood was admitted to practice in the United States courts midway of his third year in Bassett's office. The doors of the state courts swing inward to any Hoosier citizen of good moral character who wants to practice law,—a drollery of the Hoosier constitution still tolerated. The humor of being a mere "constitutional" lawyer did not appeal to Harwood, who revered the traditions and the great names of his chosen profession, and he had first written his name on the rolls of the United States District Court.

His work for Bassett grew more and more congenial. The man from Fraser was concentrating his attention on business; at least he found plenty of non-political work for Dan to do. After the troubled waters in Ranger County had been quieted and Bassett's advanced outpost in the Boordman Building had ceased to attract newspaper reporters, an important receivership to which Bassett had been appointed gave Harwood employment of a semi-legal character. Bassett had been a minor stockholder in a paper-mill which had got into difficulties through sheer bad management, and as receiver he addressed himself to the task of proving that the business could be made to pay. The work he assigned to Harwood was to the young man's liking, requiring as it did considerable travel, visits to the plant, which was only a few hours' journey from the capital, and negotiations which required the exercise of tact and judgment. However, Harwood found himself ineluctably drawn into the state campaign that fall. Bassett was deeply engaged in all the manoeuvres, and Harwood was dispatched frequently on errands to county chairmen, and his aid was welcomed by the literary bureau of the state committee. He prepared a speech whose quality he tested at small meetings in his own county, and his efforts having been favorably received he acted as a supply to fill appointments where the regular schedule failed. Toward the end of the campaign his assignments increased until all his time was taken. By studying his audiences he caught the trick of holding the attention of large crowds; his old college sobriquet of "Foghorn" Harwood had been revived and the newspapers mentioned his engagements with a casualness that implied fame. He enjoyed his public appearances, and the laughter and applause were sweet to him.

After the election Bassett admonished him not to neglect the law.

"I want you to make your way in the profession," he said, "and not let my affairs eat up all your time. Give me your mornings as far as possible and keep your afternoons for study. If at any time you have to give me a whole day, take the next day for yourself. But this work you're doing will all help you later. Lawyers these days have got to be business men; you understand that; and you want to get to the top."

Dan visited his parents and brothers as often as possible on the infertile Harrison County acres, to which the mortgage still clung tenaciously. He had felt since leaving college that he owed it to the brothers who had remained behind to wipe out the old harassing debt as soon as possible. The thought of their struggles often made him unhappy, and he felt that he could only justify his own desertion by freeing the farm. After one of these visits Bassett drew from him the fact that the mortgage was about to mature, and that another of a long series of renewals of the loan was necessary. Bassett was at once interested and sympathetic. The amount of the debt was three thousand dollars, and he proposed that Dan discharge it.

"I've never said so, but at the conclusion of the receivership I've intended paying you for your additional work. If everything goes well my own allowance ought to be ten thousand dollars, and you're entitled to a share of it. I'll say now that it will be not less than two thousand dollars. I'll advance you that amount at once and carry your personal note for the other thousand in the Fraserville bank. It's too bad you have to use your first money that way, but it's natural for you to want to do it. I see that you feel a duty there, and the folks at home have had that mortgage on their backs so long that it's taken all the spirit out of them. You pay the mortgage when it's due and go down and make a little celebration of it, to cheer them up. I'll carry that thousand as long as you like."

Miss Rose Farrell, nigh to perishing of ennui in the lonely office of the absentee steel construction agents, had been installed as stenographer in Room 66 a year earlier. Miss Farrell had, it appeared, served Bassett several terms as stenographer to one of the legislative committees of which he was chairman.

"You needn't be afraid of my telling anything," she said in reply to Dan's cautioning. "Those winters I worked at the State House I learned enough to fill three penitentiaries with great and good men, but you couldn't dig it out of me with a steam shovel. They were going to have me up before an investigating committee once, but I had burned my shorthand notes and couldn't remember a thing. Your little Irish Rose knows a few things, Mr. Harwood. I was on to your office before the 'Advertiser' sprung that story and gave it away that Mr. Bassett had a room here. I spotted the senator from Fraser coming up our pedestrian elevator, and I know all those rubes that have been dropping up to see him—struck 'em all in the legislature. He won't tear your collar if you put me on the job. And if I do say it myself I'm about as speedy on the machine as you find 'em. All your little Rose asks is the right to an occasional Wednesday matinée when business droops like a sick oleander. You needn't worry about me having callers. I'm a business woman, I am, and I guess I know what's proper in a business office. If I don't understand men, Mr. Harwood, no poor working girl does."

Bassett was pleased with Dan's choice of a stenographer. He turned over to Rose the reading of the rural newspapers and sundry other routine matters. There was no doubt of Miss Farrell's broad knowledge of the world, or of her fidelity to duty. Harwood took early opportunity to subdue somewhat the pungency of the essences with which she perfumed herself, and she gave up gum-chewing meekly at his behest. She assumed at once toward him that maternal attitude which is peculiar to office girls endowed with psychological insight. He sought to improve the character of fiction she kept at hand for leisure moments, and was surprised by the aptness of her comments on the books she borrowed on his advice from the Public Library. She was twenty-four, tall and trim, with friendly blue-gray eyes and a wit that had been sharpened by adversity.

It cannot be denied that Mrs. Bassett and Marian found Harwood a convenient reed upon which to lean. Nor was Blackford above dragging his father's secretary (as the family called him) forth into the bazaars of Washington Street to assist in the purchase of a baseball suit or in satisfying other cravings of his youthful heart. Mrs. Bassett, scorning the doctors of Fraserville, had now found a nerve specialist at the capital who understood her troubles perfectly.

Marian, at Miss Waring's school, was supposed to be preparing for college, though Miss Waring had no illusions on the subject. Marian made Mrs. Owen her excuse for many absences from school: what was the use of having a wealthy great-aunt living all alone in a comfortable house in Delaware Street if one didn't avail one's self of the rights and privileges conferred by such relationship? When a note from Miss Waring to Mrs. Bassett at Fraserville conveyed the disquieting news of her daughter's unsatisfactory progress, Mrs. Bassett went to town and dealt severely with Marian. Mrs. Owen was grimly silent when appealed to; it had never been her idea that Marian should be prepared for college; but now that the girl's mother had pledged herself to the undertaking Mrs. Owen remained a passive spectator of the struggle. Mrs. Owen was not so dull but that she surmised what had inspired this zeal for a collegiate training for Marian; and her heart warmed toward the dark young person at Wellesley, such being the contrariety of her kindly soul. To Miss Waring, a particular friend of hers and one of her admirations, Mrs. Owen said:—

"I want you to do the best you can for Marian, now that her mother's bitten with this idea of sending her to college. She's smart enough, I guess?"

"Too much smartness is Marian's trouble," replied Miss Waring. "There's nothing in the gymnasium she can't do; she's become the best French scholar we ever had, but that's about all. She's worked hard at French because she thinks it gives her a grand air. I can't imagine any other reason. She's adorable and—impossible!"

"Do the best you can for her; I want her to go to college if she can."

Miss Waring had the reputation of being strict, yet Marian slipped the cords of routine and discipline with ease. She had passed triumphantly from the kitchen "fudge" and homemade butterscotch period of a girl's existence into the realm of *marrons glacés*. Nothing bored her so much as the afternoon airings of the school under the eye of a teacher; and these she turned into larks when she shared in them. Twice in one winter she had hopped upon a passing street car and rolled away in triumph from her meek and horrified companions and their outraged duenna. She encouraged by means the subtlest, the attentions of a strange young gentleman who followed the school's peregrinations afar off. She carried on a brief correspondence with this cavalier, a fence corner in Pennsylvania Street serving as post-office.

Luck favored her astonishingly in her efforts to escape the rigors of school discipline. Just when she was forbidden to leave Miss Waring's to spend nights and Sundays at Mrs. Owen's, her mother came to town and opportunely (for Marian) fell ill, at the Whitcomb. Mrs. Bassett was cruising languidly toward the sombre coasts of Neurasthenia, and though she was under the supervision of a trained nurse, Marian made her mother's illness an excuse for moving down to the hotel to take care of her. Her father, in and out of the city caring for his multiplying interests, objected mildly but acquiesced, which was simpler and more comfortable than opposing her.

Having escaped from school and established herself at the Whitcomb, Marian summoned Harwood to the hotel on the flimsiest pretexts, many of them most ingeniously plausible. For example, she avowed her intention of carrying on her studies at the hotel during her enforced retirement from Miss Waring's, and her father's secretary, being a college man, could assist her with her Latin as well as not. Dan set tasks for her for a week, until she wearied of the pretense. She insisted that it was too stupid for her to go unattended to the hotel restaurant for her meals, and it was no fun eating in her mother's room with that lady in bed and the trained nurse at hand; so Harwood must join her for luncheon and dinner at the Whitcomb. Mrs. Owen was out of town, Bassett was most uncertain in his goings and comings, and Mrs. Bassett was beyond Harwood's reach, so he obeyed, not without chafing of spirit, these commands of Marian. He was conscious that people pointed her out in the restaurant as Morton Bassett's daughter, and he did not like the responsibility of this unauthorized chaperonage.

Mrs. Bassett was going to a sanatorium as soon as she was able to move; but for three weeks Marian was on Harwood's hands. Her bland airs of proprietorship amused him when they did not annoy him, and when he ventured to remonstrate with her for her unnecessary abandonment of school to take care of her mother, her pretty *moue* had mitigated his impatience. She knew the value of her prettiness. Dan was a young man and Marian was not without romantic longings. Just what passed between her and her mother Harwood could not know, but the hand that ruled indulgently in health had certainly not gained strength in sickness.

This was in January when the theatres were offering an unusual variety of attractions. Dan had been obliged to refuse—more harshly than was agreeable—to take Marian to see a French farce that had been widely advertised by its indecency. Her cool announcement that she had read it in French did not seem to Harwood to make an educational matter of it; but he was obliged finally to compromise with her on another play. Her mother was quite comfortable, she averred; there was no reason why she should not go to the theatre, and she forced the issue by getting the tickets herself.

That evening when they reached their seats Dan observed that Allen Thatcher sat immediately in front of them. He turned and nodded to Dan, and his eyes took in Marian. In a moment she murmured an inquiry as to who the young man was; and Harwood was aware thereafter that Marian divided her attention between Allen and the stage. Allen turned once or twice in the entr'actes with some comment on the play, and Marian was pleased with his profile; moreover he bore a name with which she had long been familiar. As the curtain fell she whispered to Harwood:—

"You must introduce me to Mr. Thatcher,—please—! His father and papa are friends, and I've heard so much about the family that I just have to know him."

Harwood looked down at her gravely to be sure it was not one of her jokes, but she was entirely serious. He felt that he must take a stand with her; if her father and mother were unaware of her venturesome nature he still had his responsibility, and it was not incumbent on him to widen her acquaintance.

"No!" he said flatly.

But Marian knew a trick or two. She loitered by her seat adjusting her wrap with unnecessary deliberation. Allen, wishing to arrange an appointment with Dan for luncheon the next day, waited for him to come into the aisle. Dan had not the slightest idea of introducing his charge to Allen or to any one else, and he stepped in front of her to get rid of his friend with the fewest words possible. But Marian so disposed herself at his elbow that he could not without awkwardness refuse her.

She murmured Allen's name cordially, leveling her eyes at him smilingly.

"I've often heard Mr. Harwood speak of you, Mr. Thatcher! He has a great way of speaking of his friends!"

Allen was not a forthputting person, and Dan's manner was not encouraging; but the trio remained together necessarily through the aisle to the foyer.

Marian took advantage of their slow exit to discuss the play and with entire sophistication, expressing astonishment that Allen was lukewarm in his praise of it. He could not agree with her that the leading woman was beautiful, but she laughed when he remarked, with his droll intonation, that the star reminded him of a dressed-up mannikin in a clothing-store window.

"That is just the kind of thing I imagined you would say. My aunt, Mrs. Owen, says that you always say something different."

"Oh, Aunt Sally! She's the grandest of women. I wish she were my aunt. I have aunts I could trade for her."

At the door Allen paused. Marian, running on blithely, gave him no opportunity to make his adieux.

"Oh, aren't you going our way?" she demanded, in a tone of invitation.

"Yes; come along; it's only a step to the hotel where Miss Bassett is staying," said Harwood, finding that they blocked the entrance and not seeing his way to abandoning Allen on the spot. He never escaped the appeal that lay in Allen; he was not the sort of fellow one would wound; and there could be no great harm in allowing him to walk a few blocks with Marian Bassett, who had so managed the situation as to make his elimination difficult. It was a cold, clear night and they walked briskly to the Whitcomb.

When they reached the hotel, Dan, who had left the conversation to Marian and Allen, breathed a sigh that his responsibility was at an end. He and Allen would have a walk and talk together, or they might go up to the Boordman Building for the long lounging parleys in which Allen delighted and which Dan himself enjoyed. But Dan had not fully gauged the measure of Marian's daring.

"Won't you please wait a minute, Mr. Harwood, until I see if poor mama needs anything. You know we all rely on you so. I'll be back in just a moment."

"So that's Morton Bassett's daughter," observed Allen when Marian had fluttered into the elevator. "You must have a lot of fun taking her about; she's much more grown-up than I had imagined from what you've said. She's almost a dangerous young person."

The young men found seats and Allen nursed his hat musingly. He had nothing whatever to do, and the chance meeting with Harwood was a bright incident in a bleak, eventless day.

"Oh, she's a nice child," replied Harwood indifferently. "But she finds childhood irksome. It gives her ladyship a feeling of importance to hold me here while she asks after the comfort of her mother. I suppose a girl is a woman when she has learned that she can tell a man to wait."

"You should write a book of aphorisms and call it 'The Young Lady's Own Handbook.' Perhaps I ought to be skipping."

"For Heaven's sake, don't! I want you as an excuse for getting away."

"I think I'd better go," suggested Allen. "I can wait for you in the office."

"Then I should pay the penalty for allowing you to escape; she can be very severe; she is a much harder taskmaster than her father. Don't desert me."

Allen took this at face value; and it seemed only ordinary courtesy to wait to say good-night to a young woman who was coming back in a moment to report upon the condition of a sick mother. In ten minutes Marian reappeared, having left her wraps behind.

"Mama is sleeping beautifully. And that's a sign that she's better."

Here clearly was an end of the matter, and Dan had begun to say good-night; but with the prettiest grace possible Marian was addressing Allen:—

"I'm terribly hungry and I sent down an order for just the smallest supper. You see, I took it for granted that you would both be just as hungry as I am, so you must come and keep me company." And to anticipate the refusal that already glittered coldly in Dan's eye, she continued, "Mama doesn't like me to be going into the restaurant alone, but she approves of Mr. Harwood."

The head waiter was already leading them to a table set for three in accordance with the order Manan had telephoned from her room. She had eliminated the possibility of discussion, and Harwood raged in his helplessness. There was no time for a scene even if he had thought it wise to precipitate one.

"It's only a lobster, you know," she said, with the careless ease of a young woman quite habituated to midnight suppers.

Harwood's frown of annoyance had not escaped her; but it only served to add to her complete joy in the situation. There were other people about, and music proceeded from a screen of palms at the end of the dining-room. Having had her way, Marian nibbled celery and addressed herself rather pointedly to Allen, unmindful of the lingering traces of Harwood's discomfiture. By the time the lobster was served she was on capital terms with Allen.

In his own delight in Marian, Allen failed utterly to comprehend Harwood's gloomy silence. Dan scarcely touched his plate, and he knew that Marian was covertly laughing at him.

"Do you know," said Allen, speaking directly to Dan, "we're having great arguments at Lüders's; we turn the universe over every day."

"You see, Miss Bassett," Allen explained to Marian; "I'm a fair carpenter and work almost every day at Louis Lüders's shop. I earn a dollar a day and eat dinner—dinner, mind you!—at twelve o'clock, out of a tin pail. You can see that I'm a laboring man—one of the toiling millions."

"You don't mean that seriously, Mr. Thatcher; not really!"

"Oh, why will you say that? Every one says just that! No one ever believes that I mean what I say!"

This was part of some joke, Marian surmised, though she did not quite grasp it. It was inconceivable that the son of the house of Thatcher should seriously seek a chance to do manual labor. Allen in his dinner jacket did not look like a laborer: he was far more her idea of a poet or a musician.

"I went to Lüders's house the other evening for supper," Allen was saying. "I rather put it up to him to ask me, and he has a house with a garden, and his wife was most amusing. We all talked German, including the kids,—three of them, fascinating little fellows. He's a cabinetmaker, Miss Bassett,—a producer of antiques, and a good one; and about the gentlest human being you ever saw. He talks about existing law as though it were some kind of devil,—a monster, devouring the world's poor. But he won't let his wife spank the children,—wouldn't, even when one of them kicked a hole in my hat! I supposed that of course there would be dynamite lying round in tomato cans; and when I shook the pepper box I expected an explosion; but I didn't see a gun on the place. He's beautifully good-natured, and laughed in the greatest way when I asked him how soon he thought of blowing up some of our prominent citizens. I really believe he likes me—strange but true."

"Better not get in too deep with those fellows," warned Dan. "The police watch Lüders carefully; he's considered dangerous. It's the quiet ones, who are kind to their families and raise cabbages, that are the most violent."

"Oh, Lüders says we've got to smash everything! He rather favors socialism himself, but he wants to tear down the court-houses first and begin again."

"You'd better be careful or you'll land in jail, Mr. Thatcher," remarked Marian, taking an olive.

"Oh, if anything as interesting as that should happen to me, I should certainly die of joy!"

"But your family wouldn't like it if you went to jail," persisted Marian, delighting in the confidences of a young gentleman for whom jails had no terrors.

"The thought of my family is disturbing, it's positively disturbing," Allen replied. "Lüders has given me a chance in his shop, and really expects me to work. Surprising in an anarchist; you'd rather expect him to press a stick of dynamite in your hand and tell you to go out and blow up a bank. Lüders has a sense of humor, you know: hence the antiques, made to coax money from the purses of the fat rich. There are more ways than one of being a cut-purse."

The lobster had been consumed, and they were almost alone in the restaurant. Marian, with her elbows on the table, was in no haste to leave, but Dan caught the eye of the hovering waiter and paid the check.

"You shouldn't have done that," Marian protested; "it was my party. I sign my own checks here."

But having now asserted himself, Dan rose, and in a moment he and Allen had bidden her good-night at the elevator door.

"You didn't seem crazy about your lobster, and you were hardly more than polite to our hostess. Sorry to have butted in. But why have you kept these tender recreations from me!"

"Oh, that child vexes my spirit sometimes. She's bent on making people do things they don't want to do. Of course the lobster was a mere excuse for getting acquainted with you; but you needn't be too set up about it: I think her curiosity about your family is responsible,—these fake newspaper stories about your sister—which is it, Hermione or Gwendolen—who is always about to marry a count. Countesses haven't been common in Indiana. We need a few to add tone to the local gossip."

"Oh," murmured Allen dejectedly: "I'm sorry if you didn't want me in the party. It's always the way with me. Nobody ever really loves me for myself alone. What does the adorable do besides midnight lobsters? I thought Aunt Sally said she was at Miss Waring's school."

"She is, more or less," growled Dan. "Her mother wants to put her through college, to please the wealthy great-aunt. Mrs. Owen has shown interest in another girl who is now at Wellesley; hence Marian must go to college, and the bare thought of it bores her to death. She's as little adapted to a course in college as one of those bright goddesses who used to adorn Olympus."

"She doesn't strike me as needing education; she's a finished product. I felt very young in the divine presence."

"She gives one that feeling," laughed Dan, his mood of impatience dissolving.

"Who's this rival who has made the higher education seem necessary for Morton Bassett's daughter?"

"She's an amazing girl; quite astonishing. If Mrs. Bassett were a wise woman she wouldn't enter Marian in competition. And besides, I think her fears are utterly groundless. Marian is delightful, with her waywardness and high-handedness; and Mrs. Owen likes originals, not feeble imitations. I should hate to try to deceive Mrs. Sally Owen—she's about the wisest person I ever saw."

"Oh, Sylvia! Mrs. Owen has mentioned her. The girl that knows all the stars and that sort of thing. But where's Morton Bassett in all this? He's rather more than a shadow on the screen?"

"Same old story of the absorbed American father and the mother with nerves"

Two afternoons later, as Harwood was crossing University Park on his way to his boarding-house, he stopped short and stared. A little ahead of him in the walk strolled a girl and a young man, laughing and talking with the greatest animation. There was no questioning their identity. It was five o'clock and quite dark, and the air was sharp. Harwood paused and waited for the two loiterers to cross the lighted space about the little park's central fountain. It seemed incredible that Marian and Allen should be abroad together in this dallying fashion. His anger rose against Allen, but he curbed an impulse to send him promptly about his business and take Marian back to the Whitcomb. Mr. Bassett was expected in town that evening and Dan saw his duty clearly in regard to Marian; she must be returned to school willy-nilly.

The young people were hitting it off wonderfully, and Marian's laughter rang out clearly upon the winter air. Her tall, supple figure, her head capped with a fur toque, and more than all, the indubitable evidence that such a clandestine stroll as this gave her the keenest delight, drove home to Harwood the realization that Marian was no longer a child, but a young woman, obstinately bent upon her own way. Allen was an ill-disciplined, emotional boy, whose susceptibilities in the matter of girls Dan had already noted. The combination had its dangers and his anger rose as he followed them at a safe distance. They prolonged their walk for half an hour, coming at last to the Whitcomb.

Harwood waylaid Allen in the hotel office a moment after Marian had gone to her room. The young fellow's cheeks were unwontedly bright from the cold or from the excitement of his encounter.

"Halloa! I was going to look you up and ask you to have dinner with me."

"You were looking for me in a likely place," replied Harwood coldly. "See here, Allen, I've been laboring under the delusion that you were a gentleman."

"Oh! Have we come to that?"

"You know better than to go loafing through town with a truant school-girl you hardly know. I suppose it's my fault for introducing you to her. I want you to tell me how you managed this. Did you telephone her or write a note? Sit down here now and let's have it out."

They drew away from the crowd and found seats in a quiet corner of the lobby.

Harwood, his anger unabated, repeated his question.

"Out with it; just how did you manage it?"

Allen was twisting his gloves nervously; he had not been conscious of transgressing any law, but he would not for worlds have invited Harwood's displeasure. He was near to tears; but he remained stubbornly silent until Harwood again demanded to know how he contrived the meeting with Marian.

"I'm sorry, old man," Allen answered, "but I can't tell you anything about it. I don't see that my crime is so heinous. She has been cooped up in the hotel all day with her sick mother, and a short walk—it was only a few blocks—couldn't have done her any harm. I think you're making too much of it."

"You were dallying there in the park, in a way to attract attention, with a headstrong, silly girl that you ought to have protected from that sort of thing. You know better than that."

Allen, enfolded in his long ulster, shuffled his feet on the tiling like a school-boy in disgrace. Deep down in his heart, Harwood did not believe that Allen had proposed the walk to Marian; it was far likelier that Marian had sought the meeting by note or telephone. He turned upon Allen with a slight relaxation of his sternness.

"You didn't write her a note or telephone her,—you didn't do either, did you?"

Allen, silent and dejected, dropped his gloves and picked them up, the color deepening in his cheeks.

"I just happened to meet her; that's all," he said, avoiding Dan's eyes.

"She wrote you a note or telephoned you?"

Silence.

"Humph," grunted Harwood.

"She's wonderfully beautiful and strong and so tremendously vivid! I think those nice girls you read of in the Greek mythology must have been like that," murmured Allen, sighing heavily.

"I dare say they were!" snapped Harwood, searching the youngster's thin, sensitive face, and meeting for an instant his dreamy eyes. He was touched anew by the pathos in the boy, whose nature was a light web of finespun golden cords thrilling to any breath of fancy. The superb health, the dash and daring of a school-girl that he had seen but once or twice, had sent him climbing upon a frail ladder of romantic dreams.

Harwood struck his hands together sharply. If he owed a duty to Marian and her family, not less he was bound to turn Allen's thoughts into safe channels.

"Of course it wouldn't do—that sort of thing, you know, Allen. I didn't mean to beat you into the dust. Let's go over to Pop June's and get some oysters. I don't feel up to our usual boarding-house discussion of Christian Science to-night."

At the first opportunity Dan suggested to Bassett, without mentioning Marian's adventure with Allen, that the Whitcomb was no place for her, and that her pursuit of knowledge under his own tutorship was the merest farce; whereupon Bassett sent her back immediately to Miss Waring's.

CHAPTER XIV
THE PASSING OF ANDREW KELTON

Andrew Kelton died suddenly, near the end of May, in Sylvia's senior year at college. The end came unexpectedly, of heart trouble. Harwood read of it in the morning newspaper, and soon after he reached his office Mrs. Owen called him on the telephone to say that she was going to Montgomery at once, and asking him to meet Sylvia as she passed through Indianapolis on her way home. Both of the morning papers printed laudatory articles on Kelton; he had been held in high esteem by all the friends of Madison College, and his name was known to educators throughout the country.

On the same afternoon Bassett appeared in town on the heels of a letter saying that Dan need not expect him until the following week.

"Thought I'd better see Fitch about some receiver business, so I came down a little ahead of time. What's new?"

"Nothing very exciting. There's a good deal of political buzz, but I don't believe anything has happened that you don't know. From the way candidates are turning up for state office our fellows must think they have a chance of winning."

Bassett was unfailingly punctilious in forecasting his appearances in town, and his explanation that legal matters had brought him down was not wholly illuminative. Dan knew that the paper-mill receivership was following its prescribed course, and he was himself, through an arrangement made by Bassett, in touch with Fitch and understood the legal status of the case perfectly. As Bassett passed through the library to his own room he paused to indulge in a moment's banter with Miss Farrell. It was not until he had opened his desk that he replied to Harwood's remark.

"A few good men on our ticket might pull through next time, but it will take us a little longer to get the party whipped into shape again and strong enough to pull a ticket through. But hope springs eternal. You have noticed that I don't talk on national affairs when the reporters come to me. In the state committee I tell them to put all the snap they can into the county organizations, and try to get good men on local tickets. When the boys out

West get tired of being licked we will start in again and do business at the old stand. I've always taken care that they shouldn't have a chance to attack my regularity."

"I've just been reading a book of Cleveland's speeches," remarked Dan.

"Solemn, but sound. He will undoubtedly go down as one of the great Presidents. I think Republicans and men of all sorts of political ideas will come to that."

"But I don't feel that all this radicalism is a passing phase. It's eating deeply into the Republicans too. We're on the eve of a revival of patriotism, and party names don't mean what they did. But I believe the Democratic Party is still the best hope of the people, even when the people go clean off their heads."

"You believe in Democracy, but you doubt sometimes whether the Democratic Party is really the custodian of the true faith of Democracy—is that it?"

"That's exactly it. And my young Republican friends feel the same way about their party."

"Well, I guess I stand about where you do. I believe in parties. I don't think there's much gained by jumping around from one party to another; and independent movements are as likely to do harm as good. I don't mind confessing to you that I had a good notion to join the Democratic schism in '96, and support Palmer and Buckner. But I didn't, and I'm not sorry I kept regular and held on. I believed the silver business would pass over; and it's out of sight. They charged me with voting the Republican ticket in '96; but that's a lie. I've never scratched a ticket since I first voted, and"—Bassett smiled his grim smile—"I've naturally voted for a good many rascals. By the way, how much are you seeing of Atwill?"

"I make a point of seeing him once a week or oftener. When I'm downtown at night I usually catch him for a late supper."

"The 'Courier' is regular, all right enough. It's a good property, and when our party gets through chasing meadow-larks and gets down to business again it will be more valuable. Was that your editorial yesterday on municipal government? Good. I'm for trying some of these new ideas. I've been reading a lot of stuff on municipal government abroad, and some of those foreign ideas we ought to try here. I want the 'Courier' to take the lead in those things; it may help"—and Bassett smiled— "it may help to make the high brows see that ours has really been the party of progress through these years when it's marched backward."

Bassett swung round slowly until his gaze fell upon the map, reminding the young man of Thatcher's interest in that varicolored oblong of paper. Dan had never mentioned Thatcher's visit to the office, feeling that if the capitalist were really the bold man he appeared to be, he would show his hand to Bassett soon enough. Moreover, Harwood's confidence in Bassett's powers had never wavered; in the management of the paper-mill receivership the senator from Fraser had demonstrated a sagacity and resourcefulness that had impressed Dan anew. Bassett possessed, in unusual degree, the astuteness and executive force of the successful American business man, and his nice feeling for the things that interest cultivated people lifted him far above the common type of political boss. Dan had yet to see a demonstration of Bassett's political venality; the bank and his other interests at Fraserville were profitable. It must be a craving for power, not money, Dan reasoned, that led Bassett into politics. Bassett turned to his desk with some letters he had taken from his pocket. It occurred to Dan that as Mrs. Owen had suggested that he accompany Sylvia to Montgomery, it would be well to mention the possibility of his leaving town for a day.

"Mrs. Owen telephoned me this morning of Professor Kelton's death. You probably read of it in to-day's papers. Mrs. Owen is an old friend of his, and went to Montgomery on the noon train. She asked me to meet the Professor's granddaughter, Miss Garrison, when she comes through here in the morning on her way home. I know her slightly, and I think I'd better go over to Montgomery with her, if you don't mind."

"Yes, certainly; I was sorry to read of Kelton's death. Mrs. Owen will feel it deeply. It's a blow to these old people when one of them drops out of the ranks. I'm glad the 'Courier' printed that capital sketch of him; much better than the 'Advertiser's.' While I think of it, I wish you would tell Atwill that I like the idea of saying a word editorially for these old citizens as they leave us. It gives the paper tone, and I like to show appreciation of fine characters like Kelton."

Bassett had turned round with a letter in his hand. He unfolded it slowly and went on, scanning it as he talked.

"I'm sorry I never knew Kelton. They say he was a very able mathematician and astronomer. It's rather remarkable that we should have kept him in Indiana. I suppose you may have seen him at Mrs. Owen's; they had a common tie in their Kentucky connections. I guess there's no tie quite like the Kentucky tie, unless it's the Virginian."

He seemed absorbed in the letter—one of a number he had taken from his bag; then he glanced up as though waiting for Dan's reply.

"No, I never saw him at Mrs. Owen's; but I did meet him once, in Montgomery. He was a fine old gentleman. You would hardly imagine him ever to have been a naval officer; he was quite the elderly, spectacled professor in his bearing and manner."

"I suppose even a man bred to the sea loses the look of a sailor if he lives inland long enough," Bassett observed.

"I think my brief interview with him rather indicated that he had been a man of action—the old discipline of the ship may have been in that," remarked Harwood. Then, fearing that he might be laying himself open to questions that he should have to avoid answering, he said: "Kelton wrote a good deal on astronomical subjects, and his textbooks have been popular. Sylvia Garrison, the granddaughter, is something of a wonder herself."

"Bright girl, is she?"

"Quite so; and very nice to look at. I met her on the train when I went to Boston with those bonds in January. She was going back to college after the holidays. She's very interesting—quite different."

"Different?" repeated Bassett vaguely, dropping back in his chair, but again referring absently to the letter.

"Yes," Dan smiled. "She has a lot of individuality. She's a serious young person; very practical-minded, I should say. They tell me she walks through mathematics like a young duchess through the minuet. Some other Wellesley girls were on the train and they did not scruple to attribute miraculous powers to her; a good sign, other girls liking her so much. They were very frank in their admiration."

"Mrs. Owen had her at Waupegan several years ago, and my wife and Marian met her there. Mrs. Bassett was greatly impressed by her fine mind. It seems to me I saw her, too, that summer; but of course she's grown up since then."

He glanced at Harwood as though for confirmation of these details, but Dan's thoughts were elsewhere. He was thinking of Sylvia speeding homeward, and of the little cottage beside the campus. His subsequent meetings with Sylvia had caused a requickening of all the impressions of his visit to Professor Kelton, and he had been recalling that errand again to-day. The old gentleman had given his answer with decision; Harwood recalled the crisp biting-off of the negative, and the Professor had lifted his head slightly as he spoke the word. Dan remembered the peace of the cottage, the sweet scents of June blowing through the open windows; and he remembered Sylvia as she had opened the door, and their colloquy later, on the campus.

"You'd better go to Montgomery with Miss Garrison and report to Mrs. Owen for any service you may render her. Does the old gentleman's death leave the girl alone?"

"Quite so, I think. She had lived with him nearly all her life. The papers mentioned no other near relatives."

"I'll be in town a day or two. You do what you can over there for Mrs. Owen."

That evening, returning to the office to clear off his desk in preparation for his absence the next day, Dan found Bassett there. This was unusual; Bassett rarely visited the office at night. He had evidently been deeply occupied with his thoughts, for when Dan entered he was sitting before his closed desk with his hat on. He nodded, and a few moments later passed through the library on his way out.

"Suppose I won't see you to-morrow. Well, I'm going to be in town a few days. Take your time."

Dan Harwood never doubted that he loved Sally Owen after that dark day of Sylvia's home-coming. From the time Sylvia stepped from the train till the moment when, late that same afternoon, just as the shadows were gathering, Andrew Kelton was buried with academic and military honors befitting his two-fold achievements, Mrs. Owen had shown the tenderness of the gentlest of mothers to the forlorn girl. The scene at the grave sank deep into Dan's memory—the patriarchal figure of Dr. Wandless, with the faculty and undergraduates ranged behind him; the old minister's voice lifted in a benediction that thrilled with a note of triumphant faith; and the hymn sung by the students at the end, boys' voices, sweet and clear, floating off into the sunset. And nothing in Dan's life had ever moved him so much as when Mrs. Owen, standing beside Sylvia and representing in her gaunt figure the whole world of love and kindness, bent down at the very end and kissed the sobbing girl and led her away.

Harwood called on Mrs. Owen at the cottage in Buckeye Lane that evening. She came down from Sylvia's room and met him in the little library, which he found unchanged from the day of his visit five years before.

"That little girl is a hero," she began. "I guess she's about the lonesomest girl in the world to-night. Andrew Kelton was a man and a good one. He hadn't been well for years, the doctor tells me; trouble with his heart, but he kept it to himself; didn't want to worry the girl. I tell you everything helps at a time like this. Admiral Martin came over to represent the Navy, and you saw the G.A.R. there; it caught me in the throat when the bugle blew good-night for Andrew. Sylvia will rally and go on and do some big thing. It's in her. I reckon she'll have to go back to college, this being her last year. Too bad the commencement's all spoiled for her."

"Yes; she won't have much heart for it; but she must get her degree."

"She'll need a rest after this. I'll go back with her, and then I'm going to take her up to Waupegan with me for the summer. There are some things to settle about her, and I'm glad you stayed. Andrew owned this house, but I shouldn't think Sylvia would want to keep it: houses in a town like this are a nuisance if you don't live where you can watch the tenants," she went on, her practical mind asserting itself.

"I suppose—" Dan began and then hesitated. It gave him a curious feeling to be talking of Sylvia's affairs in this way.

"Go on, Daniel,"—this marked a departure; she had never called him by his first name before. "I'm closer to that girl than anybody, and I'm glad to talk to you about her affairs."

"I suppose there will be something for her; she's not thrown on her own resources?"

"I guess he didn't make any will, but what he left is Sylvia's. He had a brother in Los Angeles, who died ten years ago. He was a rich man, and left a big fortune to his children. If there's no will there'll have to be an administrator. Sylvia's of age and she won't need a guardian."

Dan nodded. He knew Mrs. Owen well enough by this time to understand that she usually perfected her plans before speaking, and that she doubtless had decided exactly how Andrew Kelton's estate should be administered.

"I'm going to ask the court to appoint you administrator, Daniel. You ever acted? Well, you might as well have the experience. I might take it myself, but I'm pretty busy and there'll be some running back and forth to do. You come back in a day or two and we'll see how things stand by that time. As soon as Sylvia gets rested she'll go back to college to finish up, and then come to me for the summer."

"She might not like my having anything to do with her affairs," Dan suggested. "I shouldn't want to seem to be intruding."

"Oh, Sylvia likes you well enough. The main thing is getting somebody that you've got confidence in. I know some people here, and I guess the court will do about what we want."

"I should have to come over here frequently until everything was settled," Dan added, thinking of his duties in the city. "I suppose if you find it possible for me to serve that I shall have to get Mr. Bassett's consent; he pays for my time, you know."

"That's right, you ask him; but be sure to tell him that I want it to be that way. Morton won't make any fuss about it. I guess you do enough work for him. What's he paying you, Daniel?"

"Eighteen hundred since he got the paper-mill receivership."

She made no comment, but received the intelligence in silence. He knew from the characteristic quick movement of her eyelids that she was pondering the equity of this carefully; and his loyalty to Bassett asserting itself, he added, defensively:—

"It's more than I could begin to make any other way; and he's really generous about my time—he's made it plain that he wants me to keep up my reading."

"They don't read much after they're admitted, do they? I thought when you got admitted you knew it all."

"Not if you mean to be a real lawyer," said Dan, smiling.

"Well, I guess you had better go now. I don't want to leave Sylvia alone up there, poor little girl. I'll let you know when to come back."

CHAPTER XV
A SURPRISE AT THE COUNTRY CLUB

"That's all right. I shall be glad to have you serve Mrs. Owen in any way. It's a good deal of a compliment that she thought of you in that connection. Go ahead, and call on me if I can help you. You'll have to furnish local bondsmen. See what's required and let me know."

Such was Bassett's reply when Harwood asked his permission to serve as administrator of Andrew Kelton's estate. Bassett was a busy man, and his domestic affairs often gave him concern. He had talked to Harwood a good deal about Marian, several times in fits of anger at her extravagance. His wife retired fitfully to sanatoriums, and he had been obliged to undertake the supervision of his children's schooling. Blackford was safe for the time in a military school, and Marian had been tutored for a year at home. The idea of a college course for Marian had been, since Sylvia appeared, a mania with Mrs. Bassett. Marian had not the slightest interest in the matter, and Bassett was weary of the struggle, and sick of the idea, that only by a college career for her could Mrs. Owen's money be assured to his children. Mrs. Bassett being now at a rest cure in Connecticut, and Bassett, much away from home, and seeing nothing to be gained by keeping his daughter at Fraserville, had persuaded Miss Waring to take her as a special student, subject to the discipline of the school, but permitted to elect her own studies. It was only because Bassett was a man she liked to please that the principal accepted Marian, now eighteen years old, on this anomalous basis. Marian was relieved to find herself freed of the horror of college, but she wished to be launched at once upon a social career; and the capital and not Fraserville must be the scene of her introduction. Bassett was merely tiding over the difficult situation until his wife should be able to deal with it. Marian undoubtedly wheedled her father a good deal in the manner of handsome and willful daughters. She had rarely experienced his anger; but the remembrance of these occasions rose before her as the shadowy background of any filial awe she may be said to have had.

Bassett asked Dan to accompany him and Marian to the Country Club for dinner one evening while Harwood still waited for Mrs. Owen's summons to Montgomery. Picking up Marian at Miss Waring's, they drove out early and indulged in a loitering walk along the towpath of the old canal, not returning to the clubhouse until after seven. When they had found a table on the veranda, Dan turned his head slightly and saw Thatcher, Allen, and Pettit, the Fraserville editor, lounging in after-dinner ease at a table in a dim corner.

"Why, there's Mr. Thatcher," exclaimed Marian.

"And if that isn't Mr. Pettit! I didn't know he ever broke into a place like this."

They all bowed to the trio. Thatcher waved his hand.

"Mr. Pettit," observed Bassett dryly, "is a man of the world and likely to break in anywhere."

His manner betrayed no surprise; he asked Marian to order dinner, and bowed to a tableful of golfers, where an acquaintance was whispering his name to some guests from out of town.

It was the least bit surprising that the Honorable Isaac Pettit should be dining at the Country Club with Mr. Edward Thatcher, and yet it was possible to read too much seriousness into the situation. Harwood was immensely interested, but he knew it was Bassett's way to betray no trepidation at even such a curious conjunction of planets as this. Dan was in fact relieved that Bassett had found the men together: Bassett had seen with his own eyes and might make what he pleased of this sudden intimacy.

Marian had scorned the table d'hôte dinner, and was choosing, from the "special" offerings, green turtle soup and guinea fowl, as affording a pleasant relief from the austere regimen of Miss Waring's table. The roasting of the guinea hen would require thirty minutes the waiter warned them, but Bassett made no objection. Marian thereupon interjected a postscript of frogs' legs between soup and roast, and Bassett cheerfully acquiesced.

"You seem to be picking the most musical birds offered," he remarked amiably. "I don't believe I'd eat the rest of the olives if I were you."

"Why doesn't Allen Thatcher come over here and speak to us, I'd like to know," asked Marian. "You wouldn't think he'd ever seen us before."

The three men having dined had, from appearances, been idling at the table for some time. Pettit was doing most of the talking, regaling his two auditors with tales from his abundant store of anecdotes. At the end of a story at which Thatcher had guffawed loudly, they rose and crossed the veranda. Hearing them approaching, Bassett rose promptly, and they shook hands all round.

If there were any embarrassments in the meeting for the older men, it was concealed under the cordiality of their greetings. Pettit took charge of the situation.

"Well, sir," he boomed, "I might've known that if I came to town and broke into sassiety I'd get caught at it; you can't get away from home folks! Thatcher has filled me amply with expensive urban food in this sylvan retreat—nectar and ambrosia. I'm even as one who drinks deep of the waters of life and throws the dipper in the well. Just come to town and wander from the straight and narrow path and your next-door neighbor will catch you every time. Fact is I lectured on 'American Humor' in Churubusco last night and am lifting the spirits of Brazil to-morrow. This will be all from Ike Pettit, the Fraserville funny man, until the wheat's safe and our Chautauquas pitch their tents in green fields far away. Reminds me of what Dan Voorhees said once,—dear old Dan Voorhees,—I almost cry when I think o' Dan: well, as I was saying—"

"Didn't know you were in town, Mort," Thatcher interrupted. "I've been in Chicago a week and only got back this evening. I found your esteemed fellow townsman about to hit a one-arm lunch downtown and thought it best to draw him away from the lights of the great city."

This was apology or explanation, as one chose to take it. Bassett was apparently unmoved by it.

"I've been in town a day or two. I don't live in sleeping-cars the way you do, Ed. I keep to the main traveled road—the straight and narrow path, as our brother calls it," said Bassett.

"Well, I'm going to quit working myself to death. It's getting too hot for poker, and I'm almost driven to lead a wholesome life. The thought pains me, Mort."

Marian had opened briskly upon Allen. She wanted to know whether he had passed the school the night before with a girl in a blue hat; she had been sure it was he, and his denial only intensified her belief that she had seen him. She had wagered a box of caramels with her roommate that it was Allen; how dare he deny it and cause her to lose a dollar of her allowance? Allen said the least he could do would be to send the candy himself; a proposition which she declared, in a horrified whisper, he must put from his thoughts forever. Candy, it appeared, was contraband at Miss Waring's! Bassett, ignoring the vivacious colloquy between his daughter and Allen, continued to exchange commonplaces with Thatcher and Pettit. Marian's ease of manner amused Harwood; Allen was bending over her in his eager way; there was no question but that he admired her tremendously. The situation was greatly to her liking, and she was making the most of it. It was in her eye that she knew how to manage men. Seeing that Mr. Thatcher was edging away, she played upon him to delay his escape.

"I wish you would come up to Waupegan this summer, Mr. Thatcher. You and father are such friends, and we should all be so glad to have you for a neighbor. There are always houses to be rented, you know."

"Stranger things have happened than that, Miss Marian," replied Thatcher, eying her boldly and quite satisfied with her appearance. "My women folks want Allen and me to come across for the summer; but we like this side of the big water. Little Old United States—nothing touches it! Allen and I may take a run up into Canada sometime when it gets red hot."

"Reminds me—speaking of the heat—back in the Hancock campaign—" Pettit was beginning, but Thatcher was leaving and the editor and Allen followed perforce. In a moment they heard Thatcher's voice peremptorily demanding his motor from the steps of the entrance.

"Pettit's lecture dates must be multiplying," observed Dan carelessly.

"They seem to be," Bassett replied, indifferently.

"I can find out easily enough whether he lectured at Churubusco last night or not, or is going to invade Brazil to-morrow," Dan suggested.

"Easy, but unnecessary. I think I know what's in your mind," Bassett answered, as Marian, interested in the passing show, turned away, "but it isn't of the slightest importance one way or another."

"That was Miss Bosworth," announced Marian—"the one in the white flannel coat; she's certainly grand to look at."

"Please keep your eyes to the front," Bassett admonished; "you mustn't stare at people, Marian." And then, having dismissed Pettit, and feeling called upon to bring his daughter into the conversation, he said: "Marian, you remember the Miss Garrison your aunt is so fond of? Her grandfather died the other day and Miss Garrison had to come home. Your Aunt Sally is in Montgomery with her now. Mr. Harwood went to the funeral."

"That's too bad," said Marian, at once interested. "Sylvia's a mighty nice girl, and I guess her grandfather had just about raised her, from what she told me. I wonder what she's going to do?" she asked, turning to Harwood.

"She's going back to college to take her degree, and then Mrs. Owen is going to have her at Waupegan this summer."

"Oh! I didn't know Aunt Sally was going to open her house this summer!" said Marian, clearly surprised. "It must be just that she wants to have Sylvia with her. They're the best kind of pals, and of course Aunt Sally and the old professor were friends all their lives. I'm glad Sylvia's going to be at the lake; she will help some," she concluded.

"You don't mean that you're tired of the lake?" asked Harwood, noting the half-sigh with which she had concluded. "I thought all Waupegan people preferred it to the Maine coast or Europe."

"Oh, I suppose they do," said Marian. "But I think I could live through a season somewhere else. It will be good fun to have Aunt Sally's house open again. She must be making money out of that farm now. I suppose Sylvia's grandfather didn't have much money. Still Sylvia's the kind of girl that wouldn't much mind not having money. She isn't much for style, but she does know an awful lot."

"Don't you think a girl may be stylish and know a lot, too?" asked her father.

"I suppose it *is* possible," the girl assented, with a reluctance that caused both men to laugh.

"Let me see: Papa, you didn't see Sylvia that summer she was at the lake. That was the summer you played a trick on us and only spent a day at Waupegan. Yes; I remember now; you came home from Colorado and said hello and skipped the next morning. Of course you didn't see Sylvia."

"Oh, yes, I did," replied Bassett. "I remember her very well, indeed. I quite agree with your mother and Aunt Sally that she is an exceedingly fine girl."

"She certainly discouraged me a good deal about college. Four years of school after you're seventeen or eighteen! Not for Marian!" and she shook her head drolly.

Bassett was either absorbed in thought or he chose to ignore Marian's remark. He was silent for some time, and the girl went on banteringly with Harwood. She availed herself of all those immunities and privileges which the gods confer upon young women whom they endow with good looks. In the half-freedom of the past year she had bought her own clothes, with only the nominal supervision of Miss Waring's assistant; and in her new spring raiment she was very much the young lady, and decidedly a modish one. Dan glanced from her to the young people at a neighboring table. Among the girls in the party none was prettier or more charmingly gowned than Marian. In the light of this proximity he watched her with a new attention, and he saw that her father, too, studied her covertly, as though realizing that he had a grown daughter on his hands. Her way with Harwood was not without coquetry; she tapped his arm with her fan lightly when he refused to enter into a discussion of his attentions, of which she protested she knew much, to Miss Bosworth. He admitted having called on Miss Bosworth once; her brother was a Yale man, and had asked him to the house on the score of that tie; but Marian knew much better. She was sure that he was devoting himself to Miss Bosworth; every one said that he was becoming a great society man.

She had wearied of his big-brother attitude toward her. Except the callow youth of Fraserville and the boys she had known all the summers of her life at Waupegan, Harwood and Allen Thatcher were the only young men she knew. In her later freedom at school she had made the office telephone a nuisance to him, but he sympathized with her discreetly in her perplexities. Several times she had appealed to him to help her out of financial difficulties, confiding to him tragically that if certain bills reached Fraserville she would be ruined forever.

Marian found the Country Club highly diverting; it gave her visions of the social life of the capital of which she had only vaguely dreamed. She knew many people by sight who were socially prominent, and she longed to be of their number. It pleased her to find that her father, who was a non-resident member and a rare visitor at the club, attracted a good deal of attention; she liked to think him a celebrity. The Speaker of the House in the last session of the general assembly came out and asked Bassett to meet some men with whom he had been dining in the rathskeller; while her father was away, Marian, with elbows resting on the table, her firm, round chin touching her lightly interlaced fingers, gave a capital imitation of a girl making herself agreeable to a young man. Dan was well hardened to her cajoleries by this time; he was confident that she would have made "sweet eyes at Caliban." Harwood, smoking the cigar Bassett had ordered for him, compared favorably with other young men who had dawned upon Marian's horizon. Like most Western boys who go East to college, he had acquired the habit of careful pressing and brushing and combing; his lean face had a certain distinction, and he was unfailingly courteous and well-mannered.

"This will be tough on mama," she observed casually.

"Pray, be more explicit!"

"Oh, Aunt Sally having Sylvia up there at the lake again."

"Why shouldn't she have her there if she wants her? I thought your mother admired Sylvia. I gathered that ray of light somewhere, from you or Mrs. Owen."

"Oh, mama was beautiful to her; but I shall always think, just between you and me and that spoon, that it was Aunt Sally asking Sylvia to the lake that time that gave mama nervous prostration."

"Nonsense! I advise you, as an old friend, not to say such things: you'd better not even think them."

"Well, it was after that, when she saw that Aunt Sally had taken up Sylvia, that mama got that bug about having me go to college. She got the notion that it was Sylvia's intellectual gifts that interested Aunt Sally; and mama thought I'd better improve my mind and get into the competition."

"You thought your mother was jealous? I call that very unkind; it's not the way to speak of your mother."

"Well, if you want to be nasty and lecture me, go ahead, Mr. Harwood. You must like Sylvia pretty well yourself; you took her back to college once and had no end of a lark,—I got that from Aunt Sally, so you needn't deny it."

"Humph! Of course I like Sylvia; any one's bound to."

"But if Aunt Sally leaves her all her money, just because she's so bright, and educated, and cuts me off, then what would be the answer?"

"I shouldn't have anything to say about it; it would be Mrs. Owen that did the saying," laughed Dan. "Why didn't you meet the competition and go to college? You have brains, but you don't seem interested in anything but keeping amused."

"I suppose," she answered petulantly, "it would please you to see me go to teaching a kindergarten or something like that. Not for Marian! I'm going to see life—" and she added ruefully—"if I get the chance! Why doesn't papa leave Fraserville and come to the city? They say he can have any political office he wants, and he ought to run for governor or something like that, just on my account."

"I dare say he's just waiting for you to suggest it. Why not the presidency? You could get a lot of fun out of the White House, ordering the army around, and using the battleships to play with. The governorship and trifles like that would only bore you."

"Don't be silly. The newspapers print most horrible things about papa—"

"Which aren't true."

"Of course they're newspaper lies; but if he lets them say all those things he ought to get something to pay for it. He's only a state senator from the jayest county in Indiana. It makes me tired."

The girl's keen penetration had often surprised and it had sometimes appalled Harwood in the curious intimacy that had grown up between them. Her intuitions were active and she had a daring imagination. He wondered whether Bassett was fully aware of the problem Marian presented. Dan had never ventured to suggest a sharper discipline for the girl, except on the occasion when he had caught her walking with Allen in the park. He had regretted his interference afterward; for Bassett's anger had seemed to him out of all proportion to the offense. Like most indifferent or indulgent parents, Bassett was prone to excesses in his fitful experiments in discipline. Dan had resolved not to meddle again; but Marian was undeniably a provoking young person. It had been suggested to him of late by one or two of his intimates that in due course of events he would of course marry his employer's daughter. As she faced him across the table, the pink light of the candle-shade adding to the glow of health in her pretty cheeks, she caused him to start by the abruptness with which she said: —

"I don't see much ahead of me but to get married; do you?"

"If you put it up to me, I don't see anything ahead of you, unless you take a different view of life; you never seem to have a serious thought."

"Mr. Harwood, you can be immensely unpleasant when you choose to be. You talk to me as though I were only nine years old. You ought to see that I'm very unhappy. I'm the oldest girl at Miss Waring's—locked up there with a lot of little pigeons that coo every time you look at them. They treat me as though I were their grandmother."

"Why don't you say all these things to your father?" asked Harwood, trying to laugh. "I dare say he'll do anything you like. But please cheer up; those people over there will think we're having a terrible quarrel."

The fact that they were drawing the glances of Miss Bosworth's party pleased her; she had been perfectly conscious of it all the time.

"Well, they won't think you're making *love* to me, Mr. Harwood; there's that to console you." And she added icily, settling back in her chair as her father approached, "I hope you understand that I'm not even leading you on!"

CHAPTER XVI
"STOP, LOOK, LISTEN"

Bassett and Atwill held a conference the next day and the interview was one of length. The manager of the "Courier" came to the office in the Boordman Building at eleven o'clock, and when Harwood went to luncheon at one the door had not been opened. Miss Farrell, returning from her midday repast, pointed to the closed door, lifted her brows, and held up her forefinger to express surprise and caution. Miss Farrell's prescience was astonishing; of women she held the lightest opinion, Dan had learned; her concern was with the affairs of men. Harwood, intent upon the compilation of a report of the paper-mill receivership, was nevertheless mindful of the unwonted length of the conference. When he returned from luncheon, Bassett had gone, but he reappeared at three o'clock, and a little later Atwill came back and the door closed again. This second interview was short, but it seemed to leave Bassett in a meditative frame of mind. Wishing to discuss some points in the trial balance of the receiver's accountant, Harwood entered and found Bassett with his hat on, slowly pacing the floor.

"Yes; all right; come in," he said, as Harwood hesitated. He at once addressed himself to the reports with his accustomed care. Bassett carried an immense amount of data in his head. He understood bookkeeping and was essentially thorough. Dan constantly found penciled calculations on the margins of the daily reports from the paper-mill, indicating that Bassett scrutinized the figures carefully, and he promptly questioned any deviation from the established average of loss and gain. Bassett threw down his pencil at the end of half an hour and told Dan to proceed with the writing of the report.

"I'd like to file it personally so I can talk over the prospect of getting an order of sale before the judge goes on his vacation. We've paid the debts and stopped the flow of red ink, so we're about ready to let go."

While they were talking Miss Farrell brought in a telegram for Harwood; it was the summons from Mrs. Owen that he had been waiting for; she bade him come to Montgomery the next day. He handed the message to Bassett.

"Go ahead. I'll go over there if you like and find you the necessary bondsmen. I know the judge of the circuit court at Montgomery very well. You go in the morning? Very well; I'll stay here till you get back. Mrs. Bassett will be well enough to leave the sanatorium in a few days, and I'm going up to Waupegan to get the house ready."

"It will be pleasant for Mrs. Bassett to have Mrs. Owen there this summer. Anybody is lucky to have a woman of her qualities for a neighbor."

"She's a noblewoman," said Bassett impressively, "and a good friend to all of us."

On the train the next morning Harwood unfolded the day's "Courier" in the languidly critical frame of mind that former employees of newspapers bring to the reading of the journals they have served. He scanned the news columns and opened to the editorial page. The leader at once caught his eye. It was double-leaded,—an emphasis rarely employed at the "Courier" office, and was condensed in a single brief paragraph that stared oddly at the reader under the caption "STOP, LOOK, LISTEN." It held Harwood's attention through a dozen amazed and mystified readings. It ran thus:—

> It has long been Indiana's proud boast that money unsupported by honest merit has never intruded in her politics. A malign force threatens to mar this record. It is incumbent upon honest men of all parties who have the best interests of our state at heart to stop, look, listen. The COURIER gives notice that it is fully advised of the intentions, and perfectly aware of the methods, by which the fair name of the Hoosier State is menaced. The COURIER, being thoroughly informed of the beginnings of this movement, whose purpose is the seizure of the Democratic Party, and the manipulation of its power for private ends, will antagonize to the utmost the element that has initiated it. Honorable defeats the party in Indiana has known, and it will hardly at this late day surrender tamely to the buccaneers and adventurers that seek to capture its battleflag. This warning will not be repeated. Stop! Look! Listen!

From internal evidence Harwood placed the authorship readily enough: the paragraph had been written by the chief editorial writer, an old hand at the game, who indulged frequently in such terms as "adventurer" and "buccaneer." It was he who wrote sagely of foreign affairs, and once caused riotous delight in the reporters' room by an editorial on Turkish politics, containing the phrase, "We hope the Sultan—" But not without special authority would such an article have been planted at the top of the editorial page, and beyond doubt these lines were the residuum of Bassett's long interview with Atwill. And its aim was unmistakable: Mr. Bassett was thus paying his compliments to Mr. Thatcher. The encounter at the Country Club might have precipitated the crisis, but, knowing Bassett, Dan did not believe that the "Courier's" batteries would have been fired on so little provocation. Bassett was not a man to shoot wildly in the dark, nor was he likely to fire at all without being sure of the state of his ammunition chests. So, at least, Harwood reasoned to himself. Several of his fellow passengers in the smoking-car were passing the "Courier" about and pointing to the editorial. All over Indiana it would be the subject of discussion for a long time to come; and Dan's journalistic sense told him that in the surrounding capitals it would not be ignored.

"If Thatcher and Bassett get to fighting, the people may find a chance to sneak in and get something," a man behind Dan was saying.

"Nope," said another voice; "there won't be 'no core' when those fellows get through with the apple."

"I can hear the cheering in the Republican camp this morning," remarked another voice gleefully.

"Oh, pshaw!" said still another speaker; "Bassett will simply grind Thatcher to powder. Thatcher hasn't any business in politics anyhow and doesn't know the game. By George, Bassett does! And this is the first time he's struck a full blow since he got behind the 'Courier.' Something must have made him pretty hot, though, to have let off a scream like that."

Harwood was interested in these remarks because they indicated a prevalent impression that Bassett dominated the "Courier," in spite of the mystery with which the ownership of the paper was enveloped. The only doubt in Harwood's own mind had been left there by Bassett himself. He recalled now Bassett's remark on the day he had taken him into his confidence in the Ranger County affair. "I might have some trouble in proving it myself," Bassett had said. Harwood thought it strange that after that first deliberate confidence and his introduction to Atwill, Bassett had, in this important move, ignored him. It was possible that his relations with Allen Thatcher, which Bassett knew to be intimate, accounted for the change; or it might be due to a lessening warmth in Bassett's feeling toward him. He recalled now that Bassett had lately seemed moody,—a new development in the man from Fraser,—and that he had several times been abrupt and unreasonable about small matters in the office. Certain incidents that had appeared trivial at the time of their occurrence stood forth disquietingly now. If Bassett had ceased to trust him, there must be a cause for the change; slight manifestations of impatience in a man so habitually calm and rational might be overlooked, but Dan had not been prepared for this abrupt cessation of confidential relations. He was a bit piqued, the more so that this astounding editorial indicated a range and depth of purpose in Bassett's plans that Dan's imagination had not fathomed. He tore out the editorial and put it away carefully in his pocketbook as Montgomery was called.

A messenger was at the station to guide him to the court-house, where he found Mrs. Owen and Sylvia waiting for him in the private room of the judge of the circuit court. Mrs. Owen had, in her thorough fashion, arranged all the preliminaries. She had found in Akins, the president of the Montgomery National Bank, an old friend, and it was her way to use her friends when she needed them. At her instance, Akins and another resident freeholder had already signed the bond when Dan arrived. Dan was amused by the direct manner in which Mrs. Owen addressed the court; the terminology pertaining to the administration of estates was at her fingers' ends, and there was no doubt that the judge was impressed by her.

"We won't need any lawyer over here, Daniel; you can save the estate lawyer's fees by acting yourself. I guess that will be all right, Judge?"

His Honor said it would be; people usually yielded readily to Mrs. Owen's suggestions.

"You can go up to the house now, Sylvia, and I'll be along pretty soon. I want to make a memorandum for an inventory with Daniel."

At the bank Akins gave them the directors' room, and Andrew Kelton's papers were produced from his box in the safety vault. Akins explained that Kelton had been obliged to drop life insurance policies for a considerable amount; only one policy for two thousand dollars had been carried through. There were a number of contracts with publishers covering the copyrights in Kelton's mathematical and astronomical textbooks. The royalties on these had been diminishing steadily, the banker said, and they could hardly be regarded as an asset.

"Life insurance two thousand, contracts nothing, and the house is worth two with good luck. Take it all in—and I reckon this *is* all—we'll be in luck to pinch a little pin-money out of the estate for Sylvia. It's more than I expected. You think there ain't anything else, Mr. Akins?"

"The Professor talked to me about his affairs frequently, and I have no reason to think there's anything more. He had five thousand dollars in government bonds, but he sold them and bought shares in that White River Canneries combination. A lot of our Montgomery people lost money in that scheme. It promised fifteen per cent—with the usual result."

"Yes. Andrew told me about that once. Well, well!"

"He had money to educate his granddaughter; I don't know how he raised it, but he kept it in a special account in the bank. He told me that if he died before she finished college that was to be applied strictly to her education. There is eight hundred dollars left of that."

"Sylvia's going to teach," said Mrs. Owen. "I've been talking to her and she's got her plans all made. She's got a head for business, that girl, and nothing can shake her idea that she's got a work to do in the world. She knows what she's going to do every day for a good many years, from the way she talks. I had it all fixed to take her with me up to Waupegan for the summer; thought she'd be ready to take a rest after her hard work at college, and this blow of her grandpa dying and all; but not that girl! She's going to spend the summer taking a normal course in town, to be ready to begin teaching in Indianapolis next September. I guess if we had found a million dollars in her grandpa's box it would have been the same. When you talk about health, she laughs; I guess if there's a healthy woman on earth it's that girl. She says she doubled all her gymnasium work at college to build herself up ready for business. You know Dr. Wandless's daughter is a Wellesley woman, and keeps in touch with the college. She wrote home that Sylvia had 'em all beat a mile down there; that she just walked through everything and would be chosen for the Phi Beta Kappa—is that right, Daniel? She sort o' throws you out of your calculations, that girl does. I'd counted on having a good time with her up at the lake, and now it looks like I'd have to stay in town all summer if I'm going to see anything of her."

It was clear enough that Mrs. Owen was not interesting herself in Sylvia merely because the girl was the granddaughter of an old friend; she admired Sylvia on her own account and was at no pains to disguise the fact. The Bassett expectations were, Dan reflected, scarcely at a premium to-day!

Mr. Akins returned the papers to the safety box, and when Mrs. Owen and Harwood were alone, she closed the door carefully.

"Now, Daniel," she began, opening her hand-satchel, "I always hold that this is a funny world, but that things come out right in the end. They mostly do; but sometimes the Devil gets into things and it ain't so easy. You believe in the Devil, Daniel?"

"Well, my folks are Presbyterians," said Dan. "My own religion is the same as Ware's. I'm not sure he vouches for the Devil."

"It's my firm conviction that there is one, Daniel,—a red one with a forked tail; you see his works scattered around too often to doubt it."

Dan nodded. Mrs. Owen had placed carefully under a weight a paper she had taken from her reticule.

"Daniel,"—she looked around at the door again, and dropped her voice,—"I believe you're a good man, and a clean one. And Fitch says you're a smart young man. It's as much because you're a good man as because you've got brains that I've called on you to attend to Sylvia's business. Now I'm going to tell you something that I wouldn't tell anybody else on earth; it's a sacred trust, and I want you to feel bound by a more solemn oath than the one you took at the clerk's office not to steal Sylvia's money."

She fixed her remarkably penetrating gaze upon him so intently that he turned uneasily in his chair. "It's something somebody who appreciates Sylvia, as I think you do, ought to know about her. Andrew Kelton told me just before Sylvia started to college. The poor man had been carrying it alone till it broke him down; he had never told another soul. I reckon it was the hardest job he ever did to tell me; and I wouldn't be telling you except somebody ought to know who's in a position to help Sylvia—sort o' look out for her and protect her. I believe"—and she put out her hand and touched his arm lightly— "I believe I can trust you to do that."

"Yes, Mrs. Owen."

She waited until he had answered her, and even then she was silent, lost in thought.

"Professor Kelton didn't know, Daniel," she began gravely, "who Sylvia's father was." She minimized the significance of this by continuing rapidly. "Andrew had quit the Navy soon after the war and came out here to Madison College to teach, and his wife had died and he didn't know what to do with his daughter. Edna Kelton was a little headstrong, I reckon, and wanted her own way. She didn't like living in a country college town; there wasn't anything here to interest her. I won't tell you all of Andrew's story, but it boils down to just this, that while Edna was in New York studying music she got married without telling where, or to whom. Andrew never saw her till she was dying in a hospital and had a little girl with her,—that's Sylvia. Now, whether there was any disgrace about it Andrew didn't know; and we owe it to that dead woman and to Sylvia to believe it was all right. You see what I mean, Daniel? Now that brings me down to what I want you to know. Somebody has been keeping watch of Sylvia,—Andrew told me that."

She was thinking deeply as though pondering just how much more it was necessary to tell him, and before she spoke she picked up the folded paper and read it through carefully. "When Andrew got this it troubled him a lot: the idea that somebody had an eye on the girl, and took enough interest in her to do this, made him uneasy. Sylvia never knew anything about it, of course; she doesn't know anything about anything, and she won't ever need to."

"As I understand you, Mrs. Owen, you want some friend of hers to be in a position to protect her if any one tries to harm her; you want to shield her from any evil that might follow her from her mother's errors, if they were indeed errors. We have no right to assume that she had done anything to be ashamed of. That's the only just position for us to take in such a matter."

"That's right, Daniel. I knew you'd see it that way. It looks bad, and Andrew knew it looked bad; but at my age I ain't thinking evil of people if I can help it. If a woman goes wrong, she pays for it—keeps on paying after she's paid the whole mortgage. That's the blackest thing in the world—that a woman never shakes a debt like that the way a man can. You foreclose on a woman and take away everything she's got; put her clean through bankruptcy, and the balance is still against her; but we can't make over society and laws just sitting here talking about it. I reckon Edna Kelton suffered enough. But we don't want Sylvia to suffer. She's entitled to a happy life, and we don't want any shadows hanging over her. Now that her grandpa's gone she can't go behind what he told her,—poor man, he had trouble enough answering the questions she had a right to ask; and he had to lie to her some."

"Yes; I suppose she will be content now; she will feel that what he didn't tell her she will never know. She's not a morbid person, and won't be likely to bother about it."

"No; I ain't afraid of her brooding on what she doesn't know. It's the fear it may fly up and strike her when she ain't looking that worries me, and it worried the Professor, too. That was why he told me. I guess when he talked to me that time he knew his heart was going to stop suddenly some day. And he'd got a hint that somebody was interested in watching Sylvia— sort o' keeping track of her. And there was conscience in it; whoever it is or was hadn't got clean away from what he'd done. Now I had a narrow escape from letting Sylvia see this letter. It was stuck away in a tin box in Andrew's bedroom, along with his commissions in the Navy. I was poking round the house, thinking there might be things it would be better not to show Sylvia, and I struck this box, and there was this letter, stuck away in the middle of the package. I gave Sylvia the commissions, but she didn't see this. I don't want to burn it till you've seen it. This must have been what Andrew spoke to me about that time; it was hardly before that, and it might have been later. You see it isn't dated. He started to tear it up, but changed his mind, so now we've got to pass on it."

She pushed the letter across the table to Harwood, and he read it through carefully. He turned it over after the first reading, and the word "Declined," written firmly and underscored, held him long—so long that he started when Mrs. Owen roused him with "Well, Daniel?"

He knew before he had finished reading that it was he who had borne the letter to the cottage in Buckeye Lane, unless there had been a series of such communications, which was unlikely on the face of it. Mrs. Owen had herself offered confirmation by placing the delivery of the dateless letter five years earlier. The internal evidence in the phrases prescribing the manner in which the verbal reply was to be sent, and the indorsement on the back of the sheet, were additional corroboration. It was almost unimaginable that the letter should have come again to his hand. He realized the importance and significance of the sheet of paper with the swiftness of a lightning flash; but beyond the intelligence conveyed by the letter itself there was still the darkness to grope in. His wits had never worked so rapidly in his life; he felt his heart beating uncomfortably; the perspiration broke out upon his forehead, and he drew out his handkerchief and mopped his face.

"It's certainly very curious, very curious indeed," he said with all the calmness he could muster. "But it doesn't tell us much."

"It wasn't intended to tell anything," said Mrs. Owen. "Whoever wrote that letter, as I told you, was troubled about Sylvia. I reckon it was a man; and I guess it's fair to assume that he felt under obligations, but hadn't the nerve to face 'em as obligations. Is that the way it strikes you?"

WHOEVER WROTE THAT LETTER WAS
TROUBLED ABOUT SYLVIA

"That seems clear enough," he replied lamely. He made a pretense of rereading the letter, but only detached phrases penetrated to his consciousness. His imagination was in rebellion against the curbing to which he strove to subject it. When he had borne his answer back to Fitch's office and been discharged with the generous payment of one hundred dollars for his services as messenger, just what had been the further history of the transaction? He had so far controlled his agitation that he was able to continue discussing the letter formally with the kind old woman who had placed the clue in his hands. He was little experienced in the difficult art of conversing with half a mind, and a direct question from Mrs. Owen roused him to the necessity of heeding what she was saying. He had resolved, however, that he would not tell her of his own connection with the message that lay on the table before them. He needed time in which to consider; he must not add a pebble's weight to an avalanche that might go crashing down upon the innocent. His training had made him wary of circumstantial evidence; after all it was possible that this was not the letter he had carried to Professor Kelton. It would be very like Mrs. Owen, if she saw that anything could be gained by such a course, to go direct to Fitch and demand to know the source of the offer that had passed through his hands so mysteriously; but Fitch had not known the contents of the letter, or he had said as much to Harwood. There was also the consideration, and not the lightest, that Dan was bound in honor to maintain the secrecy Fitch had imposed upon him. The lawyer had confided the errand to him in the belief that he would accept the mission in the spirit in which it was entrusted to him, and his part in the transaction was a matter between himself and Fitch and did not concern Mrs. Owen in any way whatever. No possible benefit could accrue to Sylvia from a disclosure of his suspicion that he had borne the letter to her grandfather. Mrs. Owen had given him the letter that he might be in a position to protect Sylvia, and there was nothing incompatible between this confidence and his duty to Fitch, who continued to be a kind and helpful friend. He dreaded the outcome of an interview between this shrewd, penetrating, and indomitable woman and the lawyer. The letter, cold and colorless in what it failed to say, and torn half across to mark the indecision of the old professor, had in it a great power for mischief.

While Harwood's mind was busy with these reflections he had been acquiescing in various speculations in which Mrs. Owen had been indulging, without really being conscious of their import.

"I don't know that any good can come of keeping the letter, Daniel. I reckon we might as well tear it up. You and I know what it is, and I've been studying it for a couple of days without seeing where any good can come of holding it. You might burn it in the grate there and we'll both know it's out of the way. I guess that person feels that he done his whole duty in making the offer and he won't be likely to bother any more. That conscience was a long time getting waked up, and having done that much it probably went to sleep again. There's nothing sleeps as sound as a conscience, I reckon, and I shouldn't be a bit surprised if mine took a nap occasionally. Better burn that little document, Daniel, and we'll be rid of it and try to forget it."

"No; I don't believe I'd do that," he said slowly. "It might be better to hold on to it, at least until the estate is closed up. You can't tell what's behind it." And then, groping for a plausible reason, he added: "The author of the letter may be in a position to annoy Sylvia by filing a claim against the Professor's estate, or something of that kind. It's better not to destroy the only thing we have that might help if that should occur. I believe it's best to hold on to it till the estate's settled."

This was pretty lame, as he realized, but his caution pleased her, and she acquiesced. She was anxious to leave no ground for anyone to rob Sylvia of her money, and if there was any remote possibility that the letter might add to the girl's security she was willing that it should be retained. She sent Dan out into the bank for an envelope, and when it was brought, sealed up the letter and addressed it to Dan in her own hand and marked it private.

"You take good care of that, Daniel, and when you get the estate closed up you burn it."

"Yes, it can do no harm to hold it a little while," he said with affected lightness.

CHAPTER XVII
A STROLL ACROSS THE CAMPUS

Dan joined Mrs. Owen and Sylvia at the cottage later. He was to see them off in the morning; and he exerted himself to make Sylvia's last evening in Buckeye Lane as happy as possible. The cottage was to be left in the care of the old servant until it could be disposed of; Mary herself was to be provided for in some way—Sylvia and Mrs. Owen had decided that this was only fair and right.

After tea Mrs. Owen said she had letters to write and carried her portfolio to the library for the purpose. Dan and Sylvia being thus left to themselves, he proposed a stroll across the campus.

"There's something about a campus," he said, as they started out;— "there's a likeness in all of them, or maybe it's sentiment that binds them together. Wellesley speaks to Yale, and the language of both is understood by Madison. Ah—there's the proof of it now!"

Integer vitæ, scelerisque purus!

A dozen students lounging on the steps of the library had begun to sing the Latin words to a familiar air. Dan followed in his deep bass to the end.

"The words are the words of Horace, but the tune is the tune of Eli with thanks to Dr. Fleming," he remarked. "It's that sort of thing that makes college worth while. I'll wager those are seniors, who already feel a little heartache because their college years are so nearly over. I'm getting to be an old grad myself, but those songs still give me a twinge."

"I understand that," said Sylvia. "I'll soon be saying good-bye to girls I may never see again, or when I meet them at a reunion in five or ten years, they'll be different. College is only the beginning, after all."

"It's only the beginning, but for some fellows it's the end, too. It scares me to see how many of my classmates are already caught in the undertow. I wonder sometimes whether I'm not going under myself."

Sylvia turned toward him.

"I rather imagine that you're a strong swimmer. It would surprise me if you didn't do something pretty big. Mrs. Owen thinks you will; she's not a person for any one to disappoint."

"Oh, she has a way of thinking in large totals of people she likes, and she does like me, most unaccountably."

"She has real illusions about *me*," laughed Sylvia. "She has an idea that colleges do things by magic; and I'm afraid she will find out that the wand didn't touch me."

"You didn't need the wand's magic," he answered, "for you are a woman of genius."

"Which sounds well, Mr. Harwood; no one ever used such words to me before! I've learned one thing, though: that patience and work will make up for a good many lacks. There are some things I'm going to try to do."

They loitered in the quiet paths of the campus. "Bright College Years" followed them from the singers at the library. If there's any sentiment in man or woman the airs of a spring night in our midwestern country will call it out. The planets shone benignantly through the leaves of maple and elm; and the young grass was irregular, untouched as yet by the mower— as we like it best who love our Madison! A week-old moon hung in the sky—ample light for the first hay-ride of the season that is moving toward Water Babble to the strains of guitar and banjo and boy and girl voices. It's unaccountable that there should be so much music in a sophomore—or maybe that's a fraternity affair—Sigma Chi or Delta Tau or Deke. Or mayhap those lads wear a "Fiji" pin on their waistcoats; I seem to recall spring hay-rides as an expression of "Fiji" spirit in my own days at Madison, when I myself was that particular blithe Hellenist with the guitar, and scornful of all Barbarians!

Sylvia was a woman now. Æons stretched between to-night and that afternoon when she had opened the door for Harwood in Buckeye Lane. His chivalry had been deeply touched by Mrs. Owen's disclosure at the bank, and subsequent reflection had not lightened the burden of her confidence. Such obscurities as existed in the first paragraph of the first page of Sylvia's life's record were dark enough in any circumstances, but the darkness was intensified by her singular isolation. The commission he had accepted in her behalf from Mrs. Owen carried a serious responsibility. These things he pondered as they walked together. He felt the pathos of her black gown; but she had rallied from the first shock of her sorrow, and met him in his key of badinage. She was tall—almost as tall as he; and in the combined moon- and star-light of the open spaces their eyes met easily.

He was conscious to-night of the charm in Sylvia that he had felt first on the train that day they had sped through the Berkshires together. No other girl had ever appealed to him so strongly. It was not the charm of cleverness, for she was not clever in the usual sense; she said few bright, quotable things, though her humor was keen. She had carried into womanhood the good looks of her girlhood, and she was a person one looked at twice. Her eyes were fine and expressive, and they faced the world with an engaging candor. They had learned to laugh since we saw her first—college and contact with the world had done that for her. Her face was long, her nose a compromise of good models, her mouth a little large, but offering compensations when she smiled in her quick, responsive fashion. One must go deeper, Harwood reflected, for Sylvia's charm, and it dawned upon him that it was in the girl's self, born of an alert, clear-thinking mind and a kind and generous heart. Individuality, personality, were words with which he sought to characterize her; and as he struggled with terms, he found that she was carrying the burden of the talk.

"I suppose," she was saying, in her voice that was deeper than most women's voices, and musical and agreeable to hear,—"I suppose that college is designed to save us all a lot of hard knocks; I wonder if it does?"

"If you're asking me personally, I'll say that there are lumps on my brow where I have bumped hard, in spite of my A.B. degree. I'm disposed to think that college only postpones the day of our awakening; we've got to shoot the chutes anyhow. It is so written."

She laughed at his way of putting it.

"Oh, you're not so much older that you can frighten me. People on the toboggan always seem to be having a good time; the percentage of those whose car jumps the track isn't formidable."

"Just enough fatalities to flavor the statistics. The seniors over there have stopped singing; I dare say they're talking about life in large capital letters."

"Well, there are plenty of chances. I'm rather of the opinion that we're all here to do something for somebody. Nobody's life is just his own. Whether we want it that way or not, we are all links in the chain, and it's our business not to be the weakest."

"I'm an individualist," he said, "and I'm very largely concerned in seeing what Daniel Harwood, a poor young lawyer of mediocre abilities, can do with this thing we hear mentioned as life."

"Oh, but there's no such thing as an individualist; the idea is purely academic!" and she laughed again, but less lightly. "We're all debtors to somebody or something—to the world itself, for example."

"For the stars up there, for grass and trees, for the moon by night and the sun by day—for the gracious gift of friends?"

"A little, yes; but they don't count so much. I owe my debt to people—real human beings, who may not be as lucky as I. For a good many thousand years people have been at work trying to cheer up the world—brighten it and make it a better place to live in. I owe all those people something; it's not merely a little something; it's a tremendous lot, and I must pay these other human beings who don't know what they're entitled to. You have felt that; you have felt it just as I have, I'm sure."

"You are still in college, and that is what undergraduates are taught to call ideals, Miss Garrison. I hope you will hold on to them: I had mine, but I'm conscious of late that I'm losing my grip on them. It's inevitable, in a man's life. It's a good thing that women hold on to them longer; without woman's faith in such things the world would be a sad old cinder, tumbling aimlessly around in the void."

She stopped abruptly in the path, very tall and slim in the dusk of starlight and moonlight. He had been carrying his hat in his hand and he leaned on his stick wondering whether she were really in earnest, whether he had displeased her by the half-mocking tone in which he had spoken.

"Please don't talk this old, romantic, mediæval nonsense about women! This is the twentieth century, and I don't believe for a minute that a woman, just by being a woman, can keep the world sweet and beautiful. Once, maybe; but not any more! A woman's ideals aren't a bit better than a man's unless she stands up for them and works for them. You don't have to take that from a college senior; you can ask dear Mrs. Owen. I suppose she knows life from experience if any woman ever did, and she has held to her ideals and kept working away at them. But just being a woman, and being good, and nice, and going to church, and belonging to a missionary society—well, Mr. Harwood?"

She had changed from earnestness to a note of raillery.

"Yes, Miss Garrison," he replied in her own key; "if you expect me to take issue with you or Mrs. Owen on any point, you're much mistaken. You and she are rather fortunate over many of the rest of us in having both brains and gentle hearts—the combination is irresistible! When you come home to throw in your lot with that of about a quarter of a million of us in our Hoosier capital, I'll put myself at your disposal. I've been trying to figure some way of saving the American Republic for the plain people, and I expect to go out in the campaign this fall and make some speeches warning all good citizens to be on guard against corporate greed, invasions of sacred rights, and so on. My way is plain, the duty clear," he concluded, with a wave of his stick.

"Well," said Sylvia, "if you care enough about it to do that you must still have a few ideals lying around somewhere."

"I don't know, to be honest about it, that it's so much my ideals as a wish to help my friend Mr. Bassett win a fight."

"I didn't know that he ever needed help in winning what he really wanted to win. I have heard of him only as the indomitable leader who wins whenever it's worth while."

"Well," Dan answered, "he's got a fight on hand that he can't afford to lose if he means to stay in politics."

"I must learn all about that when I come home. I never saw Mr. Bassett but once; that was at Waupegan when I was up there with Mrs. Owen nearly five years ago. He had just come back from the West and spent only a day at the lake."

"Then you don't really know him?"

"No; they had counted on having him there for the rest of the summer, but he came one day and left the next. He didn't even see Mrs. Owen; I remember that she expressed surprise that he had come to the lake and gone without seeing her."

"He's a busy man and works hard. You were getting acquainted with Marian about that time?"

"Yes; she was awfully good to me that summer. I liked Mr. Bassett, the glimpse I had of him; he seemed very interesting—a solid American character, quiet and forceful."

"Yes, he is that; he's a strong character. He's shown me every kindness—given me my chance. I should be ashamed of myself if I didn't feel grateful to him."

They had made the complete circuit of the campus several times and Sylvia said it was time to go back. The remembrance of Bassett had turned her thoughts to Marian, and they were still talking of her when Mrs. Owen greeted them cheerily from the little veranda. They were to start for Boston in the morning, and Harwood was to stay in Montgomery a day or two longer on business connected with the estate. "Don't let my sad philosophy keep you awake, Mr. Harwood!—I've given him all my life programme, Mrs. Owen. I think it has had a depressing influence on him."

"It's merely that you have roused me to a sense of my own general worldliness and worthlessness," he replied, laughing as they shook hands.

"I guess Sylvia can tell you a good many things, Daniel," said Mrs. Owen. "I wish you'd call Myers—he's my Seymour farmer—on the long distance in the morning, and tell him not to think I won't be down to look at his corn when I get back. Tell him I've gone to college, but I'll be right down there when I get home."

CHAPTER XVIII
THE KINGDOMS OF THE WORLD

Harwood reached the capital on the afternoon of the second day after Mrs. Owen and Sylvia had gone East, and went at once to the Boordman Building. Miss Farrell was folding and sealing letters bearing Bassett's signature.

"Hello, little stranger; I'd begun to think you had met with foul play, as the hero says in scene two, act three, of 'The Dark Switch-Lantern'—all week at the Park Theatre at prices within the reach of all. Business has been good, if you press me for news, but that paper-mill hasn't had much attention since you departed this life. Everybody's saying 'Stop, Look, Listen!' When in doubt you say that,—the white aprons in the one-arm lunch rooms say it now when you kick on the size of the buns. You will find your letters in the left-hand drawer. I told that collector from the necktie foundry that he needn't wear himself to a shadow carrying bills up here; that you paid all your bills by check on the tenth of the month. As that was the twenty-ninth, you'd better frame some new by-laws to avoid other breaks like that. I can't do much lying at my present salary."

She stood with her hands clasping her belt, and continued to enlighten him on current history as he looked over his letters.

"That young Allen Thatcher has been making life a burden to me in your lamented absence. Wanted to know every few hours if you had come back, and threatened to call you up on the long distance at Montgomery, but I told him you were trying a murder case over there, and that if he didn't want to get nailed for contempt of court he'd better not interrupt the proceedings."

"You're speaking of Mr. Allen Thatcher, are you, Miss Farrell?" asked Harwood, in the tone to which the girl frequently drove him.

"The same, like the mind reader you are! Say, that boy isn't stuck on you or anything. He came up here yesterday afternoon when the boss was out and wanted to talk things over. He seemed to think I hadn't anything to do but be a sister to him and hear his troubles. Well, I've got embarrassments of my own, with that true sport his papa sending me an offer of a hundred per month to work for him. One hundred dollars a month in advance! This, Mr. Harwood, is private and confidential. I guess I haven't worked at the State House without learning a few tricks in this mortal vale of politics."

She had calculated nicely the effect of this shot. Harwood might treat her, as she said, like a step-child with a harelip, but occasionally she made him sit up. He sat up now. He remarked with the diplomatic unconcern that it was best to employ with her: —

"Refused the offer, did you, Miss Farrell?"

"I certainly did. As between a fat old sport like Ed Thatcher and a gentleman like Mr. Bassett, money doesn't count—not even with a p.w.g., or poor working girl, like me. Hush!—are we quite alone?" She bent toward the door dramatically. "What he was playing for, as neat as a hatpin in your loved one's eye, was some facts about the boss's committee work in that last session I worked at the State House. Cute of Thatcher? Well, not so awful bright! He doesn't know what he's up against if he thinks Mort Bassett can be caught on flypaper, and you can be dead sure I'm not going to sprinkle the sugar to catch our boss with. All that Transportation Committee business was just as straight as the way home; but"—Miss Farrell tapped her mouth daintily with her fingers to stifle an imaginary yawn—"but little Rose brought down her shorthand notebooks marked 'M.B. personal,' and the boss and I burned them yesterday morning early, right there in that grate in his room. That's what I think of Mr. Ed Thatcher. A pearl necklace for my birthday ought to be about right for that."

Harwood had been drinking this in as he opened and sorted his letters. He paused and stared at her absently.

"You referred to a caller a moment ago—the gentleman who annoyed you so much on the telephone. Was I to call him or anything like that?"

"He left a good many orders, but I think you were to eat food with him in the frosty halls of the University Club almost at once. He's in a state of mind. In love with the daughter of his father's enemy—just like a Park Theatre thriller. Wants you to tell him what to do; and you will pardon me for suggesting that if there's to be an elopement you write it up yourself for the 'Courier.' I was talking to a friend of mine who's on the ding-ding desk at the Whitcomb and she says the long-distance business in that tavern is painful to handle—hot words flying over the state about this Thatcher-Bassett rumpus. You may take it from me that the fight is warm, and I guess somebody will know more after the convention. But say—!"

"Um," said Harwood, whose gaze was upon the frame of a new building that was rising across the street. He was thinking of Allen. If Marian and

Allen were subjects of gossip in connection with the break between their fathers he foresaw trouble; and he was sorry, for he was sincerely devoted to the boy; and Marian he liked also, in spite of her vagaries. A great many people were likely to be affected by the personal difficulties of Thatcher and Bassett. Even quiet Montgomery was teeming, and on the way from the station he had met half a dozen acquaintances who had paused to shake hands and say something about the political situation. His ignorance of Bassett's real intentions, which presumably the defiance of the "Courier" merely cloaked, was not without its embarrassment. He had been known as a Bassett man; he had received and talked to innumerable politicians of Bassett's party in the Boordman Building; and during the four years of his identification with Bassett he had visited most of the county seats on political and business errands. The closeness of their association made all the more surprising this sudden exclusion.

"I said 'say,'" repeated Miss Farrell, lightly touching the smooth cliff of yellow hair above her brow with the back of her hand. "I was about to give you a message from his majesty our king, but if you're on a pipe dream don't let me call you home."

"Oh, yes; pardon me. What were you about to say?"

"Mr. Bassett said that if you came in before I quit to ask you to come over to the Whitcomb. Mrs. Bassett blew in to-day from that sanatorium in Connecticut where they've been working on her nerves. Miss Marian brought her back, and they've stopped in town to rest. And say," —here Miss Farrell lowered her voice,—"the Missis must try his soul a good deal! I wonder how he ever picked *her* out of the bunch?"

"That will do!" said Harwood sharply. "I'll find Mr. Bassett at the Whitcomb and I shan't have anything for you to-day."

There had been a meeting of the central committee preliminary to the approaching state convention. A number of candidates had already opened headquarters at the Whitcomb; members of Congress, aspirants for the governor's seat, to be filled two years hence, and petty satraps from far and near were visible at the hotel. If Bassett's star was declining there was nothing to indicate it in the conduct of the advance guard. If any change was apparent it pointed to an increase of personal popularity. Bassett was not greatly given to loafing in public places; he usually received visitors at such times in an upper room of the hotel; but Harwood found him established on a settee in the lobby in plain view of all seekers, and from the fixed appearance of the men clustered about him he had held this position for some time. Harwood drew into the outer edge of the crowd unnoticed for a moment. Bassett was at his usual ease; a little cheerfuler of countenance

A Hoosier Chronicle | 189

than was his wont, and yet not unduly anxious to appear tranquil. He had precipitated one of the most interesting political struggles the state had ever witnessed, but his air of unconcern before this mixed company of his fellow partisans, among whom there were friends and foes, was well calculated to inspire faith in his leadership. Some one was telling a story, and at its conclusion Bassett caught Harwood's eye and called to him in a manner that at once drew attention to the young man.

"Hello, Dan! You're back from the country all right, I see! I guess you boys all know Harwood. You've seen his name in the newspapers!"

Several of the loungers shook hands with Harwood, who had cultivated the handshaking habit, and he made a point of addressing to each one some personal remark. Thus the gentleman from Tippecanoe, who had met Dan at the congressional convention in Lafayette two years earlier, felt that he must have favorably impressed Bassett's agent on that occasion; else how had Harwood asked at once, with the most shameless flattery, whether they still had the same brand of fried chicken at his house! And the gentleman from the remote shores of the Lake, a rare visitor in town, had every right to believe, from Dan's reference to the loss by fire of the gentleman's house a year earlier, that that calamity had aroused in Dan the deepest sympathy. Dan had mastered these tricks; it rather tickled his sense of humor to practice them; but it must be said for him that he was sincerely interested in people, particularly in these men who played the great game. If he ever achieved anything in politics it must be through just such material as offered itself on such occasions as this in the halls of the Whitcomb. These men might be tearing the leader to pieces to-morrow, or the day after; but he was still in the saddle, and not knowing but that young Harwood might be of use to them some day, they greeted him as one of the inner circle.

Most of these men sincerely liked and admired Bassett; and many of them accepted the prevailing superstition as to his omniscience and invulnerability; even in the Republican camp many shared the belief that the spears of the righteous were of no avail against him. Dan's loyalty to Bassett had never been more firmly planted. Bassett had always preserved a certain formality in his relations with him; to-night he was calling him Dan, naturally and as though unconscious of the transition. This was not without its effect on Harwood; he was surprised to find how agreeable it was to be thus familiarly addressed by the leader in such a gathering.

Bassett suggested that he speak to Mrs. Bassett and Marian, who were spending a few days in town, and he found them in the hotel parlor, where Bassett joined them shortly. Mrs. Bassett and Dan had always got on well together; his nearness to her husband brought him close to the domestic circle; and he had been invariably responsive to her demands upon his time. Dan had learned inevitably a good deal of the inner life of the Bassetts, and now and then he had been aware that Mrs. Bassett was sounding him discreetly as to her husband's plans and projects; but these approaches had been managed with the nicest tact and discretion. In her long absences from home she had lost touch with Bassett's political interests and occupations, but she knew of his break with Thatcher. She prided herself on being a woman of the world, and while she had flinched sometimes at the attacks made upon her husband, she was nevertheless proud of his influence in affairs. Bassett had once, at a time when he was being assailed for smothering some measure in the senate, given her a number of books bearing upon the anti-slavery struggle, in which she read that the prominent leaders in that movement had suffered the most unjust attacks, and while it was not quite clear wherein lay Bassett's likeness to Lincoln, Lovejoy, and Wendell Phillips, she had been persuaded that the most honorable men in public life are often the targets of scandal. Her early years in Washington with her father had impressed her imagination; the dream of returning there as the wife of a Senator danced brightly in her horizons. It would mean much to Marian and Blackford if their father, like their Grandfather Singleton, should attain a seat in the Senate. And she was aware that without such party service as Bassett was rendering, with its resulting antagonisms, the virulent newspaper attacks, the social estrangements that she had not escaped in Fraserville, a man could not hope for party preferment.

Bassett had recently visited Blackford at the military school where his son was established, and talk fell upon the boy.

"Black likes to have a good time, but he will come out all right. The curriculum doesn't altogether fit him—that's his only trouble."

Bassett glanced at Harwood for approval and Dan promptly supported the father's position. Blackford had, as a matter of fact, been threatened with expulsion lately for insubordination. Bassett had confessed to Dan several times his anxiety touching the boy. To-day, when the lad's mother had just returned after a long sojourn in a rest cure, was not a fit occasion for discussing such matters.

"What's Allen doing?" asked Marian. "I suppose now that papa is having a rumpus with Mr. Thatcher I shall never see him any more."

"You shouldn't speak so, Marian. A hotel parlor is no place to discuss your father's affairs," admonished Mrs. Bassett.

"Oh, Allen's ever so much fun. He's a Socialist or something. Aunt Sally likes him ever so much. Aunt Sally likes Mr. Thatcher, too, for that matter," she concluded boldly.

"Mr. Thatcher is an old friend of mine," said Bassett soberly.

"You can be awfully funny when you want to, papa," replied Marian. "As we came through Pittsburg this morning I bought a paper that told about 'Stop, Look, Listen.' But Allen won't mind if you do whistle to his father to keep off the track."

"Mr. Thatcher's name was never mentioned by me in any such connection," replied Bassett; but he laughed when Marian leaned over and patted his cheek to express her satisfaction in her father's cleverness.

"I think it unfortunate that you have gone to war with that man," remarked Mrs. Bassett wearily.

"You dignify it too much by calling it a war," Harwood interjected. "We don't want such men in politics in this state and somebody has to deal with them."

"I guess it will be a lively scrap all right enough," said Marian, delighted at the prospect. "We're going to move to the city this fall, Mr. Harwood. Hasn't papa told you?"

Mrs. Bassett glanced at her husband with alert suspicion, thinking that perhaps in her absence he had been conniving to this end with Marian.

Bassett smiled at his daughter's adroitness in taking advantage of Harwood's presence to introduce this subject; it had been the paramount issue with her for several years.

"I shall be glad enough to stay at Fraserville the rest of my days if I get through another Waupegan summer safely," said Mrs. Bassett. "The mere thought of moving is horrible!"

"Oh, we wouldn't exactly move in coming here; we'd have an apartment in one of these comfortable new houses and come down while the legislature's in session, so we can be with papa. And there's ever so much music here now, and the theatres, and I could have a coming-out party here. You know I never had one, papa. And it would be nice to be near Aunt Sally; she's getting old and needs us."

"Yes; she undoubtedly does," said Bassett, with faint irony.

Her daughter's rapid fire of suggestions wearied Mrs. Bassett. She turned to Harwood:—

"Mr. Bassett and Marian have been telling me, Mr. Harwood, that Aunt Sally went back to college with Sylvia Garrison after Professor Kelton's death. Poor girl, it's quite like Aunt Sally to do that. Sylvia must be very forlorn, with all her people gone. I think Aunt Sally knew her mother. I hope the girl isn't wholly destitute?"

"No, the Professor left a small estate and Miss Garrison expects to teach," Dan answered.

"Dan is the administrator," remarked Bassett "I'm sure you will be glad to know that Miss Garrison's affairs are in good hands, Hallie."

"Aunt Sally is very fond of you, Mr. Harwood; I hope you appreciate that," said Mrs Bassett. "Aunt Sally doesn't like everybody."

"Aunt Sally's a brick, all right," declared Marian, as an accompaniment to Dan's expression of his gratification that Mrs. Owen had honored him with her friendship.

"It's too bad the girl will have to teach," said Mrs. Bassett; "it must be a dog's life."

"I think Miss Garrison doesn't look at it that way," Harwood intervened. "She thinks she's in the world to do something for somebody; she's a very interesting, a very charming young woman."

"Well, I haven't seen her in five years; she was only a young girl that summer at the lake. How soon will Aunt Sally be back? I do hope she's coming to Waupegan. If I'd known she was going to Wellesley, we could have waited for her in New York, and Marian and I could have gone with them to see Sylvia graduated. I always wanted to visit the college."

"It was better for you to come home, Hallie," said Mr. Bassett. "You are not quite up to sight-seeing yet. And now," he added, "Dan and I have some business on hand for an hour or so, and I'm going to send you and Marian for an automobile ride before dinner. You must quit the moment you are tired. Wish we could all go, but I haven't seen Dan much lately, and as I'm going home with you to-morrow we shan't have another chance."

When his wife and daughter had been dispatched in the motor Bassett suggested that they go to a private room he had engaged in the hotel, first giving orders at the office that he was not to be disturbed. He did not, however, escape at once from men who had been lying in wait for him in the lobby and corridors, but he made short work of them.

"I want to thresh out some things with you to-day, and I'll be as brief as possible," said Bassett when he and Harwood were alone. "You got matters fixed satisfactorily at Montgomery—no trouble about your appointment?"

"None; Mrs. Owen had arranged all that."

"You mentioned to her, did you, my offer to help?"

"Oh, yes! But she had already arranged with Akins, the banker, about the administrator's bond, and we went at once to business."

"That's all right; only I wanted to be sure Mrs. Owen understood I had offered to help you. She's very kind to my wife and children; Mrs. Bassett has been almost like a daughter to her, you know. There's really some property to administer, is there?"

"Very little, sir. The Professor had been obliged to drop part of his life insurance and there was only two thousand in force when he died. The house he lived in may bring another two. There are some publishers' contracts that seem to have no value. And the old gentleman had invested what was a large sum for him in White River Canneries."

Bassett frowned and he asked quickly:—

"How much?"

"Five thousand dollars."

"As much as that?"

Bassett's connection with White River Canneries was an incident of the politician's career to which Harwood had never been wholly reconciled. Nor was he pleasantly impressed by Bassett's next remark, which, in view of Mrs. Bassett's natural expectations,—and these Dan had frequently heard mentioned at the capital,—partook of the nature of a leading question. "That's unfortunate. But I suppose Mrs. Owen, by reason of her friendship for the grandfather, won't let the girl suffer."

"She's not the sort of girl who would be dependent in any case. She holds rather altruistic ideas in fact," remarked Harwood. "I mean," he added, seeing that Bassett waited for him to explain himself, "that Miss Garrison feels that she starts life in debt to the world—by reason of her own opportunities and so on; she expects to make payments on that debt."

"In debt?" Bassett repeated vacantly. "Oh, not literally, I see! She expects to teach and help others in that way. That's commendable. But let me see."

He had taken an unsharpened lead pencil from his pocket and was slipping it through his fingers absently, allowing its blunt ends to tap the arm of his chair at intervals. After a moment's silence he plunged into his own affairs.

"You probably saw my tip to Thatcher in the 'Courier'? I guess everybody has seen it by this time," he added grimly; and he went on as though making a statement his mind had thoroughly rehearsed: "Thatcher and I have been pretty thick. We've been in a good many business deals together. We've been useful to each other. He had more money than I had to begin with, but I had other resources—influence and so on that he needed. I guess we're quits on the business side. You may be interested to know that I never had a cent of money in his breweries and distilleries; but I've helped protect the traffic in return for support he has given some of my own enterprises. I never owned a penny in that Fraserville brewery, for instance; but I've been pointed out as its owner. They've got the idea here in Indiana that saloons are my chief joy in life; but nothing is farther from the truth. When Mrs. Bassett has been troubled about that I have always been able to tell her with a good conscience that I hadn't a penny in the business. I've frankly antagonized legislation directed against the saloon, for I've never taken any stock in this clamor of the Prohibitionists and temperance cranks generally; but I've stood consistently for a proper control. Thatcher and I got along all right until he saw that the party was coming into power again and got the senatorial bee in his bonnet. He's got the idea that he can buy his way in; and to buy a seat he's got to buy my friends. That's a clear proposition, isn't it?"

"Yes, sir; I haven't seen that he had any personal influence worth counting."

"Exactly. Now, I don't intend that Ed Thatcher shall buy a seat in the United States Senate if our party in Indiana has one to dispose of. I'm not so good myself, but when I found that Thatcher had begun to build up a little machine for himself, I resolved to show him that I can't be used by any man so long as he thinks he needs me and then kicked out when I'm in the way. And I've got some state pride, too, and with all the scandals going around in other states over the sale of seats at Washington I'm not going to have my party in the state where I was born and where I have lived all my life lend itself to the ambitions of an Ed Thatcher. I think you share that feeling?"

"The people of the whole state will commend that," replied Dan warmly. "And if you want to go to the Senate—"

"I don't want anything from my party that it doesn't want me to have," interrupted Bassett.

He rose and paced the floor. An unusual color had come into his face, but otherwise he betrayed no agitation. He crossed from the door to the window and resumed his seat.

"They've said of me that I fight in the dark; that I'm a man of secret and malign methods. The 'Advertiser' said only this morning that I have no courage; that I never make an attack where it costs me anything. I've already proved that to be a lie. My attack on Thatcher is likely to cost me a good deal. You may be sure he won't scruple to make the bill as heavy as he can. I'm talking to you freely, and I'll say to you that I expect the better element of the party to rally to my support. You see, I'm going to give you idealists a chance to do something that will count. Thatcher is not a foe to be despised. Here's his reply to my 'Stop, Look, Listen,' editorial. The sheriff served it on me just as I stepped into the elevator to come up here."

The paper Harwood took wonderingly was a writ citing Bassett to appear as defendant in a suit brought in the circuit court by Edward G. Thatcher against the Courier Publishing Company, Morton Bassett, and Sarah Owen.

Bassett stretched himself at ease in his chair and explained.

"I wanted a newspaper and he was indifferent about it at the time; but we went in together, and he consented that I should have a controlling interest. As I was tied up tight right then I had to get Mrs. Owen to help me out. It wasn't the kind of deal you want to hawk about town, and neither Thatcher nor I cared to have it known for a while that we had bought the paper. But it's hardly a secret now, of course. Mrs. Owen and I together own one hundred and fifty-one shares of the total of three hundred; Thatcher owns the rest and he was satisfied to let it go that way. He signed an agreement that I should manage the paper, and said he didn't want anything but dividends."

"Mrs. Owen's interest is subject to your wishes, of course; that goes without saying."

"Well, I guaranteed eight per cent on her investment, but we've made it lately, easily. I've now got to devise some means of getting rid of Thatcher; but we'll let him cool till after the convention. Mrs. Owen won't be back for several weeks, I suppose?"

"No; she and Miss Garrison will return immediately after the commencement exercises."

"Well, Thatcher brought that suit, thinking that if he could throw the paper into a receivership he'd run up the price when it came to be sold and shake me out. He knew, too, that it would annoy Mrs. Owen to be involved in litigation. It's surprising that he would incur her wrath himself; she's always been mighty decent to Ed and kind to his boy. But I'll have to buy her stock and let her out; it's a delicate business, and for Mrs. Bassett's sake I've got to get her aunt out as quickly as possible."

"That, of course, will be easily managed. It's too bad she's away just now."

"It was the first time I ever asked her help in any of my business affairs, and it's unfortunate. The fact is that Mrs. Bassett doesn't know of it."

He rose and crossed the room slowly with his hands thrust deep into his trousers pockets.

"But if Mrs. Owen is guaranteed against loss there's no ground for criticizing you," said Dan. "There's nothing to trouble about on that side of it, I should think."

"Oh, I'm not troubling about that," replied Bassett shortly. He shrugged his shoulders and walked to the window, gazing out on the street in silence for several minutes. Then he sat down on the edge of the bed.

"I told you, Dan, when you opened our office in the Boordman Building, that if ever the time came when you didn't want to serve me any longer you were to feel free to quit. You are under no obligations to me of any sort. I caught a bargain in you; you have been useful to me in many ways; you have carried nearly the whole burden of the paper-mill receivership in a way to win me the praise of the court and all others interested. If you should quit me to-night I should still be your debtor. I had about decided to leave you out of my calculations in politics; you have the making of a good lawyer and if you opened an office to-morrow you would find clients without trouble. You are beginning to be known, very well known for a man of your years."

Harwood demurred feebly, unheeded by Bassett, who continued steadily.

"I had thought for a time that I shouldn't encourage you to take any part in politics—at least in my affairs. The receivership has been giving you enough to do; and the game, after all, is a hard one. Even after I decided to break with Thatcher I thought I'd leave you out of it: that's why I gave you no intimation of what was coming, but put the details into Atwill's hands. I had really meant to show you a proof of that editorial, but I wasn't sure until they had to close the page that night that I was ready to make the break. I had been pretty hot that evening at the Country Club when I saw Pettit and Thatcher chumming together; I wanted to be sure I had cooled off. But I find that I've got in the habit of relying on you; I've been open with you from the beginning, and as you know I'm not much given to taking men into my confidence. But I've been leaning on you a good deal—more, in fact, than I realized."

There was no questioning Bassett's sincerity, nor was there any doubt that this appeal was having its effect on the younger man. If Bassett had been a weakling timorously making overtures for help, Harwood would have been sensible of it; but a man of demonstrated force and intelligence, who had probably never talked thus to another soul in his life, was addressing him with a candor at once disarming and compelling. It was not easy to say to a man from whom he had accepted every kindness that he had ceased to trust him; that while he had been his willing companion on fair-weather voyages, he would desert without a qualm before the tempest. But even now Bassett had asked nothing of him; why should he harden his heart against the man who had been his friend?

"You have your ideals—fine ideas of public service that I admire. Our party needs such men as you; the young fellows couldn't get away from us fast enough after '96; many of the Sons of old-time Democrats joined the Republicans. Fitch has spoken to me of you often as the kind of man we ought to push forward, and I'm willing to put you out on the firing-line, where you can work for your ideals. My help will handicap you at first,"— his voice grew dry and hard here,-"but once you have got a start you can shake me off as quick as you like. It's a perfectly selfish proposition I'm making, Harwood; it simply gets down to this, that I need your help."

"Of course, Mr. Bassett; if I can serve you in any way—"

"Anything you can do for me you may do if you don't feel that you will be debasing yourself in fighting under my flag. It's a black flag, they say—just as black as Thatcher's. I don't believe you want to join Thatcher; the question is, do you want to stick to me?"

Bassett had spoken quietly throughout. He had made no effort to play upon Harwood's sympathies or to appeal to his gratitude. He was, in common phrase, to be taken or let alone. Harwood realized that he must either decline outright or declare his fealty in a word. It was in no view a debatable matter; he could not suggest points of difference or even inquire as to the nature of the service to be exacted. He was face to face with a man who, he had felt that night of their first meeting at Fraserville, gave and received hard blows. Yet he did not doubt that if their relations terminated to-day Bassett would deal with him magnanimously. He realized that after all it was not Bassett who was on trial; it was Daniel Harwood!

He saw his life in sharp fulgurations; the farm (cleared of debt through Bassett's generosity, to be sure!) where his father and brothers struggled to wrest a livelihood from reluctant soil, and their pride and hope in him; he saw his teachers at college, men who had pointed the way to useful and honorable lives; and more than all, Sumner rose before him—Sumner who had impressed him more than any other man he had ever known. Sumner's clean-cut visage was etched grimly in his consciousness; verily Sumner would not have dallied with a man of Bassett's ilk. He had believed when he left college that Sumner's teaching and example would be a buckler and shield to him all the days of his life; and here he was, faltering before a man to whom the great teacher would have given scarce a moment's contemptuous thought. He could even hear the professor's voice as he ironically pronounced upon sordid little despots of Bassett's stamp. And only forty-eight hours earlier he had been talking to a girl on the campus at

Madison who had spoken of idealism and service in the terms of which he had thought of those things when he left college. Even Allen Thatcher, in his whimsical fashion, stood for ideals, and dreamed of the heroic men who had labored steadfastly for great causes. Here was his chance now to rid himself of Bassett; to breathe free air again! On the other hand, Bassett had himself suggested that Harwood, once in a position to command attention, might go his own gait. His servitude would be for a day only, and by it he should win eternal freedom. He caught eagerly at what Bassett was saying, grateful that the moment of his choice was delayed.

"The state convention is only three weeks off and I had pretty carefully mapped it out before the 'Courier' dropped that shot across Thatcher's bows. I've arranged for you to go as delegate to the state convention from this county and to have a place on the committee on resolutions. This will give you an introduction to the party that will be of value. They will say you are my man—but they've said that of other men who have lived it down. I want Thatcher to have his way in that convention, naming the ticket as far as he pleases, and appearing to give me a drubbing. The party's going to be defeated in November—there's no ducking that. We'll let Thatcher get the odium of that defeat. About the next time we'll go in and win and there won't be any more Thatcher nonsense. This is politics, you understand."

Harwood nodded; but Bassett had not finished; it clearly was not his purpose to stand the young man in a corner and demand a choice from him. Bassett pursued negotiations after a fashion of his own.

"Thatcher thinks he has scored heavily on me by sneaking into Fraserville and kidnaping old Ike Pettit. That fellow has always been a nuisance to me; I carried a mortgage on his newspaper for ten years, but Thatcher has mercifully taken that burden off my shoulders by paying it. Thatcher can print anything he wants to about me in my own town; but it will cost him some money; those people up there don't think I'm so wicked, and the 'Fraser County Democrat' won't have any advertisements for a while but fake medical ads. But Ike will have more room for the exploitation of his own peculiar brand of homely Hoosier humor."

Bassett smiled, and Harwood was relieved to be able to laugh aloud. He was enjoying this glimpse of the inner mysteries of the great game. His disdain of Thatcher's clumsy attempts to circumvent Bassett was complete; in any view Bassett was preferable to Thatcher. As the senator from Fraser had said, there was really nothing worse than Thatcher, with his breweries and racing-stable, his sordidness and vulgarity. Thatcher's efforts to practice Bassett's methods with Bassett's own tools was a subject for laughter. It seemed for the moment that Harwood's decision might be struck on this note of mirth. Dan wondered whether, in permitting Bassett thus to disclose his plans and purposes, he had not already nailed his flag to the Bassett masthead.

"I don't want these fellows who are old-timers in state conventions—particularly those known to be my old friends—to figure much," Bassett continued. "I'm asking your aid because you're new and clean-handed. The meanest thing they can say against you is that you're in my camp. They tell me you're an effective speaker, a number of county chairmen have said your speeches in the last campaign made a good impression. I shall want you to prepare a speech about four minutes long, clean-cut and vigorous,—we'll decide later what that speech shall be about. I've got it in mind to spring something in that convention just to show Thatcher that there are turns of the game he doesn't know yet. I'm going to give you a part that will make 'em remember you for some time, Dan."

Bassett's smile showed his strong sound teeth. He rarely laughed, but he yielded now to the contagion of the humor he had aroused in Harwood.

"It's a big chance you're giving me to get into things," replied Harwood. "I'll do my best." Then he added, in the glow of his complete surrender: "You've never asked me to do a dishonorable thing in the four years I've been with you. There's nothing I oughtn't to be glad to do from any standpoint, and I'm grateful for this new mark of your confidence."

"That's all right, Dan. There are things in store for young men in politics in this state—Republicans and Democrats," said Bassett, without elation or any show of feeling whatever. "Once the limelight hits you, you can go far—very far. I must go over to the 'Courier' office now and see Atwill."

CHAPTER XIX
THE THUNDER OF THE CAPTAINS

Marian had suggested to her mother that they visit Mrs. Owen in town before settling at Waupegan for the summer, and it was Marian's planning that made this excursion synchronize with the state convention. Mr. Bassett was not consulted in the matter; in fact, since his wife's return from Connecticut he had been unusually occupied, and almost constantly away from Fraserville. Mrs. Bassett and her daughter arrived at the capital the day after Mrs. Owen reached home from Wellesley with Sylvia, and the Bassetts listened perforce to their kinswoman's enthusiastic account of the commencement exercises. Mrs. Owen had, it appeared, looked upon Smith and Mount Holyoke also on this eastward flight, and these inspections, mentioned in the most casual manner, did not contribute to Mrs. Bassett's happiness.

Finding that her father was inaccessible by telephone, Marian summoned Harwood and demanded tickets for the convention; she would make an occasion of it, and Mrs. Owen and Sylvia should go with them. Mrs. Bassett and her family had always enjoyed the freedom of Mrs. Owen's house; it was disheartening to find Sylvia established in Delaware Street on like terms of intimacy. The old heartache over Marian's indifference to the call of higher education for women returned with a new poignancy as Mrs. Bassett inspected Sylvia's diploma, as proudly displayed by Mrs. Owen as though it marked the achievement of some near and dear member of the family. Sylvia's undeniable good looks, her agreeable manner, her ready talk, and the attention she received from her elders, were well calculated to arm criticism in a prejudiced heart. On the evening of their arrival Admiral and Mrs. Martin and the Reverend John Ware had called, and while Mrs. Bassett assured herself that these were, in a sense, visits of condolence upon Andrew Kelton's granddaughter, the trio, who were persons of distinction, had seemed sincerely interested in Mrs. Owen's protégée. Mrs. Bassett was obliged to hear a lively dialogue between the minister and Sylvia touching some memory of his first encounter with her about the stars. He brought her as a "commencement present" Bacon's "Essays." People listened to Sylvia; Sylvia had things to say! Even the gruff admiral paid her deference. He demanded to know whether it was true that Sylvia had declined a position at the Naval Observatory, which required the calculation of tides for the Nautical Almanac. Mrs. Bassett was annoyed that Sylvia had refused a position that would have removed her from a proximity to Mrs. Owen that struck her as replete with danger. And yet Mrs. Bassett was outwardly friendly, and she privately counseled Marian, quite unnecessarily, to be "nice" to Sylvia. On the same evening Mrs. Bassett was disagreeably impressed by Harwood's obvious rubrication in Mrs. Owen's good books. It seemed darkly portentous that Dan was, at Mrs. Owen's instigation, managing Sylvia's business affairs; she must warn her husband against this employment of his secretary to strengthen the ties between Mrs. Owen and this object of her benevolence.

Mrs. Bassett's presence at the convention did not pass unremarked by many gentlemen upon the floor, or by the newspapers.

"While the state chairman struggled to bring the delegates to order, Miss Marian Bassett, daughter of the Honorable Morton Bassett, of Fraser County, was a charming and vivacious figure in the balcony. At a moment when it seemed that the band would never cease from troubling the air with the strains of 'Dixie,' Miss Bassett tossed a carnation into the Marion County delegation. The flower was deftly caught by Mr. Daniel Harwood, who wore it in his buttonhole throughout the strenuous events of the day."

This item was among the "Kodak Shots" subjoined to the "Advertiser's" account of the convention. It was stated elsewhere in the same journal that "never before had so many ladies attended a state convention as graced this occasion. The wives of both Republican United States Senators and of many prominent politicians of both parties were present, their summer costumes giving to the severe lines of the balcony a bright note of color." The "Capital," in its minor notes of the day, remarked upon the perfect amity that prevailed among the wives and daughters of Republicans and Democrats. It noted also the presence in Mrs. Bassett's party of her aunt, Mrs. Jackson Owen, and of Mrs. Owen's guest, Miss Sylvia Garrison, a graduate of this year's class at Wellesley.

The experiences and sensations of a delegate to a large convention are quite different from those of a reporter at the press table, as Dan Harwood realized; and it must be confessed that he was keyed to a proper pitch of excitement by the day's prospects. In spite of Bassett's promise that he need not trouble to help elect himself a delegate, Harwood had been drawn sharply into the preliminary skirmish at the primaries. He had thought it wise to cultivate the acquaintance of the men who ruled his own county even though his name had been written large upon the Bassett slate.

In the weeks that intervened between his interview with Harwood in the upper room of the Whitcomb and the primaries, Bassett had quietly visited every congressional district, holding conferences and perfecting his plans. "Never before," said the "Advertiser," "had Morton Bassett's pernicious activity been so marked." The belief had grown that the senator from Fraser was in imminent peril; in the Republican camp it was thought that while Thatcher might not control the convention he would prove himself strong enough to shake the faith of many of Bassett's followers in the power of their chief. There had been, apparently, a hot contest at the primaries. In the northern part of the state, in a region long recognized as Bassett's stronghold, Thatcher had won easily; at the capital the contestants had broken even, a result attributable to Thatcher's residence in the county. The word had passed among the faithful that Thatcher money was plentiful, and that it was not only available in this preliminary skirmish, but that those who attached themselves to Thatcher early were to enjoy his bounty throughout his campaign—which might be protracted—for the senatorship. Bassett was not scattering largess; it was whispered that the money he had used previously in politics had come out of Thatcher's pocket and that he would have less to spend in future.

Bassett, in keeping with his forecast to Harwood, had made a point of having many new men, whose faces were unfamiliar in state conventions, chosen at the primaries he controlled, so that in a superficial view of the convention the complexion of a considerable body of the delegates was neutral. Here and there among the delegations sat men who knew precisely Bassett's plans and wishes. The day following the primaries, Bassett, closeted with Harwood in his room at the Boordman Building, had run the point of a walking-stick across every county in the state, reciting from memory just how many delegates he absolutely controlled, those he could get easily if he should by any chance need them, and the number of undoubted Thatcher men there were to reckon with. In Dan's own mingling with the crowd at the Whitcomb the night before the convention he had learned nothing to shake his faith in Bassett's calculations.

The Honorable Isaac Pettit, of Fraser, was one of the most noteworthy figures on the floor. Had he not thrown off the Bassett yoke and trampled the lord of Fraser County underfoot? Did not the opposition press applaud the editor for so courageously wresting from the despicable chieftain the control of a county long inured to slavery? Verily, the Honorable Isaac had done much to encourage belief in the guileless that such were the facts. Even the "Courier" proved its sturdy independence by printing the result of the primary without extenuation or aught set down in malice. The Honorable Isaac Pettit undoubtedly believed in himself as the savior of Fraser. He had personally led the fight in the Fraser County primaries and had vanquished Bassett! "Bassett had fought gamely," the Republican organ averred, to make more glorious the Honorable Isaac's victory. It was almost inconceivable, they said, that Bassett, who had dominated his party for years, should not be able to elect himself a delegate to a state convention.

In a statement printed in the "Courier," Bassett had accepted defeat in a commendable spirit of resignation. He and Atwill had framed that statement a week before the primaries, and Miss Rose Farrell had copied at least a dozen drafts before Bassett's critical sense was satisfied. Harwood was increasingly amused by the manifestations of Bassett's ironic humor. "I have never yet," ran the statement, "placed my own ambitions before the wishes of my party; and if, when the Democrats of Fraser County meet to choose a candidate for state senator, they are not disposed to renominate me for a seat which I have held for twelve years, I shall gladly resign to another and give my loyal support to the candidate of their choice." It was whispered that the Honorable Isaac Pettit would himself be a candidate for the nomination. The chattel mortgage scrolls in the office of the recorder of Fraser County indicated that his printing-press no longer owed allegiance to the Honorable Morton Bassett. Thatcher had treated Pettit generously, taking his unsecured note for the amount advanced to cleanse the "Fraser County Democrat" of the taint of Bassettism.

As they gathered in the convention hall many of the delegates were unable to adjust themselves to the fact that Bassett had not only failed of election as delegate from his own county, but that he was not even present as a spectator of the convention. The scene was set, the curtain had risen, but Hamlet came not to the platform before the castle. Many men sought Harwood and inquired in awed whispers as to Bassett's whereabouts, but he gave evasive answers. He knew, however, that Bassett had taken an early morning train for Waupegan, accompanied by Fitch, their purpose being to discuss in peace and quiet the legal proceeding begun to gain control of the "Courier." The few tried and trusted Bassett men who knew exactly Bassett's plans for the convention listened in silence to the hubbub occasioned by their chief's absence; silence was a distinguishing trait of Bassett's lieutenants. Among the uninitiated there were those who fondly believed that Bassett was killed, not scotched, and they said among themselves that the party and the state were well rid of him. Thatcher was to be reckoned with, but he was no worse than Bassett: with such cogitations they comforted themselves amid the noise and confusion. The old Bassett superstition held, however, with many: this was only another of the Boss's deep-laid schemes, and he would show his hand in due season and prove himself, as usual, master of the situation. Others imagined that Bassett was sulking, and these were not anxious to be the target of his wrath when he chose to emerge from his tent in full armor.

A young woman reporter, traversing the galleries to note the names and gowns of the ladies present, sought Mrs. Bassett for information as to her husband's whereabouts. When Mrs. Bassett hesitated discreetly, Marian rose promptly to the occasion:—

"Papa's gone fishing," she replied suavely.

This was not slow to reach the floor. "Papa's gone fishing" gained wide currency as the answer to the most interesting question of the day.

The Honorable Isaac Pettit, seated majestically with the Fraser County delegation, tested the acoustics of the hall at the first opportunity. While the chairman of the state central committee was endeavoring to present as the temporary chairman of the convention a patriot known as the "War Eagle of the Wabash," the gentleman from Fraser insisted upon recognition.

"Who is that preposterous fat man?" demanded Mrs. Owen, plying her palm-leaf fan vigorously.

"That's Mr. Pettit, from our town," said Mrs. Bassett. "He's an editor and lecturer."

"He's the man that defeated papa in our primaries," added Marian cheerfully. "He's awfully funny, everybody says, and I suppose his defeating papa was a joke. He's going to say something funny now."

"He doesn't need to," said Sylvia, not the least interested of the spectators. "They are laughing before he begins."

The chairman of the state committee feigned not to hear or see the delegate from Fraser, but Mr. Pettit continued to importune the chair amid much laughter and confusion. The chairman had hardened his heart, but the voice of the gentleman from Fraser alone rose above the tumult, and in a moment of comparative calm he addressed the chair unrecognized and unpermitted.

"I beg to call your attention, sir, to the presence in the gallery of many of the fair daughters of the old Hoosier State. (Applause.) They hover above us like guardian angels. They have come in the spirit that brought their sisters of old to watch true knights battle in the tourney. As a mark of respect to these ladies who do us so much honor, I ask the chair to request gentlemen to desist from smoking, and that the sergeant-at-arms be ordered to enforce the rule throughout our deliberations." (Long-continued applause.)

The state chairman was annoyed and showed his annoyance. He had been about to ingratiate himself with the ladies by making this request unprompted; he made it now, but the gentleman from Fraser sat down conscious that the renewed applause was his.

"Why don't they keep on smoking?" asked Mrs. Owen. "The hall couldn't be any fuller of smoke than it is now."

"If they would all put on their coats the room would be more beautiful," said Marian. "They always say the Republicans are much more gentlemanly than the Democrats."

"Hush, Marian; some one might hear you," Mrs. Bassett cautioned.

She did not understand her husband's absence; he rarely or never took her into his confidence in political matters. She had not known until that morning that he was not to be present at the convention. She did not relish the idea that he had been defeated in the primaries; in her mind defeat was inseparable from dishonor. The "War Eagle of the Wabash" was in excellent voice and he spoke for thirty minutes; his speech would have aroused greater enthusiasm if it had not been heard in many previous state conventions and on the hustings through many campaigns. Dan Voorhees had once expressed his admiration of that speech; and it was said that Tom Hendricks had revised the original manuscript the year he was chosen Vice-President. It was a safe speech, containing nothing that any good American might not applaud; it named practically every Democratic President except the twenty-second and twenty-fourth, whom it seemed the better part of valor just then to ignore. With slight emendations that same oration served admirably for high-school commencements, and it had a recognized cash value on the Chautauqua circuit. The peroration, closing with "Thou, too, sail on, O Ship of State!" was well calculated to bring strong men to their feet. The only complaint the War Eagle might have lodged against the Ship of State (in some imaginable admiralty court having jurisdiction of that barnacled old frigate) would have been for its oft-repeated rejection of his own piloting.

The permanent chairman now disclosed was a man of business, who thanked the convention briefly and went to work. By the time the committee on resolutions had presented the platform (on which Bassett and Harwood had collaborated) the convention enjoyed its first sensation as Thatcher appeared, moving slowly down the crowded main aisle to join the delegation of his county. His friends had planned a demonstration for his entrance, and in calling it an ovation the newspapers hardly magnified its apparent spontaneity and volume. The man who had undertaken the herculean task of driving Morton Bassett out of politics was entitled to consideration, and his appearance undoubtedly interrupted the business of the convention for fully five minutes. Thatcher bowed and waved his hand as he sat down.

The cordiality of his reception both pleased and embarrassed him. He fanned himself with his hat and feigned indifference to the admiration of his countrymen.

"Papa always gets more applause than that," Marian remarked to Sylvia. "I was at the state convention two years ago and father came in late, just as Mr. Thatcher did. They always come in late after all the stupid speeches have been made; they're surer to stir up a big rumpus that way."

Sylvia gave serious heed to these transactions of history. Her knowledge of politics was largely derived from lectures she had heard at college and from a diligent reading of newspapers. The report of the committee on resolutions—a succinct document to each of whose paragraphs the delegates rose in stormy approval—had just been read.

"I don't see how you can listen to such stuff," said Marian during a lull in the shouting. "It's only the platform and they don't mean a word of it. There's Colonel Ramsay, of Aurora,—the man with white hair who has just come on the stage. He had dinner at our house once and he's perfectly lovely. He's a beautiful speaker, but they won't let him speak any more because he was a gold bug—whatever that is. They say Colonel Ramsay has stopped gold-bugging now and wants to be governor. Sylvia, all these men that don't want to be United States Senator want to be governor. Isn't it funny? I don't see why silver money isn't just as good as any other kind, do you?"

"They told me at college," said Sylvia, "but it's rather complicated. Why didn't your father come to the convention even if he wasn't a delegate? He could have sat in the gallery; I suppose a lot of those men down there are not really delegates."

"Oh, that wouldn't be papa's way of doing things. I wish he had come, just on mama's account; she takes everything so hard. If papa ever did half the naughty things they say he does he'd be in the penitentiary good and tight. I should like to marry a public man; if I trusted a man enough to marry him I shouldn't be jarred a bit by what the newspapers said of him. I like politics; I don't know what it's all about, but I think the men are ever so interesting."

"I think so too," said Sylvia; "only I don't understand why they make so much noise and do so little. That platform they read a little bit ago seemed splendid. I read a lot of political platforms once in college—they were part of the course—and that was the best one I ever heard. It declared for laws against child labor, and I'm interested in that; and for juvenile courts and a lot of the new enlightened things. It was all fine."

"Do you think so? It sounded just like a trombone solo to me. Mr. Harwood was on that committee. Didn't you hear his name read? He's one of these high brows in politics, and father's going to push him forward so he can accomplish the noble things that interest him. Father told me Mr. Harwood would be a delegate to the convention. That's the reason I wanted to come. I hope he will make a speech; they say he's one of the best of the younger men. I heard him at the Opera House at Fraserville in the last campaign and he kept me awake, I can tell you. And funny! You wouldn't think he could be funny."

"Oh, I can see that he has humor—the lines around his mouth show that."

They had discussed the convention and its possibilities at Mrs. Owen's breakfast table and with the morning newspapers as their texts. Sylvia had gained the impression that Bassett had met a serious defeat in the choice of delegates, and she had been conscious that Mrs. Bassett was distressed by the newspaper accounts of it. Marian bubbled on elucidatively, answering all of Sylvia's questions.

"Don't you think that because papa isn't here he won't be heard from; I think I know papa better than that. He didn't think this convention would amount to enough for him to trouble with it. I told Aunt Sally not to talk much before mother about papa and politics; you will notice that Aunt Sally turned the subject several times this morning. That lawsuit Mr. Thatcher brought against papa and Aunt Sally made her pretty hot, but papa will fix that up all right. Papa always fixes up everything," she concluded admiringly.

It was in Sylvia's mind that she was witnessing a scene of the national drama and that these men beneath her in the noisy hall were engaged upon matters more or less remotely related to the business of self-government. She had derived at college a fair idea of the questions of the day, but the parliamentary mechanism and the thunder of the captains and the shouting gave to politics a new, concrete expression. These delegates, drawn from all occupations and conditions of life, were citizens of a republic, endeavoring to put into tangible form their ideas and preferences; and similar assemblies had, she knew, for years been meeting in every American commonwealth, enacting just such scenes as those that were passing under her eyes. Her gravity amused Mrs. Owen.

"Don't you worry, Sylvia; they are all kind to their families and most of 'em earn an honest living. I've attended lots of conventions of all parties and they're all about alike: there are more standing collars in a Republican convention and more whiskers when the Prohibitionists get together, but they're all mostly corn-fed and human. A few fellows with brains in their heads run all the rest."

"Look, Marian, Mr. Harwood seems to be getting ready to do something," said Sylvia. "I wonder what that paper is he has in his hand. He's been holding it all morning."

Harwood sat immediately under them. Several times men had passed notes to him, whereupon he had risen and searched out the writer to give his answer with a nod or shake of the head. When Thatcher appeared, Dan had waited for the hubbub to subside and then he left his seat to shake hands with Bassett's quondam ally. He held meanwhile a bit of notepaper the size of his hand, and scrutinized it carefully from time to time. It contained the precise programme of the convention as arranged by Bassett. Morton Bassett was on a train bound for the pastoral shades of Waupegan a hundred miles away, but the permanent chairman had in his vest pocket a copy of Bassett's scheme of exercises; even Thatcher's rapturous greeting had been ordered by Bassett. There had already been one slight slip; the eagerness of the delegates to proceed to the selection of the state ticket had sent matters forward for a moment beyond the chairman's control. A delegate with a weak voice had gained recognition for the laudable purpose of suggesting a limitation upon nominating speeches; the permanent chairman had mistaken him for another gentleman for whom he was prepared, and he hastened to correct his blunder. He seized the gavel and began pounding vigorously and the man with the weak voice never again caught his eye.

In the middle of the hall a delegate now drew attention to himself by rising upon a chair; he held a piece of paper in his hand and waved it; and the chairman promptly took cognizance of him. The chairman referred to him as the gentleman from Pulaski, but he might have been the gentleman from Vallombrosa for all that any one cared. The convention was annoyed that a gentleman from Pulaski County should have dared to flourish manuscript when there were innumerable orators present fully prepared to speak extempore on any subject. For all that any one knew the gentleman from Pulaski might be primed with a speech on the chinch bug or the Jewish kritarchy; a man with a sheet of paper in his hand was a formidable person, if not indeed a foe of mankind, and he was certainly not to be countenaced or encouraged in a hot hall on a day of June. Yet all other human beings save the gentleman from Pulaski were as nothing, it seemed, to the chairman. The Tallest Delegate, around whose lean form a frock coat hung like a fold of night, and who flung back from a white brow an immense quantity of raven hair, sought to relieve the convention of the sight and sound of the person from Pulaski. The Tallest Delegate was called smartly to order; he rebelled, but when threatened with the sergeant-at-arms subsided amid jeers. The gentleman from Pulaski was indulged to the fullest extent by the chairman, to whom it had occurred suddenly that the aisles must be cleared. The aisles were cleared and delegates were obliged to find their seats before the unknown gentleman from Pulaski was allowed to proceed. Even the War Eagle had received no such consideration. The gentleman from Pulaski calmly waited for a completer silence than the day had known. Ten men in the hall knew what was coming—not more; Miss Rose Farrell had typed ten copies of the memorandum which Harwood held in his hand!

The gentleman from Pulaski did not after all refer to his manuscript; he spoke in a high, penetrating voice that reached the farthest corner of the hall, reciting from memory:—

"Be it resolved by this convention that, whereas two years hence it will be the privilege and duty of the Indiana Democracy to elect a United States Senator to fill the seat now occupied by a Republican, we, the delegates here assembled, do hereby pledge the party's support for the office of Senator in Congress to the Honorable Edward G. Thatcher, of Marion County."

There was a moment's awed calm before the storm broke; Thatcher rose in his seat to look at the strange gentleman from Pulaski who had thus flung his name into the arena. Thatcher men rose and clamored blindly for recognition, without the faintest idea of what they should do if haply the cold eye of the chairman fell upon them. The galleries joined in the uproar; the band began to play "On the Banks of the Wabash" and was with difficulty stopped; a few voices cried "Bassett," but cries of "Thatcher" rose in a mighty roar and drowned them. The chairman hammered monotonously for order; Mr. Daniel Harwood might have been seen to thrust his memorandum into his trousers pocket; he bent forward in his seat with his eye upon the chairman. The Honorable Isaac Pettit had been for a moment nonplussed; he was unacquainted with the gentleman from Pulaski, nor had he known that an effort was to be made to commit the convention to Thatcher's candidacy; still the tone of the resolution was friendly. Thatcher, rising to his feet, was noisily cheered; his face was red and his manner betokened anger; but after glancing helplessly over the hall he sank into his seat. The chairman thumped with his gavel; it seemed for a moment that he had lost control of the convention; and now the Honorable Isaac Pettit was observed demanding to be heard. The chairman lifted his hand and the noise died away. It lay in his power to ignore the resolution wholly or to rule it out of order; the chairman was apparently in no haste to do anything.

"Good old Uncle Ike," howled some one encouragingly, and there was laughter and applause. With superb dignity Mr. Pettit appealed for silence with gestures that expressed self-depreciation, humility, and latent power in one who would, in due course, explain everything. A group of delegates in the rear began chanting stridently, "Order! Order!" and it was flung back antiphonally from a dozen other delegations.

Mr. Harwood became active and climbed upon his chair. Gentlemen in every part of the hall seemed at once anxious to speak, but the chairman was apparently oblivious of all but the delegate from Marion. The delegate from Marion, like the mysterious person from Pulaski, was a stranger to state conventions. The ladies were at once interested in the young gentleman with the red carnation in his buttonhole—a trim young fellow, in a blue serge suit, with a blue four-in-hand knotted under a white winged collar. As he waited with his eye on the chairman he put his hand to his head and smoothed his hair.

"Is Daniel going to speak?" asked Mrs. Owen. "He ought to have asked me if he's going to back Edward Thatcher for Senator."

"I always think his cowlick's so funny. He's certainly the cool one," said Marian.

"I don't know what they're talking about a Senator for," said Mrs. Bassett. "It's very unusual. If I'd known they were going to talk about that I shouldn't have come. There's sure to be a row."

The chairman seemed anxious that the delegate from Marion should be honored with the same close attention that had been secured for the stranger from Pulaski.

"I hope he'll wait till they all sit down," said Sylvia; "I want to hear him speak."

"You'll hear him, all right," said Marian. "You know at Yale they called him 'Foghorn' Harwood, and they put him in front to lead the cheering at all the big games."

Apparently something was expected of Mr. Harwood of Marion. Thatcher had left his seat and was moving toward the corridors to find his lieutenants. Half a dozen men accosted him as he moved through the aisle, but he shook them off angrily. An effort to start another demonstration in his honor was not wholly fruitless. It resulted at least in a good deal of confusion of which the chair was briefly tolerant; then he resumed his pounding, while Harwood stood stubbornly on his chair.

The Tallest Delegate, known to be a recent convert to Thatcher, was thoroughly aroused, and advanced toward the platform shouting; but the chairman leveled his gavel at him and bade him sit down. The moment was critical; the veriest tyro felt the storm-spirit brooding over the hall.

The voice of the chairman was now audible.

"The chair recognizes the delegate from Marion."

"Out of order! What's his name!" howled many voices.

The chairman graciously availed himself of the opportunity to announce the name of the gentleman he had recognized.

"Mr. Harwood, of Marion, has the floor. The convention will be in order. The gentleman will proceed."

"Mr. Chairman, I rise to a point of order."

Dan's voice rose sonorously; the convention was relieved to find that the gentleman in blue serge could be heard; he was audible even to Mr. Thatcher's excited counsellors in the corridors.

"The delegate will kindly state his point of order."

The chairman was quietly courteous. His right hand rested on his gavel, he thrust his left into the side pocket of his long alpaca coat. He was an old and tried hand in the chair, and his own deep absorption in the remarks of Mr. Harwood communicated itself to the delegates.

Dan uttered rapidly the speech he had committed to memory for this occasion a week earlier. Every sentence had been carefully pondered; both Bassett and Atwill had blue penciled it until it expressed concisely and pointedly exactly what Bassett wished to be said at this point in the convention's proceedings. Interruptions, of applause or derision, were to be reckoned with; but the speaker did not once drop his voice or pause long enough for any one to drive in a wedge of protest. He might have been swamped by an uprising of the whole convention, but strange to say the convention was intent upon hearing him. Once the horde of candidates and distinguished visitors on the platform had been won to attention, Harwood turned slowly until he faced the greater crowd behind him. Several times he lifted his right hand and struck out with it, shaking his head with the vigor of his utterance. ("His voice," said the "Advertiser's" report, "rumbles and bangs like a bowling-alley on Saturday night. There was a big bump every time a sentence rumbled down the hall and struck the rear wall of the building.")

"Sir, I make the obvious point of order that there are no vacancies to fill in the office of United States Senator, and that it does not lie within the province of the delegates chosen to this convention to pledge the party to any man. I do not question the motive of the delegate from Pulaski County, who is my personal friend; and I am animated by no feelings of animosity in demanding that the convention proceed to the discharge of its obligations without touching upon matters clearly beyond its powers. I confidently hope and sincerely believe that our party in Indiana is soon to receive a new commission of trust and confidence from the people of the old Hoosier State. But our immediate business is the choice of a ticket behind which the Hoosier Democracy will move on to victory in November like an army with banners. (Cheers.) There have been intimations in the camp of our enemy that the party is threatened with schism and menaced by factional wars; but I declare my conviction that the party is more harmonious and more truly devoted to high ideals to-day than at any time since the grand old name of Democrat became potent upon Hoosier soil. And what have we to do with leaders? Men come and men go, but principles alone are eternal and live forever. The great task of our party must be to bring the government back to the people. (Scattering applause.) But the choice of an invulnerable state ticket at this convention is our business and our only business. As for Indiana's two seats in the national Senate which we shall soon wrest from our adversaries, in due season we shall fill them with tried men and true. Sir, let us remember that whosoever maketh himself a king speaketh against Caesar. Stop, Look, Listen!"

Hardly a man in the hall so dull that this did not penetrate! Dan had given to his last words a weird, mournful intonation whose effect was startling. He jumped lightly to the floor and was in his seat before the deep boom of his voice had ceased reverberating. Then instantly it seemed that the seventeen hundred delegates had been multiplied by ten, and that every man had become a raving lunatic. This was Bassett's defiance—Bassett, who had gone fishing, but not before planting this mine for the confusion of Thatcher. A hundred men who had already committed themselves to Thatcher sought to rescue their new leader; they rose upon chairs and demanded to be heard. "Stop, Look, Listen" had suggested the idea of a locomotive bearing down upon a dangerous crossing, and Bassett's men began to whistle. The whistling increased in volume until it drowned the shouts, the cheers, and the laughter. Ladies in the galleries stopped their ears while the whistling convention earned its name. It now occurred to the chairman, who had wasted no energy in futile efforts to stay the storm, that he had a duty to perform. Even to his practiced hand the restoration of order was not easy; but by dint of much bawling and pounding he subdued the uproar. Then after impressive deliberation he said:—

"A point of order has been raised against the resolution offered by the gentleman from Pulaski. It is the ruling of the chair that the point is well taken. The resolution is out of order."

This was greeted with great applause; but the chair checked it promptly. The ten gentlemen who had copies of the Bassett programme in their pockets were not surprised by the decision. Thatcher stood at a side door and two of his men were pushing their way through the aisles to reach Pettit; for the Honorable Isaac Pettit was on his feet demanding recognition while Thatcher's delegates shouted to him to sit down; humiliation must go no farther, and if the Fraser County editor did not realize that his new chief was the victim of a vile trick, the gentleman from Fraser must be throttled, if necessary, to prevent a further affront to Thatcher's dignity. Thatcher was purple with rage; it was enough to have been made the plaything of an unscrupulous enemy once, without having one's ambitions repeatedly kicked up and down a convention hall.

The chairman, fully rehearsed in his part, showed a malevolent disposition to continue toward the friends of Thatcher an attitude at once benevolent and just. So many were demanding recognition amid cat-calling and whistling that the fairest and least partial of presiding officers might well have hesitated before singling out one gentleman when so many were eagerly, even furiously, desirous of enlightening the convention. But the presiding officer was obeying the orders communicated to him by a gentleman who was even at this moment skimming across the cool waters of Lake Waupegan. It would more fully have satisfied the chairman's sense of humor to have recognized the Honorable Isaac Pettit and have suffered an appeal from the ruling of the chair, which presumably the editor wished to demand. By this means the weakness of Thatcher might have expressed itself in figures that would have deepened Thatcher's abasement in the eyes of his fellow partisans; but this idea had been discussed with Bassett, who had sharply vetoed it, and the chairman was not a man lightly to disobey orders even to make a Hoosier holiday. He failed to see the editor of the "Fraser County Democrat" and peremptorily closed the incident. There was no mistaking his temper as he announced: —

"The chair announces that the next business in order is the call of the roll of counties for nominations for the office of secretary of state. What is the pleasure of the convention?"

Colonel Ramsay had repaired to the gallery to enjoy the proceedings with Mrs. Bassett's party. In spite of his support of the Palmer and Buckner ticket (how long ago that seems!), the Colonel had never lost touch with the main body of his party, and he carried several Indiana counties in his pocket. His relations with Bassett had never been in the least intimate, though always outwardly cordial, and there were those who looked to him to eliminate the Fraser County chief from politics. He was quite as rich as Bassett, and a successful lawyer, who had become a colonel by grace of a staff appointment in the Spanish War. He had a weakness for the poets, and his speeches were informed with that grace and sentiment which, we are fond of saying, is peculiar to Southern oratory. The Colonel, at all fitting occasions in our commonwealth, responded to "the ladies" in tender and moving phrases. He was a bachelor, and the ladies in the gallery saw in him their true champion.

"Please tell *us*—we don't understand a bit of it," pleaded Marian— "what it's all about, Colonel Ramsay."

"Oh, it's just a little joke of your father's; nothing funnier ever happened in a state convention." Colonel Ramsay grinned. "The key to the situation is right there: that Pulaski County delegate offered his resolution just to make trouble; it was a fake resolution. Of course the chairman is in the joke. This young fellow down here—yes, Harwood—made his speech to add to the gayety of nations. He had no right to make it, of course, but the word had been passed along the line to let him go through. Amazing vocal powers, that boy,—you couldn't have stopped him!"

Sylvia was aware that Colonel Ramsay's explanation had not pleased Mrs. Bassett; but Mrs. Owen evinced no feeling. Marian was enjoying Colonel Ramsay's praise of her father's adroitness. Near Sylvia were other women who had much at stake in the result of the convention. The wife of a candidate for secretary of state had invited herself to a seat beside Mrs. Bassett; the wife of a Congressman who wished to be governor, sat near, publishing to the world her intimate acquaintance with Morton Bassett's family. The appearance and conduct of these women during the day interested Sylvia almost as much as the incidents occurring on the floor; it was a new idea that politics had a bearing upon the domestic life of the men who engaged in the eternal contest for place and power. The convention as a spectacle was immensely diverting, but she had her misgivings about it as a transaction in history. Colonel Ramsay asked her politics and she confessed that she had none. She had inherited Republican prejudices from her grandfather, and most of the girls she had known in college were of Republican antecedents; but she liked to call herself an independent.

"You'd better not be a Democrat, Sylvia," Mrs. Owen warned her. "I suffered a good deal in my husband's lifetime from being one. There are still people in this town who think a Democrat's the same as a Rebel or a Copperhead. It ain't hardly respectable yet, being a Democrat, and if they don't all of 'em shut up about the 'fathers' and the Constitution, I'm going to move to Mexico where it's all run by niggers."

Sylvia had singled out several figures in the drama enacting below for special attention. The chairman had interested her by reason of his attitude of scrupulous fairness, in which she now saw the transparent irony; the banalities of the temporary chairman had touched her humor;

she watched him for the rest of the morning with a kind of awe that any one could he so dull, so timorous, and yet be chosen to address nearly two thousand American citizens on an occasion of importance. She was unable to reconcile Thatcher's bald head, ruddy neck, and heavy shoulders with Marian's description of the rich man's son, who dreamed of heroes and played at carpentry. Dan's speech had not been without its thrill for her, and she now realized its significance. It had been a part of a trick, and in spite of herself she could not share the admiration Colonel Ramsay was expressing for Harwood's share in it. He was immeasurably superior to the majority of those about him in the crowded hall; he was a man of education, a college man, and she had just experienced in her own life that consecration, as by an apostolic laying-on of hands, by which a college confers its honors and imposes its obligations upon those who have enjoyed its ministry. Yet Harwood, who had not struck her as weak or frivolous, had lent himself to-day to a bit of cheap claptrap merely to humble one man for the glorification of another. Bassett she had sincerely liked in their one meeting at Waupegan; and yet this was of his plotting and Harwood was his mouthpiece and tool. It did not seem fair to take advantage of such supreme stupidity as Thatcher's supporters had manifested. Her disappointment in Harwood—and it was quite that—was part of her general disappointment in the methods by which men transacted the serious business of governing themselves.

Harwood was conscious that he was one of the chief figures in the convention; every one knew him now; he was called here and there on the floor, by men anxious to impress themselves upon Bassett's authorized spokesman. It is a fine thing at twenty-seven to find the doors of opportunity flung wide—and had he not crossed the threshold and passed within the portal? He was Bassett's man; every one knew that now; but why should he not be Bassett's man? He would go higher and farther than Bassett: Bassett had merely supplied the ladder on which he would climb. He was happier than he had ever been before in his life; he had experienced the intoxication of applause, and he was not averse to the glances of the women in the gallery above him.

The nomination of candidates now went forward rather tamely, though relieved by occasional sharp contests. The ten gentlemen who had been favored with copies of the Bassett programme were not surprised that so many of Thatcher's friends were nominated; they themselves voted for most of them. It seemed remarkable to the uninitiated that Bassett should have slapped Thatcher and then have allowed him to score in the choice of the ticket. The "Advertiser," anxious to show Bassett as strong and malignant as possible, expressed the opinion that the Fraserville boss had not after all appreciated the full force of the Thatcher movement.

On the veranda of his Waupegan cottage Bassett and Fitch enjoyed the wholesome airs of the country. Late in the afternoon the fussy little steamer that traversed the lake paused at the Bassett dock to deliver a telegram, which Bassett read without emotion. He passed the yellow slip of paper to Fitch, who read it and handed it back.

"Harwood's a clever fellow; but you oughtn't to push him into politics. He's better than that."

"I suppose he is," said Bassett; "but I need him."

CHAPTER XX
INTERVIEWS IN TWO KEYS

Mrs. Bassett remained in bed the day following the convention, less exhausted by the scenes she had witnessed than appalled by their interpretation in the newspapers. The reappearance of Sylvia Garrison had revived the apprehensions which the girl's visit to Waupegan four years earlier had awakened. She had hoped that Sylvia's long absences might have operated to diminish Mrs. Owen's interest and she had managed in one way and another to keep them apart during the college holidays, but the death of Professor Kelton had evidently thrown Sylvia back upon Mrs. Owen. Jealous fears danced blackly in Mrs. Bassett's tired brain.

At a season when she was always busiest with her farms Mrs. Owen had made a long journey to see Sylvia graduated; and here was the girl established on the most intimate terms in the Delaware Street house, no doubt for the remainder of her life. Mrs. Owen did not lightly or often change her plans; but she had abandoned her project of spending the summer at the lake to accommodate herself to the convenience of her protégée. Mrs. Bassett's ill-health was by no means a matter of illusion; she was not well and her sojourns in sanatoriums had served to alienate her in a measure from her family. Marian had grown to womanhood without realizing her mother's ideals. She had hoped to make a very different person of her daughter, and Sylvia's reappearance intensified her sense of defeat. Even in the retrospect she saw no reason why Marian might not have pursued the course that Sylvia had followed; in her confused annoyances and agitations she was bitter not only against Marian but against Marian's father. The time had come when she must take a stand against his further dallyings in politics.

Her day at the convention hall had yielded only the most disagreeable impressions. Such incidents as had not eluded her own understanding on the spot had been freely rendered by the newspapers. It was all sordid and gross—not at all in keeping with her first experience of politics, gained in her girlhood, when her father had stood high in the councils of the nation, winning coveted positions without the support of such allies as she had seen cheering her husband's triumph on the floor of the convention. There had strayed into her hands an envelope of newspaper clippings from an agency that wished to supply her, as, its circular announced, it supplied the wives of many other prominent Americans, with newspaper comments on their husbands. As a bait for securing a client these examples of what the American press was saying of Morton Bassett were decidedly ill-chosen. The "Stop, Look, Listen" editorial had suggested to many influential journals a re-indictment of bossism with the Bassett-Thatcher imbroglio as text. It was disenchanting to find one's husband enrolled in a list of political reprobates whose activities in so many states were a menace to public safety. Her father had served with distinction and honor this same commonwealth that her husband was debasing; he had been a statesman, not a politician, not a boss. Blackford Singleton had belonged to the coterie that included such men as Hoar and Evarts, Thurman and Bayard; neither her imagination nor her affection could bridge the chasm that separated men of their type from her husband, who, in middle life, was content with a seat in the state legislature and busied himself with wars upon petty rivals. Such reflections as these did not contribute to her peace of mind.

She was alone in her room at Mrs. Owen's when Bassett appeared, late in the afternoon. Mrs. Owen was downtown on business matters; Marian, after exhausting all her devices for making her mother comfortable, had flown in search of acquaintances; and Sylvia had that day taken up her work in the normal school. Left to herself for the greater part of the warm afternoon, Mrs. Bassett had indulged luxuriously in forebodings. She had not expected her husband, and his unannounced entrance startled her.

"Well," she remarked drearily, "so you have come back to face it, have you?"

"I'm undoubtedly back, Hallie," he answered, with an effort at lightness, crossing to the bedside and taking her hand.

He had rarely discussed his political plans with her, but he realized that the rupture with Thatcher must naturally have distressed her; and there was also Thatcher's lawsuit involving her aunt, which had disagreeable possibilities.

"I'm sorry your name got into the papers, Hallie. I didn't want you to go to the convention, but of course I knew you went to please Marian. Where is Marian?"

"Oh, she's off somewhere. I couldn't expect her to stay here in this hot room all day."

The room was not uncomfortable; but it seemed wiser not to debate questions of temperature. He found a chair and sat down beside her.

"You mustn't worry about the newspapers, Hallie; they always make the worst of everything. The temptation to distort facts to make a good story is strong; I have seen it in my connection with the 'Courier.' It's lamentable, but you can't correct it in a day. I'm pretty well hardened to it myself, but I'm sorry you have let these attacks on me annoy you. The only thing to do is to ignore them. What's that you have there?"

She still clasped the envelope of clippings and thrust it at him accusingly. The calmness of his inspection irritated her and she broke out sharply:—

"I shouldn't think a man with a wife and family would lay himself open to such attacks in all the newspapers in the country. Those papers call you another such political boss as Quay and Gorman. There's nothing they don't say about you."

"Well, Hallie, they've been saying it for some time; they will go on saying it probably not only about me but about every other man who won't be dictated to by impractical reformers and pharisaical newspapers. But I must confess that this is rather hard luck!" He held up two of the cuttings. "I've undertaken to do just what papers like the New York 'Evening Post' and the Springfield 'Republican' are forever begging somebody with courage to do—I've been trying to drive a rascal out of politics. I'm glad of this chance to talk to you about Thatcher. He and I were friends for years, as you know."

"I never understood how you could tolerate that man; he's so coarse and vulgar that his wife stays abroad to keep her daughters away from him."

"Well, that's not my affair. I have had all I want of him. There's nothing mysterious about my breaking with him; he got it into his head that he's a bigger man in this state than I am. I have known for several years that he intended to get rid of me as soon as he felt he could do it safely, and be ready to capture the senatorship when he saw that our party was in shape to win again. I've always distrusted him, and I've always kept an eye on him. When he came into Fraser County and stooped low enough to buy old Ike Pettit, I thought it time to strike. You read a lot about courage in politics in such newspapers as these that have been philosophizing about me at long range. Well, I'm not going to brag about myself, but it required some courage on my part to take the initiative and read the riot act to Thatcher. I've done what men are sometimes praised for doing; but I don't want praise; I only want to be judged fairly. I've always avoided bringing business or politics home; I've always had an idea that when a man goes home he ought to close the door on everything but the interests the home has for him. I may have been wrong about that; and I'm very sorry that you have been troubled— sincerely sorry. But you may as well know the truth now, which is that

Thatcher is out of it altogether. You know enough of him to understand that he's not a man to trust with power, and I've done the state and my party a service in turning him out of doors."

He had spoken quietly and earnestly, and his words had not been without their effect. He had never been harsh with her or the children; his manner to-day was kind and considerate. He had to an extent measurably rehabilitated himself as a heroic public character, a man of honor and a husband to be proud of; but she had not spent a sleepless night and a gray day without fortifying herself against him. All day her eyes had been fixed upon an abandoned squirrel box in the crotch of an elm outside her window; it had become the repository of her thoughts, the habitation of her sorrows. She turned her head slightly so that her eyes might rest upon this tabernacle of fear and illusion, and renewed the assault refreshed.

"How is it, then, that newspapers away off in New York and Massachusetts speak of you in this outrageous fashion? They're so far away that it seems strange they speak of you at all."

He laughed with relief, feeling that the question marked a retreat toward weaker fortifications.

"You're not very complimentary, are you, Hallie? They must think me of some importance or they'd let me alone. I wouldn't subscribe to that clipping bureau if you fear we're too much in the limelight. I've been taking the service of one of these bureaus for several years, and I read every line the papers print about me. It's part of the regular routine in my office to paste them in scrapbooks."

"I shouldn't think you could burn them fast enough; what if the children should see them some day!"

"Well, you may be surprised to know that they're not all so bitter. Once in a long while I get a kind word. That bill I got through the assembly separating hardened criminals from those susceptible of reform—the indeterminate sentence law—was praised by penologists all over the country. It's all in the day's work; sometimes you're patted on the back and the next time they kick you down stairs. Without political influence you have no chance to help the good causes or defeat the bad schemes."

"Yes, I suppose that is true," she murmured weakly.

He had successfully met and turned her attack and the worst had passed; but he expected her to make some reference to Thatcher's lawsuit for the control of the "Courier" and he was not disappointed. Marian, who had a genius for collecting disagreeable information and a dramatic instinct for using it effectively, had apprised her of it. This hazarding of Mrs. Owen's favor became now the gravamen of his offense, the culmination of all his offenses. She demanded to know why he had secretly borrowed money of her aunt, when from the time of their marriage it had been understood that they should never do so. Her own fortune he had been free to use as he liked; she demanded to know why he had not taken her own money; but to ask financial favors of Aunt Sally, and this, too, without consultation, was beyond her comprehension. She was on secure ground here; he had always shared her feeling that Mrs. Owen required cautious handling, but he had nevertheless violated their compact. She rushed breathlessly and with sobs through her recital.

"And you haven't seen Aunt Sally since; you have made no effort to make it right with her!"

"As to that, Hallie, I haven't had a chance to see her; she's only been home two days and I've been away myself since. Now that I'm in her house I shall explain it all to her before I leave."

"But you haven't explained to me why you did it! It seems to me that I have a right to know how you came to do such a thing."

"Well, then, the fact is that newspapers these days are not cheap and the 'Courier' cost a lot of money. I've been pretty well tied up in telephone and other investments of late; and I have never taken advantage of my ownership of the Bassett Bank to use its money except within my reasonable credit as it would be estimated by any one else. Your own funds I have kept invested conservatively in gilt-edged securities wholly removed from speculative influences. I knew that if I didn't get the newspaper Thatcher would, so I made every possible turn to go in with him. I was fifty thousand dollars shy of what I needed to pay for my half, and after I had raked up all the money I could safely, I asked Aunt Sally if she would lend me that sum with all my stock as security."

"Fifty thousand dollars, Morton! You borrowed that much money of her!"

Her satisfaction in learning that Mrs. Owen commanded so large a sum was crushed beneath his stupendous error in having gone to her for money at all.

"Oh, she didn't lend it to me, after all, Hallie; she refused to do so; but she allowed me to buy enough shares for her to make up my quota. Thatcher and I bought at eighty cents on the dollar and she paid the same. She has her shares and it's a good investment, and she knows it. If she hadn't insisted on having the shares in her own name, Thatcher would never have known it."

He turned uneasily in his chair, and she was keenly alert at this sign of discomfiture, and not above taking advantage of it.

"So without her you are at Thatcher's mercy, are you? I haven't spoken to her about this and she hasn't said anything to me; but Marian with her usual heedlessness mentioned it, and it was clear that Aunt Sally was very angry."

"What did she say?" asked Bassett anxiously.

"She didn't say anything, but she shut her jaw tight and changed the subject. It was what she didn't say! You'd better think well before you broach the subject to her."

"I've been thinking about it. If I take her stock at par she ought to be satisfied. I'll pay more if it's necessary. And of course I'll make every effort to restore good feeling. I think I understand her. I'll take care of this, but you must stay out of it, and tell Marian to keep quiet."

"Well, Aunt Sally and Thatcher are friends. He rather amuses her, with his horse-racing, and drinking and gambling. That kind of thing doesn't seem so bad to her. She's so used to dealing with men that she makes allowances for them."

"Then," he said quickly, with a smile, eager to escape through any loophole, "maybe she will make some allowances for me! For the purpose of allaying her anger we'll assume that I'm as wicked as Thatcher."

"Well," she answered, gathering her strength for a final assault, "it doesn't look as simple as that to me. Your first mistake was in getting her into any of your businesses and the second was in making it possible for Thatcher to annoy her by all this ugly publicity of a lawsuit. And what do you think has happened on top of all this—*that girl is here*—here under this very roof!"

"That girl—what girl?"

His opacity incensed her; she had been brooding over her aunt's renewed interest in Sylvia Garrison all day and his dull ignorance was the last straw upon nerves screwed to the breaking-point. She sat up in bed and drew her dressing-gown about her as though it were the vesture of despair.

"That Garrison girl! She's not only back here, but from all appearances she's going to stay! Aunt Sally's infatuated with her. When the girl's grandfather died, Aunt Sally did everything for her—went over to Montgomery to take charge of the funeral, and then went back to Wellesley to see the girl graduate. And now she's giving up her plan of going to Waupegan for the summer to stay here in all the heat with a girl who hasn't the slightest claim on her. When the Keltons visited Waupegan four years ago I saw this coming. I wanted Marian to go to college and tried to get you interested in the plan because that was what first caught Aunt Sally's fancy—Sylvia's cleverness, and this college idea. But you wouldn't do anything about Marian, and now she's thrown away her chances, and here's this stranger graduating with honors and Aunt Sally going down there to see it! Aunt Sally's going to make a companion of her, and you can't tell what will happen! I'd like to know what you can say to your children when all Aunt Sally's money, that should rightly go to them, goes to a girl she's picked up out of nowhere. This is what your politics has got us into, Morton Bassett!"

The soberness to which this brought him at last satisfied her. She had freely expressed the anxiety caused by Sylvia's first appearance on the domestic horizon, but for a year or two, in his wife's absences in pursuit of health, he had heard little of her apprehensions. Marian's own disinclination for a college career had, from the beginning, seemed to him to interpose an insurmountable barrier to parental guidance in that direction. His wife's attitude in these new circumstances of the return of her aunt's protégée struck him as wholly unjustified and unreasonable.

"You're not quite yourself when you talk that way, Hallie. Professor Kelton was one of Aunt Sally's oldest friends; old people have a habit of going back to the friends of their youth; there's nothing strange in it. And this being true, nothing could have been more natural than for Aunt Sally to help the girl in her trouble, even to the extent of seeing her graduated. It was just like Aunt Sally," he continued, warming to his subject, "who's one of the stanchest friends anybody could have. Aunt Sally's devoted to you and your children; it's ungenerous to her to assume that a young woman she hardly knows is supplanting you or Marian. This newspaper notoriety I'm getting has troubled you and I'm sorry for it; but I can't let you entertain this delusion that your aunt's kindness to the granddaughter of one of her old friends means that Aunt Sally has ceased to care for you, or lost her regard for Marian and Blackford. If you think of it seriously for a moment you'll see how foolish it is to harbor any jealousy of Miss Garrison. Come! Cheer up and forget it. If Aunt Sally got an inkling of this you may be sure that *would* displease her. You say the girl is here in the house?"

"She's not only here, but she's here to stay! She's going to intrench herself here!"

She sent him to the chiffonier to find a fresh handkerchief. He watched her helplessly for a moment as she dried her eyes. Then he took her hands and bent over her.

"Won't you try to see things a little brighter? It's all just because you got too tired yesterday. You oughtn't to have gone to the convention; and I didn't know you were going or I should have forbidden it."

"Well, Marian wanted to go; and we were coming to town anyhow. And besides, Aunt Sally had taken it into her head to go, too. She wanted this Garrison girl to see a political convention; I suppose that was the real reason."

He laughed, gazing down into her tearful face, in which resentment lingered waveringly, as in the faces of children persuaded against their will and parting reluctantly with the solace of tears.

"You must get up for dinner, Hallie. Your doctors have always insisted that you needed variety and change; and to-morrow we'll take you up to the lake out of this heat. We have a good deal to be grateful for, after all, Hallie. You haven't any right to feel disappointed in Marian: she's the nicest girl in the state, and the prettiest girl you'll find anywhere. We ought to be glad she's so high-spirited and handsome and clever. College never was for her; she certainly was never for college! I talked that over with Miss Waring a number of times. And I don't believe Aunt Sally thinks less of Marian because she isn't a better scholar. Only a small per cent of women go to college, and I'm not sure it's a good thing. I'm even a little doubtful about sending Blackford to college; this education business is overdone, and the sooner a boy gets into harness the better."

Her deep sigh implied that he might do as he liked with his son, now that she had so completely failed with her daughter.

"Aunt Sally is very much interested in Mr. Harwood. She has put Sylvia's affairs in his hands. Could it be possible—"

He groped for her unexpressed meaning, and seeing that he had not grasped it she clarified it to his masculine intelligence.

"If there are two persons she is interested in, and they understand each other, it's all so much more formidable." And then, seeing that this also was too subtle, she put it flatly: "What if Harwood should marry Sylvia!"

"Well, that *is* borrowing trouble!" he cried impatiently. "Aunt Sally is interested in a great many young people. She is very fond of Allen Thatcher. And Allen seems to find Marian's society agreeable, more so, I fancy, than Harwood does;—why not speculate along that line? It's as plausible as the other."

"Oh, that boy! That's something we must guard against, Morton; that is quite impossible."

"I dare say it is," he replied. "But not more unlikely than that Harwood will marry this Sylvia who worries you so unnecessarily."

"Marian is going to marry somebody, some day, and that's on my mind a great deal. You have got to give more thought to family matters. It's right for Marian to marry, and I think a girl of her tastes should settle early, but we must guard her from mistakes. I've had that on my conscience several years."

"Of course, Hallie; and I've not been unmindful of it."

"And if Aunt Sally is interested in young Harwood and you think well of him yourself—but of course I don't favor him for Marian. I should like Marian to marry into a family of some standing."

"Well, we'll see to it that she does; we want our daughter to be happy— we must do the best we can for our children," he concluded largely.

She promised to appear at the dinner table, and he went down with some idea of seeing Mrs. Owen at once, to assure her of his honorable intentions toward her in the "Courier" matter; he wanted to relieve his own fears as well as his wife's as to the mischief that had been wrought by Thatcher's suit.

In the hall below he met Sylvia, just back from her first day at the normal school. The maid had admitted her, and she was slipping her parasol into the rack as he came downstairs. She heard his step and turned toward him, a slender, dark young woman in black. In the dim hall she did not at once recognize him, and he spoke first.

"Good-afternoon, Miss Garrison! I am Mr. Bassett; I believe I introduced myself to you at Waupegan—and that seems a long time ago."

"I remember very well, Mr. Bassett," Sylvia replied, and they shook hands. "You found me in my dream corner by the lake and walked to Mrs. Owen's with me. I remember our meeting perfectly."

He stood with his hand on the newel regarding her intently. She was entirely at ease, a young woman without awkwardness or embarrassment. She had disposed of their previous meeting lightly, as though such fortuitous incidents had not been lacking in her life. Her mourning hat cast a shadow upon her face, but he had been conscious of the friendliness of her smile. Her dark eyes had inspected him swiftly; he was vaguely aware of a feeling that he wanted to impress her favorably.

"The maid said Mrs. Owen and Marian are still out. I hope Mrs. Bassett is better. I wonder if I can do anything for her."

"No, thank you; she's quite comfortable and will be down for dinner."

"I'm glad to hear that; suppose we find seats here."

She walked before him into the parlor and threw back the curtains the better to admit the air. He watched her attentively, noting the ease and grace of her movements, and took the chair she indicated.

"It's very nice to see Mrs. Bassett and Marian again; they were so good to me that summer at Waupegan; I have carried the pleasantest memories of that visit ever since. It seems a long time ago and it is nearly four years, isn't it."

"Four this summer, I think. I remember, because I had been to Colorado, and that whole year was pretty full for me. But all these years have been busy ones for you, too, I hear. Your grandfather's death must have been a great shock to you. I knew him only by reputation, but it was a reputation to be proud of."

"Yes; Grandfather Kelton had been everything to me."

"It was too bad he couldn't have lived to see you through college; he must have taken a great interest in your work there, through his own training and scholarship."

"It was what he wanted me to do, and I wish he could have known how I value it. He was the best of men, the kindest and noblest; and he was a wonderful scholar. He had the habit of thoroughness."

"That, I suppose, was partly due to the discipline of the Navy. I fancy that a man trained in habits of exactness gets into the way of keeping his mind ship-shape—no loose ends around anywhere."

She smiled at this, and regarded him with rather more attention, as though his remark had given her a new impression of him which her eyes wished to verify.

"They tell me you expect to teach in the city schools; that has always seemed to me the hardest kind of work. I should think you would prefer a college position;—there would be less drudgery, and better social opportunities."

"Every one warns me that it's hard work, but I don't believe it can be so terrible. Somebody has to do it. Of course college positions are more dignified and likely to be better paid."

He started to speak and hesitated.

"Well," she laughed. "You were going to add your warning, weren't you! I'm used to them."

"No; nothing of the sort; I was going to take the liberty of saying that if you cared to have me I should be glad to see whether our state university might not have something for you. I have friends and acquaintances who could help there."

"Oh, you are very kind! It is very good of you to offer to do that; but—"

A slight embarrassment was manifest in the quick opening and closing of her eyes, a slight turning of the head, but she smiled pleasantly, happily. He liked her way of smiling, and smiled himself. He found it agreeable to be talking to this young woman with the fine, candid eyes, whose manner was so assured—without assurance! She smoothed the black gloves in her lap quietly; they were capable hands; her whole appearance and manner somehow betokened competence.

"The fact is, Mr. Bassett, that I have declined one or two college positions. My own college offered to take me in; and I believe there were one or two other chances. But it is kind of you to offer to help me."

She had minimized the importance of the offers she had declined so that he might not feel the meagreness of his proffered help; and he liked her way of doing it; but it was incredible that a young woman should decline an advantageous and promising position to accept a minor one. In the world he knew there were many hands on all the rounds of all the available ladders.

"Of course," he hastened to say, "I knew you were efficient; that's why I thought the public schools were not quite—not quite—worthy of your talents!"

Some explanation seemed necessary, and Sylvia hesitated for a moment.

"Do I really have to be serious, Mr. Bassett? So many people—the girls at college and some of my instructors and Mrs. Owen even—have assured me that I am not quite right in my mind; but I will make short work of my reasons. Please believe that I really don't mean to take myself too seriously. I want to teach in the public schools merely to continue my education; there are things to learn there that I want to know. So, you see, after all, it's neither important nor interesting; it's only—only my woman's insatiable curiosity!"

He smiled, but he frowned too; it annoyed him not to comprehend her. School-teaching could only be a matter of necessity; her plea of curiosity must cover something deeper that she withheld.

"I know," she continued, "if I may say it, ever so much from books; but I have only the faintest notions of life. Now, isn't that terribly muggy? People—and their conditions and circumstances—can only be learned by going to the original sources."

This was not illuminative. She had only added to his befuddlement and he bent forward, soliciting some more lucid statement of her position.

"I had hoped to go ahead and never have to explain, for I fear that in explaining I seem to be appraising myself too high; but you won't believe that of me, will you? If I took one of these college positions and proved efficient, and had good luck, I should keep on knowing all the rest of my life about the same sort of people, for the girls who go to college are from the more fortunate classes. There are exceptions, but they are drawn largely from homes that have some cultivation, some sort of background. The experiences of teachers in such institutions are likely to cramp. It's all right later on, but at first, it seems to me better to experiment in the wider circle. Now—" and she broke off with a light laugh, eager that he should understand.

"It's not, then, your own advantage you consult; the self-denial appeals to you; it's rather like—like a nun's vocation. You think the service is higher!"

"Oh, it would be if I could render service! Please don't think I feel that the world is waiting for me to set it right; I don't believe it's so wrong! All I mean to say is that I don't understand a lot of things, and that the knowledge I lack isn't something we can dig out of a library, but that we must go to life for it. There's a good deal to learn in a city like this that's still in the making. I might have gone to New York, but there are too many elements there; it's all too big for me. Here you can see nearly as many kinds of people, and you can get closer to them. You can see how they earn their living, and you can even follow them to church on Sunday and see what they get out of that!"

"I'm afraid," he replied, after deliberating a moment, "that you are going to make yourself uncomfortable; you are cutting out a programme of unhappiness."

"Why shouldn't I make myself uncomfortable for a little while? I have never known anything but comfort."

"But that's your blessing; no matter how much you want to do it you can't remove all the unhappiness in the world—not even by dividing with the less fortunate. I've never been able to follow that philosophy."

"Maybe," she said, "you have never tried it!" She was seeking neither to convince him nor to accomplish his discomfiture and to this end was maintaining her share of the dialogue to the accompaniment of a smile of amity.

"Maybe I never have," he replied slowly. "I didn't have your advantage of seeing a place to begin."

"But you have the advantage of every one; you have the thing that I can never hope to have, that I don't ask for: you have the power in your hands to do everything!"

His quick, direct glance expressed curiosity as to whether she were appealing to his vanity or implying a sincere belief in his power.

"Power is too large a word to apply to me, Miss Garrison. I have had a good deal of experience in politics, and in politics you can't do all you like."

"I didn't question that: men of the finest intentions seem to fail, and they will probably go on failing. I know that from books; you know it of course from actual dealings with the men who find their way to responsible places, and who very often fail to accomplish the things we expect of them."

"The aims of most of the reformers are futile from the beginning. Legislatures can pass laws; they pass far too many; but they can't make ideal conditions out of those laws. I've seen it tried."

"Yesterday, when you were able to make that convention do exactly what you wanted it to, without even being there to watch it, it must have been because of some ideal you were working for. You thought you were serving some good purpose; it wasn't just spite or to show your power. It couldn't have been that!"

"I did it," he said doggedly, as though to destroy with a single blunt thrust her tower of illusions—"I did it to smash a man named Thatcher. There wasn't any ideal nonsense about it."

He frowned, surprised and displeased that he had spoken so roughly. He rarely let go of himself in that fashion. He expected her to take advantage of his admission to point a moral; but she said instantly:—

"Then, you did it beautifully! There was a certain perfection about it; it was, oh, immensely funny!"

She laughed, tossing her head lightly, a laugh of real enjoyment, and he was surprised to find himself laughing with her. It seemed that the Thatcher incident was not only funny, but that its full humorous value had not until that moment been wholly realized by either of them.

She rose quickly. One of her gloves fell to the floor and he picked it up. The act of restoring it brought them close together, and their talk had, he felt, justified another searching glance into her face. She nodded her thanks, smiling again, and moved toward the door. He admired the tact which had caused her to close the discussion at precisely the safe moment. He was a master of the art of closing interviews, and she had placed the period at the end of the right sentence; it was where he would have placed it himself.

She had laughed!—and the novelty of being laughed at was refreshing. He and Thatcher had laughed in secret at the confusion of their common enemies in old times; but most men feared him, and he had the reputation of being a mirthless person. He had rarely discussed politics with women; he had an idea that a woman's politics, when she had any, partook of the nature of her religion, and that it was something quite emotional, tending toward hysteria. He experienced a sense of guilt at the relief he found in Sylvia's laughter, remembering that scarcely half an hour earlier he had been at pains to justify himself before his wife for the very act which had struck this girl as funny. He had met Mrs. Bassett's accusations with evasion and dissimulation, and he had accomplished an escape that was not, in retrospect, wholly creditable. He hated scenes and tiresome debates as he hated people who cringed and sidled before him.

His manner of dealing with Thatcher had been born of a diabolical humor which he rarely exercised, but which afforded him a delicious satisfaction. It was the sort of revenge one reserved for a foe capable of appreciating its humor and malignity. The answer of laughter was one to which he was unused, and he was amazed to find that it had effected an understanding of some vague and intangible kind between him and Sylvia Garrison. She might not approve of him, he had no idea that she did; but she had struck a chord whose vibrations pleased and tantalized. She was provocative and, to a degree, mystifying, and the abrupt termination of their talk seemed to leave the way open to other interviews. He thought of many things he might have said to her at the moment; but her period was not to be changed to comma or semicolon; she was satisfied with the punctuation and had, so to speak, run away with the pencil! She had tossed his political aims and strifes into the air with a bewildering dismissal, and he stood like a child whose toy balloon has slipped away, half-pleased at its flight, half-mourning its loss.

She picked up some books she had left on a stand in the hall. He stood with his hands in his pockets, watching her ascent, hearing the swish of her skirts on the stairs: but she did not look back. She was humming softly to herself as she passed out of sight.

CHAPTER XXI
A SHORT HORSE SOON CURRIED

Sylvia sat beside Bassett at dinner that night, and it was on the whole a cheerful party. Mrs. Bassett was restored to tranquillity, and before her aunt she always strove to hide her ills, from a feeling that that lady, who enjoyed perfect health, and carried on the most prodigious undertakings, had little patience with her less fortunate sisters whom the doctors never fully discharge. Mrs. Owen had returned so late that Bassett was unable to dispose of the lawsuit before dinner; she had greeted her niece's husband with her usual cordiality. She always called him Morton, and she was Aunt Sally to him as to many hundreds of her fellow citizens. She discussed crops, markets, rumors of foreign wars, prospective changes in the President's Cabinet, the price of ice, and the automobile invasion. Talk at Sally Owen's table was always likely to be spirited. Bassett's anxiety as to his relations with her passed; he had never felt more comfortable in her house.

Only the most temerarious ever ventured to ask a forecast of Mrs. Owen's plans. Marian, who had found a school friend with an automobile and had enjoyed a run into the country, did not share the common fear of her great-aunt. Mrs. Owen liked Marian's straightforward ways even when they approached rashness. It had occurred to her sometimes that there was a good deal of Singleton in Marian; she, Sally Owen, was a Singleton herself, and admired the traits of that side of her family. Marian amused her now by plunging into a description of a new flat she had passed that afternoon which would provide admirably a winter home for the Bassetts. Mrs. Bassett shuddered, expecting her aunt to sound a warning against the extravagance of maintaining two homes; but Mrs. Owen rallied promptly to her grandniece's support.

"If you've got tired of my house, you couldn't do better than to take an apartment in the Verona. I saw the plans before they began it, and it's first-class and up-to-date. My house is open to you and always has been, but I notice you go to the hotel about half the time. You'd better try a flat for a winter, Hallie, and let Marian see how we do things in town."

Instantly Mrs. Bassett was alert. This could only be covert notice that Sylvia was to be installed in the Delaware Street house. Marian was engaging her father in debate upon the merits of her plan, fortified by Mrs. Owen's unexpected approval. Mrs. Bassett raised her eyes to Sylvia. Sylvia, in one of the white gowns with which she relieved her mourning, tranquilly unconscious of the dark terror she awakened in Mrs. Bassett, seemed to be sympathetically interested in the Bassetts' transfer to the capital.

Sylvia was guilty of the deplorable sin of making herself agreeable to every one. She had paused on the way to her room before dinner to proffer assistance to Mrs. Bassett. With a light, soothing touch she had brushed the invalid's hair and dressed it; and she had produced a new kind of salts that proved delightfully refreshing. Since coming to the table Mrs. Bassett had several times detected her husband in an exchange of smiles with the young woman, and Marian and the usurper got on famously.

Mrs. Bassett had observed that Sylvia's appetite was excellent, and this had weakened her belief in the girl's genius; there was a good deal of Early-Victorian superstition touching women in Hallie Bassett! But Mrs. Owen was speaking.

"I suppose I'd see less of you all if you moved to town. Marian used to run off from Miss Waring's to cheer me up, mostly when her lessons were bad, wasn't it, Marian?"

"I love this house, Aunt Sally, but you can't have us all on your hands all the time."

"Well," Mrs. Owen remarked, glancing round the table quizzically, "I might do worse. But even Sylvia scorns me; she's going to move out to-morrow."

Mrs. Bassett with difficulty concealed her immeasurable relief. Mrs. Owen left explanations to Sylvia, who promptly supplied them.

"That sounds as though I were about to take leave without settling my bill, doesn't it? But I thought it wise not to let it get too big; I'm going to move to Elizabeth House."

"Elizabeth House! Why, Sylvia!" cried Marian.

Mrs. Bassett smothered a sigh of satisfaction. If Aunt Sally was transferring her protégée to the home she had established for working girls (and it was inconceivable that the removal could be upon Sylvia's own initiative), the Bassett prospects brightened at once. Aunt Sally was, in her way, an aristocrat; she was rich and her eccentricities were due largely to her kindness of heart; but Mrs. Bassett was satisfied now that she was not a woman to harbor in her home a girl who labored in a public school-house. Not only did Mrs. Bassett's confidence in her aunt rise, but she felt a thrill of admiration for Sylvia, who was unmistakably a girl who knew her place, and her place as a wage-earner was not in the home of one of the richest women in the state, but in a house provided through that lady's beneficence for the shelter of young women occupied in earning a livelihood.

"It's very nice there," Sylvia was saying. "I stopped on my way home this afternoon and found that they could give me a room. It's all arranged."

"But it's only for office girls and department store clerks and dressmakers, Sylvia. I should think you would hate it. Why, my manicure lives there!"

Marian desisted, warned by her mother, who wished no jarring note to mar her satisfaction in the situation.

"That manicure girl is a circus," said Mrs. Owen, quite oblivious of the undercurrent of her niece's thoughts. "When they had a vaudeville show last winter she did the best stunts of any of 'em. You didn't mention those Jewesses that I had such a row to get in? Smart girls. One of 'em is the fastest typewriter in town; she's a credit to Jerusalem, that girl. And a born banker. They've started a savings club and Miriam runs it. They won't lose any money." Mrs. Owen chuckled; and the rest laughed. There was no question of Mrs. Owen's pride in Elizabeth House. "Did you see any plumbers around the place?" she demanded of Sylvia. "I've been a month trying to get another bathroom put in on the third floor, and plumbers do try the soul."

"That's all done," replied Sylvia. "The matron told me to tell you so."

"I'm about due to go over there and look over the linen," remarked Mrs. Owen, with an air of making a memorandum of a duty neglected.

"Well, I guess it's comfortable enough," said Marian. "But I should think you could do better than that, Sylvia. You'll have to eat at the same table with some typewriter pounder. With all your education I should think it would bore you."

"Sylvia will have to learn about it for herself, Marian," said Mrs. Bassett. "I've always understood that the executive board is very careful not to admit girls whose character isn't above reproach."

Mrs. Owen turned the key of her old-fashioned coffee urn sharply upon the cup she was filling and looked her niece in the eye.

"Oh, we're careful, Hallie; we're careful; but I tell 'em not to be *too* careful!"

"Well, of course the aim is to protect girls," Mrs. Bassett replied, conscious of a disconcerting acidity in her aunt's remark.

"I'm not afraid of contamination," observed Sylvia.

"Of course not *that*," rejoined Mrs. Bassett hastily. "I think it's fine that with your culture you will go and live in such a place; it shows a beautiful spirit of self-sacrifice."

"Oh, please don't say that! I'm going there just because I want to go!" And then, smiling to ease the moment's tension, "I expect to have the best of times at Elizabeth House."

"Sylvia" — remarked Mrs. Owen, drawling the name a trifle more than usual — "Sylvia can do what she pleases anywhere."

"I think," said Bassett, who had not before entered into the discussion, "that Aunt Sally has struck the right word there. In these days a girl can do as she likes; and we haven't any business to discuss Miss Garrison's right to live at Elizabeth House."

"Of course, Sylvia, we didn't mean to seem to criticize you. You know that," said Mrs. Bassett, flushing.

"You are my friends," said Sylvia, glancing round the table, "and if there's criticizing to be done, you have the first right."

"If Sylvia is to be criticized, — and I don't understand that any one has tried it," remarked Mrs. Owen, — "I want the first chance at her myself." And with the snapping of her spectacle case they rose from the table.

They had barely settled themselves in the parlor when Harwood and Allen arrived in Allen's motor. Dan had expected his friend to resent his part in the convention, and he had sought Allen at Lüders's shop to satisfy himself that their personal relations had not been disturbed. He had found Allen, at the end of a day's work, perched upon a bench discoursing to the workmen on the Great Experiment. Allen had, it seemed, watched the convention from an obscure corner of the gallery. He pronounced Dan's speech "immense"; "perfectly bully"; he was extravagant in his praise of it. His father's success in naming the ticket had seemed to him a great triumph. Allen viewed the whole matter with a kind of detachment, as a spectator whose interest is wholly impersonal. He thought there would be a great fight between the combatants; his dad hadn't finished yet, he declared, sententiously. The incidents of the convention had convinced him that the Great Experiment was progressing according to some predestined formula. He and Harwood had dined together at the University Club and he was quite in the humor to call on the Bassetts at Mrs. Owen's; and the coming of Sylvia, as to whom Mrs. Owen had piqued his curiosity, was not to be overlooked.

He cleared the air by brushing away the convention with a word, addressed daringly to Bassett:—

"Papa's come back from fishing! *My* papa is digging bait," and they all laughed.

"Miss Garrison, you must be the greatest of girls, for you have my own ideas! Our invincible young orator here has been telling me so!"

"That was a grand speech; many happy returns of the day!" was Marian's greeting to Dan.

"You certainly have a great voice, Daniel," remarked Mrs. Owen, "and you had your nerve with you."

"You were effective from the first moment, Mr. Harwood. You ought to consider going on the lecture platform," said Mrs. Bassett.

"Oh, Dan hasn't come to that yet; its only defeated statesmen who spout in the Chautauquas," Bassett remarked.

Harwood was in fine fettle. Many men had expressed their approval of him; at the club he had enjoyed the chaffing of the young gentlemen with whom he ate luncheon daily, and whose tolerance of the universe was tinged with a certain cynicism. They liked Harwood; they knew he was a "smart" fellow; and because they liked and admired him they rallied him freely. The president of a manufacturing company had called at the Boordman Building to retain him in a damage suit; a tribute to his growing fame. Dan was a victim of that error to which young men yield in exultant moments, when, after a first brush with the pickets, they are confident of making their own terms with life. Dan's attitude toward the world was receptive; here in the Bassett domestic circle he felt no shame at being a Bassett man. All but Sylvia had spoken to him of his part in the convention, and she turned to him now after a passage with Allen that had left the young man radiant.

"You have a devoted admirer in Mr. Thatcher. He must be a difficult friend to satisfy," said Sylvia.

"Then do you think I don't satisfy him?"

"Oh, perfectly! He's a combination of optimist and fatalist, I judge. He thinks nothing matters much, for everything is coming out all right in the end."

"Then where do you place me in his scheme of things?"

"That depends, doesn't it," she replied carelessly, "on whether you are the master of the ship or only a prisoner under the hatches."

He reddened, and she added nothing to relieve his embarrassment.

"You think, then—?" And he stopped, uneasy under her gaze.

"Some of the time I don't think; I just wonder. And that's very different, isn't it?"

He realized now how much he had counted on the kind things he had expected her to say. He had plainly lost ground with her since their talk on the Madison campus, and he wanted to justify himself, to convince her of his rectitude, and of her failure to understand his part in the convention, but the time and place were unpropitious.

Allen was calling attention to the moonlight and proposing an automobile flight into the country. His car would hold them all, and he announced himself the safest of chauffeurs. Mrs. Owen declined, on the double plea that she had business to attend to and did not ride in motor cars even to please Allen Thatcher; Bassett also excused himself; so the rest set off presently under Mrs. Bassett's chaperonage.

"Are you going downtown, Morton?" asked Mrs. Owen, as they watched the motor roll away.

"No; I'd like to see you on a business matter, Aunt Sally, if you can give me a few minutes."

"Certainly, Morton; come right in."

She flashed on the lights in her office where Thomas A. Hendricks still gazed benevolently at Maud S. breaking her record.

"I owe you an apology, Aunt Sally," Bassett began at once. "I'm sorry I got you into a lawsuit, but things moved so fast that I didn't have a chance to pull you out of the way. Thatcher and I have agreed to disagree, as you doubtless know."

Mrs. Owen drew her spectacle case from her pocket (there were pockets and deep ones in all her gowns), wiped her glasses and put them on.

"You and Edward do seem to be having a little trouble. When I got home I found that summons the sheriff left here. Let me see; it was away back in '82 that I was sued the last time. Agent for a cornplanter sued me for a machine I never ordered and it wasn't worth a farthing anyhow. That was on my Greene County place. Just for that I had him arrested for trespass for going on the farm to take away the machine. He paid the costs all right, and I hope he learned better manners."

This reminiscence, recalled with evident enjoyment, was not wholly encouraging. It seemed darkly possible that she had cited a precedent applicable to every case where she was haled before a court. The chairs in Mrs. Owen's office were decidedly uncomfortable; Bassett crossed and recrossed his legs, and pressed his hand nervously to his pocket to make sure of his check-book; for he was prepared to pay his wife's aunt for her shares in the "Courier" newspaper to facilitate her elimination as a co-defendant in the suit at bar.

"It was contemptible of Thatcher to drag you into this, for he knew you took those shares merely to help me out. I'm sorry it has turned out this way, but I'm anxious to make it right with you, and I'm ready to buy your shares—at your own price, of course."

She chose a letter from the afternoon's mail, and opened it with a horn-handled paper-cutter, crumpling the envelope and dropping it over her shoulder into a big waste-paper basket. She was not apparently overcome by his magnanimity.

"Well, well," she said, glancing over the letter; "that man I've got at Waupegan is turning out better than I expected when I put him there; or else he's the greatest living liar. You never can tell about these people. Well, well!—Oh, yes, Morton; about that lawsuit. I saw Edward this afternoon and had a little talk with him about it."

"You saw Thatcher about the suit!"

"I most certainly did, Morton. I had him go down to the bank to talk to me."

"I'm sorry you took the trouble to do that. If you'd told me—"

"Oh, I'm not afraid of Edward Thatcher. If a man brings a lawsuit against me, the sooner I see him the better. I sent word to Edward and he was waiting at the bank when I got there."

"I'd given Thatcher credit for being above dragging a woman who had always been his friend into a lawsuit. He certainly owed you an apology."

"I didn't see it just that way, Morton, and he didn't apologize. I wouldn't have let him!"

She looked at him over her glasses disconcertingly, and he could think of no reply. It was possible that Thatcher had bought her stock or that she had made him bid for it. She had a reputation for driving hard bargains, and he judged from her manner that her conference with Thatcher, whatever its nature, had not been unsatisfactory. He recalled with exasperation his wife's displeasure over this whole affair; it was incumbent upon him not only to reëstablish himself with Mrs. Owen, but to do it in a way to satisfy Mrs. Bassett.

"You needn't worry about that lawsuit, Morton; there ain't going to be any lawsuit."

She gave this time to "soak in," as she would have expressed it, and then concluded:—

"It's all off; I persuaded Edward to drop the suit. The case will be dismissed in the morning."

"Dismissed? How dismissed, Aunt Sally?"

"Just dismissed; that's all there is of it. I went to see Fitch, too, and gave him a piece of my mind. He wrote me a letter I found here saying that in my absence he'd taken the liberty of entering an appearance for me, along with you, in the case. I told him I'd attend to my own lawsuits, and that he could just scratch his appearance off the docket."

The presumption of her lawyer seemed to obscure all other issues for the moment. Morton Bassett was annoyed to be kept waiting for an explanation that was clearly due him as her co-defendant; he controlled his irritation with difficulty. Her imprudence in having approached his enemy filled him with forebodings; there was no telling what compromises she might have negotiated with Edward G. Thatcher.

"I suppose you shamed him out of it?" he suggested.

"Shamed him? I *scared* him out of it! He owns a lot of property in this town that's rented for unlawful purposes, and I told him I'd prosecute him; that, and a few other things. He offered to buy me out at a good price, but he didn't get very far with that. It was a good figure, though," she added reflectively.

His spirits rose at this proof of her loyalty and he hastened to manifest his appreciation. His wife's fears would be dispelled by this evidence of her aunt's good will toward the family.

"I rather imagined that he'd be glad to quit if he saw an easy way out, and I guess you gave it to him. Now about your stock, Aunt Sally. I don't want you to be brought into my troubles with Thatcher any further. I appreciate your help so far, and I'm able now to pay for your shares. I don't doubt that Ed offered you a generous price to get a controlling interest. I'll write a check for any sum you name, and you'll have my gratitude besides."

He drew out his check-book and laid it on the table, with a feeling that money, which according to tradition is a talkative commodity, might now conclude the conversation. Mrs. Owen saw the check-book—looked at it over her glasses, apparently without emotion.

"I'm not going to sell those shares, Morton; not to you or anybody else."

"But as a matter of maintaining my own dignity—"

"Your own dignity is something I want to speak to you about, Morton. I've been watching you ever since you married Hallie, and wondering just where you'd bump. You and Edward Thatcher have been pretty thick and you've had a lot of fun out of politics. This row you've got into with him was bound to come. I know Edward better—just a little better than I know you. He's not a beautiful character, but he's not as bad as they make out. But you've given him a hard rub the wrong way and he's going to get even with you. He's mighty bitter—bitterer than it's healthy for one man to be against another. If it hadn't been for this newspaper fuss I shouldn't ever have said a word to you about it; but I advise you to straighten things up with Edward. You'd better do it for your own good—for Hallie and the children. You've insulted him and held him up to the whole state of Indiana as a fool. You needn't think he doesn't know just where you gripped that convention tight, and just where you let him have it to play with. He's got more money than you have, and he's going to spend it to give you some of your own medicine or worse, if he can. He's like a mule that lays for the nigger that put burrs under his collar. You're that particular nigger just now. You've made a mistake, Morton."

"But Aunt Sally—I didn't—"

"About that newspaper, Morton," she continued, ignoring him. "I've decided that I'll just hang on to my stock. You've built up the 'Courier' better than I expected, and that last statement showed it to be doing fine. I don't know any place right now where I can do as well with the money. You see I've got about all the farms I can handle at my age, and it will be some fun to have a hand in running a newspaper. I want you to tell 'em down at the 'Courier' office—what's his name? Atwill? Well, you tell him I want this 'Stop, Look, Listen' business stopped. If you can't think of anything smarter to do than that, you 'd better quit. You had no business to turn a newspaper against a man who owns half of it without giving him a chance to get off the track. You whistled, Morton, after you had pitched him and his side-bar buggy into the ditch and killed his horse."

"But who had put him on the track? I hadn't! He'd been running over the state for two years, to my knowledge, trying to undermine me. I was only giving him in broad daylight what he was giving me in the dark. You don't understand this, Aunt Sally; he's been playing on your feelings."

"Morton Bassett, there ain't a man on earth that can play on my feelings. I didn't let him jump on you; and I don't intend to let you abuse him. I've told you to stop nagging him, but I haven't any idea you'll do it. That's your business. If you want a big bump, you go on and get it. About this newspaper, I'm going to keep my shares, and I've told Edward that you wouldn't use the paper as a club on him while I was interested in it. You can print all the politics you want, but it must be clean politics, straight out from the shoulder."

He had lapsed into sullen silence, too stunned to interrupt the placid flow of her speech. She had not only meddled in his affairs in a fashion that would afford comfort to his enemy, but she was now dictating terms— this old woman whose mild tone was in itself maddening. The fear of incurring his wife's wrath alone checked an outburst of indignation. In all his life no one had ever warned him to his face that he was pursuing a course that led to destruction. He had always enjoyed her capriciousness, her whimsical humor, but there was certainly nothing for him to smile at in this interview. She had so plied the lash that it cut to the quick. His pride and self-confidence were deeply wounded;—his wife's elderly aunt did not believe in his omnipotence! This was a shock in itself; but what fantastic nonsense was she uttering now?

"Since I bought that stock, Morton, I've been reading the 'Courier' clean through every day, and there are some things about that paper I don't like. I guess you and Edward Thatcher ain't so particularly religious, and when you took hold of it you cut out that religious page they used to print every Sunday. You better tell Atwill to start that up again. I notice, too, that the 'Courier' sneaks in little stingers at the Jews occasionally—they may just get in by mistake, but you ought to have a rule at the office against printing stories as old as the hills about Jews burning down their clothing-stores to get the insurance. I've known a few Gentiles that did that. The only man I know that I'd lend money to without security is a Jew. Let's not jump on people just to hurt their feelings. And besides, we don't any of us know much more these days than old Moses knew. And that fellow who writes the little two-line pieces under the regular editorials—he's too smart, and he ain't always as funny as he thinks he is. There's no use in popping bird-shot at things if they ain't right, and that fellow's always trying to hurt somebody's feelings without doing anybody any good."

She opened a drawer of her desk and drew out a memorandum to refresh her memory.

"You've got a whole page and on Sundays two pages about baseball and automobiles, and the horse is getting crowded down into a corner. We"—he was not unmindful of the plural—"we must print more horse news. You tell Atwill to send his young man that does the 'Horse and Track' around to see me occasionally and I'll be glad to help him get some horse news that is news. I wouldn't want to have you bounce a young man who's doing the best he can, but it doesn't do a newspaper any good to speak of Dan Patch as a trotting-horse or give the record of my two-year-old filly Penelope O as 2:09-1/4 when she made a clean 2:09. You've got to print facts in a newspaper if you want people to respect it. How about that, Morton?"

"You're right, Aunt Sally. I'll speak to Atwill about his horse news."

He began to wonder whether she were not amusing herself at his expense; but she gave him no reason for doubting her seriousness. They might have been partners from the beginning of time from her businesslike manner of criticizing the paper. She had not only flatly refused to sell her shares, but she was taking advantage of the opportunity (for which she seemed to be prepared) to tell him how the "Courier" should be conducted!

"About farming, Morton," she continued deliberately, "the 'Courier' has fun every now and then over the poor but honest farmer, and prints pictures of him when he comes to town for the State Fair that make him look like a scarecrow. Farming, Morton, is a profession, nowadays, and those poor yaps Eggleston wrote about in 'The Hoosier Schoolmaster' were all dead and buried before you were born. Farmers are up and coming I can tell you, and I wouldn't lose their business by poking fun at 'em. That Saturday column of farm news, by the way, is a fraud—all stolen out of the 'Western Farmers' Weekly' and no credit. They must keep that column in cold storage to run it the way they do. They're usually about a season behind time—telling how to plant corn along in August and planting winter wheat about Christmas. Our farm editor must have been raised on a New York roof-garden. Another thing I want to speak of is the space they give to farmers' and stockmen's societies when they meet here. The last time the Hoosier State Mulefoot Hog Association met right here in town at the Horticultural Society's room at the State House—all the notice they got in the 'Courier' was five lines in 'Minor Mention.' The same day the State Bankers' Association filled three columns, and most of that was a speech by Tom Adams on currency reform. You might tell that funny editorial man to give Adams a poke now and then, and stop throwing chestnuts about gold bricks and green goods at farmers. And he needn't show the bad state of his liver by sarcastically speaking of farmers as honest husbandmen either; a farmer is a farmer, unless, for lack of God's grace, he's a fool! I guess the folks are coming now. I hope Allen won't knock down the house with that threshing-machine of his. That's all this time. Let me see—you'd better tell your editor to call on me now and then. What did you say his name was, Morton?"

"Atwill—Arthur P."

"Is he a son of that Ebenezer Atwill who used to be a professor in Asbury College?"

"I'm afraid not, Aunt Sally; I don't think he ever heard of Ebenezer," replied Bassett, with all the irony he dared.

CHAPTER XXII
THE GRAY SISTERHOOD

Elizabeth House was hospitable to male visitors, and Dan found Sylvia there often on the warm, still summer evenings, when the young women of the household filled the veranda and overflowed upon the steps. Sylvia's choice of a boarding-house had puzzled Dan a good deal, but there were a good many things about Sylvia that baffled him. For example, this preparation for teaching in a public school when she might have had an assistant professorship in a college seemed a sad waste of energy and opportunity. She was going to school to her inferiors, he maintained, submitting to instruction as meekly as though she were not qualified to enlighten her teachers in any branch of knowledge. It was preposterous that she should deliberately elect to spend the hottest of summers in learning to combine the principles of Pestalozzi with the methods of Dewey and Kendall.

The acquaintance of Sylvia and Allen prospered from the start. She was not only a new girl in town, and one capable of debating the questions that interested him, but he was charmed with Elizabeth House, which was the kind of thing, he declared, that he had always stood for. The democracy of the veranda, the good humor and ready give and take of the young women delighted him. They liked him and openly called him "our beau." He established himself on excellent terms with the matron to the end that he might fill his automobile with her charges frequently and take them for runs into the country. When Dan grumbled over Sylvia's absurd immolation on the altar of education, Allen pronounced her the grandest girl in the world and the glory of the Great Experiment.

Sylvia was intent these days upon fitting herself as quickly as possible for teaching, becoming a part of the established system and avoiding none of the processes by which teachers are created. Her fellow students, most of whom were younger than she, were practically all the green fruitage of high schools, but she asked no immunities or privileges by reason of her college training; she yielded herself submissively to the "system," and established herself among the other novices on a footing of good comradeship. During the hot, vexatious days she met them with unfailing good cheer. The inspiring example of her college teachers, and not least the belief she had absorbed on the Madison campus in her girlhood, that teaching is a high calling, eased the way for her at times when—as occasionally happened—she failed to appreciate the beauty of the "system."

The superintendent of schools, dropping into the Normal after hours, caught Sylvia in the act of demonstrating a problem in geometry on the blackboard for the benefit of a fellow student who had not yet abandoned the hope of entering the state university that fall. The superintendent had been in quest of a teacher of mathematics for the Manual Training School, and on appealing to the Wellesley authorities they had sent him Sylvia's name. Sylvia, the chalk still in her fingers, met his humorous reproaches smilingly. She had made him appear ridiculous in the eyes of her *alma mater*, he said. Sylvia declined his offer and smiled. The superintendent was not used to smiles like that in his corps. And this confident young woman seemed to know what she was about. He went away mystified, and meeting John Ware related his experience. Ware laughed and slapped his knee. "You let that girl alone," the minister said. "She has her finger on Time's wrist. Physician of the golden age. Remember Matthew Arnold's lines on Goethe? Good poem. Sylvia wants to know 'the causes of things.' Watch her. Great nature."

At seven o'clock on a morning of September, Sylvia left Elizabeth House to begin her novitiate as a teacher. Allen had declared his intention of sending his automobile for her every morning, an offer that was promptly declined. However, on that bright morning when the young world turned schoolward, Harwood lay in wait for her.

"This must never happen again, sir! And of course you may not carry my books—they're the symbol of my profession. Seventeen thousand young persons about like me are on the way to school this morning right here in Indiana. It would be frightfully embarrassing to the educational system if young gentlemen were allowed to carry the implements of our trade."

"You can't get rid of me now: I never get up as early as this unless I'm catching a train."

"So much the worse for you, then!"

"There will be mornings when you won't think it so much fun. It rains and snows in Indiana sometimes."

He still resented the idea of her sacrifice, as he called it, in the cause of education. They were now so well acquainted that they were not always careful to be polite in their talk; but he had an uneasy feeling that she didn't wholly approve of him. All summer, when they had discussed politics, she had avoided touching upon his personal interests and activities. His alliance with Bassett, emphasized in the state convention, was a subject she clearly avoided. This morning, as he kept time to her quick step, he craved her interest and sympathy. Her plain gray suit and simple cloth hat could not disguise her charm or grace. It seemed to him that she was putting herself a little further away from him, that she was approaching the business of life with a determination, a spirit, a zest, that dwarfed to insignificance his own preoccupation with far less important matters. She turned to glance back at a group of children they had passed audibly speculating as to the character of teacher the day held in store for them.

"Don't you think they're worth working for?" Sylvia asked.

Dan shrugged his shoulders.

"I suppose more lives are ground up in the school-teaching machine than in any other way. Go on! The girl who taught me my alphabet in the little red school-house in Harrison County earned her salary, I can tell you. She was seventeen and wore a pink dress."

"I'm sorry you don't approve of me or my clothes. Now Allen approves of me: I like Allen."

"His approval is important, I dare say."

"Yes, very. It's nice to be approved of. It helps some."

"And I suppose there ought to be a certain reciprocity in approval and disapproval?"

"Oh, there's bound to be!"

Their eyes met and they laughed lightheartedly.

"I'm going to tell you something," said Dan. "On the reciprocal theory I can't expect anything, but I'm lonesome and have no friends anyhow, so I'll give you a chance to say something withering and edged with a fine scorn."

"Good! I'll promise not to disappoint you."

"I'm going to be put on the legislature ticket to-day—to fill a vacancy. I suppose you'll pray earnestly for my defeat."

"Why should I waste prayers on that? Besides, Allen solemnly declares that the people are to be trusted. It's not for me to set my prayers against the will of the pee-pull."

"If you had a vote," he persisted, "you wouldn't vote for me?"

"I should have to know what you want to go to the legislature for before committing myself. What *are* you doing it for?"

"To do all the mischief I can, of course; to support all the worst measures that come up; to jump when the boss's whip cracks!"

She refused to meet him on this ground. He saw that any expectation he might have that she would urge him to pledge himself to noble endeavor and high achievements as a state legislator were doomed to disappointment. He was taken aback by the tone of her retort.

"I hope you will do all those things. You could do nothing better calculated to help your chances."

"Chances?"

"Your chances—and we don't any of us have too many of coming to some good sometime."

"I believe you are really serious; but I don't understand you."

"Then I shall be explicit. Just this, then, to play the ungrateful part of the frank friend. The sooner you get your fingers burnt, the sooner you will let the fire alone. I suppose Mr. Bassett has given the word that you are graciously to be permitted to sit in his legislature. He could hardly do less for you than that, after he sent you into the arena last June to prod the sick lion for his entertainment."

They were waiting at a corner for a break in the street traffic, and he turned toward her guardedly.

"You put it pretty low," he mumbled.

"The thing itself is not so bad. From what I have heard and read about Mr. Bassett, I don't think he is really an evil person. He probably didn't start with any sort of ideals of public life: you did. I read in an essay the other night that the appeal of the highest should be always to the lowest. But you're not appealing to anybody; you're just following the band wagon to the centre of the track. Stop, Look, Listen! You've come far enough with me now. The walls of my prison house loom before me. Good-morning!"

"Good-morning and good luck!"

That night Sylvia wrote a letter to one of her classmates in Boston. "I'm a school-teacher," she said,—"a member of the gray sisterhood of American nuns. All over this astonishing country my sisters of this honorable order rise up in the morning, even as you and I, to teach the young idea how to shoot. I look with veneration upon those of our sisterhood who have grown old in the classroom. I can see myself reduced to a bundle of nerves, irascible, worthless, ready for the scrap-pile at, we will say, forty-two—only twenty years ahead of me! My work looks so easy and I like it so much that I went in fright to the dictionary to look up the definition of teacher. I find that

I'm one who teaches or instructs. Think of it—I! That definition should be revised to read, 'Teacher: one who, conveying certain information to others, reads in fifty faces unanswerable questions as to the riddle of existence.' 'School: a place where the presumably wise are convinced of their own folly.' Note well, my friend: I am a gray sister, in a gray serge suit that fits, with white cuffs and collar, and with chalk on my fingers. Oh, it's not what I'm required to teach, but what I'm going to learn that worries me!"

Lüders's shop was not far from Sylvia's school and Allen devised many excuses for waylaying her. His machine being forbidden, he hung about until she appeared and trudged homeward with her. Often he came in a glow from the cabinetmaker's and submitted for her judgment the questions that had been debated that day at the shop. There was something sweet and wistful and charming in his boyishness; and she was surprised, as Harwood had been from the first, by the intelligence he evinced in political and social questions. He demanded absolute answers to problems that were perplexing wise men all over the world.

"If I could answer that," she would say to him, "I should be entitled to a monument more enduring than brass. The comfort and happiness of mankind isn't to be won in a day: we mustn't pull up the old tree till we've got a new one planted and growing."

"The Great Experiment will turn out all right yet! Some fellow we never heard of will give the lever a jerk some day, and there will be a rumble and a flash and it will run perfectly," he asserted.

The state campaign got under way in October, and Harwood was often discussed in relation to it. Allen always praised Dan extravagantly, and was ever alert to defend him against her criticisms.

"My dad will run the roller over Bassett, but Dan will be smart enough to get from under. It's the greatest show on earth—continuous vaudeville—this politics! Dan's all right. He's got more brains than Bassett. One of these days Dan will take a flop and land clean over in the Thatcher camp. It's only a matter of time. Gratitude and considerations like that are holding him back. But I'm not a partisan—not even on dad's side. I'm the philosopher who sits on the fence and keeps the score by innings."

It seemed to her, in those days and afterward, that Allen symbolized the unknown quantity in all the problems that absorbed him. His idealism was not a thing of the air, but a flowering from old and vigorous roots. His politics was a kind of religion, and it did not prove upon analysis to be either so fantastical or so fanatical as she had believed at first. As the days shortened, he would prolong their walk until the shops and factories discharged their employees upon the streets. The fine thing about the people was, he said, the fact that they were content to go on from day to day, doing the things they did, when the restraints upon them were so light,—it proved the enduring worth of the Great Experiment. Then they would plunge into the thick of the crowd and cross the Monument plaza, where he never failed to pay a tribute in his own fashion to the men the gray shaft commemorated. In these walks they spoke French, which he employed more readily than she: in his high moods it seemed to express him better than English. It amused him to apply new names to the thoroughfares they traversed. For example, he gayly renamed Monument Place the Place de la Concorde, assuring her that the southward vista in the Rue de la Méridienne, disclosing the lamp-bestarred terrace of the new Federal Building, and the electric torches of the Monument beyond, was highly reminiscent of Paris. Sylvia was able to dramatize for herself, from the abundant material he artlessly supplied, the life he had led abroad during his long exile: as a youngster he had enjoyed untrammeled freedom of the streets of Paris and Berlin, and he showed a curiously developed sympathy for the lives of the poor and unfortunate that had been born of those early experiences. He was a great resource to her, and she enjoyed him as she would have enjoyed a girl comrade. He confessed his admiration for Marian in the frankest fashion. She was adorable; the greatest girl in the world.

"Ah, sometime," he would say, "who knows!"

CHAPTER XXIII
A HOUSE-BOAT ON THE KANKAKEE

Harwood's faith in Bassett as a political prophet was badly shaken by the result of the campaign that fall. About half the Democratic candidates for state office were elected, but even more surprising was the rolling-up of a good working majority in both houses of the General Assembly. If Thatcher had knifed Bassett men or if Thatcher men had been knifed at Bassett's behest, evidence of such perfidy was difficult to adduce from the returns. Harwood was not sure, as he studied the figures, whether his party's surprising success was attributable to a development of real strength in Thatcher, who had been much in evidence throughout the campaign, or whether Bassett deserved the credit. He was disposed to think it only another expression of that capriciousness of the electorate which is often manifested in years when national success is not directly involved. While Thatcher and Bassett had apparently struck a truce and harmonized their factions, Harwood had at no time entertained illusions as to the real attitude of the men toward each other. When the *entente* between the leaders was mentioned among Thatcher's intimates they were prone to declare that Ed would "get" Bassett; it might take time, but the day of retribution would surely come.

As a candidate for the lower house in Marion County, Harwood had been thrust forward prominently into a campaign whose liveliness belied the traditional apathy of "off" years. On the Saturday night before the election, Thatcher and Bassett had appeared together on the platform at a great meeting at the capital—one of those final flourishes by which county chairmen are prone to hearten their legions against the morrow's battle. Bassett had spoken for ten minutes at this rally, urging support of the ticket and in crisp phrases giving the lie to reports of his lukewarmness. His speech was the more noteworthy from the fact that it was the first time, in all his political career, that he had ever spoken at a political meeting, and there was no questioning its favorable impression.

Bassett was, moreover, reelected to his old seat in the senate without difficulty; and Harwood ran ahead of his associates on the legislative ticket in Marion County, scoring a plurality that testified to his personal popularity.

Another campaign must intervene before the United States Senatorship became an acute issue, and meanwhile the party in the state had not in many years been so united. Credit was freely given to the "Courier" for the formidable strength developed by the Democracy: and it had become indubitably a vigorous and conservative reflector of party opinion, without estranging a growing constituency of readers who liked its clean and orderly presentation of general news. The ownership of the newspaper had become, since the abrupt termination of the lawsuit instituted by Thatcher, almost as much of a mystery as formerly. Harwood's intimate relations with it had not been revived, and neither Mrs. Owen nor Bassett ever spoke to him of the newspaper except in the most casual fashion.

Dan was conscious that the senator from Fraser had changed in the years that had passed since the beginning of their acquaintance. Bassett had outwardly altered little as he crossed the watershed of middle life; but it seemed to Dan that the ill-temper he had manifested in the Thatcher affair had marked a climacteric. The self-control and restraint that had so impressed him at first had visibly diminished. What Harwood had taken for steel seemed to him now only iron after all—and brittle iron.

During the last week of the campaign an incident occurred that shook Harwood a good deal. He had been away from the capital for several days making speeches, and finding that his itinerary would permit it, he ran into town unexpectedly one night to replenish his linen and look at his mail. An interurban car landed him in town at eleven o'clock, and he went directly to the Boordman Building. As he walked down the hall toward his office he was surprised to see a light showing on the ground-glass door of Room 66. Though Bassett kept a room at the Whitcomb for private conferences, he occasionally used his office in the Boordman for the purpose, and seeing the rooms lighted, Dan expected to find him there. He tried the door and found it locked, and as he drew out his key he heard suddenly the click of the typewriter inside. Miss Farrell was rarely at the office at night, but as Harwood opened the door, he found her busily tapping the keys of her machine. She swung round quickly with an air of surprise, stretched herself, and yawned.

"Well, I wasn't exactly looking for you, but I can't deny that I'm glad to be interrupted. Hope you don't mind my doing a small job on the side—"

As Harwood stood, suit-case in hand, blinking at her, he heard a door farther down the hall close, followed by a step in the hall outside. Harwood had seen no lights in the neighboring offices as he crossed the hall, and in his frequent long night vigils with his law books, it was the rarest thing to find any of the neighboring tenants about. He turned quickly to the door while the retreating steps were still audible.

"Oh!"

Rose had half-risen from her seat as he put his hand to the knob and her tone of alarm arrested him. Instead of flinging open the door he dropped his bag into a corner. His face flushed with sudden anger.

"I didn't suppose you'd mind my doing a little extra work out of hours, Mr. Harwood. Colonel Ramsay was in the office to see Mr. Bassett this afternoon and asked me to take some dictation for him. I guess it's about time for me to go home."

She pulled the sheet of paper from the typewriter with a sharp *brrrrr* and dropped it into a drawer with a single deft twist of the wrist.

"The Colonel didn't mention it to me," remarked Dan, feigning indifference and not looking at her. "He was making a speech at Terre Haute to-night when I left there."

He tried to minimize the disagreeable aspects of the matter. Rose had been employed by Bassett as stenographer to one of his legislative committees before Dan's relations with the politician began. Since Harwood employed her Bassett had made use of her constantly in the writing of letters. There would have been nothing extraordinary in his calling her to the office for an evening's work; it was the girl's falsehood about Ramsay and the quiet closing of the door of Bassett's inner room that disturbed Harwood. He passed into the library and Rose left without saying good-night. The incident annoyed Dan; Bassett's step had been unmistakable, and the girl's confusion had its disagreeable significance. He had not thought this of Bassett; it was inconsonant with the character of man he still believed Morton Bassett to be.

In winding up the receivership of the paper company Bassett had treated Harwood generously. Dan was out of debt; he had added forty acres of good land to his father's farm, and he kept a little money in bank. He had even made a few small investments in local securities that promised well, and his practice had become quite independent of Bassett: almost imperceptibly Bassett had ceased to be a factor in his prosperity. The office in the Boordman Building remained the same, and Bassett spent a good deal of time there. There were days when he seemed deeply preoccupied, and he sometimes buried himself in his room without obvious reason; then after an interval he would come out and throw his leg over a corner of Dan's desk and talk to him with his earlier frankness. Once he suggested that Dan might like to leave the Boordman for a new office building that was lifting the urban skyline; but the following day he came rather pointedly to Dan's desk, and with an embarrassment he rarely showed, said that of course if Dan moved he should expect to go with him; he hoped Dan had understood that. A few days later he entrusted Dan with several commissions that he seemed to have devised solely to show his good will and confidence.

Harwood was happy these days. He was still young and life had dealt kindly with him. Among lawyers he was pointed to as a coming light of the bar; and in politics he was the most conspicuous man of his age in the state. He was invited to Harrison County that fall to deliver an address at a reunion of the veterans of his father's regiment, and that had pleased him. He had more than justified the hopes of his parents and brothers, and they were very proud of him. While they did not understand his apostasy from the family's stern Republicanism, this did not greatly matter when Dan's name so often came floating home in the Indianapolis newspapers. His mother kept careful track of his social enthrallments; her son was frequently among those present at private and public dinners; and when the president of Yale visited Indiana, Dan spoke at the banquet given in his honor by the alumni; and not without emotion does a woman whose life has been spent on a humble farm find that her son has won a place among people of distinction in a city which is to her the capital of the Universe. There were times when Dan wished to be free of Bassett. He had reached a point where Bassett was not only of little service to him, but where he felt he was of little use to Bassett. And it was irksome to find that all the local newspapers, except the "Courier," constantly identified the Boordman Building with Bassett's political activities.

Amid all the agitations of the campaign Dan had seen as much as possible of Sylvia. The settlement of Andrew Kelton's estate gave him an excuse for consulting her frequently, but he sought her frankly for the pleasure of seeing her. He found that she was a good deal at Mrs. Owen's, and it was pleasanter to run in upon her there than at Elizabeth House, where they must needs share the parlor with other callers. Often he and Allen met at Mrs. Owen's and debated the questions that were forever perplexing young Thatcher's eager mind,—debates that Mrs. Owen suffered to run so far and then terminated with a keen observation that left no more to be said, sending them to the pantry to forage for food and drink. Thatcher had resented for a time Harwood's participation in his humiliation at the convention; but his ill-feeling had not been proof against Allen's warm defense. Thatcher's devotion to his son had in it a kind of pathos, and it was not in him to vent his spleen against his son's best friend.

A few days after the election Thatcher invited Harwood to join him and Allen in a week's shooting in the Kankakee where he owned a house-boat that Allen had never seen.

"Come up, Dan, and rest your voice. It's a good place to loaf, and we'll take John Ware along as our moral uplifter. Maybe we'll pot a few ducks, but if we don't we'll get away from our troubles for a little while anyhow."

The house-boat proved to be commodious and comfortable, and the ducks scarce enough to make the hunter earn his supper. I may say in parenthesis that long before Thatcher's day many great and good Hoosiers scattered birdshot over the Kankakee marshes—which, alack! have been drained to increase Indiana's total area of arable soil. "Lew" Wallace and other Hoosier generals and judges used to hunt ducks on the Kankakee; and Maurice Thompson not only camped there, but wrote a poem about the marshes,—a poem that *is* a poem,—all about the bittern and the plover and the heron, which always, at the right season, called him away from the desk and the town to try his bow (he was the last of the toxophilites!) on winged things he scorned to destroy with gunpowder. (Oh what a good fellow you were, Maurice Thompson, and what songs you wrote of our lakes and rivers and feathered things! And how I gloated over those songs of fair weather in old "Atlantics" in my grandfather's garret, before they were bound into that slim, long volume with the arrow-pierced heron on its cover!)

John Ware, an ancient and honorable son of the tribe of Nimrod, was the best of comrades. The striking quality in Ware was his beautiful humanness, which had given him a peculiar hold upon men. Thatcher was far from being a saint, but, like many other cheerful sinners in our capital, he had gone to church in the days when Ware occupied the First Congregational pulpit. A good many years had passed since Ware had been a captain of cavalry, chasing Stuart's boys in the Valley of Virginia, but he was still a capital wing shot. A house-boat is the best place in the world for talk, and the talk in Thatcher's boat, around the sheet-iron stove, was good those crisp November evenings.

On Sunday Ware tramped off to a country church, taking his companions with him. It was too bad to miss the ducks, he said, but a day's peace in the marshes gave them a chance to accumulate. That evening he talked of Emerson, with whom he had spoken face to face in Concord in that whitest of houses. We shouldn't bring this into our pages if it hadn't been that Ware's talk in that connection interested Thatcher greatly. And ordinarily Thatcher knew and cared less about Emerson than about the Vedic Hymns. Allen was serenely happy to be smoking his pipe in the company of a man who had fought with Sheridan, heard Phillips speak, and talked to John Brown and Emerson. When Ware had described his interview with the poet he was silent for a moment, then he refilled his pipe.

"It's odd," he continued, "but I've picked up copies of Emerson's books in queer places. Not so strange either; it seems the natural thing to find loose pages of his essays stuck around in old logging-camps. I did just that once, when I was following Thoreau's trail through the Maine woods. Some fellow had pinned a page of 'Compensation' on the door of a cabin I struck one night when it was mighty good to find shelter,—the pines singing, snowstorm coming on. That leaf was pretty well weather-stained; I carried it off with me and had it framed—hangs in my house now. Another time I was doing California on horseback, and in an abandoned shack in the Sierras I found Emerson's 'Poems'—an old copy that somebody had thumbed a good deal. I poked it out of some rubbish and came near making a fire of it. Left it, though, for the next fellow. I've noticed that if one thing like that happens to you there's bound to be another. Is that superstition, Thatcher? I'm not superstitious,—not particularly,—but we've all got some of it in our hides. After that second time—it was away back in the seventies, when I was preaching for a spell in 'Frisco—I kept looking for the third experience that I felt would come."

"Oh, of course it did come!" cried Allen eagerly.

"Well, that third time it wasn't a loose leaf torn out and stuck on a plank, or just an old weather-stained book; it was a copy that had been specially bound—a rare piece of work. I don't care particularly for fine bindings, but that had been done with taste,—a dark green,—the color you get looking across the top of a pine wood; and it seemed appropriate. Emerson would have liked it himself."

The sheet-iron stove had grown red hot and Harwood flung open the door. The glow from the fire fell full upon the dark, rugged face and the white hair of the minister, who was sitting on a soap-box with his elbows on his knees. In a gray flannel shirt he looked like a lumberman of the North. An unusual tenderness had stolen into his lean, Indian-like face.

"That was a long while after that ride in the Sierras. Let me see, it was more than twenty years ago,—I can't just place the year; no difference. I'd gone up into the Adirondacks to see my folks. I told you about our farm once, Allen,—not far from John Brown's old place. It isn't as lonesome up there now as it was when I was a boy; there were bully places to hide up there; I used to think of that when I was reading Scott and Cooper. Brown could have hid there forever if he'd got out of Virginia after the raid. Nowadays there are too many hotels, and people go canoeing in ironed collars. No good. My folks were all gone even then, and strangers lived in my father's house. From the old place I moved along, walking and canoeing it. Stopped on Saturday in a settlement where there was a church that hadn't been preached in since anybody could remember. Preached for 'em on Sunday. An old Indian died, while I was there, and I baptized and buried him. But that wasn't what kept me. There was a young woman staying at the small boarding-house where I stopped—place run by a man and his wife. Stranger had brought her there early in the summer. City people—they told the folks they came from New York. They were young, well-appearing folks—at least the girl was. The man had gone off and left her there, and she was going to have a child soon and was terribly ill. They called me in one day when they thought the woman was dying. The country doctor wasn't much good—an old fellow who didn't know that anything particular had happened in his profession since Harvey discovered the circulation of the blood. I struck off to Saranac and got a city doctor to go and look at the woman. Nice chap he was, too. He stayed there till the woman's troubles were over. Daughter born and everything all right. She never mentioned the man who had left her there. Wouldn't answer the doctor's questions and didn't tell me anything either. Strange business, just to drop in on a thing like that."

It occurred to Harwood that this big, gray, kindly man had probably looked upon many dark pictures in his life. The minister appeared to be talking half to himself, and there had been abrupt pauses in his characteristically jerky recital. There was a long silence which he broke by striking his hands together abruptly, and shaking his head.

"The man that kept the boarding-house was scared for fear the woman wasn't straight; didn't like the idea of having a strange girl with a baby left on his hands. I had to reason some with that fellow; but his wife was all right, and did her full duty by the girl. She was a mighty pretty young girl, and she took her troubles, whatever they were, like what you'd call a true sport, Ed."

Thatcher, stretched out on a camp bed at the side of the room, chewing a cigar, grunted.

"Well," the minister continued, "I was around there about three weeks; put in all my vacation there. Fact is I hated to go off and leave that girl until I was sure I couldn't do anything for her. But she was getting out of the woods before I left, and I offered to help her any way I could. She didn't seem to lack for money; a couple of letters with money came for her, but didn't seem to cheer her much. There was a beast in the jungle,—no doubt of that,—but she was taking good care to hide him. Didn't seem to care much about taking care of herself, even when she must have known that it looked bad for her. She was a flighty, volatile sort of creature; made a lot of what I'd done for her in bringing over the doctor. That doctor was a brick, too. Lots of good people in the world, boys. Let me see; Dan, feel in that shooting-coat of mine on the nail behind you and you'll find the book I started to tell you about. Thanks. You see it's a little banged up because I've carried it around with me a good deal—fishing-trips and so on; but it's acquired tone since I began handling it—the green in that leather has darkened. 'Society and Solitude.' There's the irony of fate for you.—Where had I got to? When I went in to say good-bye we had quite a talk. I thought maybe there was some message I could carry to her friends for her, but she was game and wouldn't hear to it. She wanted the little girl baptized, but said she hadn't decided what to name her; asked me if I could baptize a baby without having a real name. She was terribly cut up and cried about it. I said I guessed God Almighty didn't care much about names, and if she hadn't decided on one I'd name the baby myself and I did: I named the little girl—and a mighty cute youngster she was, too—I named her Elizabeth— favorite name of mine;—just the mother, lying there in bed, and the man and woman that kept the boarding-house in the room. The mother said she wanted to do something for me; and as I was leaving her she pulled this book out and made me take it."

"I suppose it was a favorite book of hers and all that," suggested Dan.

"I don't think anybody had ever opened that book," replied Ware, smiling. "It was brand-new—not a scratch on it."

"And afterward?" asked Allen, anxious for the rest of the story.

"Well, sir, I passed through there four years afterward and found the same people living in the little cottage there at that settlement. Strange to say, that woman had stayed there a couple of years after the baby was born. Hadn't any place to go, I reckon. Nobody ever went near her, they said; but finally she picked up and left; took the baby with her. She had never been well afterward, and finally, seeing she hadn't long to live, she struck out for home. Wanted to die among her own people, maybe. I don't know the rest of the story, Allen. What I've told you is all I know,—it's like finding a magazine in a country hotel where you haven't anything to read and dip into the middle of a serial story. I never told anybody about that but my wife. I had a feeling that if that woman took such pains to bury herself up there in the wilderness it wasn't my business to speak of it. But it's long ago now—most everything that an old chap like me knows is!"

Thatcher rose and crossed to the stove and took the book. He turned it over and scrutinized it carefully, scanned the blank pages and the silk-faced lids in the glow from the stove, and then handed it to Allen.

"What does that say there, that small gold print on the inside of the cover?"

"That's the binder's name—Z. Fenelsa."

Allen closed the book, passed his hand over the smooth covers, and handed it back to Ware.

"What did you say the woman's name was, Ware?" asked Thatcher.

"Didn't say, but the name she went by up there was Forbes. She told me it was an assumed name. The people she stayed with told me they never knew any better."

Several minutes passed in which no one spoke. The minister lapsed into one of his deep reveries. Thatcher stood just behind him peering into the fire. Suddenly he muttered under his breath and almost inaudibly, "Well, by God!"

CHAPTER XXIV
A WASHINGTON'S BIRTHDAY BALL

The Bassetts moved to the capital that winter, arriving with the phalanx of legislators in January, and establishing themselves in a furnished house opportunely vacated by the Bosworths, who were taking the Mediterranean trip. Bassett had been careful to announce to the people of Fraserville that the removal was only temporary, and that he and his family would return in the spring, but Marian held private opinions quite at variance with her father's published statements.

Mrs. Bassett's acquiescence had been due to Mrs. Owen's surprising support of Marian's plan. In declaring that she would never, never consent to live in a flat, Mrs. Bassett had hoped to dispose of Marian's importunities, to which Bassett had latterly lent mild approval. When, however, Mrs. Owen suggested the Bosworth house, which could be occupied with the minimum of domestic vexation, Mrs. Bassett promptly consented, feeling that her aunt's interest might conceal a desire in the old lady's breast to have some of her kinsfolk near her. Mrs. Bassett had not allowed her husband to forget the dangerous juxtaposition of Sylvia Garrison to Mrs. Owen's check-book. "That girl," as Mrs. Bassett designated Sylvia in private conversation with her husband, had been planted in Elizabeth House for a purpose. Her relief that Sylvia had not been settled in the Delaware Street residence had been of short duration: Mrs. Bassett saw now that it was only the girl's adroit method of impressing upon Mrs. Owen her humility and altruism. Still Mrs. Bassett was not wholly unhappy. It was something to be near at hand where she could keep track of Sylvia's movements; and the social scene at the capital was not without its interest for her. She was not merely the wife of Morton Bassett, but the only child of the late Blackford Singleton, sometime Senator in Congress. She was moreover the niece of Sally Owen, and this in itself was a social asset. She showed her husband the cards that were left at their door, and called his attention to the fact that the representative people of the capital were looking them up. He made the mistake of suggesting that the husbands of most of the women who had called had axes to grind at the State House,—a suggestion intended to be humorous; but she answered that many of her callers were old friends of the

Singletons, and she expressed the hope that he would so conduct himself as to adorn less frequently the newspaper headlines; the broad advertisement of his iniquities would be so much worse now that they were in the city, and with Marian's future to consider, and all.

It should be said that Marian's arrival had not gone unheeded. The society columns of the capital welcomed her, and the "Advertiser" reproduced her photograph in a picture hat. She began at once to be among those included in all manner of functions. Allen danced cheerfully to her piping and she still telephoned to Harwood when she thought of ways of using him. Mrs. Owen had declared her intention of giving a "party" to introduce Marian to the society of the capital. Sally Owen had not given a "party" since Mrs. Bassett's coming out, but she brought the same energy and thoroughness to bear upon a social affair that characterized her business undertakings. In preparing the list (in itself a task) and in the discussion of details, it was necessary of course to consult Marian,—one usually heard Marian's views whether one consulted her or not,—but she and her aunt were on the best of terms, and Mrs. Owen was sincerely anxious to satisfy her in every particular. On half a dozen evenings Allen or Dan brought Sylvia to the Delaware Street house to meet Marian and plan the coming event. No one would have imagined, from the zest with which Sylvia discussed such deep questions as the employment of musicians, the decorating of the hall, the german favors and the refreshments, that she had been at work all day in a schoolroom that had been built before ventilation was invented.

When Sylvia was busy, she was the busiest of mortals, but when she threw herself heart and soul into play, it was with the completest detachment. She accomplished wonderful things in the way of work after schoolhours if she received warning that either of her faithful knights meditated a descent upon her. During these councils of war to plan Marian's belated début, Sylvia might snowball Allen or Dan or both of them all the way from Elizabeth House to Mrs. Owen's door, and then appear demurely before that amiable soul, with cheeks aglow and dark eyes flashing, and Mrs. Owen would say: "This school-teaching ain't good for you, Sylvia; it seems to be breaking down your health." That was a lively quartette—Sylvia, Marian, Allen, and Dan!

Dan, now duly sworn to serve the state faithfully as a legislator, had been placed on several important committees, and a busy winter stretched before him. Morton Bassett's hand lay heavily upon the legislature; the young man had never realized until he took his seat in the lower house how firmly Bassett gripped the commonwealth. Every committee appointment in both houses had to be approved by the senator from Fraser. Dan's selection as chairman of the committee on corporations both pleased and annoyed him. He would have liked to believe himself honestly chosen by the speaker on the score of fitness; but he knew well enough that there were older men, veteran legislators, more familiar with the state's needs and dangers, who had a better right to the honor. The watchful "Advertiser" had not overlooked his appointment. On the day the committees were announced it laid before its readers a cartoon depicting Bassett, seated at his desk in the senate, clutching wires that radiated to every seat in the lower house. One desk set forth conspicuously in the foreground was inscribed "D.H." "The Lion and Daniel" was the tag affixed to this cartoon, which caused much merriment among Dan's friends at the round table of the University Club.

Miss Bassett's début was fixed for Washington's Birthday, and as Mrs. Owen's house had no ballroom (except one of those floored attics on which our people persist in bestowing that ambitious title) she decided that the Propylæum alone would serve. Pray do not reach for your dictionary, my friend! No matter how much Greek may have survived your commencement day, you would never know that our Propylæum (reared by the women of our town in North Street, facing the pillared façade of the Blind Institute) became, on its completion in 1890, the centre of our intellectual and social life. The club "papers" read under that roof constitute a literature all the nobler for the discretion that reserves it for atrabilious local criticism; the later editions of our *jeunesse dorée* have danced there and Boxed and Coxed as Dramatic Club stars on its stage. "Billy" Sumner once lectured there on "War" before the Contemporary Club, to say nothing of Mr. James's appearance (herein before mentioned), which left us, filled with wildest surmise, on the crest of a new and ultimate Darien. Nor shall I omit that memorable tea to the Chinese lady when the press became so great that a number of timorous Occidentals in their best bib and tucker departed with all possible dignity by way of the fire-escape. So the place being historic, as things go in a new country, Mrs. Owen did not, in vulgar parlance, "hire a hall," but gave her party in a social temple of loftiest consecration.

It was a real winter night, with a snowstorm and the jangle of sleigh-bells outside. The possibilities of a hall famed for its many brilliant entertainments had never been more fully realized than on this night of Marian Bassett's presentation. The stage was screened in a rose-hung lattice that had denuded the conservatories of Newcastle and Richmond; the fireplace was a bank of roses, and the walls were festooned in evergreens. Nor should we overlook a profile of the father of his country in white carnations on a green background, with all the effect of a marble bas-relief,—a fitting embellishment for the balcony,—done by the florist from Allen's design and under Allen's critical eye.

In the receiving line, established in one of the lower parlors, were Mrs. Owen, Mr. and Mrs. Morton Bassett, the Governor and his wife (he happened just then to be a Republican), Colonel and Mrs. Vinning (retired army people), and the pick of the last October's brides and their young husbands. We may only glance hurriedly at the throng who shook Mrs. Owen's hand, and were presented to Mr. and Mrs. Bassett and by them in turn to their daughter. Every one remarked how stunning the hostess looked (her gown was white, and in the latest fashion, too,—none of your quaint old lace and lavender for Aunt Sally!), and what amusing things she said to her guests as they filed by, knowing them all and in her great good heart loving them all! It is something to be an Aunt Sally where the name is a synonym for perpetual youth and perpetual kindness and helpfulness. (And if Aunt Sally didn't live just a little way down my own street, and if she hadn't bribed me not to "put her in a book" with a gift of home-cured hams from her Greene County farm last Christmas, there are many more things I should like to say of her!)

Since the little affair of the "Courier" Morton Bassett had fought shy of his wife's aunt; but to-night he stood beside her, enjoying, let us hope, the grim humor of his juxtaposition to the only person who had ever blocked any of his enterprises. Nothing escaped Mrs. Bassett, and her heart softened toward her politician husband as she saw that next to her aunt and Marian (a daughter to be proud of to-night!) Morton Bassett was the person most observed of all observers. She noted the glances bent upon him by the strangers to whom he was introduced, and many acquaintances were at pains to recall themselves to him. Her husband was a presentable man anywhere, and she resolved to deal more leniently with his offenses in future. The governorship or a seat in the United States Senate would amply repay her for the heartaches so often communicated by the clipping bureau.

Mrs. Bassett prided herself on knowing who's who in her native state and even she was satisfied that the gathering was representative. The "list" had not been submitted for her approval; if it had been she might have deleted certain names and substituted others. She was unable, for example, to justify the presence of the senior Thatcher, though her husband assured her in a tone of magnanimity that it was all right; and she had never admired Colonel Ramsay, though to be sure nearly every one else did. Was not the Colonel handsome, courteous, genial, eloquent, worthy of all admiration? Mrs. Owen had chosen a few legislators from among her acquaintances, chiefly gentlemen who had gallantly aided some of her measures at earlier sessions of the assembly. This accounted for the appearance of a lone Prohibitionist who by some miracle appeared biennially in the lower house, and for a prominent labor leader whom Mrs. Owen liked on general principles. The statesman who has already loomed darkly in these pages as the Tallest Delegate was taller than ever in a dress coat, but in all ways a citizen of whom Vermillion County had reason to be proud. John Ware and Admiral Martin, finding themselves uncomfortable in the crowd, rescued Thatcher and adjourned with him to a room set apart for smokers. There they were regarded with mild condescension by young gentlemen who rushed in from the dance, mopping their brows and inhaling cigarettes for a moment, wearing the melancholy air becoming to those who support the pillars of society.

At ten o'clock the receiving line had dissolved and the dance was in full swing above. Sylvia had volunteered to act as Mrs. Owen's adjutant, and she was up and down stairs many times looking after countless details. She had just dispatched Allen to find partners for some out-of-town girls when Morton Bassett accosted her in the hall.

"I'm thirsty, Miss Garrison; which punch bowl do you recommend to a man of my temperate habits?"

She turned to the table and took a glass from Mrs. Owen's butler and held it up.

"The only difference between the two is that one is pink. I put it in myself. Your health and long life to Marian," said Sylvia.

"I'm going to take this chance to thank you for your kind interest in Marian's party. We all appreciate it. Even if you didn't do it for us but for Mrs. Owen, we're just as grateful. There's a lot of work in carrying off an affair like this."

He seemed in no hurry and apparently wished to prolong the talk. They withdrew out of the current of people passing up and down the stairway.

"You are not dancing?" he asked.

"No; I'm not here socially, so to speak. I'm not going out, you know; I only wanted to help Mrs. Owen a little."

"Pardon me; I hadn't really forgotten. You are a busy person; Marian tells me you have begun your teaching. You don't show any evidences of wear."

"Oh, I never was so well in my life!"

"You will pardon me for mentioning it here, but—but I was sorry to hear from Mr. Harwood that the teaching is necessary."

He was quite right, she thought, in saying that the time and place were ill-suited to such a remark. He leaned against the wall and she noticed that his lids drooped wearily. He seemed content to linger there, where they caught fitfully glimpses of Marian's bright, happy face in the dance. Mrs. Owen and Mrs. Bassett were sitting in a group of dowagers at the other end of the ballroom, identifying and commenting upon the season's débutantes.

"I suppose you are very busy now," Sylvia remarked.

Yes; this will be a busy session."

"And I suppose you have more to do than the others; it's the penalty of leadership."

He flushed at the compliment, changed his position slightly, and avoided her eyes for a moment. She detected in him to-night something that had escaped her before. It might not be weariness after all that prompted him to lean against the wall with one hand carelessly thrust into his pocket; he was not a man to show physical weariness. It seemed, rather, a stolid indifference either to the immediate scene or to more serious matters. Their meeting had seemed accidental; she could not believe he had contrived it. If the dance bored him she was by no means his only refuge; many present would have thought themselves highly favored by a word from him. A messenger brought Sylvia a question from Mrs. Owen. In turning away to answer she gave him a chance to escape, but he waited, and when she was free again she felt that he had been watching her.

He smiled, and stood erect as though impelled by an agreeable thought.

"We don't meet very often, Miss Garrison, and this is hardly the place for long conversations; you're busy, too; but I'd like to ask you something."

"Certainly, Mr. Bassett!"

The newest two-step struck up and she swung her head for a moment in time to it and looked out upon the swaying forms of the dancers.

"That's Marian's favorite," she said.

"That afternoon, after the convention, you remember—"

"Of course, Mr. Bassett; I remember perfectly."

"You laughed!"

They both smiled; and it seemed to him that now, as then, it was a smile of understanding, a curious reciprocal exchange that sufficed without elucidation in words.

"Well!" said Sylvia.

"Would you mind telling me just why you laughed?"

"Oh! That would be telling a lot of things."

Any one seeing them might have thought that this middle-aged gentleman was taking advantage of an opportunity to bask in the smile of a pretty girl for the sheer pleasure of her company. He was purposely detaining her, but whether from a wish to amuse himself or to mark his indifference to what went on around him she did not fathom. The fact was that Sylvia had wondered herself a good deal about that interview in Mrs. Owen's house, and she was not quite sure why she had laughed.

"I'd really like to know, Miss Garrison. If I knew why you laughed at me—"

"Oh, I didn't laugh at you! At least—it wasn't just you alone I was laughing at!"

"Not at me?"

His look of indifference vanished wholly; he seemed sincerely interested as he waited for her reply, delayed a moment by the passing of a group of youngsters from the ballroom to the fresher air of the hall.

"I know perfectly well this isn't a good place to be serious in; but I laughed—Do you really want to know?"

"Yes, please. Don't try to spare my feelings; they're pretty badly shot up anyhow."

"It must have been because it struck me as funny that a man like you— with all your influence and power—your capacity for doing big things— should go to so much trouble merely to show another man your contempt for him. Just a moment"—she deliberated an instant, lifting her head a trifle,—"it was funny, just as it would be funny if the United States went to war to crush a petty, ignorant pauper power; or it would be like using the biggest pile driver to smash a mosquito. It was ridiculous just because it seemed so unnecessarily elaborate—such a waste of steam."

She had spoken earnestly and quickly, but he laughed to assure her that he was not offended.

"So that was it, was it?"

"I think so; something like that. And you laughed too that day!"

"Yes; why did I laugh?" he demanded.

"Because you knew it was grotesque, and not to be taken at all seriously as people did take it. And then, maybe—maybe I thought it funny that you should have employed Mr. Harwood to pull the lever that sent the big hammer smashing down on the insect."

"So that was it! Well, maybe it wasn't so unnecessary after all; to be frank, I didn't think so. In my conceit I thought it a good stroke. That's a secret; nobody else knows that! Why shouldn't I have used Mr. Harwood—assuming that I did use him?"

"Can you stand any more? Shan't we talk of something else?"

Their colloquy had been longer than Sylvia found comfortable: every one knew Bassett; every one did not know her. She was a comparative stranger in the city, and it was not wholly kind in him to make her conspicuous; yet he seemed oblivious to his surroundings.

"You cast an excellent actor for an unworthy part, that's all."

"I was debasing him? Is that what you think?" he persisted.

"Yes," she answered steadily, meeting his eyes.

"You like him; you believe in him?"

"He has ability," she answered guardedly.

"Then I've done nothing to thwart him in the use of it. He's the best advertised young man in the state in either political party. He's in a place now where he can make good."

His smile was grave; it was impossible to answer him in the key of social small talk.

"The 'Advertiser' seems to think that he's in the legislature to do what you tell him to."

"He doesn't have to do it, does he? He owes me nothing—absolutely nothing. He can kick me down stairs to-morrow if he wants to. It was understood when he came into my office that he should be free to quit me whenever he liked. I'd like you to know that."

She was embarrassed by the direct look that accompanied this. Her opinions could not interest him one way or another, and he was going far in assuming that she was deeply concerned in Harwood's welfare. The incongruity of their talk was emphasized by the languorous strains of the newest popular waltz that floated over them from the ballroom.

"If it were any of my affair—which it certainly isn't—I should tell him to stand by you—to say no to you if need be and yet remain your friend."

"You think, then, that I am not beyond reclamation—that I might be saved—pulled out of the mire?"

"No man is beyond reclamation, is he? I think not; I believe not."

The music ceased; the dancers were demanding a repetition of the number. Bassett stood his ground stubbornly.

"Well, I've asked him to do something for me—the only thing I have ever asked him to do that wasn't straight."

There was no evading this; she wondered whether he had deliberately planned this talk, and what it was leading to. In any view it was inexplicable. His brow knit and there was a curious gravity in his eyes as they sought hers searchingly.

"That's his affair entirely, Mr. Bassett," she replied coldly. "He and I are good friends, and of course I should hate to see him make a mistake."

"But the mistake may be mine; let us say that it is mine."

"I had an idea that you didn't make mistakes. Why should you make the serious mistake of asking a good man to do a bad thing?"

"The natural inference would be that I'm a bad man, wouldn't it?"

"It wouldn't be my way of looking at it. All you need is courage to be a great man—you can go far!"

He smiled grimly.

"I need only one thing, you say;—but what if it's the thing I haven't got?"

"Get it!" she replied lightly. "But your defiance in the convention wasn't worthy of you; it was only a piece of bravado. You don't deserve to be abused for that,—just scolded a little. That's why I laughed at you that afternoon; I'm going to laugh at you now!"

The music had ceased again and Allen and Marian flashed out upon them in the highest spirits.

"Well, I like this!" cried Marian. "What are you two talking so long about? Oh, I saw you through three dances at least!"

"Miss Garrison has been laughing at me," said Bassett, smiling at his daughter. "She doesn't take me at all seriously—or too seriously: I don't know which!"

"How could she take you seriously!" demanded Marian. "I never do! Sylvia, where on earth is our little Daniel? It's nearly time for the cotillion. And if Dan Harwood doesn't show up for that I'll never forgive him in this world."

"The cotillion?" repeated Bassett, glancing at his watch. "Hasn't Dan got here yet? He had a committee meeting to-night, but it ought to have been over before now."

Sylvia noted that the serious look came into his eyes again for an instant.

"He oughtn't to have had a committe meeting on the night of my party. And it's a holiday too."

"And after all the rehearsing we've done at Aunt Sally's the cherry-tree figure absolutely has to have him," said Allen. "Maybe I'd better send a scout to look him up or run over to the State House myself."

"Oh, he'll be here," murmured Sylvia.

Dan had undoubtedly intended to appear early at the dance, and she wondered whether his delay might not be due to the crisis in his relations with Bassett of which the politician had hinted. As she ran off with Allen to make sure the apparatus for the german was in order, she wished Bassett had not spoken to her of Harwood.

Sylvia and Allen had despaired of Dan when at a quarter of twelve he appeared. He met their reproaches cheerfully, and airily explained his delay.

"State's business! Can you imagine me fresh from Richelieu's cabinet, with a trail of dead horses on the road behind me? In plain prose I didn't get home to dress until eleven, and the snow makes it hard going."

He had dressed with care nevertheless and had never looked better. Sylvia sent Allen ahead to begin clearing the floor for the cotillion, and followed more slowly with Harwood.

"I suppose," he remarked, half to himself, "that I really oughtn't to do it."

"What—you hesitate now after keeping the stage waiting!"

"It may be a case for an understudy. There are reasons why."

"Then—you have done it?"

They were at the turn of the stair and Sylvia paused. He was conscious of a quick catch in her breath. Her eyes met his for an instant searchingly.

"Yes; I have done it," he answered, and looked at her wonderingly.

A moment later he had made his peace with Mrs. Owen and paid his compliments to Mrs. Bassett at the favor table, heaped high with beribboned hatchets and bunches of cherries for the first figure.

Morton Bassett had heard praise of his daughter from many lips, but he watched her joyous course through the cherry-tree figure in the german with an attention that was not wholly attributable to fatherly pride. Harwood's white-gloved hand led her hither and thither through the intricate maze; one must have been sadly lacking in the pictorial sense not to have experienced a thrill of delight in a scene so animate with grace, so touched with color. It was ungracious to question the sincerity of those who pronounced Marian the belle of the ball when Colonel Ramsay, the supreme authority in Hoosier pulchritude, declared her to be the fairest rose in a rose-garden of girls. He said the same thing to the adoring parents of a dozen other girls that night. (The Colonel was born in Tecumseh County, on our side of the Ohio, and just plays at being a Kentuckian!) Mothers of daughters, watching the dance with a jealous eye on their own offspring, whispered among themselves that as likely as not Marian's tall, broad-shouldered cavalier was the man chosen of all time to be her husband. He was her father's confidential man, and nothing could stay his upward course.

Bassett saw it all and guessed what they were thinking. Sylvia flashed across his vision now and then. He overheard people asking who she was, and he caught the answers, that she was a girl Mrs. Owen had taken up; a public school-teacher, they believed, the daughter of an old friend. Sylvia, quite unconscious of this interest, saw that the figures she had done so much toward planning were enacted without a hitch. The last one, the Pergola, with real roses, if you must know, well deserved Colonel Ramsay's compliment. "You can't tell," said the Colonel in his best manner, "where the roses end and the girls begin!"

It was two o'clock when Harwood, after taking Mrs. Owen down to supper, found himself free. He met Thatcher in the lower hall, muffled in astrakhan and swearing softly to himself because his carriage had been lost in the blizzard.

"Well; how are things going with you, young man?"

"Right enough. I'm tired and it's about bed-time for me."

"Haven't got House Bill Ninety-five in your pockets have you?" asked Thatcher with a grin. "A reporter for the 'Advertiser' was in here looking for you a minute ago. He said your committee had taken a vote to-night and he wanted to know about it. Told him you'd gone home. Hope you appreciate that; I'm used to lying to reporters. You see, my son, I ain't in that deal. You understand? That bill was fixed up in Chicago, and every corporation lawyer that does business in the old Hoosier State has his eye on it. I'm not asking any questions; Lord, no! It's up to you. Grand party; that's a nice girl of Bassett's. My wagon here? All right. Good-night, Dan! Good-night, Bassett!"

Harwood turned and found himself face to face with Bassett, who was loitering aimlessly about the hall.

"Good-evening, sir," he said, and they shook hands mechanically.

"How are you? Party about over?"

"I should like to speak to you to-night, Mr. Bassett. It need take but a minute."

"Better now, if it's important," replied Bassett carelessly.

"We voted on House Bill Ninety-five in committee to-night: the majority report will be against it."

"So? What was the matter with it?"

"It's crooked, that's all. I wouldn't stand for it; two members were willing to support it, and there will be a minority report. It's that same bill that was jumped on so hard at the last session, only it's been given a fresh coat of paint."

"It seems to have taken you several weeks to find that out. There's nothing wrong with that bill. It merely frames a natural and reasonable right into a statute. Those labor cranks at the State House have been trying to scare you."

"No, sir; that thing's dead wrong! You not only know it's wrong, but you misled me about it. That public benefit clause is put in there to throw dust in the eyes of the people; it makes possible the very combination and absorption of industries that the party is pledged to fight. I have bawled against those things in every county in Indiana!"

Bassett nodded, but showed no irritation. His manner irritated Harwood. The younger man's lips twitched slightly as he continued.

"And the fact that you were behind it has leaked out; the 'Advertiser' is on to it and is going to go after it to-morrow. House Bill Ninety-five is an outrage on the party honor and an affront to the intelligence of the people. And moreover your interest in having me made chairman of the committee that had to pass on it doesn't look good."

"Well, sir, what are you going to do about it? I'm not particularly interested in that bill; but a lot of our friends are behind it, and we've got to take care of our friends," said Bassett, without raising his voice.

Their relations were practically at an end; and Bassett did not care. But Dan felt the wrench; he felt it the more keenly because of Bassett's impassiveness at this moment of parting.

"You've been a kind friend to me, sir; you've—"

Bassett laid his hand with an abrupt gesture upon Harwood's arm, and smiled a curious, mirthless smile.

"None of that! I told you, when the time came for you to go, you need shed no tears at the parting. Remember, you don't owe me anything; we're quits."

"I hoped you wouldn't see it just this way; that you would realize the danger of that bill—to the party, to yourself!"

"You can score heavily by showing up the bill for what you think it is. Go ahead; it's your chance. I haven't a word to say to you."

He folded his white gloves and put them away carefully in his breast pocket.

"Good-night, sir!"

"Good-night, Harwood!"

The dancing continued above. Mrs. Owen insisted on seeing her last guest depart, but begged Harwood to take Sylvia home at once. As they left a few minutes later Dan caught a glimpse of Bassett sitting alone in the smoking-room.

On the way to Elizabeth House Dan told Sylvia what had happened.

The carriage plunged roughly through the drifting snow. Sleet drove sharply against the windows.

"He lied to me about it; and I thought that with all his faults he would play square with me. The whole corporation lobby is back of the bill. I was stupid not to have seen it earlier; I've been a dull ass about a lot of things. But it's over now; I'm done with him."

"I'm glad—glad you met it squarely—and glad that you settled it quickly. I'm glad"—she repeated slowly—"but I'm sorry too."

"Sorry?"

"Oh, I'm so sorry for him!"

CHAPTER XXV
THE LADY OF THE DAGUERREOTYPE

"Daniel doesn't seem to be coming," remarked Mrs. Owen. "He hardly ever misses a Sunday afternoon."

"He's working hard. I had no idea legislators had to work so hard," said Sylvia.

They sat in Mrs. Owen's office, which was cosier than the sitting-room, and the place where she seemed most comfortable. Since we looked at her desk last a file-hook has been added to its furniture, and on it hang impaled a few cuttings from agricultural newspapers. The content of these clippings will ultimately reach the "Courier's" readers,—there is no doubt of that, as Mrs. Owen and Mr. Atwill now understand each other perfectly. It was the first Sunday in March and a blustery day, with rain and sleet alternating at the windows and an impudent wind whistling in the chimneys. Hickory logs snapped pleasantly in the small fireplace that was a feature of the room. Sylvia had dined with her friend, and the day being of the sort that encourages confidences, they had prolonged their talk.

"When did you see Daniel last?" asked Mrs. Owen casually.

"Last night," replied Sylvia, meeting her friend's eyes easily. "He dropped in for a little while. He wanted to talk about his stand on that corporation bill."

"Well, he and Morton have broken up housekeeping. Daniel has climbed on to the other side of the breastworks."

Sylvia smiled. "Yes, that's about it. But I think he has acted quite finely about it."

"You mean he didn't jump on Morton as he might have done—didn't make a grand stand play of it?"

"Yes; he might have made capital for himself out of the corporation bill, but he didn't. He made his report without bringing personalities into it."

"And the bill was passed over the governor's veto! That was Morton's way of showing that he didn't need Daniel."

"Very likely. I'm rather glad it happened that way."

"Glad Daniel got a licking?"

"Oh, not just that; but it shows him that if he's going to be the people's champion he will have to be unhorsed pretty often. If all these things could be accomplished easily, there wouldn't be any glory in success. It's not an easy thing to drive a man like Mr. Bassett out of politics, or even to defeat the dangerous measures he introduces in the legislature. If it were easy to get rid of them, such men wouldn't last long. Besides, I'm a little afraid it wasn't half so much Dan's patriotism that was involved as it was his vanity. He was bitter because he found that Mr. Bassett had deceived him and was trying to use him. But in view of Mr. Bassett's many kindnesses to him he wouldn't make a personal matter of it in the House. Dan's opposition was based on legal defects in that bill,—points that were over the heads of most of the legislators,—but he is now determined to keep up the fight. He finds that Mr. Bassett is quite able to do as he pleases even without his services. He felt that he dealt with him magnanimously in keeping his antagonism to the corporation bill on the high plane of its legal unsoundness. Mr. Bassett ignored this, and merely secured the passage of the bill by marshaling all the votes he needed in both parties."

"That's a new scheme they say Morton has introduced into Indiana— this getting men on both sides to vote for one of these bad bills. That shuts up the party newspapers, and neither side can use that particular thing as ammunition at the next election. Instead of talking about House Bill Ninety-five in the next campaign, they will howl about the tariff on champagne, or pensions for veterans of the Black Hawk War. They're all tarred with the same stick and don't dare call attention to the other fellow. Daniel had better get out of politics," she ended leadingly.

"Please, no! He'd better stay in and learn how to make himself count. So far as Mr. Bassett is concerned, I think that for some reason he had gone as far with Dan as he cared to. I think he was prepared for the break."

Mrs. Owen was wiping her spectacles on a piece of chamois skin she kept in her desk for the purpose, and she concluded this rite with unusual deliberation.

"How do you figure that out, Sylvia?"

"This must be confidential, Aunt Sally; I have said nothing to Dan about it; but the night of your party Mr. Bassett was in a curious frame of mind."

"It seemed to me he was particularly cheerful. I thought Morton had as good a time as anybody."

"Superficially, yes; but I had a long talk with him—in the hall, after the dancing had begun. I think in spite of his apparent indifference to the constant fire of his enemies, it has had an effect on him. He's hardened—or, if he was always hard, he doesn't care any longer whether he wears the velvet glove or not. That attack on Mr. Thatcher in the convention illustrates what I mean. His self-control isn't as complete as most people seem to think it is; he lets go of himself like a petulant child. That must be a new development in him. It doesn't chime with the other things you hear of him as a shrewd, calculating manager, who strikes his enemies in the dark. He was in an evil humor that night or he wouldn't have talked to me as he did. He was ugly and vindictive. He was not only glad he had put Dan in the way of temptation, but he wanted me to know that he had done it. He seemed to be setting his back to the wall and daring the world."

"Well, well," said Mrs. Owen. "Morton has seemed a little uneasy lately. But there don't seem to be any reason why he should have picked you out to jump on. You never did anything to Morton."

"Yes," said Sylvia, smiling; "I laughed at him once! I laughed at him about the way he had treated Mr. Thatcher. We stopped right there, with the laugh; he laughed too, you know. And he took that up again at the party—and I had to explain what my laugh meant."

"Oh, you explained it, did you?"

And Sylvia recounted the interview.

"I guess Morton hasn't been laughed at much, and that was why he remembered it and wanted to talk to you again. I suspect that Hallie scolds him when she doesn't pet him. Most folks are afraid of Morton; that's why he could take care of that corporation bill with the 'Advertiser' jumping him the way it did. Well, well! That must have been quite a day for Morton. You laughed at him, and when the rest of you went off in Allen's automobile that night I ran the harrow over him a few times myself. Well, well!"

Mrs. Owen smiled as though recalling an agreeable experience. "As long as there are old stumps in a field that you must plough around I haven't got much use for the land. When the corn comes up you don't see the stumps, just sitting on the fence and looking over the scenery; but when you go to put the plow through again, your same old stumps loom up again, solider than ever. I guess Daniel will come out all right; he was raised on a farm and ought to know how to drive a straight furrow. By the way, they telephoned me from Elizabeth House last night that there's a vacant room there. Who's moved out?"

Mrs. Owen always prolonged the E of Elizabeth, and never referred to the House except by its full title.

"Rose Farrell has left. Went unexpectedly, I think. I didn't know she was going."

"Let me see. She's that girl that worked for Morton and Daniel. What's she leaving for?"

"I'm going to see if I can't get her back," replied Sylvia evasively.

"Why Rose has been at Elizabeth House for two years and under the rules she can stay a year longer. She ain't getting married, is she?"

"I think not," replied Sylvia. "I'm going to look her up and get her back if possible."

"You do that, Sylvia. It ain't just your place, but I'll be glad if you'll see what's the matter. We don't want to lose a girl if we can help it."

Mrs. Owen rose and transferred a pile of paperbound books from a shelf to her desk. Sylvia recognized these as college catalogues and noted bits of paper thrust into the leaves as markers.

"I've been looking into this business some since we went down to college. I had a lot of these schools send me their catalogues and they're mighty interesting, though a good deal of it I don't understand. Sylvia" (Sylvia never heard her name drawled as Mrs. Owen spoke it without a thrill of expectancy)—"Sylvia, there's a lot of books being written, and pieces in the magazines all the time, about women and what we have done or can't do. What do you suppose it's all leading up to?"

"That question is bigger than I am, Aunt Sally. But I think the conditions that have thrown women out into the world as wage-earners are forcing one thing—just one thing, that is more important now than any other—it's all summed up in the word efficiency."

"Efficiency?"

Mrs. Owen reached for the poker and readjusted the logs; she watched the resulting sparks for a moment, then settled herself back in her chair and repeated Sylvia's word again.

"You mean that a woman has got to learn how to make her jelly jell? Is that your notion?"

"Exactly that. She must learn not to waste her strokes. Any scheme of education for Swoman that leaves that out works an injury. If women are to be a permanent part of the army of wage-earning Americans they must learn to get full value from their minds or hands—either one, it's the same. The trouble with us women is that there's a lot of the old mediæval taint in us."

"Mediæval? Say that some other way, Sylvia."

"I mean that we're still crippled—we women—by the long years in which nothing was expected of us but to sit in ivy-mantled casements and work embroidery while our lords went out to fight, or thrummed the lute under our windows."

"Well, there was Joan of Arc: she delivered the goods."

"To be sure; she does rather light up her time, doesn't she?" laughed Sylvia.

"Sylvia, the day I first saw a woman hammer a typewriter in a man's office, I thought the end had come. It seemed, as the saying is, 'agin nater'; and I reckon it was. Nowadays these buildings downtown are full of women. At noontime Washington Street is crowded with girls who work in offices and shops. They don't get much pay for it either. Most of those girls would a lot rather work in an office or stand behind a counter than stay at home and help their mothers bake and scrub and wash and iron. These same girls used to do just that,—help their mothers,—coming downtown about once a month, or when there was a circus procession, and having for company some young engine-wiper who took them to church or to a Thanksgiving matinée and who probably married them some day. A girl who didn't marry took in sewing for the neighbors, and as like as not went to live with her married sister and looked after her babies. I've seen all these things change. Nowadays girls have got to have excitement. They like spending their days in the big buildings; the men in the offices jolly them, the men bookkeepers and clerks seem a lot nicer than the mechanics that live out in their neighborhood. When they ain't busy they loaf in the halls of the buildings flirting, or reading novels and talking to their bosses' callers. They don't have to soil their hands, and you can dress a girl up in a skirt and shirt-waist so she looks pretty decent for about two weeks of her wages. They don't care much about getting married unless they can strike some fellow with an automobile who can buy them better clothes than they can buy themselves. What they hanker for is a flat or boarding-house where they won't have any housekeeping to do. Housekeeping! Their notions of housekeeping don't go beyond boiling an egg on a gas range and opening up a sofa to sleep on. You're an educated woman, Sylvia; what's going to come of all this?"

"It isn't just the fault of the girls that they do this, is it? Near my school-house there are girls who stay at home with their mothers, and many of them are without any ambition of any kind. I'm a good deal for the girl who wants to strike out for herself. The household arts as you knew them in your youth can't be practised in the home any more on the income of the average man. Most women of the kind we're talking about wear ready-made clothes—not because they're lazy, but because the tailor-made suits which life in a city demands can't be made by any amateur sempstress. They're turned out by the carload in great factories from designs of experts. There's no bread to bake in the modern mechanic's home, for better bread and cake are made more cheaply in the modern bakeshop. Wasn't there really a good deal of nonsense about the pies that mother used to make—I wonder? There were perhaps in every community women who were natural cooks, but our Mary used to drive grandfather crazy with her saleratus biscuits and greasy doughnuts. A good cook in the old times was famous all over the community because the general level of cooking was so low. Women used to take great pride in their preservings and jellyings, but at the present prices of fruit and sugar a city woman would lose money making such things. It's largely because this work can't be done at home that girls such as we have at Elizabeth House have no sort of manual dexterity and have to earn a poor living doing something badly that they're not interested in or fitted for. Women have one terrible handicap in going out into the world to earn their living; it's the eternal romance that's in all of us," said Sylvia a little dreamily. "I don't believe any woman ever gets beyond that." It was a note she rarely struck and Mrs. Owen looked at her quickly. "I mean, the man who may be always waiting just around the corner."

"You mean every girl has that chance before her? Well, a happy marriage is a great thing—the greatest thing that can happen to a woman. My married life was a happy one—very happy; but it didn't last long. It was my misfortune to lose my husband and the little girl when I was still young. They think I'm hard—yes, a good many people do—because I've been making money. But I had to do something; I couldn't sit with my hands folded; and what I've done I've tried to do right. I hope you won't leave love and marriage out of your life, Sylvia. In this new condition of things that we've talked about there's no reason why a woman shouldn't work—do things, climb up high, and be a woman, too. He'll be a lucky man who gets you to stand by him and work for him and with him."

"Oh," sighed Sylvia, "there are so many things to do! I want to know so much and do so much!"

"You'll know them and do them; but I don't want you to have a one-sided life. Dear Sylvia," and Mrs. Owen bent toward the girl and touched her hand gently, "I don't want you to leave love out of your life."

There was an interval of silence and then Mrs. Owen opened a drawer and drew out a faded morocco case. "Here's a daguerreotype of my mother and me, when I was about four years old. Notice how cute I look in those pantalets—ever see those things before? Well, I've been thinking that I'm a kind of left-over from daguerreotype times, and you belong to the day of the kodak. I'm a dingy old shadow in a daguerreotype picture, in pantalets, cuddled up against my mother's hoopskirt. You, Sylvia, can take a suit-case and a kodak and travel alone to Siam; and you can teach in a college alongside of men and do any number of things my mother would have dropped dead to think about. And," she added quizzically, "it gives me heart failure myself sometimes, just thinking about it all. I can't make you throw your kodak away, and I wouldn't if I could, any more than I'd want you to sit up all night sewing clothes to wear to your school-teaching when you can buy better ones already made that have real style. It tickles me that some women have learned that it's weak-minded to massage and paraffine their wrinkles out—those things, Sylvia, strike me as downright immoral. What I've been wondering is whether I can do anything for the kind of girls we have at Elizabeth House beyond giving them a place to sleep, and I guess you've struck the idea with that word efficiency. No girl born to-day, particularly in a town like this, is going back to make her own soap out of grease and lye in her back yard. But she's got to learn to do something well or she'll starve or go to the bad; or if she doesn't have to work she'll fool her life away doing nothing. Now you poke a few holes in my ideas, Sylvia."

"Please, Aunt Sally, don't think that because I've been to college I can answer all those questions! I'm just beginning to study them. But the lady of the daguerreotype in hoops marks one era, and the kodak girl in a short skirt and shirt-waist another. Women had to spend a good deal of time proving that their brains could stand the strain of higher education—that they could take the college courses prescribed for men. That's all been settled now, but we can't stop there. A college education for women is all right, but we must help the girl who can't go to college to do her work well in the office and department store and factory."

"Or to feed a baby so it won't die of colic, and to keep ptomaine poison out of her ice box!" added Mrs. Owen.

"Exactly," replied Sylvia.

"Suppose a girl like Marian had gone to college just as you did, what would it have done for her?"

"A good deal, undoubtedly. It would have given her wider interests and sobered her, and broadened her chances of happiness."

"Maybe so," remarked Mrs. Owen; and then a smile stole over her face. "I reckon you can hardly call Marian a kodak girl. She's more like one of these flashlight things they set off with a big explosion. Only time I ever got caught in one of those pictures was at a meeting of the Short-Horn Breeders' Association last week. They fired off that photograph machine to get a picture for the 'Courier'—I've been prodding them for not printing more farm and stock news—and a man sitting next to me jumped clean out of his boots and yelled fire. I had to go over to the 'Courier' office and see the editor—that Atwill is a pretty good fellow when you get used to him—to make sure they didn't guy us farmers for not being city broke. As for Marian, folks like her!"

"No one can help liking her. She's a girl of impulses and her impulses are all healthy and sound. And her good fellowship and good feeling are inexhaustible. She came over to see me at Elizabeth House the other evening—had Allen bring her in his machine and leave her. The girls were singing songs and amusing themselves in the parlor, and Marian took off her hat and made herself at home with them. She sang several songs, and then got to 'cutting up' and did some of those dances she's picked up somewhere—did them well too. But with all her nonsense she has a lot of good common sense, and she will find a place for herself. She will get married one of these days and settle down beautifully."

"Allen?"

"Possibly. The Bassetts don't seem troubled by Allen's attentions to Marian; but the real fight between Mr. Thatcher and Mr. Bassett hasn't come yet."

"Who says so?"

"Oh, it's in the air; every one says so. Dan says so."

"I've warned Morton to let Edward Thatcher alone. The United States Senate wouldn't be ornamented by having either one of them down there. I met Colonel Ramsay—guess he's got the senatorial bee in his hat, too—coming up on the train from Louisville the other day. There's only one qualification I can think of that the Colonel has for going to the Senate—he would wring tears out of the galleries when he made obituary speeches about the dead members. When my brother Blackford was senator, it seemed to me he spent most of his time acting as pallbearer for the dead ones. But what were we talking about, Sylvia? Oh, yes. I'm going to send those catalogues over to your room, and as you get time I want you to study out a scheme for a little school to teach what you call efficiency to girls that have to earn their living. I don't mean school-teaching, but a whole lot of things women ought to be doing but ain't because they don't know how. Do you get the idea?"

"A school?" asked Sylvia wonderingly.

"A kind of school."

"It's a splendid, a beautiful idea, but you need better advice than I can give you. They talk a good deal now about vocational training, and it's going to mean a great deal to women."

"Well, we must get hold of all the latest ideas, and if there's any good in us old daguerreotypes, we'll keep it, and graft it on to the kodak."

"Oh, I hope there will always be ladies of the daguerreotype! One thing we women have to pray to be saved from is intolerance toward our sisters. You know," continued Sylvia with a dropping of her voice and a tilting of her head that caused Mrs. Owen to laugh,—"you know we are not awfully tolerant. And there's a breadth of view, an ability to brush away trifles and get to the heart of things, that we're just growing up to. And magnanimity—I think we fall short there. I'm just now trying to cultivate a sisterly feeling toward these good women for whom Jane Austen and Sir Roger de Coverley and the knitting of pale-blue tea cosies are all of life— who like mild twilight with the children singing hymns at the piano and the husband coming home to find his slippers set up against the baseburner. That was beautiful, but even they owe something to the million or so women to whom Jane Addams is far more important than Jane Austen. It might be more comfortable if the world never moved, but unfortunately it does seem to turn over occasionally."

"I notice that you can say things like that, Sylvia, without waving your hands, or shouting like an old woman with a shawl on her head swinging a broom at the boys in her cherry tree. We've got to learn to do that. It was some time after I went into business, when Jackson Owen died, before I learned that you couldn't shoo men the way you shoo hens. You got to drop a little corn in a fence corner and then throw your apron over 'em. It strikes me that if you could catch these girls that go to work in stores and offices young enough you might put them in the way of doing something better. There are schools doing this kind of thing, but I'd like to plant one right here in Indiana for the kind of girls we've got at Elizabeth House. They haven't much ambition, most of 'em; they're stuck right where they are. I'd like to see what can be done toward changing that, and see it started in my lifetime. And we must do it right. Think it over as you get time." She glanced at the window. "You'd better stay all night, Sylvia; it's getting dark."

"No, I must run along home. The girls expect me."

"That school idea's just between you and me for the present," Mrs. Owen remarked as she watched Sylvia button her mackintosh. "Look here, Sylvia, don't you need some money? I mean, of course, don't you want to borrow some?"

"Oh, never! By the way, I didn't tell you that I expect to make some? The publisher of one of grandfather's textbooks came to see me about the copyright, and there were some changes in the book that grandfather thought should be made and I'm going to make them. There's a chance of it's being adopted in one or two states. And then, I want to make a geometry of my own. All the textbooks make it so hard—and it really isn't. The same publisher told me he thought well of my scheme, and I'm going ahead with it."

"Well, don't you kill yourself writing geometries: I should think teaching the youngsters would be a full job."

"That's not a job at all, Aunt Sally; that's just fun. And you know I'm not going to do it always. I'm learning things now that I needed to know. I only wish my mind were as sound as my health."

"You ought to wear heavier flannels, though; it's a perfect scandal what girls run around in nowadays."

She rested her hands on Sylvia's shoulders lightly, smiled into her face, and then bent forward and kissed her.

"I don't understand why you won't wear rubbers, but be sure you don't sit around all evening in wet stockings."

A gray mist was hastening nightfall, though the street lamps were not yet lighted. The glow of Mrs. Owen's kindness lingered with Sylvia as she walked toward Elizabeth House. She was constantly surprised by her friend's intensely modern spirit—her social curiosity, and the breadth and sanity of her views. This suggestion of a vocational school for young women had kindled Sylvia's imagination, and her thoughts were upon it as she tramped homeward through the slush. To establish an institution such as Mrs. Owen had indicated would require a large sum of money, and there were always the Bassetts, the heirs apparent of their aunt's fortune. Any feeling of guilt Sylvia may have experienced by reason of her enforced connivance with Mrs. Owen for the expenditure of her money was mitigated by her belief that the Bassetts were quite beyond the need of their aunt's million, the figure at which Mrs. Owen's fortune was commonly appraised.

She was thinking of this when a few blocks from Mrs. Owen's she met Morton Bassett. The electric lamp overhead was just sputtering into light as he moved toward her out of an intersecting street. His folded umbrella was thrust awkwardly under his arm, and he walked slowly with bent head. The hissing of the lamp caused him to lift his eyes. Sylvia paused an instant, and he raised his hat as he recognized her.

"Good evening, Miss Garrison! I've just been out for a walk. It's a dreary evening, isn't it?"

Sylvia explained that she had been to Mrs. Owen's and was on her way home, and he asked if he might go with her.

"Marian usually walked with me at Fraserville, but since we've been here, Sunday seems to be her busy day. I find that I don't know much about the residential district; I can easily lose myself in this part of town."

During these commonplaces she wondered just where their conversation at Marian's ball had left them; the wet street was hardly a more favorable place for serious talk than the crowded Propylæum. The rain began to fall monotonously, and he raised his umbrella.

"Some things have happened since our last talk," he observed presently.

"Yes?" she replied dubiously.

"I want to talk to you of them," he answered. "Dan has left me. You know that?"

"Yes; I know of it."

"And you think he has done quite the fine thing about it—it was what you would have had him do?"

"Yes, certainly. You practically told me you were putting him to the test. You weren't embarrassed by his course in any way; you were able to show him that you didn't care; you didn't need him."

"You saw that? You read that in what followed?"

"It was written so large that no one could miss it. You are the master. You proved it again. I suppose you found a great satisfaction in that. A man must, or he wouldn't do such things."

"You seem to understand," he replied, turning toward her for an instant. "But there may be one thing you don't understand."

There was a moment of silence, in which they splashed on slowly through the slush.

"I liked Dan; I was fond of him. And yet I deliberately planned to make him do that kind of thing for me. I pulled him out of the newspaper office and made it possible for him to study law, just that I might put my hand on him when he could be useful. Please understand that I'm not saying this in the hope that you will intercede to bring him back. Nothing can bring him back. I wouldn't let him come back to me if he would starve without my help."

Sylvia was silent; there was nothing with which she could meet this.

"What I mean is," he continued, "that I'm glad he shook me; I had wondered from the beginning just when it would come, and when I saw his things going out of my office, it satisfied something in me. I wonder whether there's some good in me after all that made me glad in spite of myself that he had the manhood to quit."

Bassett was a complex character; his talk and manner at Marian's ball had given her a sense of this which he was now confirming. Success had not brought him happiness; the loss of Dan had been a blow to him, and she felt the friendlessness and isolation of this man whom men feared. He had spoken doggedly, gruffly, and if she had marveled at their talk at the dance, her wonder was the greater now. It was inconceivable that Morton Bassett should come to her with his difficulties. If his conscience troubled him, or if he was touched with remorse for his conduct toward Dan Harwood, she was unable to see why he should make his confession to her. It seemed that he had read her thoughts, for he spoke roughly, as though defending himself from an attack.

"You like him; you've known him for several years; you know him probably better than you know any other man."

"I suppose I do, Mr. Bassett," said Sylvia; "we are good friends, but—that's all."

He stopped short, and she felt his hand touch her arm for an instant lightly—it was almost like a caress, there in the rain-swept street with the maple boughs swishing overhead in the cold west wind.

He quickened his pace now, as though to mark a new current in his thoughts.

"There's a favor I want to ask of you, Miss Garrison. Dan talked to me once or twice about your grandfather's estate. He owned some shares in a business I had helped to organize, the White River Canneries. The scheme failed for many reasons; the shares are worthless. I want you to let me pay you back the money Professor Kelton paid for them. I should have to do it privately—it would have to be a matter between you and me."

A SUDDEN FIERCE ANGER BURNED IN HER HEART

"Oh, no! Dan explained that to me; he didn't hold you responsible. He said the company failed, that was all. You are kind to offer, but I can't think of accepting it."

"Very well," he said quietly. And then added, as though to explain himself more fully: "Your grandfather and Mrs. Owen were old friends. He wasn't a business man. I promoted the canneries scheme and I was responsible for it, no matter what Harwood says about it."

She had experienced sharp alternations of pity and apprehension in this brief walk. He was a prominent man; almost, it might be said, a notorious character. The instinct of self-protection was strong in her; what might lie behind his confidences, his blunt confessions, and his offer of help, she did not know. They had reached Elizabeth House, and she paused on the broad steps under the shelter of the veranda. With her back toward the door she looked down upon him as he stood on the sidewalk, his umbrella deeply shadowing his head and shoulders. She stood before him like a vestal guarding her temple from desecration. She was conscious of a sharp revulsion of feeling, and a sudden fierce anger burned in her heart. She spoke with a quick, passionate utterance.

"There is something you can do for me, Mr. Bassett. I'm going to bring Rose Farrell back to this house. I want you to let her alone!"

He stood dumbly staring at the door as it closed upon her. He lingered a moment, the rain beating down upon him, and then walked slowly homeward.

CHAPTER XXVI
APRIL VISTAS

"Is it *possible*? *Is* it possible!"

Colonel Ramsay's entrances were frequently a bit theatrical, and on a particular afternoon in April, as he opened the door of Dan Harwood's new office in the Law Building, the sight of Miss Farrell at the typewriter moved him to characteristic demonstrations. Carefully closing the door and advancing, hat in hand, with every appearance of deepest humility, he gazed upon the young woman with a mockery of astonishment.

"Verily, it is possible," he solemnly ejaculated. "And what is it that our own poet says:—

"'When she comes home again! A thousand ways
I fashion to myself the tenderness
Of my glad welcome: I shall tremble—yes—'"

"Stop trembling, Colonel, and try one of our new office chairs, warranted to hold anybody but Brother Ike Pettit without fading away."

The Colonel bent over Miss Farrell's hand reverently and sat down.

"I've been trying to earn an honest living practicing law down at home and this is the first chance I've had to come up and see what the late lamented legislature left of the proud old Hoosier State. Is Dan locked up inside there with some lucrative client?"

"I regret to say that I don't believe there's a cent in his present caller."

"Hark!" At this moment a roar was heard from the inner room on which "private" was printed in discreet letters. The Colonel was at once alert.

"'Ask me no more; the moon may draw the sea'
But Isaac Pettit's jokes shall shake the land,—

with apologies to the late Laureate. So the boys are finding their way up here, are they? I'll wait an hour or two till that compendium of American humor has talked Dan to sleep. So you and Dan left your Uncle Morton all alone in gloomy splendor in the Boordman Building!"

"Mr. Harwood made me an offer and I accepted it," replied Rose. "This is a free country and a P.W.G. can work where she pleases, can't she?"

"P.W.G.?"

"Certainly, a poor working-girl"—Rose clasped her hands and bowed her head—"if the initials fail to illuminate."

The Colonel inspected the room, and his eyes searched Miss Farrell's desk.

"Let me see, I seem to miss something. It must be the literary offerings that used to cluster about the scene of your labors. Your selections in old times used to delight me. No one else of my acquaintance has quite your feeling for romance. I always liked that one about the square-jawed American engineer who won the Crown Princess of Piffle from her father in a poker game, but decided at the last minute to bestow her upon his old college friend, the Russian heir-apparent, just to preserve the peace of Europe. I remember I found you crying over the great renunciation one day."

"Oh, I've passed that all up, Colonel. I'm strong for the pale high-brow business now. I'm doing time in all the night classes at Elizabeth House where I board, and you'll hardly know your little Rose pretty soon."

"Fitting yourself for one of the learned professions?"

"Scarcely. Just fitting myself to be decent," replied Rose in a tone that shifted the key of the conversation—a change which the Colonel respected.

"That's right, Rose. This is a good place for you, and so is Mrs. Owen's boarding-house. By the way, who's this school-teacher Aunt Sally has taken up—saw her at the party-great chum of the old lady's."

"You must mean Miss Sylvia."

"Sylvia?"

"Miss Sylvia Garrison. Colonel Ramsay," continued Rose earnestly, resting an elbow lightly on her typewriter, "you and I are old pals—you remember that first winter I was over at the State House?"

"Very well, Rose."

"Well, it wasn't a good place for me to be. But I was a kid and hadn't much sense. I've learned a good deal since then. It ain't so easy to walk straight; so many people are careless about leaving banana peelings lying round."

The Colonel nodded.

"You needn't apologize to me, Rose. It's all right now, is it?"

"You can be dead sure of it, Colonel. Miss Garrison caught me by the heel of my shoe, just as I was going down the third time, and yanked me back. There's a good many cheap imitations of human beings loose around this world, but that's a woman, I can tell you!"

"Glad you struck a good friend, Rose. You did well to come along with Harwood."

"Well, she fixed that, too, after I cut loose from *him*—you understand? I guess Miss Garrison and Mr. Harwood are pretty good friends."

"Oh!" ejaculated Ramsay. "So there's that, is there?"

"I hope so; they're all white and speak the same language. This is on the dead. I'm only talking to you because you're an old friend."

An occasional roar from within testified to Mr. Pettit's continued enjoyment of his own jokes.

"You know," Rose continued, "I learned a good deal those winters I spent at the State House, when I was stenog to certain senate committees. I see where you stand now, all right, Colonel. I always knew you didn't belong in that bunch of lobbyists that was always gum-shoeing through the marble halls of the State House. Thatcher sends somebody around to look me up every little while to see if he can't coax something out of me,—something he can use, you know."

"Thatcher oughtn't to do that. If you want me to, I'll pull him off."

"No; I guess I can take care of myself. He"—Rose indicated the inner office with a slight movement of the head, "he never tries to pump me. He ain't that kind of a fighter. But everybody that's anywhere near the inside knows that Thatcher carries a sharp knife. He's going to shed some pink ink before he gets through. Are you on?"

They exchanged a glance.

"Something that isn't nice?"

Rose nodded.

"I hate to see that sort of thing brought into the game. But they'll never find anything. The gentleman we are referring to works on noiseless rollers." Colonel Ramsay indicated the closed door by an almost imperceptible gesture of interrogation; and Rose replied by compressing her lips and shaking her head.

"He isn't in on that; he's a gentleman, you know; not a mud-slinger."

"He might have to stand for anything Thatcher springs. Thatcher has developed into a shrewd and hard fighter. The other crowd don't laugh at him any more; it was his work that got our legislative ticket through last fall when Bassett passed the word that we should take a licking just to magnify his importance. Is Thatcher in town now?"

"No; that boy of his with the bad lung had to go off to the Adirondacks, and he went with him."

The inner door opened at this moment, disclosing the Honorable Isaac Pettit, who greeted Ramsay effusively.

"What is immortality, gentlemen!" the Honorable Isaac Pettit inquired, clinging to the Colonel's hand. "We had a little social gathering for our new pastor up at Fraser the other night, and I sprung a new game on the old folks. Offered a prize for anybody who could name all the Vice-Presidents of the United States since Lincoln's administration, and they couldn't even get past Grant—and Schuyler Colfax being right off our own Hoosier pastures! Then we tried for the Democratic candidates for President, beginning back at the war, and they couldn't even start. One young chap piped up and said Jeff Davis—oh, Lord!—which reminds me that the teaching of history in the public schools ain't what it ought to be. They hadn't heard of Hancock, and when somebody said Blaine, the teacher of the infant class in our Sunday School said Blaine who? That reminds me of one time when I met Dan Voorhees, than whom God Almighty never made a nobler soul; I met Dan down here in the lobby of the old Bates House, carrying a 'Harper's Weekly' with one of Tom Nast's cartoons spread wide open. You know Dan had—"

Colonel Ramsay had been edging toward the door of Harwood's private room, and he now broke in upon the editor's reminiscences.

"You tell that story to Miss Farrell, Ike. I'm spouting myself to-night, at a Christian Endeavor rally at Tipton, and want to see Dan a minute."

Miss Farrell was inured to Pettit's anecdotes of Dan Voorhees, and the Fraserville editor continued, unmindful of the closing of the door upon Dan and Ramsay.

Ramsay pushed his fedora to the back of his head and inspected Dan's new furniture.

"Well, you did it! You've cut loose from your base and burned your bridges behind you. I would have brought my congratulations sooner, but I've had a long jury case on hand. You did it, my boy, and you did it like a gentleman. You might have killed him if you had wanted to."

"I don't want to kill anybody," smiled Dan. "I want to practice law."

"That's a laudable ambition, but you can't go back on us now. What we've needed for a long time was a young man of about your make-up who wasn't afraid."

"Don't rub it in, Colonel. I was a mighty long time seeing the light, and I don't deserve any praise from anybody. I mean what I say about practicing law. I'm a free man now and any political work I do is going to be along the lines of the simple, childish ideas I brought home from college with me. I had begun to feel that all this political idealism was sheer rubbish, but I put the brakes on before I got too far downhill. If a few of us who have run with the machine and know the tricks will turn and help the bewildered idealists, we can make idealism effective. Most of the people don't want a handful of crooks to govern them, but there's a kind of cheap cynicism abroad that discourages the men who are eager to revolt. There are newspapers that foster that sentiment, and scores of men who won't take time to go to a caucus keep asking what's the use. Now, as for Bassett, I'm not going to bite the hand that fed me; I'm simply going to feed myself. Pettit was just in here to sound me as to my feelings toward Thatcher. Quite frankly, I'm not interested in Thatcher as a senatorial possibility."

"That's all right; but if you had to make a choice between Thatcher and Bassett?"

Dan shrugged his shoulders impatiently.

"You mustn't exaggerate the importance of my influence. I don't carry United States senatorships around in my pocket."

"You're the most influential man of your age in our state. I'm not so sure you wouldn't be able to elect any man you supported if the election were held to-morrow."

"You've mastered the delicate art of flattery, Colonel; when the time comes, I'll be in the fight. It's not so dead certain that our party's going to have a senator to elect—there's always that. But all the walls are covered with handwriting these days that doesn't need interpreting by me or any other Daniel. Many of the younger men all over this state in both parties are getting ready to assert themselves. What we want—what you want, I believe—is to make this state count for something in national affairs. Just changing parties doesn't help anything. I'd rather not shift at all than send some fellow to the Senate just because he can capture a caucus. It's my honest conviction that any man can get a caucus vote if he will play according to the old rules. You and I go out over the state bawling to the people that they are governing this country. We appeal to them for their votes when we know well enough that between Thatcher and Bassett as Democrats, and 'Big' Jordan and Ridgefield in the Republican camp, the people don't stand to win. It may tickle you to know that I've had some flattering invitations lately to join the Republicans—not from the old guard, mind you, but from some of the young fellows who want to score results for policies, not politicians. I suppose, after all, Colonel, I'm only a kind of academic Democrat, with no patience whatever with this eternal hitching of our ancient mule to the saloons and breweries just to win. In the next campaign I'm going to preach my academic Democracy all the way from Lake Michigan to the Ohio River, up and down and back and forth—and I'm going to do it at my own expense and not be responsible to any state committee or anybody else. That's about where I stand."

"Good; mighty good, Dan. All the rest of us want is for you to holler that in your biggest foghorn voice and you'll find the crowd with you."

"But if the crowd isn't with me, it won't make a bit of difference; I shall bark just the same."

"Now that we've got down to brass tacks, I'll tell you what I've thought ever since Bassett got his clamps on the party: that he really hasn't any qualities of leadership; that grim, silent way of his is a good deal of a bluff. If anybody ever has the nerve to set off a firecracker just behind him, he'll run a mile. The newspapers keep flashing him up in big headlines all the time, and that helps to keep the people fooled. The last time I saw him was just after he put through that corporation bill you broke on, and he didn't seem to have got much fun out of his victory; he looked pretty gray and worried. It wasn't so easy pulling through House Bill Ninety-five; it was the hardest job of Mort's life; but he had to do it or take the count. And Lord! he certainly lost his head in defeating those appropriation bills; he let his spite toward the governor get the better of him. It wasn't the Republican governor he put in the hole; it was his own party."

"That's the way with all these men of his type on both sides; they have no real loyalty; they will sacrifice their parties any time just to further personal ends, or in this case it would seem to have been out of sheer bad temper. I didn't use to think Bassett had any temper or any kind of emotional organization. But when he's mad it's the meanest kind of mad, blind and revengeful."

"He's forced an extra session—he's brought that on us. Just chew on that a minute, Dan. A Republican governor has got to reassemble a Democratic legislature merely to correct its own faults. It looks well in print, by George! Speaking of print, how did he come to let go of the 'Courier,' and who owns that sheet anyway? I thought when Thatcher sprung that suit and dragged our Aunt Sally into it, the Wabash River would run hot lava for the next forty years. But that night of the ball she and Mort stood there on the firing-line as though nothing had ever happened."

Harwood grinned and shook his head gravely.

"There are some things, Colonel, that even to a good friend like you I can't give away. Besides, I promised Atwill not to tell."

"All right, Dan. And now, for fear you may think I've got something up my sleeve, I want to say to you with my hand on my heart that I don't want any office now or ever!"

"Now, Colonel, be very careful!" laughed Dan.

"No; I'm not up here on a fishing-trip. But I want you to know where I stand and the friendly feeling of a whole lot of people toward you. You say the younger men are getting tired of the old boss system; I'll tell you that a lot of the old fellows too are beginning to get restless. The absurdity of the whole game on both sides is beginning to get into the inner consciousness of the people. You know if I had stayed regular when the free-silver business came on I might have been in a position now to play for the governorship — which is the only thing I ever wanted; rather nice to be governor of your own state, and have your name scratched on a slab at the State House door; it's even conceivable, Daniel, that a man might do a little good — barely possible," he concluded dryly. "I'm out of it now for good; but anything I can do to help you, don't wait to write, just telephone me. Now —"

"I'm not so sure you can't make it yet; I'd like to see you there."

"Thanks, Daniel; but like you I'm in the ranks of the patriots and not looking for the pie counter. Here's another matter. Do you mind telling me what you're up to in this White River Canneries business? I notice that you've been sticking the can-opener into it."

"Yes; that protest of the original stockholders against the reorganization is still pending. As administrator of the estate of Professor Kelton — you remember him — Madison College — I filed a petition to be let into the case. It's been sleeping along for a couple of years — stockholders too poor to put up a fight. I've undertaken to probe clear into the mire. I've got lots of time and there's lots of mire!"

"Good. They say the succotash and peaches were all cooked in the same pot, and that our Uncle Mort did the skimming."

"So they say; but believe me, I can attack him without doing violence to my professional conscience. White River Canneries was never in the Boordman office to my knowledge. This isn't vengeance on my part; it's my duty to get what I can for the estate."

"Well, some of our farmers down my way got soaked in that deal, but it never seemed worth while to waste their money in litigation. I'll be glad to turn the claims I have in my office over to you; the more you have, the stronger fight you can make."

"Good. I welcome business. I'm going to see if I can't get to the bottom of the can."

As a *révolté* Dan had attracted more attention than he liked, in all the circumstances. Now that the legislature had adjourned, he was anxious to give his energy to the law, and he did not encourage political pilgrims to visit his office. He felt that he had behaved generously toward his old chief when the end came, and the promptness with which Bassett's old guard sought to impeach his motives in fighting the corporation bill angered him. Threats of retaliation were conveyed to him from certain quarters; and from less violent sources he heard much of his ingratitude toward the man who had "made" him. He had failed in his efforts to secure the passage of several measures whose enactment was urged by the educational and philanthropic interests of the community, and this was plainly attributable to the animosity aroused by his desertion of the corporation bill. He had not finished with this last measure, which had been passed by Bassett's bi-partisan combination over the governor's veto. The labor organizations were in arms against it and had engaged Dan to attack it in the courts.

Sylvia's approval of his course had been as cordial as he could have asked, and as the spring advanced they were much together. They attended concerts, the theatre, and lectures, as often as she had time for relaxation, and they met pretty regularly at Mrs. Owen's dinner table on Sunday—often running out for long tramps in the country afterward, to return for supper, and a renewal of their triangular councils. The Bassetts were to continue at the Bosworth house until June, and when Marian dashed in upon these Sunday symposiums—sometimes with a young cavalier she had taken out for a promenade—she gave Dan to understand that his difficulties with her father made not the slightest difference to her.

"But, mama!" She spoke of her mother as of one whose views must not weigh heavily against the world's general good cheer—"mama says she *never* trusted you; that there was just that something about you that didn't seem quite—" Marian would shake her head and sigh suggestively, whereupon Mrs. Owen would rebuke her and send her off to find the candy in the sideboard.

Allen, relegated for a time to a sanatorium in the Adirondacks, amused himself by telegraphing to Marian daily; and he usually managed to time a message to reach Mrs. Owen's Sunday dinner table with characteristic remembrances for all who might be in her house. To Dan he wrote a letter commending his course in the legislature.

"I always knew you would get on Dad's side one of these days. The Great Experiment is making headway. Don't worry about me. I'm going to live to be a hundred. There's really nothing the matter with my lungs, you know. Dad just wanted an excuse to come up here himself (mother and the girls used me as an excuse for years, you remember). He's doing big stunts tramping over the hills. You remember that good story Ware told us that night up in the house-boat? You wouldn't think Dad would have so much curiosity, but he's been over there to look at that place Ware told about. He's left me now to go down to New York to see the lights. . . . I'm taking quite a literary turn. You know, besides Emerson and those chaps who camped with him up here, Stevenson was here, too,—good old R.L.S.!"

Several times Sylvia, Marian, and Dan collaborated in a Sunday round robin to Allen, in the key of his own exuberances.

CHAPTER XXVII
HEAT LIGHTNING

"We'll finish the peaches to-night, and call it a day's work," remarked Mrs. Owen. "Sylvia, you'd better give another turn to the covers on those last jars. There's nothing takes the heart out of a woman like opening a can of fruit in January and finding mould on top. There, Annie, that's enough cinnamon. Put in too much and your peaches will taste like a drug store."

Spicy odors floated from the kitchen of Mrs. Owen's house on Waupegan. The August afternoon sun struck goldenly upon battalions of glasses and jars in the broad, screened veranda, an extension of the kitchen itself. The newly affixed labels announced peach, crab-apple, plum, and watermelon preserves (if the mention of this last item gives you no thrill, so much the worse for you!); jellies of many tints and flavors, and tiny cucumber pickles showing dark green amid the gayer colors. Only the most jaded appetite could linger without sharp impingements before these condensations and transformations of the kindly fruits of the earth.

In Mrs. Owen's corps of assistants we recognize six young women from Elizabeth House—for since the first of July Elizabeth House has been constantly represented on Waupegan, girls coming and going in sixes for a fortnight at the farm. Mrs. Owen had not only added bedrooms to the rambling old farmhouse to accommodate these visitors, but she had, when necessary, personally arranged with their employers for their vacations.

On the face of it, the use of her farm as a summer annex to the working girls' boarding-house in town was merely the whim of a kind-hearted old woman with her own peculiar notions of self-indulgence. A cynical member of the summer colony remarked at the Casino that Mrs. Owen, with characteristic thrift, was inveigling shop-girls to her farm and then putting them to work in her kitchen. Mrs. Owen's real purpose was the study of the girls in Elizabeth House with a view to determining their needs and aptitude: she was as interested in the woman of forty permanently planted behind a counter as in the gayest eighteen-year-old stenographer. An expert had built for her that spring a model plant for poultry raising, an industry of which she confessed her own ignorance, and she found in her battery of incubators the greatest delight.

"When a woman has spent twenty years behind a counter, Sylvia, or working a typewriter, she hasn't much ahead of her. What's the matter with ducks?"

They made prodigious calculations of all sorts that summer, and continued their study of catalogues. Mrs. Owen expected to visit the best vocational schools in the country during the fall and winter. The school could not be a large one, but it must be wisely planned. Mrs. Owen had already summarized her ideas on a sheet of paper in the neat, Italian script which the daguerreotype ladies of our old seminaries alone preserve for us. The students of the proposed school were to be girls between fifteen and eighteen, who were driven by necessity into shops, factories, and offices. None should be excluded for lack of the knowledge presupposed in students ready for high school, and the general courses were to be made flexible so that those who entered deficient might be brought to a fixed standard. The vocational branches were the most difficult, and at Sylvia's suggestion several well-known authorities on technical education were called into conference. One of these had visited Waupegan and expressed his enthusiastic approval of Mrs. Owen's plans. She was anxious to avoid paralleling any similar work, public or private. What the city schools did in manual training was well enough, and she did not mean to compete with the state's technical school, or with its reformatory school for erring girls. The young girl about to take her place behind the ribbon counter, or at a sewing-machine in a garment factory, or as a badly equipped, ignorant, and hopeless stenographer, was the student for whom in due course the school should open its doors. Where necessary, the parents of the students were to be paid the wages their daughters sacrificed in attending school during the two-year course proposed. The students were to live in cottages and learn the domestic arts through their own housekeeping, the members of each household performing various duties in rotation. The school was to continue in session the year round, so that flower—and kitchen—gardening might take rank with dressmaking, cooking, fruit culture, poultry raising, and other branches which Mrs. Owen proposed to have taught.

"I can't set 'em all up in business, but I want a girl that goes through the school to feel that she won't have to break her back in an overall factory all her life, or dance around some floor-walker with a waxed mustache. They tell me no American girl who has ever seen a trolley car will go into a kitchen to work—she can't have her beaux going round to the back door. Sylvia, we've got to turn out cooks that are worth going to kitchen doors to see! Now, I've taught you this summer how to make currant jelly that you needn't be ashamed of anywhere on earth, and it didn't hurt you any. A white woman can't learn to cook the way darkies do, just by instinct.

That's a miracle, by the way, that I never heard explained—how these colored women cook as the good ones do—those old-fashioned darkies who take the cook book out of your hand and look at it upside down and grin and say, 'Yes, Miss Sally,' when they can't read a word! You catch a clean, wholesome white girl young enough, and make her understand that her kitchen's a laboratory, and her work something to be proud of, and she'll not have any trouble finding places to work where they won't ask her to clean out the furnace and wash the automobile."

The Bassetts had opened their cottage early and Morton Bassett had been at the lake rather more constantly than in previous summers. Marian was off on a round of visits to the new-found friends that were the fruit of her winter at the capital. She was much in demand for house parties, and made her engagements, quite independently of her parents, for weeks and fortnights at widely scattered mid-Western resorts. Mrs. Bassett was indulging in the luxury of a trained nurse this summer, but even with this reinforcement she found it impossible to manage Marian. It need hardly be said that Mrs. Owen's philanthropic enterprises occasioned her the greatest alarm. It was enough that "that girl" should be spending the summer at Waupegan, without bringing with her all her fellow boarders from Elizabeth House.

Mrs. Bassett had now a tangible grievance against her husband. Blackford's course at the military school he had chosen for himself had been so unsatisfactory that his father had been advised that he would not be received for another year. It was now Mrs. Bassett's turn to cavil at her husband for the sad mess he had made of the boy's education. She would never have sent Blackford to a military school if it had been her affair; she arraigned her husband for having encouraged the boy in his dreams of West Point.

Blackford's father continuing indifferent, Mrs. Bassett rose from bed one hot August day filled with determination. Blackford, confident of immunity from books through the long vacation, was enjoying himself thoroughly at the lake. He was a perfectly healthy, good-natured lad, whose faults were much like those of the cheerful, undisciplined Marian. His mother scanned the reports of Blackford's demerits and decided that he required tutoring immediately. She thereupon reasoned that it would score with her aunt if she employed "that girl" to coach the delinquent Blackford. It would at any rate do no harm to manifest a friendly interest in her aunt's protégée, who would doubtless be glad of a chance to earn a little pin-money. She first proposed the matter to her aunt, who declared promptly that it must be for Sylvia to say; that Sylvia was busy writing a book (she was revising her grandfather's textbook), besides helping to entertain the Elizabeth House guests; but when the matter was referred to Sylvia, she cheerfully agreed to give Blackford two hours a day.

Sylvia quickly established herself on terms of good comradeship with her pupil. Blackford was old enough to find the proximity of a pretty girl agreeable, and Sylvia was sympathetic and encouraging. When he confided to her his hopes of a naval career (he had finally renounced the Army) Sylvia sent off to Annapolis for the entrance requirements. She told him of her Grandfather Kelton's service in the Navy and recounted some of the old professor's exploits in the Civil War. The stories Sylvia had heard at her grandfather's knee served admirably as a stimulus. As the appointments to Annapolis had to be won in competitive examinations she soon persuaded him that the quicker he buckled down to hard study the sooner he would attain the goal. This matter arranged, Mrs. Bassett went back to bed, where she received Sylvia occasionally and expressed her sorrow that Mrs. Owen, at her time of life, should be running a boarding-house for a lot of girls who were better off at work. Her aunt was merely making them dissatisfied with their lot. She did not guess the import of the industries in Mrs. Owen's kitchen, as reported through various agencies; they were merely a new idiosyncracy of her aunt's old age, a deplorable manifestation of senility.

Sylvia was a comfortable confessor; Mrs. Bassett said many things to her that she would have liked to say to Mrs. Owen, with an obscure hope that they might in due course be communicated to that inexplicable old woman. And Sylvia certainly was past; the difficult art of brushing hair without tangling and pulling it, thereby tearing one's nerves to shreds—as the nurse did. Mrs. Owen's visits were only occasional, but they usually proved disturbing. She sniffed at the nurse and advised her niece to get up. She knew a woman in Terre Haute who went to bed on her thirtieth birthday and left it only to be buried in her ninetieth year. Sylvia was a far more consoling visitor to this invalid propped up on pillows amid a litter of magazines, with the cool lake at her elbow. Sylvia did not pooh-pooh Christian Science and New Thought and such things with which Mrs. Bassett was disposed to experiment. Sylvia even bestowed upon her a boon in the shape of the word "psychotherapy." Mrs. Bassett liked it, and declared that if she read a paper before the Fraserville Woman's Club the next winter—a service to which she was solemnly pledged—psychotherapy should be her subject. Thus Mrs. Bassett found Sylvia serviceable and comforting. And the girl knew her place, and all.

Morton Bassett found Sylvia tutoring his son one day when he arrived at Waupegan unexpectedly. Mrs. Bassett explained the arrangement privately in her own fashion.

"You seem to take no interest in your children, Morton. I thought Blackford was your particular pride, but the fact that he was practically expelled from school seemed to make not the slightest impression on you. I thought that until you *did* realize that the boy was wasting his time here, I'd take matters into my own hands. Miss Garrison seems perfectly competent; she tells me Blackford is very quick—all he needs is application."

"I hadn't got around to that yet, Hallie. I'd intended taking it up this week. I'm very busy," murmured Bassett.

His wife's choice of a tutor seemed inconsistent with her earlier animosity toward Sylvia, but he shrank from asking explanations. Mrs. Bassett had grown increasingly difficult and arbitrary.

"That's the American father all over! Well, I've done my duty."

"No doubt it's a good arrangement. We've got to keep Blackford in hand. Where's Marian?"

"She's visiting the Willings at their place at Whitewater. She's been gone a week."

"The Willings? Not those Burton Willings? How did that happen;—I don't believe we care to have her visit the Willings."

"They are perfectly nice people," she replied defensively, "and Marian knew their daughter at school. Allen Thatcher is in the party, and they're all people we know or know about."

"Well, I don't want Marian visiting around promiscuously. I know nothing about the family, but I don't care for Willing. And we've had enough of young Thatcher. Marian's already seen too much of him."

"Allen's a perfectly nice fellow. It isn't fair to dislike him on his father's account. Allen isn't a bit like his father; but even if he were you used to think well enough of Ed Thatcher."

This shot was well aimed, and Bassett blinked, but he felt that he must exercise his parental authority. If he had been culpable in neglecting Blackford he could still take a hand in Marian's affairs.

"So I did," he replied. "But I'm going to telegraph Marian to come home. What's the Willings' address?"

"Oh, you'll find it on a picture postal card somewhere about. I'll write Marian to come home; but I wouldn't telegraph if I were you, Morton. And if you don't like my employing Miss Garrison, you can get rid of her: I merely felt that *something* had to be done. I turn it all over to you," she ended mournfully.

"Oh, I have no objections to Miss Garrison. We'll see how Blackford gets on with her."

Bassett was troubled by other things that summer than his son's education. Harwood's declaration of war in the White River Canneries matter had proved wholly disagreeable, and Fitch had not been able to promise that the case might not come to trial, to Bassett's discomfiture. It was a hot summer, and Bassett had spent a good deal of time in his office at the Boordman Building, where Harwood's name no longer adorned the door of Room 66. The 'Advertiser' continued to lay on the lash for his defeat of the appropriations necessary to sustain several important state institutions while he carried through his corporation bill. They were saying in some quarters that he had lost his head, and that he was now using his political power for personal warfare upon his enemies. Thatcher loomed formidably as a candidate for the leadership, and many predicted that Bassett's power was at last broken. On the other hand, Bassett's old lieutenants smiled knowingly; the old Bassett machine was still in perfect running order, they said, as Thatcher would learn when he felt the wheels grinding him.

Bassett saw Sylvia daily, and he was wary of her at first. She had dealt him a staggering blow that rainy evening at the door of Elizabeth House—a blow which, from her, had an effect more poignant than she knew. That incident was ended, however, and he felt that he had nothing to fear from her. No one appreciates candor so thoroughly as the man who is habitually given to subterfuge, evasion, and dissimulation. Sylvia's consent to tutor Blackford indicated a kindly feeling toward the family. It was hardly likely that she would report to Mrs. Bassett his indiscretions with Rose Farrell. And his encounters with Sylvia had moreover encouraged the belief that she viewed life broadly and tolerantly.

There was little for a man of Bassett's tastes to do at Waupegan. Most of the loungers at the Casino were elderly men who played bridge, which he despised; and he cared little for fishing or boating. Tennis and golf did not tempt him. His wife had practically ceased to be a figure in the social life of the colony; Marian was away, and Blackford's leisure was spent with boys of his own age. Morton Bassett was lonely.

It thus happened that he looked forward with growing interest to Sylvia's daily visits to his house. He found that he could mark her progress from Mrs. Owen's gate round the lake to his own cottage from the window of a den he maintained in the attic. He remained there under the hot shingles, conscious of her presence in his house throughout her two hours with Blackford. Once or twice he took himself off to escape from her; but on these occasions he was surprised to find that he was back on the veranda when Sylvia emerged from the living-room with her pupil. She was always cheery, and she never failed to say something heartening of Blackford's work.

A number of trifling incidents occurred to bring them together. The cook left abruptly, and Mrs. Bassett was reduced to despair. Bassett, gloomily pacing his veranda, after hearing his wife's arraignment of the world in general and domestic servants in particular, felt the clouds lift when Sylvia came down from a voluntary visit to the invalid. He watched her attack the problem by long-distance telephone. Sensations that were new and strange and sweet assailed him as he sat near in the living-room of his own house, seeing her at the telephone desk by the window, hearing her voice. Her patience in the necessary delays while connection was made with the city, her courtesy to her unseen auditors, the smile, the occasional word she flung at him—as much as to say, of course it's bothersome but all will soon come right!—these things stirred in him a wistfulness and longing such as the hardy oak must feel when the south wind touches its bare boughs with the first faint breath of spring.

"It's all arranged—fixed—accomplished!" Sylvia reported at last. "There's a cook coming by the afternoon train. You'll attend to meeting her? Please tell Mrs. Bassett it's Senator Ridgefield's cook who's available for the rest of the summer, as the family have gone abroad. She's probably good— the agent said Mrs. Ridgefield had brought her from Washington. Let me see! She must have Thursday afternoon off and a chance to go to mass on Sunday. And you of course stand the railroad fare to and from the lake; it's so nominated in the bond!"

She dismissed the whole matter with a quick gesture of her hands.

Their next interview touched again his domestic affairs. He had telegraphed Marian to come home without eliciting a reply, and the next day he found in a Chicago newspaper a spirited and much-beheadlined account of the smashing of the Willings' automobile in a collision. It seemed that they had run into Chicago for a day's shopping and had met with this misadventure on one of the boulevards. The Willings' chauffeur had been seriously injured. Miss Marian Bassett, definitely described as the daughter of Morton Bassett, the well-known Indiana politician, had been of the party. Allen Thatcher was another guest of the Willings, a fact which added to Bassett's anger. He had never visited his hatred of Thatcher upon Allen, whom he had regarded as a harmless boy not to be taken seriously; but the conjunction of his daughter's name with that of his enemy's son in a newspaper of wide circulation in Indiana greatly enraged him. It was bound to occasion talk, and he hated publicity. The Willings were flashy people who had begun to spend noisily the money earned for them by an automobile patent. The indictment he drew against Marian contained many "counts." He could not discuss the matter with his wife; he carefully kept from her the newspaper story of the smash-up. The hotel to which the Willings had retired for repairs was mentioned, and Bassett resolved to go to Chicago and bring Marian home.

The best available train passed Waupegan Station at midnight, and he sat alone on his veranda that evening with anger against Marian still hot in his heart. He had yet to apprise Mrs. Bassett of his intended journey, delaying the moment as long as possible to minimize her inevitable querulous moanings. Blackford was in his room studying, and Bassett had grimly paced the veranda for half an hour when the nurse came down with a request that he desist from his promenade, as it annoyed Mrs. Bassett in her chamber above.

He thereupon subsided and retired to the darkest corner of the veranda. A four-hour vigil lay before him, and he derived no calm from the still stars that faintly shadowed the quiet waters below. He was assailed by torments reserved for those who, having long made others writhe without caring that they suffered, hear the swish of the lash over their own heads. He had only lately been conscious of his growing irritability. He hated men who yield to irritation; it was a sign of weakness, a failure of self-mastery. He had been carried on by a strong tide, imagining that he controlled it and guided it. He had used what he pleased of the apparatus of life, and when any part of the mechanism became unnecessary, he had promptly discarded it. It angered him to find that he had thrown away so much, that the mechanism was no longer as responsive as it had been. The very peace of the night grated upon him.

A light step sounded at the end of the veranda. A figure in white was moving toward the door, and recognizing Sylvia, he rose hastily and advanced to meet her.

"Is that you, Mr. Bassett? I ran over with a new grammar for Blackford that he will like better than the one he's using. I've marked his lesson so he can look it over before I come in the morning. How is Mrs. Bassett?"

"She's very tired and nervous to-night. Won't you sit down?"

"Thank you, no. If it isn't too late I'll run up and see Mrs. Bassett for a moment."

"I think you'd better not. The nurse is trying to get her to sleep."

"Oh, then of course I shan't stop," and Sylvia turned to go. "How soon will Marian be home?"

"To-morrow evening; I'm going up to get her to-night," he answered harshly.

"You are going to the Willings to come home with her?" asked Sylvia, surprised by his gruffness.

He spoke in a lower tone.

"You didn't see to-day's papers? She's been to Chicago with those Willings and their machine was smashed and the chauffeur hurt. I'm going to bring her back. She had no business to be visiting the Willings in the first place, and their taking her to Chicago without our consent was downright impudence. I don't want Mrs. Bassett to know of the accident. I'm going up on the night train."

It satisfied his turbulent spirit to tell her this; he had blurted it out without attempting to conceal the anger that the thought of Marian roused in him.

"She wasn't hurt? We should be glad of that!"

Sylvia lingered, her hand on the veranda rail. She seemed very tall in the mellow starlight. His tone had struck her unpleasantly. There was no doubt of his anger, or that Marian would feel the force of it when he found her.

"Oh, she wasn't hurt," he answered dully.

"It's very unfortunate that she was mixed up in it. I suppose she ought to come home now anyhow."

"The point is that she should never have gone! The Willings are not the kind of people I want her to know. It was a great mistake, her ever going."

"Yes, that may be true," said Sylvia quietly. "I don't believe—"

"Well—" he ejaculated impatiently, as though anxious for her to speak that he might shatter any suggestion she made. Before she came he had sharply vizualized his meeting with Marian and the Willings. He was impatient for the encounter, and if Sylvia projected herself in the path of his righteous anger, she must suffer the consequences.

"If I were you I shouldn't go to Chicago," said Sylvia calmly. "I think your going for Marian would only make a disagreeable situation worse. The Willings may not be desirable companions for her, but she has been their guest, and the motor run to Chicago was only an incident of the visit. We ought to be grateful that Marian wasn't hurt."

"Oh, you think so! You don't know that her mother had written for her to come home, and that I had telegraphed her."

"When did you telegraph her?" asked Sylvia, standing her ground.

"Yesterday; yesterday morning, in care of Willing at his farm address."

"Then of course she didn't get your message; she couldn't have had it if the accident happened in time for this morning's Chicago papers. It must have taken them all day to get from their place to Chicago." "If she had been at the Willings' where we supposed she was she would have, got the message. And her mother had written—twice!"

"I still think it would be a serious mistake in all the circumstances for you to go up there in a spirit of resentment to bring Marian home. It's not exactly my business, Mr. Bassett. But I'm thinking of Marian; and you could hardly keep from Mrs. Bassett the fact that you went for Marian. It would be sure to distress her."

"Marian needs curbing; she's got to understand that she can't go gallivanting over the country with strangers, getting her name in the newspapers. I'm not going to have it; I'm going to stop her nonsense!"

His voice had risen with his anger. Sylvia saw that nothing was to be gained by argument.

"The main thing is to bring Marian home, isn't it, Mr. Bassett?"

"Most certainly. And when I get her here she shall stay; you may be sure of that!"

"I understand of course that you want her back, but I hope you will abandon the idea of going for her yourself. Please give that up! I promise that she shall come home. I can easily take the night train and come back with her. What you do afterward is not my affair, but somehow I think this is. Please agree to my way of doing it! I can manage it very easily. Mrs. Owen's man can take me across to the train in the launch. I shan't even have to explain about it to her, if you'd rather I didn't. It will be enough if I tell her I'm going on business. You will agree, won't you—please?"

It was not in his heart to consent, and yet he consented, wondering that he yielded. The rescue of Marian from the Willings was taken out of his hands without friction, and there remained only himself against whom to vent his anger. He was curiously agitated by the encounter. The ironic phrases he had already coined for Marian's discomfiture clinked into the melting-pot. Sylvia was turning away and he must say something, though he could not express a gratitude he did not feel. His practical sense grasped one idea feebly. He felt its imbecility the moment he had spoken.

"You'll allow me, of course, to pay your expenses. That must be understood."

Sylvia answered over her shoulder.

"Oh, yes; of course, Mr. Bassett. Certainly."

He meant to accompany her to Mrs. Owen's door, but before he could move she was gone, running along the path, a white, ghost-like figure faintly discernible through the trees. He walked on tiptoe to the end of the veranda to catch the last glimpse of her, and waited till he caught across the quiet night the faint click of Mrs. Owen's gate. And he was inexpressibly lonely, now that she had gone.

He opened the door of the living-room and found his wife standing like an accusing angel by the centre table. She loomed tall in her blue tea-gown, with her brown braids falling down her back.

"Whom were you talking to, Morton?" she demanded with ominous severity.

"Miss Garrison came over to bring a book for Blackford. It's a grammar he needed in his work."

He held up the book in proof of his assertion, and as she tossed her head and compressed her lips he flung it on the table with an effort to appear at ease.

"She wanted him to have it before his lesson in the morning."

"She certainly took a strange time to bring it over here."

"It struck me as very kind of her to trouble about it. You'll take cold standing there. I supposed you were asleep."

"I've no doubt you did, Morton Bassett; but how do you suppose I could sleep when you were talking right under my window? I had already sent word about the noise you were making on the veranda."

"We were not talking loudly; I didn't suppose we were disturbing you."

"So you were talking quietly, were you! Will you please tell me what you have to talk to that girl about that you must whisper out there in the dark?"

"Please be reasonable, Hallie. Miss Garrison was only here a few minutes. And as I knew noises on the veranda had disturbed you I tried to speak in a low tone. We were speaking of Blackford."

"Well, I'd like you to know that I employed that girl to remedy your mistakes in trying to educate Blackford, and if she has any report to make she can make it to me."

"Very well, then. It was only a few days ago that you told me you had done all you were going to do about Blackford; you gave me to understand that you washed your hands of him. You're nervous and excited,—very unnecessarily excited,—and I insist that you go back to bed. I'll call Miss Featherstone."

"Miss Featherstone is asleep and you needn't bother her. I'm going to send her away at the end of her week anyhow. She's the worst masseuse I ever had; her clumsiness simply drives me frantic. But I never thought you would treat me like this—entertaining a young woman on the veranda when you thought I was asleep and out of the way. I'm astonished at Miss Garrison; I had a better opinion of her. I thought she knew her place. I thought she understood that I employed her out of kindness; and she's abused my confidence outrageously."

"You can't speak that way of that young woman; she's been very good to you. She's come to see you nearly every day and shown you many kindnesses. It is kind of her to be tutoring Blackford at all when she came to the lake for rest."

"For rest!"

She gulped at the enormity of this; it was beyond belief that any intelligent being could have been deceived in a matter that was as plain as daylight to any understanding. "You think she came here for rest! Don't you know that she's hung herself around Aunt Sally's neck, and that she's filling Aunt Sally's head with all manner of wild ideas? She's been after Aunt Sally's money ever since she saw that she could influence her. Did you ever know of Aunt Sally's taking up any other girl? Has she ever traveled over the country with Marian or shown any such interest in her own flesh and blood?"

"Please quiet yourself. You'll have Blackford and the nurse down here in a minute. You know perfectly well that Aunt Sally started Elizabeth House long before she had ever heard of this girl, and you know that your aunt is a vigorous, independent woman who is not led around by anybody."

Her nostrils quivered and her eyes shone with tears. She leveled her arm at him rigidly.

"I saw you walking with that girl yesterday! When she left here at noon you came down from the den and walked along to Aunt Sally's gate with her. I could see you through the trees from my bed, laughing and talking with her. I suppose it was then you arranged for her to come and sit with you on the veranda when you thought I was asleep!"

He took a step toward her and seized the outstretched hand roughly.

"You are out of your senses or you wouldn't speak in this way of Miss Garrison. She's been a kind friend to you all summer; you've told me yourself self how she's gone up to brush your hair and do little things for you that the nurse couldn't do as well. You've grown morbid from being ill so long, but nothing was ever more infamous than your insinuations against Miss Garrison. She's a noble girl and it's not surprising that Aunt Sally should like her. Everybody likes her!"

Having delivered this blow he settled himself more firmly on his feet and glared.

"Everybody likes her!" she repeated, snatching away her hand. "I'd like to know how you come to know so much about her."

"I know enough about her: I know all about her!"

"Then you know more than anybody else does. Nobody else seems to know *anything* about her!" she ended triumphantly.

"There you go again with insinuations! It's ungenerous, it's unlike you."

"Morton Bassett," she went on huskily, "if you took some interest in your own children it would be more to your credit. You blamed me for letting Marian go to the Willings' and then telegraphed for her to come home. It's a beautiful relationship you have established with your children! She hasn't even answered your telegram. But I suppose if she had you'd have kept it from me. The newspapers talk about your secretive ways, but they don't know you, Morton Bassett, as I do. I suppose you can't imagine yourself entertaining Marian on the veranda or walking with her, talking and laughing, as I saw you with that girl."

"Well, thank God there's somebody I can talk and laugh with! I'm glad to be able to tell you that Marian will be home to-morrow. You may have the satisfaction of knowing that if you *would* let her go to the Willings' with Allen Thatcher I can at least bring her back after you failed to do it."

"So you did hear from her, did you! Of course you couldn't have told me: I suppose you confide in Miss Garrison now," she ended drearily.

His wife's fatigue, betrayed in her tired voice, did not mitigate the stab with which he wished to punish her references to Sylvia. And he delivered it with careful calculation.

"You are quite right, Hallie. I did speak to Miss Garrison about Marian. Miss Garrison has gone to bring Marian home. That's all; go to bed."

CHAPTER XXVIII
A CHEERFUL BRINGER OF BAD TIDINGS

The announcement that Harwood was preparing to attack the reorganization of the White River Canneries corporation renewed the hopes of many victims of that experiment in high finance, and most of the claims reached Dan's office that summer. The legal points involved were sufficiently difficult to evoke his best energies, and he dug diligently in the State Library preparing his case. He was enjoying the cool, calm heights of a new freedom. Many older men were eking out a bare living at the law, and the ranks were sadly overcrowded, but he faced the future confidently. He meant to practice law after ideals established by men whose names were still potent in the community; he would not race with the ambulance to pick up damage suits, and he refused divorce cases and small collection business. He meant to be a lawyer, not a scandal-hunting detective or pursuer of small debtors with a constable's process.

He tried to forget politics, and yet, in spite of his indifference, hardly a day passed that did not bring visitors to his office bent upon discussing the outlook. Many of these were from the country; men who, like Ramsay, were hopeful of at last getting rid of Bassett. Some of his visitors were young lawyers like himself, most of them graduates of the state colleges, who were disposed to take their politics seriously. Nor were these all of his own party. He found that many young Republicans, affected by the prevailing unrest, held practically his own views on national questions. Several times he gathered up half a dozen of these acquaintances for frugal dinners in the University Club rathskeller, or they met in the saloon affected by Allen's friends of Lüders's carpenter shop. He wanted them to see all sides of the picture, and he encouraged them to crystallize their fears and hopes; more patriotism and less partisanship, they all agreed, was the thing most needed in America.

Allen appeared in Dan's office unexpectedly one hot morning and sat down on a chair piled with open lawbooks. Allen had benefited by his month's sojourn in the Adirondacks, and subsequent cruises in his motor car had tanned his face becomingly. He was far from rugged, but he declared that he expected to live forever.

"I'm full of dark tidings! Much has happened within forty-eight hours. See about our smash-up in Chicago! Must have read it in the newspapers?"

"A nice, odorous mess," observed Dan, filling his pipe. "I'm pained to see that you go chasing around with the plutocrats smashing lamp-posts in our large centres of population. That sort of thing is bound to establish your reputation as the friend of the oppressed. Was the chauffeur's funeral largely attended?"

"Pshaw; he was only scratched; we chucked him into the hospital to keep him from being arrested, that was all. Look here, old man, you don't seem terribly sympathetic. Maybe you didn't notice that it was *my* car that got smashed! It looked like a junk dealer's back yard when they pulled us out. I told them to throw it into the lake: I've just ordered a new car. I never cared for that one much anyhow."

"Another good note for the boys around Lüders's joint! You're identified forever with the red-necked aristocrats who smash five thousand dollar motors and throw them away. You'd better go out in the hall and read the sign on the door. I'm a lawyer, not a father confessor to the undeserving rich."

"This is serious, Dan," Allen remonstrated, twirling his straw hat nervously. "All that happened in connection with the smash-up didn't get into the newspapers."

"The 'Advertiser' had enough of it: they printed, published, and uttered an extra with Marian's picture next to yours on the first page! You can't complain of the publicity you got out of that light adventure. How much space do you think it was worth?"

"Stop chaffing and hear me out! I'm up against a whole lot of trouble, and I came to get your advice. You see, Dan, the Bassetts didn't know Marian was going on that automobile trip. Her mother had written her to leave the Willings' and go home—twice! And her father telegraphed—after we left the farm. She never got the telegram. Then, when Mr. Bassett read of the smash in the papers, I guess he was warm clear through. You know he doesn't cut loose very often; and—"

"And he jumped on the train and went to Chicago to snatch Marian away from the Willings? I should think he would have done just that."

"No; oh, no! He sent Sylvia!" cried Allen. "Sylvia came up on the night train, had a few words privately with Marian, took luncheon with the Willings, all as nice as you please, and off she went with Marian."

Harwood pressed his thumb into his pipe-bowl and puffed in silence for a moment. Allen, satisfied that he had at last caught his friend's attention, fanned himself furiously with his hat.

"Well," said Dan finally, "there's nothing so staggering in that. Sylvia's been staying at the lake: I suppose Mrs. Bassett must have asked her to go up and bring Marian home when the papers screamed her daughter's name in red ink. I understand that Mrs. Bassett's ill, and I suppose Bassett didn't like to leave her. There's nothing fuddlesome in that. Sylvia probably did the job well. She has the habit. What is there that troubles you about it, Allen?"

His heart had warmed at the mention of Sylvia, and he felt more kindly toward Allen now that she had flashed across his vision. Many times a day he found Sylvia looking up at him from the pages of his books; this fresh news brought her near. Sylvia's journey to Chicago argued an intimacy with the Bassetts that he did not reconcile with his knowledge of her acquaintance with the family. He was aroused by the light touch of Allen's hand on his knee. The young man bent toward him with a bright light in his eyes.

"You know," he said, "Marian and I are engaged!"

"You're what?" bellowed Dan.

"We're engaged, old man; we're engaged! It happened there at the Willings'. You know I think I loved her from the very first time I saw her! It's the beautifullest thing that ever came into my life. You don't know how happy I am: it's the kind of happiness that makes you want to cry. Oh, you don't know; nobody could ever know!"

Dan rose and paced the floor, while Allen stood watching him eagerly and pouring his heart out. Dan felt that tragedy loomed here. He did not doubt Allen's sincerity; he was not unmoved by his manner, his voluble description of all the phases of his happiness. Allen, with all his faults and weaknesses, had nevertheless a sound basis of character. Harwood's affection for him dated from that first encounter in the lonely Meridian Street house when the boy had dawned upon him in his overalls and red silk stockings. He had never considered Allen's interest in Marian serious; for Allen had to Dan's knowledge paid similar attentions to half a dozen other girls. Allen's imagination made a goddess of every pretty girl, and Dan had settled down to the belief that his friend saw in Marian only one of the many light-footed Dianas visible in the city thoroughfares, whom he invested with deific charms and apostrophized in glowing phrases. But that he should marry Marian—Marian, the joyous and headstrong; Marian the romping, careless Thalia of Allen's bright galaxy! She was ill-fitted for marriage, particularly to a dreamy, emotional youngster like Allen. And yet, on the other hand, if she had arrived at a real appreciation of Allen's fineness and gentleness and had felt his sweetness and charm, why not?

Dan's common sense told him that quite apart from the young people themselves there were reasons enough against it. Dan had imagined that Allen was content to play at being in love; that it satisfied the romantic strain in him, just as his idealization of the Great Experiment and its actors expressed and satisfied his patriotic feelings. The news that he had come to terms of marriage with Marian was in all the circumstances dismaying, and opened many dark prospects. Allen stood at the window staring across the roofs beyond. He whirled round as Dan addressed him.

"Have you spoken to Mr. Bassett? You know that will be the first thing, Allen."

"That's exactly what I want you to help me about? He's at Waupegan now, and of course I've got to see him. But you know this row between him and dad makes it hard. You know dad would do anything in the world for me—dear old dad! Of course I've told *him*. And you'd be surprised to see the way he took it. You know people don't know dad the way I do. They think he's just a rough old chap, without any fine feeling about anything. And mother and the girls leaving him that way has hurt him; it hurts him a whole lot. And when I told him last night, up at that big hollow cave of a house, how happy I was and all that, it broke him all up. He cried, you know—dad cried!"

The thought of Edward G. Thatcher in tears failed to arrest the dark apprehensions that tramped harshly through Dan's mind. As for Bassett, Dan recalled his quondam chief's occasional flings at Allen, whom the senator from Fraser had regarded as a spoiled and erratic but innocuous trifler. Mrs. Bassett, Dan was aware, valued her social position highly. As the daughter of Blackford Singleton she considered herself unassailably a member of the upper crust of the Hoosier aristocracy. And Dan suspected that Bassett also harbored similar notions of caste.

Independently of the struggle in progress between Thatcher and Bassett, it was quite likely that the Bassetts would look askance at the idea of a union between their daughter and Edward Thatcher's son, no matter what might be said in Allen's favor. Bassett's social acceptance was fairly complete, and he enjoyed meeting men of distinction. He was invariably welcomed to the feasts of reason we are always, in our capital, proffering to the great and good of all lands who pause for enlightenment and inspiration in our empurpled Athens. He was never ignored in the choice of those frock-coated and silk-hatted non-partisan committees that meet all trains at the Union Station, and quadrennially welcome home our eternal candidates for the joyous office of Vice-President of the Republic. He kept his dress suit packed for flight at Fraserville free of that delicate scent of camphor that sweetens the air of provincial festivals. Thatcher never, to the righteous, sensitive, local consciousness, wholly escaped from the maltster's taint, in itself horrible and shocking; nor did his patronage of budding genius in the prize ring, or his adventures (often noisily heralded) as a financial pillar of comic opera, tend to change or hide the leopard's spots in a community where the Ten Commandments haven't yet been declared unconstitutional, save by plumbers and paperhangers. Women who had never in their lives seen Mrs. Thatcher admired her for remaining in exile; they knew she must be (delectable phrase!) a good woman.

"You know dad has had an awful lonely time of it, Dan, and if he has done things that haven't sounded nice, he's as sorry as anybody could ask. You know dad never made a cent in his life at poker, and his horses have come near busting him lots of times. And sentiment against breweries over here would astonish people abroad. It's that old Puritan strain, you know. You understand all that, Dan."

Dan grinned in spite of himself. It was hardly less than funny to attempt a defense of Ed Thatcher by invoking the shades of the Puritans. But Thatcher did love his boy, and Dan had always given him full credit for that.

"Never mind the breweries; tell me the rest of it."

"Well," Allen continued, "dad always tells me everything, and when I spoke of Marian he told me a lot of things. He wants to put Bassett out of business and go to the Senate. Dad's set his heart on that. I didn't know that any man could hate another as he hates Bassett. That business in the state convention cut him deep;—no, don't you say a word! Dad hasn't any feeling against you; he thinks you're a fine fellow, and he likes to feel that when you quit Bassett you put yourself on his side. Maybe he's wrong, but just for my sake I want you to let him think so. But he's got it in for Bassett; he's got his guns all loaded and primed. Dad's deeper than you think. They used to say that dad was only second fiddle to Bassett, but you'll see that dad knows a thing or two."

Dan drummed his desk. This reference to Thatcher's ambitions only kindled his anger and he wished that Allen would end his confidences and take himself off. But he pricked up his ears as Allen went on.

"I'm telling you this just to show you how it mixes up things for Marian and me. I came to you for help, old man; and I want you to see how hard it is for me to go to Mr. Bassett and tell him I want to marry Marian."

"Just a minute, Allen. Are you quite sure that Marian has made up her mind to marry you; that she really wants to marry anybody?"

"I tell you it's all fixed! You don't imply that Marian is merely amusing herself at my expense! It wouldn't be like you to think that. I have always thought you liked Marian and saw how superb she is."

"Of course I like Marian," said Dan hastily. "My one hope is that both of you will be happy; and the difficulties you have suggested only make that more important. You will have to wait. I'm not sure but that you had better keep this to yourselves for a while—maybe for a long time. It would be wise for you to talk to Aunt Sally. She's a good friend of yours, and one of the wisest of women."

It was not in Allen's eye that he sought wisdom. With him, as with most people who ask advice, advice was the last thing he wanted. It was his way to unbosom himself, however, and he forged ahead with his story, with what seemed to Harwood a maddening failure to appreciate its sinister import. "You remember that when we were up there on the Kankakee, John Ware told a story one night—a mighty good story about an experience he had once?"

"Yes; he told a lot of stories. Which one do you mean?"

"Oh, the best one of all—about the woman in the Adirondacks. You haven't forgotten that?"

"No; I do remember something about it."

"You may not have noticed that while Ware was telling the story dad got up from the bed in the corner and walked over to the stove, after Ware had asked you—it was you, wasn't it?—to reach into the pocket of his coat over your head and get the book he was talking about—it was you he spoke to, wasn't it?"

"Yes; it comes back to me now," replied Dan, frowning.

"Well, I remember, because it struck me as odd that dad should be interested; it was Emerson, you know; and dad looked at the book in the light from the stove and asked me what the name was down in the inside of the cover. It was the binder's name in small letters,—Z. Fenelsa. Well, there's a long story about that. It's a horrible story to know about any man; but dad had been trying to find something he could use on Bassett. He's had people—the sort you can get to do such jobs—going over Bassett's whole life to find material. Dad says there's always something in every man's life that he wants to hide, and that if you keep looking you can find it. You see—"

"I don't like to see," growled Harwood. "It's an ugly idea." And then, with sudden scorn for Thatcher's views on man's frailty, he said with emphasis: "Now, Allen, it's all right for you to talk to me about Marian, and your wish to marry her; but don't mix scandal up in it. I'm not for that. I don't want to hear any stories of that kind about Bassett. Politics is rotten enough at best without tipping over the garbage can to find arguments. I don't believe your father is going to stoop to that. To be real frank with you, I don't think he can afford to."

"You've got to hear it; you can't desert me now. I'm away up in the air this morning, and even if you do hate this kind of thing, you've got to see where dad's hatred of Bassett puts Marian and me."

"It puts you clean out of it; away over the ropes and halfway home! That's where it puts you," boomed Harwood.

"Well, you've got to listen, and you've got to tell me what to do. Dad had already investigated Bassett's years in New York, when he was a young man studying in the law school down there. But they could get about so far and no farther. It's a long time ago and all the people Bassett knew at that time had scattered to the far corners of the earth. But that book struck dad all of a heap. It fitted into what he had heard about Bassett as a dilettante book collector; even then Bassett was interested in such things. And you know in that account of him you wrote in the 'Courier' that I told you I had read on the other side that first time we met? Well, when dad and I went to the Adirondacks it was only partly on my account; he met a man up there who had been working up Bassett's past, and dad went over all the ground himself. It was most amazing that it should all come out that way, but he found the place, and the same man is still living at the house where the strange woman stayed that Ware told about. I know it's just as rotten as it can be, but dad's sure Bassett was the man who took that woman there and deserted her. It fits into a period when Bassett wasn't in New York and he wasn't at Fraserville. They've found an old file of the Fraserville paper at the State Library that mentions the fact that Bassett's father was very ill—had a stroke—and they had hard work locating Bassett, who was the only child. There's only one missing link in the chain of evidence, and that's the woman herself, and her child that was born up there. Ware told us that night how he failed to get track of them later, and dad lost the trail right there too. But that's all I need tell you about it. That's what I've got hanging over me. And dad won't promise not to use it on Bassett if he has to."

Harwood's face had gone white, but he smiled and knit his fingers together behind his head with an air of nonchalance that he did not feel. He knew that Thatcher meant to drive Bassett out of politics, but he had little faith in Thatcher's ability to do so. He discredited wholly the story Allen had so glibly recited. By Allen's own admission the tale was deficient in what Harwood's lawyer's instinct told him were essentials. The idea that Bassett could ever have been so stupid as to leave traces of any imaginable iniquities plain enough for Thatcher to find them after many years was preposterous. The spectacle of the pot calling the kettle black, never edifying, aroused Dan's ire against Thatcher. And Bassett was not that sort; his old liking for the man stirred to life again. Even the Rose Farrell incident did not support this wretched tissue of fabrication. He had hated Bassett for that; but it was not for the peccable Thatcher to point a mocking finger at Achilles's heel.

"Well," said Allen impatiently.

"Well," Dan blurted contemptuously, "I think your father's stooped pretty low, that's all. You can tell him for me that if he's digging in the muck-pile for that sort of thing, I'm done with him; I'm not only done with him, but if he attempts to use any such stuff as that, I'll fight him; I will raise a war on him that won't be forgotten in this state through all eternity. You tell him that; tell him you told me your story and that's what I said about it."

"But, Dan, old man—" began Allen pleadingly.

Harwood shook his head until his cowlick bobbed and danced.

"You'd better get out of here, Allen. If you think you can marry Morton Bassett's daughter with that kind of a scandal in your pocket, I tell you you're mad—you've plumb gone insane! Great God, boy, you don't know the meaning of the words you use. You handle that thing like a child with a loaded pistol. Don't you see what that would mean—to Marian, to Blackford, to Mrs. Bassett—to Aunt Sally! Now, you want my advice, or you said you did, and I'm going to give you some. You go right down to that bank over there on the corner and buy a steamer ticket and a long letter of credit. Then take the first train for New York and go back to your mother and stay there till I send for you to come home. I mean that—every word of it. If you don't skip I'm damned if I don't go to Bassett and tell him this whole rotten story."

Allen, the tears glistening in his frightened eyes, turned toward the door.

"Good-bye, Dan, old man; I'm sorry it had to end this way. I'm disappointed, that's all."

He paused after opening the door, hoping to be called back, but Harwood had walked to the window and stood with his hands in his pockets staring into the street.

CHAPTER XXIX
A SONG AND A FALLING STAR

This was on Friday, and Harwood took the afternoon train for Waupegan. He had found that when he was tired or lonely or troubled he craved the sight of Sylvia. Sylvia alone could restore his equanimity; Sylvia who worked hard but never complained of weariness; Sylvia who saw life steadily and saw it whole, where he caught only fitful, distorted glimpses. Yes; he must see Sylvia. Not only must he see her but there were things he meant to say to her.

He needed Sylvia. For several months he had been sure of that. He loved her and he meant to marry her. Since leaving college he had indulged in several more or less ardent flirtations, but they had ended harmlessly; it was very different with Sylvia! He had realized all that spring that she was becoming increasingly necessary to him; he needed her solace and her inspiration. He thrust one or two new books on the prevailing social unrest into his suit case and added a box of candy, smiling at the combination. Sylvia with all her ideals was still so beautifully human. She was quite capable of nibbling bon-bons to the accompaniment of a vivacious discussion of the sorrows of the world—he had seen her do just that! With her ideals of life and service, she would not be easily won; but he was in the race to win. Yes, there were things he meant to say to Sylvia, and in the tedious journey through the hot afternoon to Waupegan he formulated them and visualized the situations in which he should utter them.

Dan reached Waupegan at six o'clock and went to one of the little inns at the lakeside near the village. He got into his flannels, ate supper, and set off for Mrs. Owen's with his offerings on the seven o'clock boat. In the old days of his intimacy with Bassett he had often visited Waupegan, and the breach between them introduced an element of embarrassment into his visit. He was very likely to meet his former chief, who barely bowed to him now when they met in hotels or in the streets of the capital.

Jumping aboard the steamer just as it was pulling out, he at once saw Bassett sitting alone in the bow. There were only a few other passengers, and hearing Dan's step on the deck behind him, Bassett turned slightly, nodded, and then resumed his inspection of the farther shore lines. A light overcoat lay across his knees, and the protruding newspapers explained his visit to the village. Dan found a seat on the opposite side of the deck, resolved to accept Bassett's own definition of their relations—markedly expressed in Bassett's back and shoulders that were stolidly presented to him. Dan, searching out the lights that were just beginning to blink on the darkling shores, found the glimmering lanterns of Mrs. Owen's landing. Sylvia was there! It was Sylvia he had come to see, and the coldness with which Morton Bassett turned his back upon him did not matter in the least. It was his pliability in Bassett's hands, manifested at the convention where he had appeared as the boss's spokesman, that had earned him Sylvia's first rebuke.

He was thinking of this and of Sylvia when Bassett left his chair and crossed the deck. Dan barely turned his head, thinking he was merely changing his seat for a better view; but as Bassett stopped in front of him, Dan rose and pushed forward a chair.

"No, thank you; I suppose you came up on the evening train. I just wondered whether you saw Fitch to-day."

"No, sir; I didn't see him; I didn't know he wanted to see me."

"He was here yesterday and probably hadn't had time to see you before you left town. He had a proposition to make in that Canneries case."

"I didn't know that, of course, or I should have waited. I've never had any talk with him about the Canneries business."

"So he said."

Bassett clapped his hand savagely upon his hat suddenly to save it from the breeze that had been roused by the increasing speed of the boat. He clearly disliked having to hold his hat on his head. Dan marked his old chief's irritation. There were deep lines in Bassett's face that had only lately been written there.

"I'll see him Monday. I only ran up for a day or two. It's frightfully hot at home."

Neither the heat, nor Harwood's enterprise in escaping from it, interested Bassett, who lifted his voice above the thumping of the machinery to say:—

"I told Fitch to talk to you about that suit of yours and fix it up if we can come to terms. I told him what I'd stand for. I'm not afraid of the suit, and neither is Fitch, and I want you to understand that. My reasons for getting rid of it are quite apart from the legal questions."

"It will save time, Mr. Bassett, if you tell Fitch that the suit won't be dropped until all the claims I represent are paid in full. Several of your associates in the reorganization have already sounded me on that, and I've said no to all of them."

"Oh, you have, have you?" There was a hard glitter in Bassett's eyes and his jaws tightened.

"All right, then; go ahead," he added, and walked grimly back to his chair.

When the steamer stopped at his landing, Bassett jumped off and began the ascent to his house without looking at Harwood again. Dan felt that it had been worth the journey to hear direct from Bassett the intimations of a wish to compromise the Canneries case. And yet, while the boat was backing off, it was without exultation that he watched Bassett's sturdy figure slowly climbing the steps. The signs of wear, the loss of the politician's old elasticity, touched a chord of pity in Harwood's breast. In the early days of their acquaintance it had seemed to him that Bassett could never be beaten; and yet Dan had to-night read defeat in his face and manner. The old Morton Bassett would never have yielded an inch, never have made overtures of compromise. He would have emerged triumphant from any disaster. Harwood experienced something of the sensations of a sculptor, who, having begun a heroic figure in the grand manner of a Michael Angelo, finds his model shrinking to a pitiful pygmy. As Bassett passed from sight he turned with a sigh toward the red, white and blue lanterns that advertised Mrs. Owen's dock to the mariner.

"Well, well, if it isn't Daniel," exclaimed Mrs. Owen, as Harwood greeted her and Sylvia on her veranda. "One of the farm hands quit to-day and you can go to work in the morning, Daniel."

"Not if I'm strong enough to run, Aunt Sally. I'm going to have forty-eight hours' vacation if I starve to death the rest of my life."

Rose Farrell had told him that Mrs. Owen was entertaining the Elizabeth House girls in installments, and he was not surprised to find the veranda filled with young women. Some of them he knew and Sylvia introduced him to the others.

"When's Rose coming up?" asked Sylvia, balancing herself on the veranda rail. "You know she's expected."

"Do I know she's expected? Didn't I have a note from you, Aunt Sally, ordering me to send her up? She's coming just as soon as I get back, but I think of staying forever."

"A man has come and he's come to stay forever," murmured one of the young women.

"Oh, you're an event!" laughed Sylvia. "But don't expect us to spoil you. The sport for to-morrow is tomato pickles, and the man who skipped to-day left because Aunt Sally wanted him to help scald and peel the tomats. Your job is cut out for you."

"All right," he replied humbly. "I'll do anything you say but plough or cut wood. My enchanted youth on the farm was filled with those delights, and before I go back to that a swift Marathon runner must trip me."

He was aware presently that one by one the girls were slipping away; he saw them through the windows settling themselves at the round table of the living-room, where Mrs. Owen was reading a newspaper. Not more than a quarter of an hour had passed when he and Sylvia found themselves alone.

"I haven't scarlet fever or anything," he remarked, noting the flight with satisfaction.

"I suppose we might go inside, too," suggested Sylvia obtusely.

"Oh, I came up for the fresh air! Most of my nights lately have been spent in a hot office with not even a June bug for company. How are the neighbors?"

"The Bassetts? Oh, Mrs. Bassett is not at all well; Marian is at home now; Blackford is tutoring and getting ready to take the Annapolis examinations the first chance he gets."

"I saw Allen to-day," he remarked carelessly.

She said nothing. He moved his chair nearer.

"He told me things that scared me to death—among others that he and Marian are engaged."

"Yes, Marian told me that."

"Ah! She really takes it seriously, does she?"

"Yes, she takes it seriously; why shouldn't she?"

"It's the first time she ever took anything seriously; that's all."

"Please don't speak of her like that, Dan. You know she and I are friends, and I thought you and she were friends too. She always speaks of you in the very kindest way. Your leaving Mr. Bassett didn't make any difference with her. And you are the greatest of Blackford's heroes next to Nelson and Farragut."

Dan laughed.

"So it isn't Napoleon, and Grant and Custer any more? I'm glad he's settled down to something."

"He's a fine boy with a lot of the right stuff in him. We've been having some lessons together."

"Tutoring Blackford? You'll have to explain the psychological processes that brought that about."

"Oh, they're simple enough. He hadn't done well in school last year; Mrs. Bassett was troubled about it. I take him for a couple of hours every morning. Mrs. Bassett engaged me, and Mr. Bassett approved of the plan. Allen probably told you all the news, but he didn't know just how I came to go to Chicago cago to bring Marian home. It was to keep the news of that automobile smash from Mrs. Bassett, and to save Marian's own dignity with the Willings."

"Oh! You went at her father's instance, did you?"

"Yes. I offered to go when I found that he was very angry and likely to deal severely and ungenerously with Marian. I thought it would be better for me to go."

"As near as I can make out, you've taken the Bassetts on your shoulders. I didn't suppose Aunt Sally would stand for that."

"Aunt Sally doesn't know why I went to Chicago. I assume Mrs. Bassett knows I went to bring Marian home, but I don't know what Mr. Bassett told her about it, and I haven't seen her since. It's possible my going may have displeased her. Blackford came here for his lessons this morning."

Dan moved uneasily. The domestic affairs of the Bassetts did not interest him save as they involved Sylvia. It was like Sylvia to help them out of their scrapes; but Sylvia was not a person that he could scold or abuse.

"You needed rest and it's too bad you've had to bother with their troubles. Bassett was on the boat as I came over. He had a grouch. He doesn't look like a happy man."

"I don't suppose he is altogether happy. And I've begged Marian not to tell him she wants to marry Allen. That would certainly not cheer him any, right now."

"I'm glad you had a chance to do that. I told Allen to skip right out for Europe and hang on to his mother's apron strings till I send for him. This old Capulet and Montague business doesn't ring quite true in this twentieth century; there's something unreal about it. And just what those youngsters can see in each other is beyond me."

"You must be fair about that. We haven't any right to question their sincerity."

"Oh, Allen is sincere enough; but you'll have to show me the documents on Marian's side of it. She sees in the situation a great lark. The fact that her father and Thatcher are enemies appeals to her romantic instincts."

"I think better of it than that, Dan. She's a fine, strong, loyal girl with a lot of hard common sense. But that doesn't relieve the situation of its immediate dangers. She's promised me not to speak to her father yet—not until she has my consent. When I see that it can't be helped, I'm going to speak to Mr Bassett about it myself."

"You seem to be the good angel of the Bassett household," he remarked sullenly. A lover's jealousy stirred in his heart, he did not like to think of Sylvia as preoccupied with the affairs of others, and he saw no peace or happiness ahead for Marian and Allen. "It's all more wretched than you imagine. This war between Thatcher and Bassett has passed the bounds of mere political rivalry. There's an implacable hatred there that's got to take its course. Allen told me of it this morning when he was trying to enlist me in his cause with Marian. It's hideous—a perfectly rotten mess. Thatcher is preparing a poisoned arrow for Bassett. He's raked up an old scandal, an affair with a woman. It makes my blood run cold to think of its possibilities."

"But Mr. Thatcher wouldn't do such a thing; he might threaten, but he wouldn't really use that sort of weapon!"

"You don't know the man, Sylvia. He will risk anything to break Bassett down. There's nothing respectable about Thatcher but his love for Allen, and that doesn't redeem everything."

"But you won't let it come to that. You have influence enough yourself to stop it. Even if you hated him you would protect Mrs. Bassett and the children."

"I could do nothing of the kind, Sylvia. Now that I've left Bassett my influence has vanished utterly. Besides, I'm out of politics. I hate the game. It's rotten—rotten clean through."

"I don't believe it's quite true that you have lost your influence. I read the newspapers, and some of them are saying that you are the hope of your party, and that you have a large following. But you wouldn't do that, Dan; you wouldn't lend yourself to such a thing as that!"

"I'm not so sure," he replied doggedly, angry that they should be discussing the subject at all, though to be sure he had introduced it. "A man's family has got to suffer for his acts; it's a part of the punishment. I'd like to see Bassett driven out of politics, but I assure you that I don't mean to do it. There's no possibility of my having the chance. He put me in the legislature to use me; and I'm glad that's all over. As I tell you, I'm out of the game."

"I don't sympathize with that at all, Dan; you not only ought to stay in, but you ought to do all you can to make it impossible for men like Bassett and Thatcher to have any power. The honor of the state ought to be dear to all of us; and if I belonged to a party I think I should have a care for its honor too."

The time was passing. It was not to discuss politics that he had gone to Waupegan.

"Come," he said. "Let's find a canoe and get out under the stars."

Sylvia went for a wrap, and they had soon embarked, skimming along in silence for a time till they were free of the shores. There was no moon, but the stars shone brilliantly; a fitful west wind scarcely ruffled the water. Along the deep-shadowed shores the dock lanterns twinkled, and above and beyond them the lamps of the cottages flashed and vanished. Dan paddled steadily with a skilled, splashless stroke. The paddle sank noiselessly and rose to the accompaniment of a tinkling drip as the canoe parted the waters. There is nothing like a canoe flight under stars to tranquilize a troubled and perplexed spirit, and Dan was soon won to the mood he sought. It seemed to him that Sylvia, enfolded in the silvery-dim dusk in the bow, was a part of the peace of sky and water. They were alone, away from the strifes and jars of the world, shut in together as completely as though they had been flung back for unreckoned ages into a world of unbroken calm. The peace that Wordsworth sought and sang crept into their blood, and each was sensible that the other knew and felt it and that it was grateful to them both.

Sylvia spoke, after a time, of immaterial things, or answered his questions as to the identity of the constellations mapped in the clear arch above.

"I dream sometimes of another existence," she said, "as I suppose every one does, when I knew a quiet lake that held the stars as this does. I even think I remember how it looked in winter, with the ice gleaming in the moonlight, and of snow coming and the keen winds piling it in drifts. It's odd, isn't it? those memories we have that are not memories. The metempsychosis idea must have some substance. We have all been somebody else sometime, and we clutch at the shadows of our old selves, hardly believing they are shadows."

"It's a good deal a matter of imagination, isn't it?" asked Dan, idling with the paddle.

"Oh, but I haven't a bit of that. That's one thing I'm not troubled with, and I'm sorry for it. When I look up at the stars I think of the most hideous formula for calculating their distances from the earth. When I read in a novel that it was a night of stars, I immediately wonder what particular stars. It used to make dear Grandfather Kelton furiously indignant to find a moon appearing in novels contrary to the almanac; he used to check up all the moons, and he once thought of writing a thesis on the 'Erroneous Lunar Calculations of Recent Novelists,' but decided that it didn't really make any difference. And of course it doesn't."

As they discussed novels new and old, he drew in his paddle and crept nearer her. It seemed to him that all the influences of earth and heaven had combined to create this hour for him. To be talking to her of books that interpreted life and of life itself was in itself something sweet; he wished such comradeship as this, made possible by their common interests in the deep, surging currents of the century in which they lived, to go on forever.

Their discussion of Tolstoy was interrupted by the swift flight of a motor boat that passed near, raising a small sea, and he seized the paddle to steady the canoe. Then silence fell upon them.

"Sylvia" he said softly, and again, "Sylvia!" It seemed to him that the silence and the beauty of the night were his ally, communicating to her infinite longings hidden in his heart which he had no words to express. "I love you, Sylvia; I love you. I came up to-night to tell you that."

"Oh, Dan, you mustn't say it—you must never say it!" The canoe seemed to hang between water and stars, a motionless argosy in a sea of dreams.

"I wanted to tell you before you came away," he went on, not heeding; "I have wanted to tell you for a long time. I want you to marry me. I want you to help me find the good things; I want you to help me to stand for them. You came just when I needed you; you have already changed me, made a different man of me. It was through you that I escaped from my old self that was weak and yielding, and I shall do better; yes, I shall prove to you that I am not so weak but that I can strive and achieve. Every word you ever spoke to me is written on my heart. I need you, Sylvia!"

"You're wrong, you're terribly wrong about all that; and it isn't fair to let you say such things. Please, Dan! I hoped this would never come—that we should go on as we have been, good friends, talking as we were a while ago of the fine things, the great things. And it will have to be that way—there can be nothing else."

"But I will do my best, Sylvia! I'm not the man you knew first; you helped me to see the light. Without you I shall fall into the dark again. I had to tell you, Sylvia. It was inevitable that I should tell you; I wonder I kept it to myself so long. Without you I should go adrift—no bearings, no light anywhere."

"You found yourself, Dan; that was the way of it. I saw it and appreciated it—it meant more to me than I can tell you. I knew exactly how it was that you started as you did; it was part of your fate; but it made possible the finer thing. It's nothing in you or what you've done or may do. But I have my own work to do. I have cut a pattern for my own life, and I must try to follow it. I think you understand about that—I told you that night when we talked of our aims and hopes on the campus at Montgomery that I wanted to do something for the world. And I must still go on trying to do that. It's a poor, tiny little gleam; but I must follow the gleam."

"But there's nothing in that that we can't do together. We can go on seeking it together," he pleaded.

"I hope it may be so. We must go on being the good friends we are now. You and Aunt Sally are all I have—the best I have. I can't let you spoil that," she ended firmly, as though, after all, this were the one important thing.

There was nothing here, he reasoned, that might not be overcome. The work that she had planned to do imposed no barrier. Men and women were finding out the joy of striving together; she need give up nothing in joining her life to his. He touched the hand that lay near and thrilled to the contact of her lingers.

"Please, Dan!" she pleaded, drawing her hand away. "I mean to go on with my life as I have begun it. I shall never marry, Dan,—marriage isn't in my plan at all. But for you the right woman will come some day—I hope so with all my heart. We must understand all this now. And I must be sure, oh, very sure, that you know how dear it is to have had you say these things to me."

"But I shall say them again and always, Sylvia! This was only the beginning; I had to speak to-night; I came here to say these things to you. I am able to care for you now—not as I should like to, but I'm going to succeed. I want to ease the way for you; I mean that you mustn't go back to teaching this fall!"

"There, you see"—and he knew she smiled in her patient, sweet way that was dear to him—"you want to stop my work before it's begun! You see how impossible it would be, Dan!"

"But you can do other things; there are infinite ways in which you can be of use, doing the things you want to do. The school work is only a handicap,—drudgery that leads to nothing."

He knew instantly that he had erred; and that he must give her no opportunity to defend her attitude toward her work. He returned quickly to his great longing and need.

"Without you I'm a failure, Sylvia. If it hadn't been for you I should never have freed myself of that man over there!" And he lifted his arm toward the lights of the Bassett landing on the nearer shore.

"No; you would have saved yourself in any case; there's no questioning that. You were bound to do it. And it wasn't the man; it was the base servitude that you came to despise."

"Not without you! It was your attitude toward me, after that cheap piece of melodrama I figured in in that convention, that brought me up with a short turn. It all came through you—my wish to measure up to your ideal."

"That's absurd, Dan. If I believed that I should think much less of you; I really should!" she exclaimed. "It was something finer and higher than that; it was your own manhood asserting itself. That man over there," she went on more quietly, "is an object of pity. He's beset on many sides. It hurt him to lose you. He's far from happy."

"He has no claim upon happiness; he doesn't deserve happiness," replied Dan doggedly.

"But the break must have cost you something; haven't you missed him just a little bit?"

It was clear from her tone that she wished affirmation of this. The reference to his former employer angered him. He had been rejoicing in his escape from Morton Bassett, and yet Sylvia spoke of him with tolerance and sympathy. The Bassetts were coolly using her to extricate themselves from the embarrassments resulting from their own folly; it was preposterous that they should have sent Sylvia to bring Marian home. And his rage was intensified by the recollection of the pathos he had himself felt in Bassett that very evening, as he had watched him mount the steps of his home. Sylvia was causing the old chords to vibrate with full knowledge that, in spite of his avowed contempt for the man, Morton Bassett still roused his curiosity and interest. It was unfair for Sylvia to take advantage of this.

"Bassett's nothing to me," he said roughly.

"He seems to me the loneliest soul I ever knew," replied Sylvia quietly.

"He deserves it; he's brought himself to that."

"I don't believe he's altogether evil. There must be good in him."

"It's because he's so evil that you pity him; it's because of that that I'm sorry for him. It's because we know that he must be broken upon the wheel before he realizes the vile use he has made of his power that we are sorry for him. Why, Sylvia, he's the worst foe we have—all of us who want to do what we call the great things—ease the burdens of the poor, make government honest, catch the gleam we seek! Even poor Allen, when he stands on the Monument steps at midnight and spouts to me about the Great Experiment, feels what Morton Bassett can't be made to feel."

"But he may yet see it; even he may come to see it," murmured Sylvia.

"He's a hard, stubborn brute; it's in the lines of his back—I was studying him on the boat this evening, and my eyes followed him up the steps after they dropped him at his dock. It's in those strong, iron hands of his. I tell you, what we feel for him is only the kind of pity we have for those we know to be doomed by the gods to an ignominious end. He's not worth our pity. He asks no mercy and he won't get any."

He was at once ashamed of the temper to which he had yielded, and angry at himself for having broken the calm of the night with these discordant notes. Sylvia's hand touched the water caressingly, waking tiny ripples.

"Sylvia," he said when he was calm again, "I want you to marry me."

"I have told you, Dan, that I can never marry any one; and that must be the end of it."

"But your work can go on—" he began, ready for another assault upon that barrier.

A sailboat loitering in the light wind had stolen close upon them, and passed hardly a paddle's length away. Dan, without changing his position, drove the canoe toward the shore with a few strokes of the paddle, then steadied himself to speak again. Sylvia's eyes watched the sails vanishing like ghosts into the dark.

"That won't do, Sylvia: that isn't enough. You haven't said that you don't care for me; you haven't said that you don't love me! And I can't believe that your ambitions alone are in the way. Believe me, that I respect them; I should never interfere with them. There must be some other reason. I can't take no for an answer; this night was made for us; no other night will ever be just like this. Please, dear, if there are other reasons than my own poor spirit and the little I can offer, let me know it. If you don't care, it will be kinder to say it now! If that is the reason—even if there's some other man—let me know it now. Tell me what it is, Sylvia!"

It was true that she had not said she did not care. Her silence now at the direct question stirred new fears to life in his breast, like the beat of startled wings from a thicket in November.

Only the lights of the sailboat were visible now, but suddenly a girl's voice rose clear and sweet, singing to the accompaniment of guitar and mandolin. The guitar throbbed; and on its deep chords the mandolin wove its melody. The voice seemed to steal out of the heart of the night and float over the still waters. The unseen singer never knew the mockery of the song she sang. It was an old song and the air was one familiar the world round. And it bore the answer to Dan's question which Sylvia had carried long in her heart, but could not speak. She did not speak it then; it was ordained that she should never speak it. And Dan knew and understood.

"Who is Sylvia, what is she,
That all the swains adore her?"

"Who is Sylvia?" Dan knew in that hour the answer of tears!

The song ceased. When Dan saw Sylvia's head lift, he silently took the paddle and impelled the canoe toward the red, white, and blue lanterns that defined Mrs. Owen's landing. They were within a hundred yards of the intervening green light of the Bassett dock when a brilliant meteor darted across the zenith, and Dan's exclamation broke the tension. Their eyes turned toward the heavens—Sylvia's still bright with tears, Dan knew, though he could not see her face.

"Poor lost star!" she murmured softly.

Dan was turning the canoe slightly to avoid the jutting shore that made a miniature harbor at the Bassett's when Sylvia uttered a low warning. Dan, instantly alert, gripped his paddle and waited. Some one had launched a canoe at the Bassett boathouse. There was a stealthiness in the performance that roused him to vigilance. He cautiously backed water and waited. A word or two spoken in a low tone reached Dan and Sylvia: two persons seemed to be embarking.

A canoe shot out suddenly from the dock, driven by a confident hand.

"It must be Marian; but there's some one with her," said Sylvia.

Dan had already settled himself in the stern ready for a race.

"It's probably that idiot Allen," he growled. "We must follow them."

Away from the shore shadows the starlight was sufficient to confirm Dan's surmise as to the nature of this canoe flight. It was quite ten o'clock, and the lights in the Bassett house on the bluff above had been extinguished. It was at once clear to Dan that he must act promptly. Allen, dismayed by the complications that beset his love-affair, had proposed an elopement, and Marian had lent a willing ear.

"They're running away, Sylvia; we've got to head them off." He bent to his paddle vigorously. "They can't possibly get away."

But it was not in Marian's blood to be thwarted in her pursuit of adventure. She was past-mistress of the canoeist's difficult art, and her canoe flew on as though drawn away into the dark on unseen cords.

"You'd better lend a hand," said Dan, and Sylvia turned round and knelt, paddling Indian fashion. The canoe skimmed the water swiftly. It was in their thoughts that Marian and Allen must not land at Waupegan, where their intentions would be advertised to the world. The race must end before the dock was reached. At the end of a quarter of an hour Dan called to Sylvia to cease paddling.

"We've passed them; there's no doubt of that," he said, peering into the dark.

"Maybe they're just out for fun and have turned back," suggested Sylvia.

"I wish I could think so. More likely they're trying to throw us off. Let's check up for a moment and see if we hear them again."

He kept the canoe moving slowly while they listened for some sign of the lost quarry. Then suddenly they heard a paddle stroke behind them, and an instant later a canoe's bow brushed their craft as lightly as a hand passing across paper. Dan threw himself forward and grasped the sides firmly; there was a splashing and wobbling as he arrested the flight. A canoe is at once the most docile and the most intractable of argosies. Sylvia churned the water with her paddle, seeking to crowd the rocking canoes closer together, while Marian endeavored to drive them apart.

"Allen!" panted Dan, prone on the bottom of his canoe and gripping the thwarts of the rebellious craft beside him, "this must end here."

"Let us go!" cried Allen stridently. "This is none of your business. Let us go, I say."

Finding it impossible to free her canoe, Marian threw down her paddle angrily. They were all breathless; Dan waited till the canoes rode together quietly. Sylvia had brought an electric lamp which Dan now flashed the length of the captive canoe. It searched the anxious, angry faces of the runaways, and disclosed two suit cases that told their own story.

"I told you to keep away from here, Allen. You can't do this. It won't do," said Dan, snapping off the light; "you're going home with us, Marian."

"I won't go back; you haven't any right to stop me!"

"You haven't any right to run away in this fashion," said Sylvia, speaking for the first time. "You would cause endless trouble. It's not the way to do it."

"But it's the only way out," stormed Allen. "There's no other way. Dan told me himself I couldn't speak to Mr. Bassett, and this is the only thing we could do."

"Will you kindly tell me just what you intended doing?" asked Dan, still gripping the canoe.

"I'd spoken to the minister here in the village. Marian was going to spend the night at his house and we were to be married in the morning as soon as I could get a license."

"You can't get a marriage license in Waupegan; your minister ought to know that."

"No; but we could have driven over early to the county seat and got it; I tell you I had it all fixed. You let go of that canoe!"

"Stand by, Sylvia," said Dan with determination.

He steadied himself a moment, stepped into Marian's canoe, and caught up her paddle.

"Wait here, Sylvia. I'm going to land Allen over there at that dock with the two white lights, and I'll come back with Marian and we'll take her home. Flash the light occasionally so I shan't lose you."

A few minutes later when Allen, sulky and breathing dire threats, had been dropped ashore, Harwood paddled Marian home, Sylvia trailing behind.

It was near midnight when Sylvia, having hidden Marian's suit case in Mrs. Owen's boathouse, watched the tearful and wrathful Juliet steal back into her father's house.

Allen lodged at the inn with Dan that night and, duly urged not to make a fool of himself again, went home by the morning train.

CHAPTER XXX
THE KING HATH SUMMONED HIS PARLIAMENT

The Great Seal of the Hoosier Commonwealth, depicting a sturdy pioneer felling a tree while behind him a frightened buffalo gallops madly into oblivion, was affixed to a proclamation of the governor convening the legislature in special session on the 20th of November. It was Morton Bassett's legislature, declared the Republican press, brought back to the capital to do those things which it had left undone at the regular session. The Democratic newspapers proved conclusively that the demands of the state institutions said to be in dire need were the fruit of a long period of Republican extravagance, for which the Democratic Party, always prone to err on the side of frugality, was in no wise responsible. The Republican governor had caused the legislative halls to be reopened merely to give a false impression of Democratic incompetence, but in due season the people would express their opinion of that governor. So reasoned loyal Democrats. Legislatures are not cheap, taken at their lowest valuation, and a special session, costing something like one hundred thousand of the people's dollars, is an extravagance before which a governor may well hesitate. This particular convocation of the Hoosier lawmakers, summoned easily enough by a stroke of the pen, proved to be expensive in more ways than one.

On the third day of the special session, when the tardiest member, hailing from the remote fastnesses of Switzerland County, was just finding his seat, and before all the others had drawn their stationery and registered a generous computation of their mileage, something happened. The bill for an act entitled an act to lift the lid of the treasure chests was about to be read for the first time when a page carried a telegram to Morton Bassett in the senate chamber.

Senator Bassett read his message once and again. His neighbors on the floor looked enviously upon the great man who thus received telegrams without emotion. It seemed, however, to those nearest him, that the bit of yellow paper shook slightly in Bassett's hand The clerk droned on to an inattentive audience. Bassett put down the telegram, looked about, and then got upon his feet. The lieutenant-governor, yawning and idly playing with his gavel, saw with relief that the senator from Fraser wished to interrupt the proceedings.

"Mr. President."

"The senator from Fraser."

"Mr. President, I ask leave to interrupt the reading of the bill to make an announcement."

"There being no objection, the senator will make his announcement."

Senators who had been smoking in the cloakroom, or talking to friends outside the railing, became attentive. The senator from Fraser was little given to speech, and it might be that he meant at this time to indicate the attitude of the majority toward the appropriations asked by the governor. In any event, it was always wise to listen to anything Morton Bassett had to say.

The senator was unusually deliberate. Even when he had secured the undivided attention of the chamber he picked up the telegram and read it through again, as though to familiarize himself with its contents.

"Mr. President, I have just received the following message from a personal friend in Washington: 'The Honorable Roger B. Ridgefield, United States Senator from Indiana, while on a hunting trip in Chesapeake Bay with a party of Baltimore friends, died suddenly this morning. The death occurred at a point remote from the telegraph. No particulars have yet been received at Washington.' It is with profound sorrow, Mr. President, that I make this announcement. Though Senator Ridgefield had long been my political antagonist, he had also been, for many years, a valued personal friend. The Republican Party has lost one of its great leaders, and the State of Indiana a son to whom men of all parties have given their ungrudging admiration. Mr. President, I move that the senate do now adjourn to meet at ten o'clock to-morrow morning."

Even before the motion could be put, Bassett was passing about among the desks. The men he spoke to nodded understandingly. A mild, subdued excitement reigned in the chamber. It flashed through the mind of every Democratic member that that death in the Chesapeake had brought a crisis in the war between Bassett and Thatcher. In due course the assembly, convened in joint session, would mourn decorously the death of a statesman who had long and honorably represented the old Hoosier State in the greatest tribunal on earth; and his passing would be feelingly referred to in sonorous phrases as an untoward event, a deplorable and irreparable loss to the commonwealth. To Republicans, however, it was a piece of stupendous ill-luck that the Senator should have indulged in the childish pastime of duck shooting at an inconvenient season when the Democratic majority in the general assembly would be able to elect a successor to complete his term of office.

When the gavel fell, adjourning the senate, gentlemen were already seeking in the Federal Constitution for the exact language of the section bearing upon this emergency. If the Republican governor had not so gayly summoned the legislature he might have appointed a Senator of his own political faith to serve until the next regular session, following the elections a year hence. It was ungenerous and disloyal of Roger B. Ridgefield to have taken himself out of the world in this abrupt fashion. Before the first shock had passed, there were those about the State House who, scanning the newspaper extras, were saying that a secret fondness for poker and not an enthusiasm for ducks had led the Honorable Roger B. Ridgefield to the remote arm of the Chesapeake, where he had been the guest of a financier whose influence in the upper house of Congress was notoriously pernicious. This did not, however, alter the immediate situation. The language of the Federal and State Constitutions was all too explicit for the Republican minority; it was only in recess that a governor might fill a vacancy; and beyond doubt the general assembly was in town, lawfully brought from the farm, the desk, the mine, and the factory, as though expressly to satisfy the greed for power of a voracious Democracy.

Groups of members were retiring to quiet corners to discuss the crisis. Bassett had already designated a committee room where he would meet his followers and stanch adherents. Thatcher men had gone forth to seek their chief. The Democrats would gain a certain moral strength through the possession of a Senator in Congress. The man chosen to fill the vacancy would have an almost irresistible claim upon the senatorship if the Democrats should control the next legislature. It was worth fighting for, that dead man's seat!

The full significance of the news was not wasted upon Representative Harwood. The house adjourned promptly, and Dan hastened to write telegrams. He wired Colonel Ramsay, of Aurora, to come to the capital on the first train. Telegrams went flying that afternoon to every part of Indiana.

Thatcher read the evening papers in Chicago and kept the wires hot while he waited for the first train for Indianapolis.

One of his messages, addressed to Harwood, read:

"Breakfast with me to-morrow morning at my house. Strictly private. This is your big chance."

Harwood, locked in his office in the Law Building, received this message by telephone, and it aroused his ire. His relations with Thatcher did not justify that gentleman in tendering him a strictly private breakfast, nor did he relish having a big chance pointed out to him by Mr. Thatcher. It cannot be denied that Dan, too, felt that Senator Ridgefield had chosen a most unfortunate season for exposing himself to the ravages of the pneumococcus. He kept away from the State House and hotels that evening, having decided to take no part in the preliminary skirmishes until he had seen Ramsay, who would bring a cool head and a trained hand to bear upon this unforeseen situation.

He studied the newspapers as he ate breakfast alone at the University Club early the next morning. The "Advertiser" had neatly divided its first page between the Honorable Roger B. Ridgefield, dead in a far country, and the Honorable Morton Bassett, who, it seemed, was very much alive at the Hoosier capital. A double column headline conveyed this intelligence:—

BASSETT IS HIMSELF AGAIN

Harwood, nibbled his toast and winnowed the chaff of speculation from the grains of truth in this article. He had checked off the names of all the Bassett men in both houses of the assembly, and listed Thatcher's supporters and the doubtful members. Bassett would undoubtedly make a strong showing in a caucus, but whether he would be able to command a majority remained to be seen. There were men among the doubtful who would be disposed to favor Thatcher because he had driven a wedge into the old Bassett stone wall. No one else had ever succeeded in imperiling the security of that impregnable stronghold. The thought of this made Harwood uncomfortable. It was unfortunate from every standpoint that the legislature should be called upon to choose a Senator without the usual time for preparation. Dan had already been struck by the general air of irresponsibility that prevailed among the legislators. Many of the members had looked upon the special session as a lark; they seemed to feel that their accountability to their constituents had ended with the regular session.

The "Courier," Dan observed, printed an excellent biographical sketch of the dead Senator, and its news article on the Democratic opportunity was seemly and colorless. The state and federal statutes bearing upon the emergency were quoted in full, but the names of Bassett and Thatcher did not appear, nor were any possible successors to Ridgefield mentioned. Dan opened to the editorial page, and was not surprised to find the leading article a dignified eulogy of the dead Senator. Then his eye fastened upon an article so placed that it dominated the whole page. It was the old "Stop, Look, Listen!" editorial, reproduced with minute citation of the date of original publication.

Dan flinched as though a cupful of ice water had struck him in the face. Whatever scandalous knowledge touching Bassett's public or private life Thatcher might possess, it was plain that Bassett was either ignorant of it or knew and did not fear exposure. In either event, the republication of the "Stop, Look, Listen!" article was an invitation to battle.

It was in no happy frame of mind that Harwood awaited the coming of Ramsay.

CHAPTER XXXI
SYLVIA ASKS QUESTIONS

The Wares had asked Sylvia to dine with them on Friday evening a fortnight later, and Harwood was to call for her at the minister's at nine o'clock. Sylvia went directly to the Wares' from school, and on reaching the house learned that Mrs. Ware had not come home and that the minister was engaged with a caller in the parlor. Sylvia, who knew the ways of the house well, left her wraps in the hall and made herself comfortable in the study, that curious little room that was never free from the odor of pipe smoke, and where an old cavalry sabre hung above the desk upon which in old times many sermons had been written. A saddle, a fishing-rod, and a fowling-piece dwelt together harmoniously in one corner, and over the back of a chair hung a dilapidated corduroy coat.

It had been whispered in orthodox circles that Ware had amused himself one winter after his retirement by profanely feeding his theological library into the furnace. However true this may be, few authors were represented in his library, and these were as far as possible compressed in one volume. Shakespeare, Milton, Emerson, Arnold, and Whittier were always ready to his hand; and he kept a supply of slender volumes of Sill's "Poems" in a cupboard in the hall and handed them out discriminatingly to his callers. The house was the resort of many young people, some of them children of Ware's former parishioners, and he was much given to discussing books with them; or he would read aloud—"Sohrab and Rustum," Lowell's essay on Lincoln, or favorite chapters from "Old Curiosity Shop"; or again, it might be a review article on the social trend or a fresh view of an old economic topic. The Wares' was the pleasantest of small houses and after Mrs. Owen's the place sought oftenest by Sylvia.

"There's a gentleman with Mr. Ware: he's been here a long time," said the maid, lingering to lay a fresh stick of wood on the grate fire.

Sylvia, warming her hands at the blaze, heard the faint blur of voices from the parlor. She surveyed the room with the indifference of familiarity, glanced at a new magazine, and then sat down at the desk and picked up a book she had never noticed before. She was surprised to find it a copy of "Society and Solitude" that did not match the well-thumbed set of Emerson—one of the few "sets" Ware owned. She passed her hand over the green covers, that were well worn and scratched in places. The fact that the minister boasted in his humorous way of never wasting money on bindings caused Sylvia to examine this volume with an attention she would not have given it in any other house. On the fly leaf was written in pencil, in Ware's rough, uneven hand, an inscription which covered the page, with the last words cramped in the lower corner. These were almost illegible, but Sylvia felt her way through them slowly, and then turned to the middle of the book quickly with an uncomfortable sense of having read a private memorandum of the minister's. The margins of his books she knew were frequently scribbled over with notes that meant nothing whatever to any one but Ware himself. After a moment her eyes sought again irresistibly the inscription. She re-read it slowly:—

> "The way of peace they know not; and there is no judgment in their goings; they have made them crooked paths; whosoever goeth therein shall not know peace. Tramping in Adirondacks. Baptized Elizabeth at Harris's."

It was almost like eavesdropping to come in this way upon that curiously abrupt Ware-like statement of the minister's: "Tramping in Adirondacks. Baptized Elizabeth at Harris's."

The discussion in the parlor had become heated, and occasionally words in a voice not Ware's reached Sylvia distinctly. Some one was alternately beseeching and threatening the minister. It was clear from the pauses in which she recognized Ware's deep tones that he was yielding neither to the importunities nor the threats of his blustering caller. Sylvia had imagined that the storms of life had passed over the retired clergyman, and she was surprised that such an interview should be taking place in his house. She was about to retreat to the dining-room to be out of reach of the voices when the parlor door opened abruptly and Thatcher appeared, with anger unmistakably showing in his face, and apparently disposed to resume in the hall the discussion which the minister had terminated in the library. Thatcher seemed balder and more repellent than when she had first seen him on the floor of the convention hall on the day Harwood uttered Bassett's defiance. Sylvia rose with the book still in her hand and walked to the end of the room; but any one in the house might have heard what Thatcher was saying.

"That's the way with you preachers; you talk about clean politics, and when we get all ready to clean out a bad man, you duck; you're a lot of cowardly dodgers. I tell you, I don't want you to say a word or figure in this thing at all; but you give me that book and I'll scare Mort Bassett out of town. I'll scare him clean out of Indiana, and he'll never show his head again. Why, Ware, I've been counting on it, that when you saw we were in a hole and going to lose, you'd come down from your high horse and help me out. I tell you, there's no doubt about it; that woman's the woman I'm looking for! I guessed it the night you told that story up there in the house-boat."

"Quit this business, Ed," the minister was saying; "I'm an old friend of yours. But I won't budge an inch. I'd never breathed a word of that story before and I shouldn't have told it that night. It was so far back that I thought it was safe. But your idea that Bassett had anything to do with that is preposterous. Your hatred of him has got the better of you, my friend. Drop it: forget it. If you can't whip him fair, let him win."

"Not much I won't; but I didn't think you'd go back on me; I thought better of you than that!"

Thatcher strode to the door and went out, slamming it after him.

The minister peered into the library absently, and then, surprised to find Sylvia, advanced to meet her, smiling gravely. He took both her hands, and held them, looking into her face.

"What's this you've been reading? Ah, that book!" The volume slipped into his hands and he glanced at it, frowning impatiently. "Poor little book. I ought to have burned it years ago; and I ought to have learned by this time to keep my mouth shut. They've always said I look like an Indian, but an Indian never tells anything. I've told just one story too many. *Mea maxima culpa!*"

He sat down in the big chair beside his desk, placed the book within reach, and kept touching it as he talked.

"I saw Mr. Thatcher," said Sylvia. "He seemed very much aroused. I couldn't help hearing a word now and then."

"That's all right, Sylvia. I've known Thatcher for years, and last fall I went up to his house-boat on the Kankakee for a week's shooting. Allen and Dan Harwood were the rest of the party—and I happened to tell the story of this little book—an unfinished story. We ought never to tell stories until they are finished. And it seems that Thatcher, with a zeal worthy of a better cause, has been raking up the ashes of an old affair of Bassett's with a woman, and he's trying to hitch it on to the story I told him about this book. He says by shaking this at Bassett he can persuade him that he's got enough ammunition to blow him out of the water. But I don't believe a word of it; I won't believe such a thing of Morton Bassett. And even if I did, Thatcher can't have that book. I owe it to the woman whose baby I baptized up there in the hills to keep it. And the woman may be living, too, for all I know. I think of her pretty often. She was game; wouldn't tell anything. If a man had deceived her she stood by him. Whatever she was—I know she was not bad, not a bit of it—the spirit of the hills had entered into her—and those are cleansing airs up there. I suppose it all made the deeper impression on me because I was born up there myself. When I strike Adirondacks in print I put down my book and think a while. It's a picture word. It brings back my earliest childhood as far as I can remember. I call words that make pictures that way moose words; they jump up in your memory like a scared moose in a thicket and crash into the woods like a cavalry charge. I can remember things that happened when I was three years old: one day father shot a deer in our cornfield and I recall it perfectly. The general atmosphere of the old place steals over me yet. The very thought of the pointed spruces, the feathery tamaracks, all the scents and sounds of summer, and the long, white winters, does my soul good now. The old Hebrews understood the effect of landscape on character. They knew most everything, those old chaps. 'I will lift up mine eyes unto the hills from whence cometh my help.' Any strength there is in me dates back to the hills of my youth. I'd like to go back there to die when the bugle calls."

Mrs. Ware had not yet come in. Ware lighted the lamp and freshened the fire. While he was doing this, Sylvia moved to a chair by the table and picked up the book. What Ware had said about the hills of his youth, the woods, the word tamarack that he had dropped carelessly, touched chords of memory as lightly as a breeze vibrates a wind harp. Was this merely her imagination that had been stirred, or was it indeed a recollection? Often before she had been moved by similar vague memories or longings, whatever they were. They had come to trouble her girlhood at Montgomery, when the snow whitened the campus and the wind sang in the trees. She was grateful that the minister had turned his back. Her hands trembled as she glanced again at the scribbled fly leaf; and more closely at the words penciled at the bottom: "Baptized Elizabeth at Harris's." Thatcher wanted this book to use against Bassett. Bassett was a collector of fine bindings; she had heard it spoken of in the family. It was part of Marian's pride in her father that he was a bookish man. When the minister returned to his seat Sylvia asked as she put down the book:—

"Who was Elizabeth?"

And then, little by little, in his abrupt way, he told the story, much as he had told it that night on the Kankakee, with pauses for which Sylvia was grateful—they gave her time for thought, for filling in the lapses, for visualizing the scene he described. And the shadow of the Morton Bassett she knew crept into the picture. She recalled their early meetings, that first brief contact on the shore of the lake; their talk on the day following the convention when she had laughed at him; that wet evening when they met in the street and he had expressed his interest in Harwood and the hope that she might care for the young lawyer. With her trained habits of reasoning she rejected this or that bit of testimony as worthless; but even then enough remained to chill her heart. Her hands were cold as she clasped them together. Who was Elizabeth? Ah, who was Sylvia? The phrase of the song that had brought her to tears that starry night on the lake when Dan Harwood had asked her to marry him smote her again. Her grandfather's evasion of her questions about her father and mother, and the twinges of heartache she had experienced at college when other girls spoke of their homes, assumed now for the first time a sinister meaning. Had she, indeed, come into the world in dishonor, and had she in truth known that far hill country, with its evergreens and glistening snows?

Ware had finished his story, and sat staring into the crackling fire. At last he turned toward Sylvia. In the glow of the desk lamp her face was white, and she gazed with unseeing eyes at the inscription in the book.

The silence was still unbroken when a few minutes later Mrs. Ware came in with Harwood, whom she had met in the street and brought home to dinner.

Dan was full of the situation in the legislature, and the table talk played about that topic.

"We're sparring for time, that's all, and the people pay the freight! The deadlock is clamped on tight. I never thought Thatcher would prove so strong. I think we could shake loose enough votes from both sides to precipitate a stampede for Ramsay, but he won't hear to it. He says he wants to do the state one patriotic service before he dies by cleaning out the bosses, and he doesn't want to spoil the record by taking the senatorship himself. Meanwhile Bassett stands fast and there's no telling when he'll break through Thatcher's lines."

"Thatcher was here to see me to-day—the third time. He won't come back. You know what he's after?" said Ware.

"Yes; I understand," Dan answered.

"There won't be anything of that kind, will there, Dan?"

Dan shrugged his shoulders, and glanced at Sylvia and Mrs. Ware.

"Mrs. Ware knows about it; I had to tell her," remarked the minister, chuckling. "When Ed Thatcher makes two calls on me in one week, and one of them at midnight, there's got to be an explanation. And Sylvia heard him raving before I showed him out this afternoon."

Sylvia's plate was untouched; her eyes searched those of the man who loved her before she spoke.

"That's an ethical point, Mr. Ware. If it were necessary to use that,—if every other resource failed,—would you use it?"

"No! Not if Bassett's success meant the utter destruction of the state. I don't believe a word of it. I haven't the slightest confidence in Thatcher's detective work, and the long arm of coincidence has to grasp something firmer than my pitiful little book to convince me."

Dan shook his head.

"He doesn't need the book, Mr. Ware. I've seen the documents in the case. Most of the evidence is circumstantial, but you remember what your friend Thoreau said about circumstantial evidence—something to the effect that it's sometimes pretty convincing, as when you find a trout in the milk."

"But has Thatcher found the trout?"

"Well, no; he hasn't exactly found the trout, but there's enough, there's altogether too much!" ended Dan despairingly. "The caucus doesn't meet again till to-morrow night, when Thatcher promises to show his hand. I'm going to put in the time trying to persuade Ramsay to come round."

"You might take it yourself, Dan," suggested Mrs. Ware.

"Oh, I'm not eligible; I'm a little shy of being old enough! And besides, I couldn't allow Ramsay to prove himself a better patriot than I am. There are plenty of fellows who have no such scruples, and we've got to look out or Bassett will shift suddenly to some man of his own if he finds he can't nominate himself."

"But do you think he has any idea what Thatcher has up his sleeve?" asked Ware.

"It's possible; I dare say he knows it. He's always been master of the art of getting information from the enemy's camp. But Thatcher has shown remarkable discretion in managing this. He tells me solemnly that nobody on earth knows his intentions except you, Allen, and me. He's saving himself for a broadside, and he wants its full dramatic effect."

Sylvia had hardly spoken during this discussion; but the others looked at her curiously as she said:—

"I don't think he has it to fire; it's incredible; I don't believe it."

"Neither do I, Sylvia," said the minister earnestly.

The talk at the Wares' went badly that evening. Harwood's mind was on the political situation. As he sat in the minister's library he knew that in upper chambers of the State House, and in hotels and boarding-houses, members of the majority in twos and threes, or here and there a dozen, were speculating and plotting. The deadlock was becoming intolerable. Interest in the result was keen in all parts of the country, and the New York and Chicago newspapers had sent special representatives to watch the fight. Dan was sick of the sight and sound of it. In the strict alignment of factions he had voted with Thatcher, yet he told himself he was not a Thatcher man. He had personally projected Ramsay's name one night in the hope of breaking the Bassett phalanx, but the only result was to arouse Thatcher's wrath against him. Bassett's men believed in Bassett. The old superstition as to his invulnerability had never more thoroughly possessed the imaginations of his adherents. Bassett was not only himself again, but his iron grip seemed tighter than ever He was making the fight of his life, and he was beyond question a "game" fighter, the opposition newspapers that most bitterly opposed Bassett tempered their denunciations with this concession. Dan fumed at this, such bosses were always game fighters, they had to be, and the readiness of Americans to admire the gameness of the Bassetts deepened his hostility. The very use of sporting terminology in politics angered him. In his mind the case was docketed not as Thatcher *versus* Bassett, but as Thatcher and Bassett *versus* the People. It all came to that. And why should not the People—the poor, meek, long-suffering People, the "pee-pul" of familiar derision—sometimes win? His pride in the state of his birth was strong; his pride in his party was only second to it. He would serve both if he could. Not only must Bassett be forever put down, but Thatcher also; and he assured himself that it was not the men he despised, but the wretched, brutal mediæval system that survived in them. And so pondering, it was no wonder that Dan brought no joy to John Ware's library that night. The minister himself seemed unwontedly preoccupied; Sylvia stared at the fire as though seeking in the flames answers to unanswerable questions. Mrs. Ware sought vainly to bring cheer to the company:

Shortly after eight o'clock, Sylvia rose to leave.

"Aunt Sally got home from Kentucky this afternoon, and I must drop in for a minute, Dan, if you don't mind."

Sylvia hardly spoke on the way to Mrs. Owen's. Since that night on the lake she had never been the same, or so it seemed to Dan. She had gone back to her teaching, and when they met she talked of her work and of impersonal things. Once he had broached the subject of marriage,—soon after her return to town,—but she had made it quite clear that this was a forbidden topic. The good comradeship ship and frankness of their intercourse had passed, and it seemed to his despairing lover's heart that it could never be regained. She carried her head a little higher; her smile was not the smile of old. He shrank from telling her that nothing mattered if she cared for him as he believed she did. She gave him no chance, for one thing, and he had never in his bitter self-communing found any words in which to tell her so. More than ever he needed Sylvia, but Sylvia had locked and barred the doors against him.

Mrs. Owen received them in her office, and the old lady's cheeriness was grateful to both of them.

"So you've been having supper with the Wares, have you, while I ate here all by myself? A nice way to treat a lone old woman,—leaving me to prop the 'Indiana Farmer' on the coffee pot for company! I had to stay at Lexington longer than I wanted to, and some of my Kentucky cousins held me up in Louisville. I notice, Daniel, that there are some doings at the State House. I must say it was a downright sin for old Ridgefield to go duck shooting at his time of life and die just when we were getting politics calmed down in this state. When I saw that old 'Stop, Look, Listen!' editorial printed like a Thanksgiving proclamation in the 'Courier,' I knew there was trouble. I must speak to Atwill. He's letting the automobile folks run the paper again."

She demanded to know when Dan would have time to do some work for her; she had disposed of her Kentucky farm and was going ahead with her scheme for a vocational school to be established at Waupegan. This was the first that Dan had heard of this project, and its bearing upon the hopes of the Bassetts as the heirs apparent of Mrs. Owen's estate startled him.

"I want you to draw up papers covering the whole business, Daniel, but you've got to get rid of your legislature first. I thought of a good name for the school, Sylvia. We'll call it Elizabeth House School, to hitch it on to the boarding-house. I want you and Daniel to go down East with me right after

Christmas to look at some more schools where they do that kind of work. We'll have some fun next spring tearing up the farm and putting up the new buildings. Are Hallie and Marian in town, Sylvia?"

"No, they're at Fraserville," Sylvia replied. "And I had a note from Blackford yesterday. He's doing well at school now."

"Well, I guess you did that for him, Sylvia. I hope they're all grateful for that."

"Oh, it was nothing; and they paid me generously for my work."

"Humph!" Mrs. Owen sniffed. "Children, there are things in this world that a check don't settle."

There were some matters of business to be discussed. Dan had at last received an offer for the Kelton house at Montgomery, and Mrs. Owen thought he ought to be able to screw the price up a couple of hundred dollars.

"I'm all ready to close the estate when the sale is completed," said Dan. "Practically everything will be cleaned up when the house is sold. That Canneries stock that we inventoried as worthless is pretty sure to pan out. I've refused to compromise."

"That's right, Daniel. Don't you compromise that case. This skyrocket finance is all right for New York, but we can't allow it here in the country where folks are mostly square or trying to be."

"It seems hard to let the house go," said Sylvia. "It's given Mary a home and we'll have to find a place for her."

"Oh, that's all fixed," remarked Mrs. Owen. "I've got work for her at Elizabeth House. She can do the darning and mending. Daniel, have you brought the papers from Andrew's safety box over here?"

"Yes, Aunt Sally; I did that the last time I was in Montgomery. I wanted to examine the abstract of title and be ready to close this sale if you and Sylvia approved of it."

"Well, well," Mrs. Owen said, in one of those irrelevances that adorned her conversation.

Dan knew what was in her mind. Since that night on Waupegan, blessed forever by Sylvia's tears, the letter found among Professor Kelton's papers had led him through long, intricate mazes of speculation. It was the torn leaf from a book that was worthless without the context; a piece of valuable evidence, but inadmissible unless supported and illuminated by other testimony.

SYLVIA MUST KNOW JUST WHAT WE KNOW

Sylvia had been singularly silent, and Mrs. Owen's keen eyes saw that something was amiss. She stopped talking, as much as to say, "Now, if you young folks have anything troubling you, now's your time to come out with it."

An old clock on the stair landing boomed ten. Mrs. Owen stirred restlessly. Sylvia, sitting in a low chair by the fire, clasped her hands abruptly, clenched them hard, and spoke, turning her head slowly until her eyes rested upon Dan.

"Dan," she asked, "did you ever know—do you know now—what was in the letter you carried to Grandfather Kelton that first time I saw you—the time I went to find grandfather for you?"

Dan glanced quickly at Mrs. Owen.

"Answer Sylvia's question, Daniel," the old lady replied.

"Yes; I learned later what it was. And Aunt Sally knows."

"Tell me; tell me what you know about it," commanded Sylvia gravely, and her voice was clear now.

Dan hesitated. He rose and stood with his arm resting on the mantel.

"It's all right, Daniel. Now that Sylvia has asked, she must know just what we know," said Mrs. Owen.

"The letter was among your grandfather's papers. It was an offer to pay for your education. It was an unsigned letter."

"But you know who wrote it?" asked Sylvia, not lifting her head.

"No; I don't know that," he replied earnestly; "we haven't the slightest idea."

"But how did you come to be the messenger? Who gave you the letter?" she persisted quietly.

"Daniel never told me that, Sylvia. But if you want to know, he must tell you. It might be better for you not to know; you must consider that. It can make no difference now of any kind."

"It may make a difference," said Sylvia brokenly, not lifting her head; "it may make a great deal of difference. That's why I speak of it; that's why I must know!"

"Go on, Daniel; answer Sylvia's question."

"Mr. Fitch gave it to me. It had been entrusted to him for delivery by a personal friend or a client: I never knew. He assured me that he had no idea what the letter contained; but he knew of course where it came from. He chose me for the errand, I suppose, because I was a new man in the office, and a comparative stranger in town. I remember that he asked me if I had ever been in Montgomery, as though to be sure I had no acquaintances there. I carried back a verbal answer—which was stipulated in the letter. The answer was 'No,' and in what way Mr. Fitch passed it on to his client I never knew."

"You didn't tell me those things when we found the letter, Daniel," said Mrs. Owen reproachfully.

The old lady opened a drawer, found a chamois skin, and polished her glasses slowly. Dan walked away as though to escape from that figure with averted face crouching by the fire. But without moving Sylvia spoke again, with a monotonous level of tone, and her question had the empty ring of a lawyer's interrogatory worn threadbare by repetition to a succession of witnesses:—

"At that time was Mr. Bassett among the clients of Wright and Fitch, and did you ever see him in the office then, or at any time?"

Mrs. Owen closed the drawer deliberately and raised her eyes to Dan's affrighted gaze.

"Daniel, you'd better run along now. Sylvia's going to spend the night here."

Sylvia had not moved or spoken again when the outer door closed on Harwood.

CHAPTER XXXII
"MY BEAUTIFUL ONE"

Miss Farrell was surprised to find her employer already in his office when she unlocked the door at eight o'clock the next morning, and her surprise was increased when Harwood, always punctilious in such matters, ignored the good-morning with which she greeted him. The electric lights over Dan's desk were burning, a fact not lost upon his stenographer. It was apparent that Harwood had either spent the night in his office or had gone to work before daylight. Rose's eyes were as sharp as her wits, and she recognized at a glance the file-envelopes and papers relating to the Kelton estate, many of them superscribed in her own hand, that lay on Harwood's desk.

She snapped off the lights with an air that implied reproof, or could not have failed of that effect if the man at the desk had been conscious of the act. He was hopelessly distraught and his face appeared no less pallid in daylight than in the electric glare in which Rose had found him. As the girl warmed her hands at the radiator in the reception room the telephone chimed cheerily. The telephone provides a welcome companionship for the office girl: its importunities and insolences are at once her delight and despair. Rose took down the receiver with relief. She parleyed guardedly with an unseen questioner and addressed Harwood from the door in the cautious, apologetic tone with which wise office girls break in upon the meditations of their employers.

"Pardon me, Mr. Harwood. Shall I say you're engaged. It's Mr. Thatcher."

Dan half-turned and replied with a tameness Rose had not expected.

"Say what you please, Rose; only I don't want to talk to him or see him, or anybody."

The clock in the court-house tower boomed nine sombrely. Dan distrusted its accuracy as he distrusted everything in the world that morning. He walked listlessly to the window and compared the face of the clock with his watch. He had thought it must be noon; but the hour of the day did not matter greatly.

"It's all right," said Rose meekly from the door. "I told him you were probably at the State House."

"Whom? Oh, thank you, Rose." And then, as though to ease her conscience for this mild mendacity, he added: "I believe I did have an engagement over there at nine."

"He said—" Rose began warily; and then gave him an opportunity to cut her short.

"What did he say?"

"Oh, he was hot! He said if you came in before he found you, to say that if you and Ramsay didn't help him deliver the freight to-day he would get action to-morrow; that that's the limit."

"He said to-morrow, did he? Very well, Rose. That's all."

Rose, virtuously indexing the letter-book, saw Harwood as he idly ranged the rooms try the hall door to make sure it was bolted. Then he stood at the window of his own room, staring at nothing. The telephone chimed cheerfully at intervals. Ramsay sought him; Thatcher had stationed one of his allies at a telephone booth in the State House corridor to call the office at regular intervals. Newspaper reporters demanded to know where Harwood could be found; the governor, rankling under the criticism he had brought upon his party by the special session, wished to see Harwood to learn when, if possible, the legislature would take itself home. To these continual importunities Rose replied in tones of surprise, regret, or chagrin, as the individual case demanded, without again troubling her employer. The index completed, she filed papers, smoothed her yellow hair at the wash stand, exchanged fraternal signals with a girl friend in the office opposite, and read the "Courier's" report of the senatorial struggle with complete understanding of its intricacies.

"Rose!"

It was twelve o'clock when Harwood called her. He had brushed aside the mass of documents she had noted on her arrival, and a single letter sheet lay before him. Without glancing up he bade her sit down. She had brought her notebook prepared to take dictation. He glanced at it and shook his head. The tired, indifferent Harwood she had found at the end of his night vigil had vanished; he was once more the alert, earnest young man of action she admired.

"Rose, I want to ask you some questions. I think you will believe me if I say that I shouldn't ask them if they were not of importance—of very great importance."

"All right, Mr. Harwood."

Her eyes had fallen upon the letter and her lids fluttered quickly. She touched her pompadour with the back of her hand and tightened the knot of her tie.

"This is on the dead, Rose. It concerns a lot of people, and it's important for me to know the truth. And it's possible that you may not be able to help; but if you can't the matter ends here."

He rose and closed the door of his room to shut out the renewed jingle of the telephone.

"I want you to look at this letter and tell me whether you ever saw it before."

She took it from him, glanced at the first line indifferently, looked closely at the paper, and gave it back, shaking her head.

"We never had anything like that in the office, paper or machine either. That's heavier than the stationery you had over in the Boordman Building, and that's a black ribbon; we've always used purple copying-ribbons. And that letter wasn't copied; you can tell that."

"That doesn't answer my question, Rose. I want to know whether you ever saw that letter before. Perhaps you'd better take another look at it."

"Oh, I can tell any of my work across the street! I don't know anything about that letter, Mr. Harwood."

Her indifference had yielded to respectful indignation. She set her lips firmly, and her blue eyes expressed surprise that her employer should be thus subjecting her to cross-examination.

"I understand perfectly, Rose, that this is unusual, and that it is not quite on the square. But this is strictly between ourselves. It's on the dead, you understand."

"Oh, I'd do anything for you that I'd do for anybody, yes, sir—I'd do more: but I refused ten thousand dollars for what I know about what happened in the Transportation Committee that winter I was its stenog. That's a lot of money; it would take care of me for the rest of my life; and you know Thatcher kept after me until I had to tell him a few things I'd do to him if he didn't let me alone. I'll answer your question straight," and she looked him in the eye, "I never saw that letter before, and I don't know anything about it. Is that all?"

"To go back again, Rose," resumed Dan patiently, "not many girls would have the strength to resist a temptation like that, as you did. But this is a very different case. I need your help, but it isn't for myself that I'm trying to trace that letter. If it weren't a matter of actual need I shouldn't trouble you—be sure of that."

"I always thought you were on the square, but you're asking me to do something you wouldn't do yourself. And I've told you again that I don't know anything about that letter; I never saw it before."

She tapped the edge of the desk to hide the trembling of her fingers. The tears shone suddenly in her blue eyes.

Dan frowned, but the frown was not for Rose. She had already betrayed herself; he was confident from her manner that she knew. The prompt denial of any knowledge of the fateful sheet of paper for which he had hoped all night had not been forthcoming. But mere assumptions would not serve him; he had walked in darkness too long not to crave the full light. The pathos of this girl's loyalty had touched him; her chance in life had been the slightest, she had been wayward and had erred deeply, and yet there were fastnesses of honor in her soul that remained unassailable.

Her agitation distressed him; he had never seen her like this; he missed the little affectations and the droll retorts that had always amused him. She was no longer the imperturbable and ready young woman whose unwearying sunniness and amazing intuitions had so often helped him through perplexities.

"As a matter of your own honor, Rose, you wouldn't tell me. But if the honor of some one else—"

She shook her head slowly, and he paused.

"No," she said. "I'm only a poor little devil of a stenog and I've been clear down,—you know that,—but I won't do it. I turned down Thatcher's ten thousand dollars, and I turned it down hard. The more important that letter is, the less I know about it. I'll go into court and swear I never saw or heard of it before. I don't know anything about it. If you want me to quit, it's all right; it's all right, Mr. Harwood. You've been mighty good to me and I hate to go; but I guess I'd better quit."

He did not speak until she was quite calm again. As a last resource he must shatter her fine loyalty by an appeal to her gratitude.

"Rose, if some one you knew well—some one who had been the kindest of friends, and who had lent you a hand when you needed it most—were in danger, and I needed your help to protect—that person—would you tell me?"

Their eyes met; she looked away, and then, as she met his gaze again, her lips parted and the color deepened in her face.

"You don't mean—" she began.

"I mean that this is to help me protect a dear friend of yours and of mine. I shouldn't have told you this if it hadn't been necessary. It's as hard for me as it is for you, Rose. There's a great deal at stake. Innocent people will suffer if I'm unable to manage this with full knowledge of all the facts. You think back, six years ago last spring, and tell me whether you have any knowledge, no matter how indefinite, as to where that letter was written."

"You say," she began haltingly, "there's a friend of mine that I could help if I knew anything about your letter? You'll have to tell me who it is."

"I'd rather not do that; I'd rather not mention any names, not even to you."

She was drying her eyes with her handkerchief. Her brows knit, she bent her head for an instant, and then stared at him in bewilderment and unbelief, and her lips trembled.

"You don't mean my friend—my beautiful one!—not the one who picked me up out of the dirt—" She choked and her slender frame shook—and then she smiled wanly and ended with the tears coursing down her cheeks. "My beautiful one, who took me home again and kissed me—she kissed me here!" She touched her forehead as though the act were part of some ritual, then covered her eyes.

"You don't mean"—she cried out suddenly,—"you don't mean it's that!"

"No; it's not that; far from *that*," replied Dan sadly, knowing what was in her mind.

He went out and closed the door upon her. He called Mrs. Owen on the telephone and told her he would be up immediately. Then he went back to Rose.

"It was like this, Mr. Harwood," said the girl, quite composed again. "I knew him—pretty well—you know the man I mean. After that Transportation Committee work I guess he thought he had to keep his hand on me. He's like that, you know. If he thinks anybody knows anything on him he watches them and keeps a tight grip on them, all right. You know that about him?"

Dan nodded. He saw how the web of circumstance had enmeshed him from the beginning. All the incidents of that chance visit to Fraserville to write the sketch of Bassett for the "Courier" lived in his memory. Something had been said there about Madison College; and his connection with Fitch's office had been mentioned, and on the fears thus roused in Morton Bassett, he, Daniel Harwood, had reared a tottering superstructure of aims, hopes, ambitions, that threatened to overwhelm him! But now, as the first shock passed, he saw all things clearly. He would save Sylvia even though Bassett must be saved first. If Thatcher could be silenced in no other way, he might have the senatorship; or Dan would go direct to Bassett and demand that he withdraw from the contest. He was not afraid of Morton Bassett now.

"I had gone to work for that construction company in the Boordman where you found me. It was his idea to move me into your office—I guess you thought you picked me out; but he gave me a quiet tip to ask you for the job. Well, he'd been dropping into the construction office now and then to see me—you know the boss was never in town and I hadn't much to do. He used to dictate letters—said he couldn't trust the public stenogs in the hotels; and one day he gave me that letter to copy. He had written it out in lead pencil beforehand, but seemed mighty anxious to get it just right. After I copied it he worked it over several times, before he got it to suit him. He said it was a little business he was attending to for a friend. We burnt up the discards in the little old grate in the office. He had brought some paper and envelopes along with him, and I remember he held a sheet up to the light to make sure it didn't have a watermark. He threw down a twenty-dollar gold piece and took the letter away with him. After I had moved into your office he spoke of that letter once: one day when you were out he asked me how much money had been mentioned in the letter."

"When was that, Rose?"

"A few days after the state convention when you shot the hot tacks into Thatcher. He had been at Waupegan, you remember."

Dan remembered. And he recalled also that Bassett had seen Sylvia at Mrs. Owen's the day following the convention, and it was not astonishing that the sight of her had reminded him of his offer to pay for her education. His own relation to the matter was clear enough now that Rose had yielded her secret.

Rose watched him as he drew on his overcoat and she handed him his hat and gloves. Her friend, "the beautiful one," would not suffer; she was confident of this, now that Harwood was fully armed to protect her.

"Keep after Ramsay by telephone until you find him. Tell him to come here and wait for me if it's all day. If you fail to catch him by telephone, go out and look for him and bring him here."

In a moment he was hurrying toward Mrs. Owen's.

CHAPTER XXXIII
THE MAN OF SHADOWS

The dome was a great blot against the stars when, shortly after eight o'clock that evening, Sylvia entered the capitol.

All night, in the room she had occupied on that far day of her first visit to Mrs. Owen, Sylvia had pondered. It is not for us to know what passed in that still chamber between her and her friend; but it was the way of both women to meet the truth squarely. They discussed facts impersonally, dispassionately, and what Sylvia had assumed, her old friend could not controvert. Not what others had done, not what others might do, but what course Sylvia should follow—this was the crux of the situation.

"I must think it out; I must think it out," Sylvia kept repeating. At last Mrs. Owen left her lying dressed on the bed, and all night Sylvia lay there in the dark. Toward morning she had slept, and later when Mrs. Owen carried up her breakfast she did not refer to her trouble except to ask whether there was any news. Mrs. Owen understood and replied that there was nothing. Sylvia merely answered and said: "Then there is still time." What she meant by this her kind old friend did not know; but she had faith in her Sylvia. Dan came, but he saw Mrs. Owen only. Later Sylvia asked what he had said, and she merely nodded when Rose's story was repeated. Again she said: "Yes; there is still time."

Sylvia had kept her room all day, and Mrs. Owen had rigidly respected her wish to be alone. She voluntarily appeared at the evening meal and talked of irrelevant things: of her school work, of the sale of the house at Montgomery, of the projected school at Waupegan.

"I'm going out for a while," she said, after an hour in the little office. "I shan't be gone long, Aunt Sally; don't trouble about me. I have my key, you know."

When she had gone, Mrs. Owen called one of the colored men from the stable and gave him a line to Harwood, with a list of places where Dan might be found. Her message was contained in a single line:—

"Sylvia has left the house. Keep an eye out for her; she told me nothing."

Sylvia found consolation and courage in the cold night air; her old friends the stars, whose names she had learned before she knew her letters, did not leave her comfortless. They had unconsciously contributed to her gift for seeing life in long vistas. "When you are looking at the stars," Professor Kelton used to say, "you are not thinking of yourself." It was not of herself that Sylvia was thinking.

She prolonged her walk, gathering strength as the exercise warmed her blood, planning what she meant to do, even repeating to herself phrases she meant to use. So it happened that Mrs. Owen's messenger had found Dan at the State House and delivered the note, and that Dan, called from a prolonged conference with Ramsay, saw Sylvia's unmistakable figure as she reached the top of the stairway, watched her making inquiries of a lounger, saw men staring at her. It crossed his mind that she was seeking him, and he started toward her; but she had stopped again to question one of the idlers in the hall. He saw her knock at a door and knew it was Bassett's room—a room that for years had been set apart for the private councils of the senator from Fraser. As Sylvia knocked, several men came out, as though the interruption had terminated an interview. The unveiled face of the tall, dark girl called for a second glance; it was an odd place for a pretty young woman to be seeking Morton Bassett. They looked at each other and grinned.

A single lamp on a table in the middle of the high-ceilinged room shed a narrow circle of light that deepened the shadows of the walls. Bassett, standing by a window, was aware of a lighter step than was usual in this plotting chamber. He advanced toward the table with his hands in his pockets, waited till Sylvia was disclosed by the lamp, stopped abruptly, stared at her with eyes that seemed not to see her. Then he placed a chair for her, muttering:—

"I thought you would come."

It seemed to her that a sigh broke from him, hidden by the scraping of the chair across the bare floor. He crossed and recrossed the floor several times, as though now that she had come he had dismissed her from his thoughts. Then as he passed near her with slow, heavy step she spoke.

"I came to talk to you, Mr. Bassett. Please turn on the other lights."

"Pardon me," he said; and she heard his fingers fumbling for the switch by the door. In a moment the room was flooded from the chandelier overhead, and he returned, and sat down by the table without looking at her.

"I shouldn't have come here, but I knew of no other way. It seemed best to see you to-night."

"It's all right," he replied indifferently.

He sat drooping, as though the light had in itself a weight that bore him down. His face was gray; his hands hung impotently from the arms of his chair. He still did not meet her eyes, which had taken in every line of his figure, the little details of his dress, even the inconspicuous pearl pin thrust through the loose ends of his tie. A man opened the door hurriedly and peered in: Bassett was wanted elsewhere, he said. Without rising Bassett bade him wait outside. The man seemed to understand that he was to act as guard, and he began patrolling the corridor. The sound of his steps on the tiles was plainly distinguishable as he passed the door.

"It's all right now," Bassett explained. "No one will come in here."

He threw his arm over the back of his chair and bent upon Sylvia a glance of mingled curiosity and indifference.

"I understand," she said quietly, "that nothing has been done. It is not yet too late. The situation here is as it has been?"

"Yes; if you mean out *there*. They are waiting for me."

"I suppose Mr. Harwood is there, and Mr. Thatcher."

He blinked at the names and changed his position slightly.

"I dare say they are," he answered coldly.

"I thought it best to see you and talk to you; and I'm glad I knew before it was too late."

His eyes surveyed her slowly now from head to foot. Why was she glad she had known before it was too late? Her calmness made him uneasy, restless. It was a familiar characteristic of Morton Bassett that he met storm and stress stoically. He was prepared for scorn, recrimination, tears; but this dark-eyed girl, sitting before him in her gray walking-dress and plain hat with a bunch of scarlet flowers showing through the veil she had caught up over them, seemed in no danger of yielding to tears. Her voice fell in cool, even tones. He had said that he expected her, but she did not know what manner of meeting he had been counting on in his speculations. After a long look he passed his hand across his face.

"I hope you haven't thought—you didn't think I should let them bring you into it."

He spoke as though this were something due her; that she was entitled to his reassurance that the threatened cataclysm should not drag her down with him. When she made no reply he seemed to feel that he had not made himself clear, and he repeated, in other terms, that she need not be concerned for the outcome; that he meant to shield her.

"Yes; I supposed you would do that; I had expected that."

"And," he went on, as though to anticipate her, to eliminate the necessity for her further explanations, "you have a right to ask what you please. Or we can meet again to arrange matters. I am prepared to satisfy your demands in the fullest sense."

His embarrassment had passed. She had sought the interview, but he had taken charge of it. Beyond the closed door the stage waited. This was the briefest interlude before the moment of his triumphant entrance.

Sylvia smiled, an incredulous smile, and shook her head slowly, like a worn, tired mother whose patience is sorely taxed by a stubborn, unyielding child at her knee. Her lips trembled, but she bent her head for a moment and then spoke more quickly than before, as though overriding some inner spirit that strove rebelliously within her breast.

"I know—almost all I ever need to know. But there are some things you must tell me now. This is the first—and the last—time that I shall ever speak to you of these things. I know enough—things I have stumbled upon—and I have built them up until I see the horror, the blackness. And I want to feel sure that you, too, see the pity of it all."

Her note of subdued passion roused him now to earnestness, and he framed a disavowal of the worst she might have imagined. He could calm her fears at once, and the lines in his face relaxed at the thought that it was in his power to afford her this relief.

"I married your mother. There was nothing wrong about it. It was all straight."

"And you thought, oh, you thought I came for that—you believed I came to have you satisfy me of her honor! I never doubted her!" and she lifted her head proudly. "And that is what you thought I came for?" The indignation that flashed in her first stammered sentences died falteringly in a contemptuous whisper.

Her words had cut him deep; he turned away aimlessly, fingering some papers on the table beside him. Then he plunged to the heart of the matter, as though in haste to exculpate himself.

"I never meant that it should happen as it did. I knew her in New York when we were both students there. My father had been ill a long time; he was bent upon my marrying the daughter of his old friend Singleton, a man of wealth and influence in our part of the state. I persuaded your mother to run away and we were married, under an assumed name,—but it was a marriage good in law. There's no question of that, you understand. Then I left her up there in the Adirondacks, and went home. My father's illness was prolonged, and his condition justified me in asking your mother to wait. She knew the circumstances and agreed to remain away until I saw my way clear to acknowledging her and taking her home. You were born up there. Your mother grew impatient and hurt because I could not go back to her. But I could not—it would have ruined all my chances at home. When I went to find my wife she had disappeared. She was a proud woman, and I suppose she had good cause for hating me."

He told the story fully, filling in the gaps in her own knowledge. He did not disguise the fact of his own half-hearted search for the woman he had deserted. He even told of the precautions he had taken to assure himself of the death of Edna Kelton by visiting Montgomery to look at her grave before his marriage to Hallie Singleton. He had gone back again shortly before he made the offer to pay for Sylvia's schooling, and had seen her with her grandfather in the little garden among the roses.

Outside the guard slowly passed back and forth. Sylvia did not speak; her seeming inattention vexed and perplexed him. He thought her lacking in appreciation of his frankness.

"Thatcher knows much of this story, but he doesn't know the whole," he went on. "He believes it was irregular. He's been keeping it back to spring as a sensation. He's told those men out there that he can break me; that at the last minute he will crush me. They're waiting for me now—Thatcher and his crowd; probably chuckling to think how at last they've got me cornered. That's the situation. They think they're about rid of Morton Bassett."

"You left her; you deserted her; you left her to die alone, unprotected, without even a name. You accepted her loyalty and fidelity, and then threw her aside; you slunk away alone to her grave to be sure she wouldn't trouble you again. Oh, it is black, it is horrible!"

Sylvia was looking at him with a kind of awed wonder in her eyes. For an instant there had been a faint suggestion of contrition in his tone, but it was overwhelmed by his desire for self-justification. It was of himself he was thinking, not of the deed in itself, not of the woman he had left to bear her child in an alien wilderness.

"I tried to do what I could for you. I want you to know that. I meant to have cared for you, that no harm should come to you," he said, and the words jarred upon his own ears as he spoke them.

In her face there was less of disdain than of marvel. He wished to escape from her eyes, but they held him fast. Messengers ran hurriedly through the corridors; men passed the door talking in tones faintly audible; but the excitement in the rival camps communicated nothing of its intensity to this quiet chamber. Men had feared Morton Bassett; this girl, with her wondering dark eyes, did not fear him. But he was following a course he had planned for this meeting, and he dared not shift his ground.

"I don't want you to think that I haven't been grieved to see you working for your living; I never meant that you should do that. Hereafter that will be unnecessary; but I am busy to-night. To-morrow, at any time you say, we will talk of those things."

There was dismissal in his manner and tone. He was anxious to be rid of her. The color deepened in her olive cheeks, but she bent upon him once more her patient, wondering, baffling smile.

"Please never propose such a thing again, Mr. Bassett. There is absolutely nothing of that kind that you can do for me."

"You want to make it hard for me; but I hope you will think better of that. It is right that I should make the only reparation that is possible now."

This rang so false and was so palpably insincere that he was relieved when she ignored it.

"You said a moment ago that your enemies, waiting out there, thought they had you beaten. I want you to tell me just how you propose to meet Mr. Thatcher's threat."

"What am I going to do?" he broke out angrily. "I'm going into that caucus and beat Thatcher's game; I'm going to tell his story first! But don't misunderstand me; I'm going to protect you. I know men, and those men will respect me for coming out with it. I haven't been in politics all these years to be beaten at last by Ed Thatcher. I've pledged votes enough to-day to give me a majority of three on the next ballot; but I'll explode Thatcher's bombshell in his own hands. I'm all prepared for him; I have the documents—the marriage certificate and the whole business. But you won't suffer; you won't be brought into it. That's what I'm going to do about it!"

The failure of his declaration to shake her composure disturbed him; perhaps after all his contemplated *coup* was not so charged with electricity as he had imagined. Nothing in his bald statement of his marriage to her mother and the subsequent desertion had evoked the reproach, the recrimination, for which he had steeled himself when she entered the room. He felt his hold upon the interview lessening. He had believed himself expert in calculating effects, yet apparently she had heard his announcement, delivered with a brutal directness, without emotion.

"This isn't quite all, Mr. Bassett," Sylvia began after a moment. "You have offered me reparation, or what you called by that name. You can't deny that I have a right to be satisfied with that reparation."

"Certainly; anything in reason. It is for you to name the terms; I expect you to make them—adequate."

"Let us go back a moment," she began, smiling at the care with which he had chosen his last word. "Last night I fought out for myself the whole matter of your scoundrelly, cowardly treatment of my mother. You can make no reparation to her. The time passed long ago for that. And there is absolutely nothing you can do for me. I will accept nothing from you, neither the name you denied to her nor money, now or later. So there is only one other person whose interest or whose happiness we need consider."

He stared at her frowning, not understanding. Once more, as on that day when she had laughed at him, or again when she had taken the affairs of his own household into her hands, he was conscious of the strength that lay in her, of her power to drive him back upon himself. Something of his own masterful spirit had entered into her, but with a difference. Her self-control, her patient persistence, her sobriety of judgment, her reasoning mind, were like his own. She was as keen and resourceful as he, and he was eager for the explanation she withheld, as though, knowing that she had driven in his pickets, he awaited the charge of her lines. He bent toward her, feeling her charm, yielding to the fascination she had for him.

"No," he said gently and kindly. "I don't see; I don't understand you."

She saw and felt the change in him; but she was on guard against a reaction. He could not know how her heart throbbed, or how it had seemed for a moment that words would not come to her lips.

"It is to you; it is to yourself that you must make the reparation. And you must make it now. There may never be a time like this; it is your great opportunity."

"You think, you ask—" he began warily; and she was quick to see that the precise moment for the full stroke had not come; that the ground required preparation.

"I think," she interrupted, smiling gravely, "that you want me to be your friend. More than that, we have long been friends. And deep down in your heart I believe you want my regard; you want me to think well of you. And I must tell you that there's a kind of happiness—for it must be happiness—that comes to me at the thought of it. Something there is between you and me that is different; somehow we understand each other."

His response was beyond anything she had hoped for; a light shone suddenly in his face. There was no doubt of the sincerity of the feeling with which he replied:—

"Yes; I have felt it; I felt it the first day we met!"

"And because there is this understanding, this tie, I dare to be frank with you: I mean to make your reparation difficult. But you will not refuse it; you will not disappoint me. I mean, that you must throw away the victory you are prepared to win."

He shook his head slowly, but he could not evade the pleading of her eyes.

"I can't do it; it's too much," he muttered. "It's the goal I have sought for ten years. It would be like throwing away life itself."

"Yes; it would be bitter; but it would be the first sacrifice you ever made in your life. You have built your life on lies. You have lurked in shadows, hating the light. You have done your work in the dark, creeping, hiding, mocking, vanishing. What you propose doing to-night in anticipating the blow of your enemy is only an act of bravado. There is no real courage in that. When you thrust Dan Harwood into the convention to utter your sneer for you, it was the act of a coward. And that was contemptible cowardice. You picked him up, a clean young man of ideals, and tried to train him in your cowardly shadow ways. When the pricking of your conscience made you feel some responsibility for me, you manifested it like a coward. You sent a cowardly message to the best man that ever lived, not knowing, not caring how it would wound him. And you have been a great thief, stealing away from men the thing they should prize most, but you have taught them to distrust it—their faith in their country—even more, their faith in each other! The shadows have followed you to your own home. You have hidden yourself behind a veil of mystery, so that your own wife and children don't know the man you are. You have never been true to anything—not to yourself, not to those who should be near and dear to you. And you have sneered at the people who send you here to represent them; you have betrayed them, not once but a hundred times; and you know it hasn't paid. You are the unhappiest man in the world. But there's a real power in you, or you could never have done the things you have done—the mean and vile things. You have brains and a genius for organizing and managing men. You could never have lasted so long without the personal qualities that a man must have to lead men. And you have led them, down and down."

To all appearances she had spoken to dull ears. Occasionally their eyes had met, but his gaze had wandered away to range the walls. When she ceased he moved restlessly about the room.

"You think I am as bad as that?" he asked, pausing by the table and looking down at her.

"You are as bad—and as good—as that," she replied, the hope that stirred in her heart lighting her face.

He shrugged his shoulders and sat down.

"You have the wit to see that the old order of things is passing; the old apparatus you have learned to operate with a turn of the hand is out of date. Now is your chance to leave the shadow life and begin again. It's not too late to win the confidence—the gratitude even—of the people who now distrust and fear you. The day of reckoning is coming fast for men like you, who have made a mystery of politics, playing it as a game in the dark. I don't pretend to know much of these things, but I can see that men of your type are passing out; there would be no great glory for you in waiting to be the last to go. And there are things enough for you to do. If you ally yourself with the good causes that cry for support and leadership, you can be far more formidable than you have ever been as a skulking trickster; you can lead men up as you have led them down."

"The change is coming; I have seen it coming," he replied, catching at the one thing it seemed safest to approve.

But she was not to be thwarted by his acquiescence in generalities. He saw that she had brought him back to a point whence he must elect his course, but he did not flinch at the flat restatement of her demand.

"You have done nothing to deserve the senatorship; you are not the choice of the people of this state. You must relinquish it; you must give it up!"

The earnestness with which she uttered her last words seemed, to her surprise, to amuse him.

"You think," he said, "that I should go back and make a new start by a different route? But I don't know the schedule; my transportation is good on only one line." And he grinned at his joke.

"Oh, you will have to pay your fare!" she replied quickly. "You've never done that."

His grin became a smile, and he said: "You want me to walk if I can't pay my way!"

"Yes," she laughed happily, feeling that her victory was half won; "and you would have to be careful to stop, look, and listen at the crossings!"

The allusion further eased the stress of the hour; humor shone in his gray eyes. He consulted his watch, frowned, bent his eyes upon the floor, then turned to her with disconcerting abruptness.

"I haven't been half the boss you think me. I've been hedged in, cramped, and shackled. All these fellows who hop the stick when I say 'Jump' have their little axes I must help grind. I've fooled away the best years of my life taking care of these little fellows, and I've spent a lot of money on them. It's become a little monotonous, I can tell you. It's begun to get on my nerves, for I have a few; and all this hammering I've taken from the newspapers has begun to make me hot. I know about as much as they do about the right and wrong of things; I suppose I know something about government and the law too!"

"Yes," Sylvia assented eagerly.

He readjusted himself in his chair, crossing his legs and thrusting his hands into his trousers pockets.

"It *would* be rather cheerful and comfortable," he continued musingly, as though unburdening himself of old grievances, "to be free to do as you like once in a lifetime! Those fellows in Thatcher's herd who have practically sold out to me and are ready to deliver the goods to-night are all rascals, swung my way by a few corporations that would like to have me in Washington. It would be a good joke to fool them and elect a man who couldn't be bought! It's funny, but I've wondered sometimes whether I wasn't growing tired of the old game."

"But the new game you can play better than any of them. It's the only way you can find peace."

With a gesture half-bold, half-furtive, he put out his hand and touched lightly the glove she had drawn off and laid on the table.

"You believe in me; you have some faith left in me?"

"Yes."

Her hand touched his; her dark eyes searched the depths of his soul— sought and found the shadows there and put them to flight. When she spoke it was with a tenderness that was new to all his experience of life; he had not known that there could be balm like this for a bruised and broken spirit. This girl, seeking nothing for herself, refusing anything he could offer, had held up a mirror in which he saw himself limned against dancing, mocking shadows. Nothing in her arraignment had given him a sharper pang than her reference to his loneliness, his failure to command sympathy and confidence in his home relationships. No praise had ever been so sweet to him as hers; she not only saw his weaknesses and dealt with them unsparingly, but she recognized also the strength he had wasted and the power he had abused. She saw life in broad vistas as he had believed he saw it; he was not above a stirring of pride that she appreciated him and appraised his gifts rightly. He had long played skillfully upon credulity and ignorance; he had frittered away his life in contentions with groundlings. It would be a relief, if it were possible, to deal with his peers, the enlightened, the far-seeing, and the fearless, who strove for great ends. So he pondered, while outside the sentinel kept watch like a fate.

"Yes," Sylvia was saying slowly, "you can make restitution. But not to the dead—not to my mother asleep over there at Montgomery, oh, not to me! What is done is past, and you can't go back. There's no going back in this world. But you can go on—you can go on and up—"

"No! You don't see that; you don't believe that?"

"Yes, I believe it. The old life—the life of mystery and duplicity is over; you will never go back to the old way."

"The old way?" he repeated.

"The old unhappy way."

"Up there at the lake you knew I was unhappy; you knew things weren't right with me?"

"Things weren't right because you were wrong! Success hadn't made you happy. The shadows kept dancing round you. Mrs. Bassett's troubles came largely from worrying about you. In time Marian and Blackford will begin to see the shadows. I should think—I should think"—and he saw that she was deeply moved—"that a man would want the love of his children; I should think he would want them to be proud of him."

"His children; yes; I haven't thought enough of that."

She had so far controlled herself, but an old ache throbbed in her heart. "In college, when I heard the girls talking of their homes, it used to hurt me more than you can ever know. There were girls among my friends whose fathers were fine men,—some of them great and famous; and I used to feel sure that my father would have been like them. I felt—that I should have been proud of him." And suddenly she flung her arms upon the table and bowed her face upon them and wept.

He stood beside her, patiently, helplessly. The suggestion of her lonely girlhood with its hovering shadow smote him the more deeply because it emphasized the care she had taken to subordinate herself throughout their talk.

"Do you think you could ever be proud of me?—that you might even care a little, some day?" he asked, bending over her.

"Oh, if it could be so!" she whispered brokenly, so low that he bent closer to hear.

The room was very still. Sylvia rose and began drawing on her glove, not looking at him. She was afraid to risk more; there was, indeed, nothing more to say. It was for him to make his choice. He was silent so long that she despaired. Then he passed his hand across his face like one roused from sleep.

"Wait a moment," he said, "and I will walk home with you."

He went to the door and dispatched the guard on an errand; then he seated himself at the table and picked up a pad of paper. He was still writing when Harwood entered. Sylvia and Dan exchanged a nod, but no words passed between them. They watched the man at the table, as he wrote with a deliberation that Dan remembered as characteristic of him. When he had finished, he copied what he had written, put the copy in his breastpocket and buttoned his coat before glancing at Harwood.

"If I withdraw my name, what will happen?" he asked quietly.

"Ramsay will be nominated, sir," Dan answered.

Bassett studied a moment, fingering the memorandum he had written; then he looked at Dan quizzically.

"Just between ourselves, Dan, do you really think the Colonel's straight?"

"If he isn't, he has fooled a lot of people," Dan replied.

He had no idea of what had happened, but he felt that all was well with Sylvia. It seemed a long time since Bassett had called him Dan!

"Well, I guess the Colonel's the best we can do. I'm out of it. This is my formal withdrawal. Hand it to Robbins—you know him, of course. It tells him what I want done. My votes go to Ramsay on the next ballot. I look to you to see that it's played square. Give the Colonel my compliments. That's all. Good-night."

Harwood called Robbins from the room where Bassett's men lounged, waiting for the convening of the caucus, and delivered the message. As he hurried toward Thatcher's headquarters he paused suddenly, and bent over the balcony beneath the dome to observe two figures that were slowly descending one of the broad stairways. Morton Bassett and Sylvia were leaving the building together. A shout rang out, echoing hollowly through the corridors, and was followed by scattering cheers from men who were already hastening toward the senate chamber where the caucus sessions were held.

Somehow Morton Bassett's sturdy shoulders, his step, quickened to adapt it to the pace of his companion, did not suggest defeat. Dan still watched as the two crossed the rotunda on their way to the street. Bassett was talking; he paused for an instant and looked up at the dome, as though calling his companion's attention to its height.

Sylvia glanced up, nodded, and smiled as though affirming something Bassett had said; and then the two vanished from Dan's sight.

CHAPTER XXXIV
WE GO BACK TO THE BEGINNING

"Sylvia was reading in her grandfather's library when the bell tinkled."

With these words our chronicle began, and they again slip from the pen as I begin these last pages. When Morton Bassett left her at the door of Elizabeth House she had experienced a sudden call of the truant spirit. Sylvia wanted to be alone, to stand apart for a little while from the clanging world and take counsel of herself. Hastily packing a bag she caught the last train for Montgomery, walked to the Kelton cottage, and roused Mary, who had been its lone tenant since the Professor's death. She sent Mary to bed, and after kindling a fire in the grate, roamed about the small, comfortable rooms, touching wistfully the books, the pictures, the scant bric-à-brac. She made ready her own bed under the eaves where she had dreamed her girlhood dreams, shaking from the sheets she found in the linen chest the leaves of lavender that Mary had strewn among them. The wind rose in the night and slammed fitfully a blind that, as long as she could remember, had uttered precisely that same protest against the wind's presumption. It was all quite like old times, and happy memories of the past stole back and laid healing hands upon her.

She slept late, and woke to look out upon a white world. Across the campus floated the harsh clamor of the chapel bell, and she saw the students tramping through the swirling snow just as she had seen them in the old times, the glad and happy times when it had seemed that the world was bounded by the lines of the campus, and that nothing lay beyond it really worth considering but Centre Church and the court-house and the dry-goods shop where her grandfather had bought her first and only doll. She bade Mary sit down and talk to her while she ate breakfast in the little dining-room; and the old woman poured out upon her the gossip of the Lane, the latest trespasses of the Greek professor's cow, the escapades of the Phi Gamma Delta's new dog, the health of Dr. Wandless, the new baby at the house of the Latin professor, the ill-luck of the Madison Eleven, and like matters that were, and that continue to be, of concern in Buckeye Lane. Rumors of the sale of the cottage had reached Mary, but Sylvia took pains to reassure her.

"Oh, you don't go with the house, Mary! Mrs. Owen has a plan for you. You haven't any cause for worry. But it's too bad to sell the house. I'd like to get a position teaching in Montgomery and come back here and live with you. There's no place in the world quite like this."

"But it's quiet, Miss, and the repairs keep going on. Mr. Harwood had to put a new downspout on the kitchen; the old one had rusted to pieces. The last time he was over—that was a month ago—he came in and sat down to wait for his train, he said; and I told him to help himself to the books, but when I looked in after a while he was just sitting in that chair out there by the window looking out at nothing. And when I asked him if he'd have a cup of tea, he never answered; not till I went up close and spoke again. He's peculiar, but a good-hearted gentleman. You can see that. And when he paid me my wages that day he made it five dollars extra, and when I asked him what it was for, he smiled a funny kind of smile he has, and said, 'It's for being good to Sylvia when she was a little girl.' He's peculiar, very peculiar, but he's kind. And when I said I didn't have to be paid for that, he said all right, he guessed that was so, but for me to keep the money and buy a new bonnet or give it to the priest. A very kind gentleman, that Mr. Harwood, but peculiar."

The sun came out shortly before noon. Sylvia walked into town, bought some flowers, and drove to the cemetery. She told the driver not to wait, and lingered long in the Kelton lot where snow-draped evergreens marked its four corners. The snow lay smooth on the two graves, and she placed her flowers upon them softly without disturbing the white covering. A farmboy whistling along the highway saw her in the lonely cemetery and trudged on silently, but he did not know that the woman tending her graves did not weep, or that when she turned slowly away, looking back at last from the iron gates, it was not of the past she thought, nor of the heartache buried there, but of a world newly purified, with long, broad vistas of hope and aspiration lengthening before her. But we must not too long leave the bell— an absurd contrivance of wire and knob—that tinkled rather absently and eerily in the kitchen pantry. Let us repeat once more and for the last time:—

Sylvia was reading in her grandfather's library when the bell tinkled.

Truly enough, a book lay in her lap, but it may be that, after all, she had not done more than skim its pages—an old "Life of Nelson" that had been a favorite of her grandfather's. Sylvia rose, put down the book, marked it carefully as on that first occasion which so insistently comes back to us as we look in upon her. Mary appeared at the library door, but withdrew, seeing that Sylvia was answering the bell.

Some one was stamping vigorously on the step, and as Sylvia opened the door, Dan Harwood stood there, just as on that other day; now, to be sure, he seemed taller than then, though it must be only the effect of his long ulster.

"How do you do, Sylvia," he said, and stepped inside without waiting for a parley like that in which Sylvia had engaged him on that never-to-be-forgotten afternoon in June. "You oughtn't to try to hide; it isn't fair for one thing, and hiding is impossible for another."

"It's too bad you came," said Sylvia, "for I should have been home to-morrow. I came just because I wanted to be alone for a day."

"I came," said Dan, laughing, "because I didn't like being alone."

"I hope Aunt Sally isn't troubled about me. I hadn't time to tell her I was coming here; I don't believe I really thought about it; I simply wanted to come back here once more before the house is turned over to strangers."

"Oh, Aunt Sally wasn't worried half as much as I was. She said you were all right; she has great faith in your ability to take care of yourself. I'm pretty sure of it, too," he said, and bent his eyes upon her keenly.

There was nothing there to dismay him; her olive cheeks still glowed with color from her walk, and her eyes were clear and steady.

"Did you see the paper—to-day's paper?" he asked, when they were seated before the fire.

"No," she replied, folding her arms and looking at the point of her slipper that rested against the brass fender.

"You will be glad to know that the trouble is all over. Ramsay has the senatorship, all but the confirmation of the joint session, which is merely a formality. They've conferred on me the joy of presenting his name. Ramsay is clean and straight, and thoroughly in sympathy with all the new ideas that are sound. Personally I like him. He's the most popular and the most presentable man we have, and his election to the Senate will greatly strengthen the party."

He did not know how far he might speak of the result and of the causes that had contributed to it. He was relieved when she asked, very simply and naturally,—

"I suppose Mr. Bassett made it possible; it couldn't have been, you couldn't have brought it about, without him."

"If he hadn't withdrawn he could have had the nomination himself! Thatcher's supporters were growing wobbly and impatient. We shouldn't any of us care to see Thatcher occupy a seat in the Senate that has been filled by Oliver Morton and Joe MacDonald and Ben Harrison and Dave Turpie. We Hoosiers are not perfect, but our Senators first and last have been men of brains and character. Ramsay won't break the apostolic succession; he's all right."

"You think Mr. Bassett might have had it; you have good reason for believing that?" she asked.

"I could name you the men who were ready to go to him. He had the stampede all ready, down to the dress rehearsal. He practically gave away a victory he had been working for all his life."

"Yes; he is like that; he can do such things," murmured Sylvia.

"History has been making rapidly in the past twenty-four hours. Bassett has bought Thatcher's interest in the 'Courier,' and he proposes editing it himself. More than that, he was at my office this morning when I got there, and he asked me, as a special favor to him, to take a few shares in the company to qualify me as secretary of the corporation, and said he wanted me to help him. He said he thought it about time for Indiana to have a share in the general reform movement; talked about it as though this were something he had always intended doing, but had been prevented by press of other matters. He spoke of the Canneries case and wanted to know if I cared to reconsider my refusal to settle it. He put it quite impersonally—said Fitch told him he couldn't do more than prolong the litigation by appeals, and that in the end he was bound to be whipped. And I agreed, on terms that really weren't generous on my part. He said all right; that he wanted to clear up all his old business as quickly as possible. As he left my office I almost called him back to throw off the last pound I had exacted; he really made me feel ashamed of my greed. The old spell he had for me in the beginning came back again. I believe in him; I never believed in any man so much, Sylvia! And if he does throw his weight on the right side it will mean a lot to every good cause men and women are contending for these days. It will mean a lot to the state, to the whole country."

"And so much, oh, so much to him!"

Just what had passed between Bassett and Sylvia he only surmised; but it was clear that the warmth with which he had spoken of his old employer was grateful to Sylvia. He had not meant to dwell upon Bassett, and yet the brightening of her eyes, her flash of feeling, the deep inner meaning of her ejaculation, had thrilled him.

"I've said more than I meant to; I didn't come to talk of those things, Sylvia."

"I'm glad you thought I should like to know—about him. I'm glad you told me."

They were quiet for a little while, then he said, "Sylvia!" very softly.

"Not that, Dan; please! I can't bear to hear that. It will break my heart if you begin that!"

She rose and faced him, her back to the wall.

He had come to complete the declaration which the song had interrupted on the lake, and at the first hint the chords that had been touched by the unknown singer vibrated sharply, bringing back her old heartache. He crossed to her quickly that he might show her how completely the memory of that night had been obliterated; that it had vanished utterly and ceased to be, like the ripple stirred to a moment's life by the brush of a swallow's wing on still water. He stood beside her and took both her hands in his strong clasp.

"We are going to be married, Sylvia; we are going to be married, here, now, to-day!"

"No, no!"

She turned away her head, but his arms enfolded her; he bent down and kissed her forehead, her eyes, and her lips last of all.

"Yes; here and now. Unless you say you don't care for me, that you don't love me. If you say those things I shall go away."

She did not say them. She clung to him and looked long into his face, and kissed him.

Harwood had chosen the hour well. Sylvia had met bravely the great crisis of her life, and had stood triumphant and satisfied, weary but content in the clear ether to which she had climbed; but it was a relief to yield herself at last to the sway of emotions long checked and stifled. Save for her grandfather's devoted kindness, and the friendship of Mrs. Owen, her experiences of affection had been singularly meagre. She had resolved that if Dan should speak of love again she would be strong enough to resist him; but she had yielded unhesitatingly at a word. And it was inexpressibly sweet to yield, to feel his strong arms clasping her, to hear his protestations and assurances, to know that her life had found shelter and protection. She knew that she had never questioned or doubted, but that her faith had grown with her love for him. Not only had he chosen the hour well, but there was a fitness in his choice of place. The familiar scene emphasized her sense of dependence upon him and gave a sweet poignancy to the memories of her childhood and youth that were enshrined within the cottage walls.

In this room, in the garden outside, on the campus across the Lane, she had known the first tremulous wonderings and had heard the first whispered answers to life's riddles and enigmas; and now she knew that in Love lives the answer to all things.

After a little she rested her hands on his shoulders, half-clinging to him, half-repelling him, and he pressed his hands upon her cheeks, to be ready for the question he had read in her eyes.

"But," she faltered, "there are things I have promised to do for Aunt Sally; we shall have to wait a long time!"

"Not for Aunt Sally," he cried happily. "Here she is at the door now. I left her and John Ware at Dr. Wandless's."

"Well, well!" exclaimed Mrs. Owen, advancing into the room and throwing open her coat. "You said you meant to get back to the city in time to catch that limited for New York, and you haven't got much margin, Daniel, I can tell you that!"

It seemed to the people who heard of it afterward a most romantic marriage, that of Sylvia and Dan Harwood; but whatever view we may take of this, it was certainly of all weddings the simplest. They stood there before the mantel above which still hung the broken half of a ship's wheel. Mrs. Owen, very tall and gaunt, was at one side, and Dr. Wandless at the other; and old Mary, abashed and bewildered, looked on with dilated eyes and crossed herself at intervals.

John Ware drew a service book from his pocket, and his fingers trembled as he began. For none in the room, not even for Sylvia, had this hour deeper meaning than for the gray soldier. He read slowly, as though this were a new thing in the world, that a man and a woman had chosen to walk together to the end of their days. And once his voice broke. He who, in a hill country far away, had baptized this woman into the fold of Christ the Shepherd, wavered for an instant as he said:—

"Elizabeth, wilt thou have this man—"

Sylvia lifted her head. She had not expected this, nor had Dan; but Dr. Wandless had already stepped forward to give her in marriage, and as she repeated her name after the minister, she felt the warm, reassuring pressure of Dan's hand.

And so they went forth together from the little cottage by the campus where they had first met; nor may it have been wholly a fancy of Dr. Wandless's that the stars came out earlier that white, winter evening to add their blessing!

A POSTSCRIPT BY THE CHRONICLER

Those who resent as an impertinence the chronicler's intrusion upon the scene may here depart and slam the door, if such violence truly express their sentiments. Others, averse to precipitous leavetaking, may linger, hat in hand, for the epilogue.

I attended a public hearing by the senate committee on child labor at the last session of the general assembly, accompanying my neighbor, Mrs. Sally Owen, and we found seats immediately behind Mr. and Mrs. Daniel Harwood.

"There's E-lizabeth and Daniel," remarked Mrs. Owen, as they turned round and nodded to us. I found it pleasant to watch the Harwoods, who are, as may have been surmised, old friends of mine. The meeting gathered headway, and as one speaker after another was presented by the chairman, I observed that Mrs. Harwood and her husband frequently exchanged glances of approval; and I'm afraid that Mrs. Harwood's profile, and that winning smile of hers, interested me quite as much as the pleas of those who advocated the pending bill. Then the representative of a manufacturers' organization inveighed against the measure, and my two friends became even more deeply absorbed. It was a telling speech, by one of the best-known lawyers in the state. Once I saw Dan's cowlick shake like the plume of an angry warrior as his wife turned toward him inquiringly. When the orator concluded, I saw them discussing his arguments in emphatic whispers, and I was so pleased with the picture they made that I failed to catch the name of the speaker whom the chairman was introducing. A nudge from Mrs. Owen caused me to lift my eyes to the rostrum.

"The next speaker is Mrs. Allen Thatcher," announced the chairman, beaming inanely as a man always does when it becomes his grateful privilege to present a pretty woman to an audience. Having known Marian a long time, it was almost too much for my composure to behold her there, beyond question the best-dressed woman in the senate chamber, with a single American Beauty thrust into her coat, and a bewildering rose-trimmed hat crowning her fair head. A pleasant sight anywhere on earth, this daughter of the Honorable Morton Bassett, sometime senator from Fraser; but her appearance in the legislative hall long dominated by her father confirmed my faith in the ultimate adjustments of the law of compensations. I had known Marian of old as an expert golfer and the most tireless dancer at Waupegan; but that speech broke all her records.

Great is the emotional appeal of a pretty woman in an unapproachable hat, but greater still the power of the born story-teller! I knew that Marian visited Elizabeth House frequently and told stories of her own or gave recitations at the Saturday night entertainments; but this was Marian with a difference. She stated facts and drove them home with anecdotes. It was a vigorous, breathless performance, and the manufacturers' attorney confessed afterward that she had given him a good trouncing. When she concluded (I remember that her white-gloved hand smote the speaker's desk with a sharp thwack at her last word), I was conscious that the applause was started by a stout, bald gentleman whom I had not noticed before. I turned to look at the author of this spontaneous outburst and found that it was the Honorable Edward G. Thatcher, whose unfeigned pride in his daughter-in-law was good to see.

When the applause had ceased, Mrs. Owen sighed deeply and ejaculated: "Well, well!"

As we walked home Aunt Sally grew talkative. "I used to say it was all in the Book of Job and believed it; but there are some things that Job didn't know after all. When I put Marian on the board of trusteees of E-lizabeth House School, it was just to make good feeling in the family, and I didn't suppose she would attend a meeting; but she's one of the best women on that job. And E-lizabeth"—I loved the way she drawled the name, and repeated it—"E-lizabeth says they couldn't do without her. I guess between 'em those girls will make E-lizabeth House School go right. That investment will be a dividend payer. And there's Morton Bassett, that I never took much stock in, why, he's settled down to being a decent and useful citizen. There ain't a better newspaper in the country than the 'Courier,' and that first editorial, up at the top of the page every morning, he writes himself, and it's got a smack to it—a kind of pawpaw and persimmon flavor that shows it's honest. I guess settling up that Canneries business cost him some money, but things had always come too easy for Morton. And now that they've moved down here, Hallie's cheered up a good deal, and she shows signs of being cured of the sanatorium habit."

We were passing round the Monument, whose candelabra flooded the plaza with light, and Mrs. Owen inveighed for a moment against automobiles in general as we narrowly escaped being run down by a honking juggernaut at Christ Church corner.

"It seems Morton has grown some," she resumed. "He's even got big enough to forgive his enemies, and John Ware says only great men do that. You've noticed that 'Hoosier Folks at Home' column in the 'Courier'? Well, Ike Pettit runs that; Morton brought him to town on purpose after Edward Thatcher closed out the Fraserville paper. I read every word of that column every day. It gives you a kind of moving-picture show of cloverfields, and children singing in the country schools, and rural free delivery wagons throwing off magazines and newspapers, and the interurban cars cutting slices out of the lonesomeness of the country folks. It's certainly amazing how times change, and I want to live as long as I can and keep on changing with 'em! Why, these farmers that used to potter around all winter worrying over their debts to the insurance companies are now going to Lafayette every January to learn how to make corn pay, and they're putting bathrooms in their houses and combing the hay out of their whiskers. They take their wives along with 'em to the University, so they can have a rest and learn to bake bread that won't bring up the death-rate; and when those women go home they dig the nails out of the windows to let the fresh air in, and move the melodeon to the wood-pile, and quit frying meat except when the minister stops for dinner. It's all pretty comfortable and cheerful and busy in Indiana, with lots of old-fashioned human kindness flowing round; and it's getting better all the time. And I guess it's always got to be that way, out here in God's country."